In 1992, after being fired from a top secret nuclear facility, a top KGB man buried a nuclear suitcase. Sixteen years later he has found a buyer for it. Travelling with the buyer is an undercover policeman, working for MI6. But as their shadowy journey across Europe begins, it becomes clear that their man may be suffering from Stockholm Syndrome and the whole operation is very likely to be thrown into jeopardy . . .

ABOUT THE AUTHOR

Gerald Seymour spent fifteen years as an international television news reporter with ITN, covering Vietnam and the Middle East, and specialising in the subject of terrorism across the world. Seymour was on the streets of Londonderry on the afternoon of Bloody Sunday, and was a witness to the massacre of Israeli athletes at the Munich Olympics.

Gerald Seymour is now a full time writer, and six of his novels have been filmed for television in the UK and US. TRAITOR'S KISS is his twenty-first novel.

For more information about Gerald Seymour and his books, visit his Facebook page at
www.facebook.com/GeraldSeymourAuthor

Traitor's Kiss

Gerald Seymour

HODDER

First published in Great Britain in 2003 by Bantam
Press, a division of Transworld Publishers

This paperback edition first published in 2014

1

Copyright © Gerald Seymour 2003

The right of Gerald Seymour to be identified as the Author
of the Work has been asserted by him in accordance with
the Copyright, Designs and Patents Act 1988.

All rights reserved. No part of this publication may be reproduced, stored
in a retrieval system, or transmitted, in any form or by any means without
the prior written permission of the publisher, nor be otherwise circulated
in any form of binding or cover other than that in which it is published and
without a similar condition being imposed on the subsequent purchaser.

All characters in this publication are fictitious and any resemblance
to real persons, living or dead, is purely coincidental.

A CIP catalogue record for this title is available from the British Library.

Book ISBN 978 1 444 76041 5
eBook ISBN 978 1 444 76042 2

Printed and bound by Clays Ltd, St Ives plc

Hodder & Stoughton policy is to use papers that are natural, renewable
and recyclable products and made from wood grown in sustainable
forests. The logging and manufacturing processes are expected to
conform to the environmental regulations of the country of origin.

Hodder & Stoughton Ltd
338 Euston Road
London NW1 3BH

www.hodder.co.uk

For Alfie

PROLOGUE

August 1998

He held the package tightly, as if he were reluctant to let it go. His calloused and scarred fingers gripped the envelope of cheap brown paper; the tips indented the paper, such was the tightness with which he held it. There was no writing on the envelope, nothing to indicate to whom it should be delivered.

'I was in my cabin. We needed fuel, and I was using the calculator, working out the exchange rate, and then he was just there, no knock. One moment the door was closed, the next it was open and he was filling it, and he took this from inside his jacket, and . . .'

Mowbray, the veteran, said quietly, 'I think it's better, Mr Harris, if we just start at the beginning. In your own time.' He smiled reassuringly.

The head of Russia Desk, Bertie Ponsford, beamed. Behind Harris, her pencil poised, Alice North sat with the shorthand pad on her knee. At the end of the table, detached from the rest of them, was the naval officer who wore slacks and a blazer and had loosened his tie as if to relax the stranger. In a cabinet the tape-recorder was already turning, but it was general practice to keep recorders and microphones, which intimidated civilians, out of sight. It was mid-morning, and coffee and a plate of digestive biscuits were on the table. A cup had been poured by Alice for Harris, but he had not touched it: to have lifted the cup and drunk the coffee would necessitate releasing his hold on the envelope that had brought them together.

'Yes, from the beginning.' Ponsford had a deceptively gentle voice, but his features were those of a scavenging fox. 'You are Frederick Harris, part-owner with two others of the *Marie Eugenie*, ocean-going trawler, home port of Hull, and thirteen days ago, on the thirtieth of July, you *strayed* into Russian territorial waters, going after cod. Do people call you Fred or Freddie, Mr Harris?'

'Fred.'

'Well, Fred, there you are, hauling in the cod, and that's the beginning, so let's take it from there, please.'

The room chosen for the meeting was off Pall Mall. In a cul-de-sac out of sight of the gentlemen's clubs, watering-holes and restaurants, the house had a fine Georgian façade, and the ground-floor reception rooms boasted exquisite moulded ceilings, high sash windows and antique furniture – all except this room. Here, the furnishings and décor were deliberately tacky, so that the location should not appear too grand. The table was covered by a plastic sheet adorned with patterns of primroses, the chairs were steel-tube-framed with canvas seats, the thin carpet was bright yellow, except at the door where generations of feet had pounded it to a faded orange. Few of those summoned to a meeting with representatives of the Secret Intelligence Service and personnel from the military were at ease, and the presentation of the room was designed to minimize inevitable apprehension.

'Well, you know how it is.' Harris shrugged. 'It's partly the stocks and also the quotas, but the North Sea is fished out. I've got a mortgage on the boat that's killing me. I've got to go where the money is, got to take the chance. Another couple of years like the last two, and I'm gone. There's been trawling in my family for the last hundred and twenty years – it won't happen for my kids. So we go up north, give it a try there. We'd gone by the North Cape, that's Norwegian, and kept on east, got as far as the East Bank, which is Russian. We're thirty sea miles off the coast, well out into the Barents Sea, and we'd got a really good catch in. It was foul weather, just right for us, thick fog and visibility down to a hundred metres, couldn't have been better. Then, in the space of five minutes, there were two calls over the radio. The first was from their Fisheries Protection lot: we should identify ourselves. The second was from a Russian vessel: they'd a casualty on board, needed help, and giving a position. I put it all together, says to myself that we'll use the casualty as the reason for us being there, and come out smelling of roses, or sweeter.

2

'The catch was in the holds, the nets were stowed, and we sailed to the distress call. It was one of their research ships, on its way up to north of Spitzbergen, and a crewman had double-fractured his leg. The weather was too bad to get a helicopter out, and they didn't want to turn back and lose out on their schedule. So, we're like the Angel Michael showing up. The guy was transferred on board and I told their skipper that I'd run him straight back into Murmansk. We got a crate of vodka for our trouble. I radioed ashore and told the Fisheries Protection what I was doing. We made it into Murmansk, the guy was taken off to hospital, and instead of having the *Marie Eugenie* impounded and me being in court, we were everybody's favourite flavour. Get me straight, Murmansk isn't a place I'd take my wife for a weekend break, but they made us really welcome. Couldn't do enough for us – the next morning I'd one hell of a hangover.

'Fuel's dirt cheap there, a fraction of what it is at home, so I loaded up to the top. I was waiting on the tide, working out what the diesel was going to cost me, scratching through every pound sterling that I'd got on board, and what my crew had . . . and then he was in the door of my cabin. He was in uniform, quite a high-ranking officer of the regular navy, not merchant. We'd had harbour people on board, shabby sort of folk, but this one was immaculate. Well-pressed tunic, crease in his trousers, clean shirt, tie, like he worked in an office, not on a warship. But he looked as if he were about to shit himself – sorry – very tense and stressed up. There wasn't any preamble. I looked at him and he looked at me, big staring eyes. Just for a moment there was real fear in his face. He said, blurted it out, but a whisper, in English: "I have a communication that I request you pass to your intelligence authorities." I'm a hundred sea miles from Norwegian waters, I've got an illegal catch on board, and then he's in my cabin talking espionage. I suppose I went white. A moment like that, and the big word that belts you is *provocation*, or it's a set-up, a sting. I don't know what to say . . . What I can tell you, him and me, equally, we were both about to shit ourselves. He had what I'd call an honest face – there wasn't anything devious about him. I'm not a great judge of people, I can pick a crewman but that's about it. He had a face that I reckoned sincere. He must have realized that I thought he was

3

bad news. He looked over his shoulder, satisfied himself that we weren't overheard, then said, sort of simple: "I am taking a very much greater risk than I am asking of you." I had to believe him – but what if he were followed? What if he were being watched? I must have nodded, maybe I held my hand out. He took this envelope out from inside his jacket, and he gave it me. I asked him who he was, but he just shook his head. The only other thing he said was: "Please . . . please . . . see that it gets to those authorities . . . please." Then he was gone and I'd the envelope in my hand. When I looked out of the porthole I saw him scramble up on to the quay and he just walked away, like nothing had happened. My first thought was to chuck the envelope over the side. But it was his face that stopped me. Then I moved fast across my cabin, fast like I'd a ferret down my trousers. I opened my safe double quick, and I locked it in there, right at the back.

'Within an hour I'd paid off the diesel and we'd slipped the moorings. We went up the Kola inlet like we were in a regatta race, couldn't get clear of Murmansk fast enough. All the time I was thinking that if a cutter or a patrol-boat came out towards us, I was going to be back in my cabin, getting the safe open and heaving that packet as far as I could chuck it – but there wasn't any cutter or patrol-boat. Twenty sea miles up the inlet is Severomorsk, where the nuke submarines are and the heavy cruisers, the big naval base. I was shaking like a leaf as we passed it, couldn't hold the wheel steady, and the other boys – none of them had seen him come on board or leave – thought it was the hangover. Then I saw him. He was a tiny figure out on the end of a groin, all alone, and he must have been waiting there to see us leave. I needed the binoculars to check it was him. He didn't wave to us, just smoked a cigarette, and when we'd gone by him he turned away and kept walking.

'We nearly bust the old engine getting across the North Sea, full power, then offloaded the catch at Peterhead, and went on down south to home. My wife's cousin is a policeman there. I told him the bones of it and an inspector from Special Branch came round to the house to see me. I'd taken the envelope off the *Marie Eugenie* and it was under the mattress of the spare bed. I didn't tell the Branch man any more than I'd said to her cousin. He wanted to take it. No way. I

4

said I'd deliver it personally because that's what was asked of me. So the Branch man made the arrangements and here I am.'

He pushed the envelope hard across the table.

'Well done, Fred,' Ponsford said. 'I cannot, even if I wished to, fault your actions. Alice will see you out, and your travel expenses will be met. Good sailing in the future, but not to Murmansk.'

'Thank you, Mr Harris.' Mowbray leaned forward and shook the trawler skipper's roughened hand.

Harris asked, 'What did he mean, in this day and age, about risk?'

Mowbray smiled comfortingly. 'Nothing for you to worry about. As I'm sure you will, put the whole matter out of your mind. Leave it to us.'

When the door had closed behind him and the beat of his heavy shoes had been lost in a distant corridor, the three men stared at the envelope. It lay sandwiched between a coffee cup and the plate of biscuits.

As the senior man it was Bertie Ponsford's privilege to snatch up the envelope. In his hand he seemed to weigh its significance and its bulk. He tore open the flap and spilled a sheaf of papers on to the table. The naval officer stood back, knowing his time would come. The top sheet of perhaps fifty pages was covered with a handwritten scrawl and on its reverse side were two pen-drawn maps. The pages scattered on the primroses were printed or typed, or were covered in photocopied diagrams.

Mowbray felt his pulse pound. He was in his sixty-first year but he recognized the excitement he had known on his first overseas assignment for the Service thirty-four years earlier. The handwritten page was given to him. He read, and the adrenaline coursed through him, as it had in the old days.

Dear Sirs,
It is a good friend who is contacting you, a friend who has become your ally for the cause of truth, honesty and justice. I have embarked on this course of struggle, having thought long and hard of the consequences. I have made a mature decision to reach out towards you for your hand. I have at my disposal materials on many subjects of interest and importance to your government and I wish to pass these materials to

5

you. I enclose details of the dead drops you should use, and maps of
their locations, and later we should meet face to face. I ask that, in
working with me, you observe all the rules of professional tradecraft.
Protect me. I wish you long life and good health.
Your Friend.

Mowbray's mind blurred with the images of a man whose face he could not picture, burdened with fear, isolation and the bitterness that had caused him to write this letter. He blinked.

Ponsford had shuffled together the remaining sheets and had passed them to the naval officer, who slumped down at the table with them and retrieved a pair of half-moon spectacles from his breast pocket to study them.

'Well, what does our customer think?' Ponsford boomed.

'Of course, I'll need more time.' The naval officer shrugged.

As if talking to an idiot, Ponsford repeated the question, more slowly. 'But, what do you think?'

'It's submarine material. I'd say it's a taster. Kilo-class submarines are the best part of twenty years old, but refitting. These top pages are about what they're doing to reduce hydrodynamic noise. Then it goes on to describe their progress in the concept of co-axial contra-rotating propellers. It's technical, it's detail, it's interesting. What's undeniable, he has access. I'd say he's a staff officer, probably a captain, third rank, and well placed.'

Mowbray didn't know about hydrodynamics, nor about co-axial contra-rotating propellers. He smiled icily. 'Is it new?'

The naval officer grimaced. 'I'd say it's new, and I'd say that it's confirmation of what we believed but could not have been sure of. Is "valuable" good enough?'

Ponsford said that 'valuable' would be satisfactory.

It was arranged that they would meet again in a week, when the customer from naval intelligence had had more time. Briefcases were filled, Alice's notepad was back in her handbag, coats were retrieved from hooks. Mowbray bit at his lip – each year the Service spent millions, tens of millions, around the world seeking to bribe, suborn, trick, deceive military officers of potentially hostile powers into sharing their nation's closest secrets, and the money always trickled down the plug-hole. The ones that mattered, always, were the 'walk-ins', who just pitched up without warning or invitation. In more than three decades with the Service, Mowbray had seen millions disappear without reward and now, in the twilight of his career, a 'walk-in' had appeared. He ground his hands together, cracked and flexed his fingers, and savoured the moment.

A frown had settled on the naval officer's forehead. 'I am just trying to work out what sort of man he'd be. A little piece of scum, I suppose. I have to say, if he was one of mine I'd reckon slow garotting was too good for him.'

'But he's not one of yours, he's one of theirs,' Mowbray, tart, interrupted. 'We don't talk about scum, we talk about an asset.'

'Why? Why would he betray . . .'

Mowbray stood to his full height, took the stature of a lecturer, pontificated as if to a class of recruits. 'We call it MICE. Every agent from the other side that we run is governed by MICE. That's Money, Ideology, Compromise or Ego. MICE is the formula that governs each last one of them, and frankly I don't give a damn which motivates our "Friend". See you in a week.'

Half an hour later, after the naval officer had left and after arrangements had been agreed with Bertie Ponsford, Mowbray stood on the pavement, Alice beside him, searching for a vacant taxi that would run them out to Heathrow and the plane back to his Station, Warsaw. Alice had come up with the code-name, the only time she'd spoken. The skipper had described how fast he'd gone to his safe to bury the package. It was her habit only to speak when she had something relevant to say, and that was a principal reason that he'd demanded of Personnel that she be transferred to Poland with him. Ferret, she'd said, was from the fourteenth-century old-French word *furet*, which in turn originated from the Latin and was literally translated as 'thief'.

It was a warm afternoon and the summer sunshine had brought smiles to the faces of the pedestrian hordes who jostled them for pavement space. He did not feel the sunshine. A cold seemed to cling to him because he reflected on a man, with neither a face nor a name, who had put trust in him. *Protect me.* The thief among the files of the Northern Fleet would be Codename Ferret. The cold bit at his bones. At his side, Alice waved down the taxi. He shuddered. Unless he was protected, and they rarely were, a bullet to end the pain of torture was the only long-term future of an asset. He settled heavily on to the back seat of the taxi.

I

Q. Where is the home of the Russian navy's Baltic Fleet?
A. Kaliningrad.

The present
It wasn't there.

Gabriel Locke, twenty-eight years old and in the last year of his first overseas posting, straightened, pushed out his legs in front of him, eased back on the bench and looked around him.

Coming through the entry gate to the Middle Castle were the German tourists. He estimated there were more than a hundred. He'd seen their two coaches stop in the car park near the river and he'd studied them for a few moments, before walking ahead of them towards the gate of perfect arched symmetry with the wooden portcullis over it. His training was to observe. It had been dinned into him on the IONEC course that he should always approach a dead drop with extreme caution, and should never go close to it before guaranteeing to himself that he was not watched. The Germans were elderly, boisterous, wore bright clothes and were festooned with cameras. What was now Poland, and what had been East Prussia more than half a century before, was popular, these days, as a destination for a retired generation of Germans from the West: it was about heritage, and visiting a place where they had been born, or where their parents had lived, and it was about cost.

When he had scanned them he had seen nothing to make him wary. He had made his careful half-moon arc across the cobbled courtyard of the Middle Castle, had then waited for a party of school-children to move on from the bench, and had sat down. He had chewed a peppermint, then leaned forward and run his right hand along the bottom of the bench's slats. There had been nothing there.

Had he made a mistake?

Locke – he was Daffyd to his parents, but had used his second name, Gabriel, from the time he'd left home – had been to the castle at Malbork twice before. He had come up from Warsaw in the third week of July and in the third week of May. On both days the court-yard had also been filled with Germans – with the same bright laughter, the same adoration of this medieval heap of redbrick-built Teutonic splendour. He had slipped his hand under the close-set slats and had felt the package fastened there with chewing-gum. After discreetly pocketing it, he had walked off, like any tourist, to resume his tour. At Malbork, on the Nogat river, to the south-east of Gdansk, the religious order of the Knights of the Cross had constructed the largest castle in Europe. Locke, always the careful man, did not believe in unnecessary risk-taking. His belief and care in preparation – the reason he had sailed through the induction tests laid in front of him by the Service – had dictated that he should read the abbreviated history of the castle, which he was tasked to visit every two months to collect from the dead drop. It was the first time there was nothing for him to retrieve. The Germans, in their noisy phalanx, were advancing towards him, led by the siren calls of the guides, drawn to four larger-than-life statues fashioned in bronze. The statues were representations of four of the warlords who had ruled the surrounding countryside six hundred years before. He glanced up at the sheened faces of the armour-clad men. Hermann von Salza, Siegfried von Feuchtwangen, Winrich von Kniprode and Markgraf Albrecht stood on an extended plinth of marble, each with his own pedestal; they wore chainmail under long tunics, they had close-fitting helmets, and double-bladed swords hung from broad belts. Von Feuchtwangen – for all the sternness of the visage the sculptor had given him – suffered the handicap of having lost, to recent pillage, his right hand, sliced off at the wrist. They were all men of brutal appearance, and on his three visits Locke had reflected that they would have meted out brutal treatment to any spy who threatened them.

But Gabriel Locke had not made a mistake.

It was the correct day of the third week in September. It was the correct location, as laid down by the previous communication. It was the only bench. There was no margin of error. His eyes searched the four high walls of the courtyard as he looked for a watcher, a man or a woman, but there was none that he could identify. He steeled himself, bent forward and tried to make the movement seem casual. His right hand snaked under the slats to feel for the package. It wasn't there. He wriggled further along the bench and all the time his fingers probed for it. The tourists advanced. The guide had stopped her chatter and eyed him. He felt a flush on his face, and a bead of sweat, brought on by embarrassment. Then his fingers had reached the far end of the underneath of the bench seat. Two ladies, heavy and supported by medical sticks, lurched closer to him. Still nothing. They dropped down beside him and he was squeezed to the extremity of the bench. He smiled at them, and was ignored, then stood up. He had no more business on the bench. His instinct was to kneel, or lie down full length on the grit in front of it and peer under the slats, but that would have been ridiculous and unnecessary.

He could not escape the conclusion: the dead drop had not been serviced.

Locke stepped two paces forward and his place was immediately taken by an old man whose left trouser leg was folded up at the knee where the amputation had been made and who took the weight on a wooden crutch. He hesitated. In his short, bright career he had not before known failure. Debatable, of course, whether the failure was his . . . No reason for him to blame himself . . . He had done nothing wrong. This was, in his opinion, the stuff of dinosaurs. In the third year of the new millennium it was pathetic that he should be required to drive every two months from Warsaw to Malbork Castle and scuffle like an idiot under a bench to collect a package. On the other occasions he had been here, after he had pocketed the package he had trailed round the treasures of the castle and visited the Amber Collection of caskets and wine cups, cutlery and jewellery made by seventeenth- and eighteenth-century craftsmen, and the Porcelain Collection from the workshops of Korzec and Baranowka, and the Weapons Collection. He had wandered through the Grand Master's Palace and the cloister corridors of the High Castle, and marvelled at the skill of the reconstruction of the castle after the Red Army's shelling at the end of the last war, and he'd treated himself to light lunches before hitting the road.

He walked away, and anger burned in him.

Locke had never met the agent, Codename Ferret. Too junior to be taken inside the loop, he did not know his name nor had he been shown a photograph. He was merely a courier. Being outside the need-to-know circle, he was expressly forbidden to open the package once he had made the pick-up and was required to deliver it, still sealed, to his Station chief at the embassy. It was a small consolation that his Station chief – Ms Libby Weedon – was also denied access to the material that he had twice brought back. The papers, whatever they contained, went to London in the bag that was fastened by handcuff and chain to a messenger's wrist. He was a child of the computerized age and it was, to him, as obvious as the inevitability of night following day that material should be transmitted electronically having been suitably encoded. Only rarely in his six years as a member of the Service, which he had joined with such pride, had he been obliged to work the Neanderthal procedures of the few old warriors still existing at Vauxhall Bridge Cross. His day was wasted. He assumed that Codename Ferret was either in a meeting, had a head cold, or was in a warm apartment and had gotten his leg over. For a young man, when his Welsh temper was roused, Gabriel Locke was short of charity.

There was a fall-back. The sparse file of papers available to him in the Service's quarters at the embassy dictated that if the Malbork Castle dead drop was not utilized another location should be checked seven days later.

As he drove out of the town, over the bridge above the Nogat river, he had no idea of the consequences to many people of his wasted journey.

There was little protection from the autumn cold when the wind knifed from Beinn Odhar Mhor and cut south along the small stream's gully that dropped down to Loch Shiel. The Highlands' mountain wind fell fiercely at that time of year, but the artist did not feel it. The autumn was the best time for Billy Smith because the wind and heavy rainclouds conjured the threatening skyscapes with their pillars of light. Dark, scudding cloud and shafts of low sun thrown down made the vistas that he sought out. Huddled between yellow lichen-coated boulders above the tree line, his view was of white caps on the loch, then the rock-scarred cliffs of Sgurr Ghiubhsachain and up to the black purple of the clouds above. He was not among the boulders for warmth but to protect himself from the wind's buffeting as he painted. His paper was held by steel chrome clips to a legless Formica table-top, his paints were on a palette beside his left elbow, and at his right side was a jar once long ago filled with coffee but now holding the water he had taken from the loch before he had climbed to the vantage-point. He never worked from memory, always climbed as if it were important to him to experience the power of the elements that raked this wilderness. He worked methodically, would be there till dusk, or until he could no longer see the paper, and then he would come down the steep, precarious slope, easily and with confidence, and go to the little tin-roofed hut that was his home.

It was a good restaurant, as good as any in that south-coastal town. The season was over and the visitors remaining were eking out their pensions and would not have patronized the one he had chosen. With the summer gone, the town's traders and this restaurant's owner were able to evaluate their successes and failings of the last five months, and they had not been well treated by the weather. For that reason, each time Hamilton Protheroe raised his hand he was given immediate and undivided attention. Champagne had been drunk while they sat on stools at the bar and chose the Italian-style dishes, and a Chianti bottle was now nearly empty on the table. He was a con-man. He deceived older ladies, widows and divorced. He made them laugh and smile, and sometimes bedded them after lunch, and when he had had use of their credit cards and their chequebooks, he slid away and out of their lives, and moved on to the next town with a new name but the same flattering, winning patter. That summer, unlike the traders and the restaurant owner, he had prospered. His conquests had been in Bournemouth, Swanage, Weymouth and Lyme Regis, and he had now reached Budleigh Salterton. He had enough secreted away to live in comfort in the North through the winter, and next spring he would start to play the predator again on the far extremes of the south coast – Folkestone, Rye and Eastbourne – where police files on him were aged and forgotten. The woman now opposite him, as the light outside faded on their long lunch, had been targeted ten days earlier: the rings on her fingers and the size of the stones set in them had marked her out in the hotel lounge as being suitable for attention. He made her laugh, and when he poured the wine for her she allowed his fist to brush against her arm, set with bracelets. She had a wallet in her handbag that held a bank of credit and cash cards. The sad, barren creatures always slept after he'd had sex with them.

It was raining, which hastened the dusk that crept over the cemetery. Peter Flint had no foreman to oversee him, or a manager who would have clocked him in in the morning and out at the end of the afternoon. For six days a week he worked until he could no longer see the weeds in the earth around the headstones, or pick up the grass snips he cut with shears. He had no need of supervision in this place of the dead. It was called Tyne Cot. This was his home, not the farmhouse on the far side of Passchendaele village where he rented a room under the rafters. Home was among the geometric patterns of white stones quarried at Portland and carried eighty years earlier to this Belgian field. The stones he cared for most, which took the greatest part of his day, were those on which had been carved 'A Soldier of the Great War' and 'Known unto God'. His home, the largest of the Commonwealth War Graves cemeteries, contained 11,908 graves and a memorial with the names of 34,808 men listed as missing in action in the last twelve months of the war-to-end-all-wars. He was not a social man and liked to work, his wheelbarrow, hoe, trowel and shears close by him, away from the other men. He had come to love this place and he never tired of gazing down the gentle slope, over the regimented stones, towards the poplars and the sunken pillboxes that had taken so many of these lives. When the evening came and he could no longer work, long after the other gardeners had gone, he would lock away his wheelbarrow and tools, switch on the headlight of his bicycle, then pedal away down the road to the farmhouse and his room. He did not need company, he was content.

*   *   *

He wheeled the trolley back down the corridor along which, a few minutes earlier, it had been stampeded when *en route* from the ambulance reception bay to A&E. The hospital was less than a dozen miles from the M6 motorway and received more than its share of road-accident victims. The casualty who had been on the trolley Colin Wicks now pushed – a young man in a good suit, what was left of it, and a white shirt made revolting with his blood – had looked, as he was wheeled in by the shouting, running team, to have little future. Wicks pushed the trolley down the corridor and out through swing doors into the dropping gloom, unravelled the hose, turned on the tap and drove the gore from the trolley's cradle. It was always him who did it, hosed down the trolleys, because the others on the shift were too squeamish for that work. It upset them, but not him. When the cradle was cleaned he would take disinfectant and a stiff brush and would scour its canvas surface; he would let it dry in the evening air, then wheel it back to the ambulance bay, and it would be there for the next victim who had been impatient or tired or had drunk too much or had simply been unlucky. The last of the water cascaded off the trolley and down to the drain at his feet. As he bent to turn off the tap, he saw the flash in the water and knelt to retrieve it, a cufflink. It would have been given to the casualty by a grandfather, a father, or a lover. He used his own handkerchief to dry it, and examined it to make certain that no blood was left staining it. He would take it back to A&E and give it to a nurse. He didn't feel good about finding it, or bad about the condition of the young man who had worn it in his cuff. In his life, he was long past feeling emotions.

None of them – Billy, Ham, Lofty or Wickso – knew of the consequences that would follow from the empty space under a faraway castle's bench.

He pressed the key. Electronically, the signal was sent. FERRET: NO SHOW. His finger hovered, and in that macro-second the signal, in cypher, travelled from the Service's suite of rooms in the embassy on Warsaw's Al Roz street, near to the Park Ujazdowski, and hurtled across the airspace of western Europe until it was sucked down by the dishes and antennae on the roof of Vauxhall Bridge Cross over-looking the Thames.

He went through the procedure of shutting down the secure computer. A few years back, in the days before Gabriel Locke had been accepted into the Secret Intelligence Service, there would have been a technician to handle the transmission. In those days, those years, the officers of the Service would not have been trusted to write, encode, and transmit their messages from the field. He understood the way the computers worked and what they could do for him. He had even written a paper, passed on by his Station chief for consideration by Administration, on how the computers could be upgraded at a minimal cost. To Locke it was pitiful that older inadequate men could not master the new technology.

The signal was sent. He closed the door to the cypher room behind him, checked the double lock was engaged, and went through to the outer room where the two girls, Amanda and Christine, had their desks.

Libby Weedon's door was open. He was sidling past it, hoping not to be noticed, but her voice, deep and with the clarity of a broadcaster, snatched at him. He was summoned inside. He was told he looked 'pissed off', and then she smiled in her prim, severe way and told him it was not his fault that Ferret hadn't travelled . . . of course it was not his fault . . . and she reminded him not to forget George, who would be waiting out in the second-floor lobby . . . of course he wouldn't . . . and she pointedly mentioned the ambassador's reception later that evening. She glanced up at him from her screen and a little of the severity was replaced by a tinge of coyness. He knew Libby Weedon was in her forty-third year, and that there was no sign of any romantic entanglement in her life. Well, she fancied him. Drunk, or across lit candles at dinner, or sweating after a workout in the embassy's basement gymnasium, he thought she might have pushed the 'fancying' further. He repeated that he wouldn't forget George, and had not forgotten that there was a three-line whip on the ambassador's drinks party. She was heavy in the hips and the chest, but she had good skin and her throat wasn't lined – she was as old as his aunts, who lived marooned lives on the west Wales coast. He thought she was lonely and had only her work for comfort.

Outside, in the open-plan area, he grinned, winked, and gave a little wave to Amanda and Christine. He took his heavy coat and slipped out. In the corridor he pressed the code into the console on the wall and pushed open the door of inch-thick steel bars that separated the Service's quarters from the rest of the embassy offices, and with his heel slammed it shut after him.

Across the lobby, on a thinly upholstered bench, George waited. A heavy-set man, balding and with the jowl to go with his fifty-nine years, George was the punctual one: a wristwatch could have been set by his movements. Long ago, and he'd told Locke most of his life story on the two previous occasions they'd met, he'd been a detective sergeant in the Metropolitan Police, but on retirement eleven years earlier he had decided to augment his pension with paid travel. He was a courier for the Service. Not a week went by when he wasn't in the air. Long-haul or short, it barely mattered to him. On the flights of the national carrier, George went business class; the front row of the section and the seat beside him were always unfilled, even if it meant turning away paying passengers. Libby Weedon had said that a hostile counter-intelligence service would know from George's arrival and departure from their capital city that the Service were running an operation on their territory. For all his weight the courier would have been hard to spot in a crowd and he dressed down in street-market jeans, a well-used shirt with a quiet tie poking up above his pullover, and a faded green anorak. To Locke, he was another example of the *old* world still inhabited by a part of the Service. On his knee was a battered briefcase, scratched and well-used, like any businessman's, except that its fastening lock was reinforced with a discreet padlock and a fine chain hung between the handle and George's wrist, where it disappeared under the cuff of his anorak. At the sight of him, George flipped open the briefcase, making ready to receive the package, then withdrew a little pad of docket sheets from the inside pocket of the anorak.

Locke said curtly, 'Sorry, George, nothing for you.'

'Beg your pardon, Mr Locke?'

'As I said, George, I've nothing for you.'

That should have been simple enough, but a fog of puzzlement hazed the courier's forehead, and his eyes closed sharply, then opened again. 'Oh, I see, nothing – nothing for me.'

17

'That's right.'

George stood, and the frown gouged his brow deeper. 'Well, that's a turn-up . . . Every two months I've been coming, sixteen trips, and never gone away empty-handed.' His eyes screwed as if in suspicion. 'You absolutely sure, Mr Locke?'

The query annoyed Locke. Patronizingly, he rolled his eyes to the ceiling light. 'Yes, I am sure, George. I think I would know whether I had a package for you, or not. I have today driven halfway across this bloody country and back – so give me the credit for knowing whether or not I have anything for you.'

George murmured, understated criticism, 'There was always something for me when Mr Mowbray was here.'

'Mr Mowbray is not here, and has not been here for many months,' Locke said evenly. 'I expect I'll see you in a week's time, but you'll have it confirmed.'

The handcuff was unlocked, taken off the wrist and, with the chain, was dropped into the briefcase. George scowled. 'Yes, maybe, in a week . . . if nothing's happened – or gone belly-up.'

'I'm sure it hasn't,' Locke said quickly.

He followed George down the flights of stairs, through the main doors, and waved desultorily to him as the courier climbed, still frowning, into the embassy car. He realized that he, too, was merely a courier. They were equally ignorant of Ferret. 'Gone belly-up'? What could have gone belly-up? Nothing ever went belly-up with Ferret.

Locke drove into the centre. Danuta would be waiting for him. Their favourite trysting place, at the end of his working day, was where they could get the best coffee in the city. The little bar had a daft long name, Sklep z Kawq Pozegnanie z Afrykq, but the coffee choice was unrivalled in the city, thirty different varieties, and better than any place he knew in London. With Danuta, sitting opposite her and holding her long and elegantly thin fingers, and sipping the *caffè latte* in the big bowl cups, he could lose the day's irritation. Danuta designed websites, was as in love with the *new* world as he was. They were together, a fact known only to Libby Weedon. They would drink coffee and discuss her day before he went to the chore of the ambassador's party. Then he would go back to his apartment where Danuta would be waiting for him – and the fact that an agent had not filled a dead drop would be erased from his mind.

She was tied up at the quayside. Heavy hawsers held her fast. Once she had offloaded her cargo of lemons, brought from Palermo on the Italian island of Sicily, she would sail again on the midnight tide from her costly moorings at the port of Bilbao. Out in the Bay of Biscay she would ride out the storms that were forecast and would wait for the agents to find her another cargo. She might wait, tossed and forgotten, for several days because she was a vessel with the mark of death on her, for whom the breaker's yard beckoned, as suitable work was hard to come by.

With her cargo taken off by the docks' cranes, and her holds empty, she was high in the water. The *Princess Rose*, call sign 9HAJ6, had been launched in 1983 from the Den Helder yard of the Netherlands, and in the nineteen years since she had slipped out from the Wadden See, through the Marsdiep channel, she had performed as an overladen but willing baggage mule for her Cyprus-based owners. She had flown the convenience flag of Malta as she had plied around the Mediterranean, the eastern Atlantic European coastline, the Bay of Biscay, the North Sea and the Baltic. She was now worth no more than a hundred thousand American dollars, and her future was uncertain.

With the lemons in lorries and heading for French fruit-juice and soft-drinks factories she towered in her rusting glory above the quay. No care, no tenderness, no love or respect had been wasted on her. She was doomed, a liability to her owners, and soon she would be gone, probably on the one great voyage of her life to the Indian Ocean beaches of Pakistan where the demolition teams would pick her apart and destroy the memory of her.

In the night or in the morning, tossed in the Biscay, or the following night or the following day – or in a week – the owners' orders would be given to the master and his crew by radio. None of them knew where those orders would take them, and none of them believed that the orders would lead to anything more than the dreary routine of sailing to a familiar port, loading a cargo, then sailing to another familiar port, then unloading. Such was the life of the *Princess Rose* in her dying days.

Rupert Mowbray had been born to take his place on a stage, to have a spotlight shining at his face, a microphone on the lectern his hands gripped, notes in front of him that he did not need to refer to because he was the master of his subject, and an audience hushed and hanging on his words.

'You may call me – should you wish to, and it will be your privilege – an old *fart*. I would not take offence. You might also call me – because this is a free country, and I value the liberty of speech and have spent my adult life attempting to ensure it – an unreconstructed warrior of the conflict between East and West, between dictatorship and democracy. I would be proud if you did. The Cold War lives. It is about us at all times, and should concern defence analysts, students such as yourselves of international relations, and the men and women tasked with protecting our society. Perhaps you do not believe me – then I quote for you the words of Colonel General Valery Mironov who, from his vantage-point as the Kremlin's deputy defence minister, remarked in a rare interview, "The Cold War still goes on. Only one definite period of it is over." Yes, cuts have been made, but I can assure you that the knife has only been taken to the flab of the body of the Russian military. Key armoured units, the most advanced squadrons of the air force, and the fleet of nuclear-missile-carrying long-range submarines still have every devalued rouble thrown at them that the state can muster. Friendship, trust, cooperation do not exist. It would be folly to relax our guard.'

He sipped from his water glass. Rupert Mowbray, now professor of the newly formed Department of Strategic Studies, had returned in glory to University College, London, from which he had graduated thirty-six years before. A niche had been found him. The deputy provost had been lunched by the Service's director, and it had been arranged that a place be manufactured to support his retirement. He had a room, a secretary, a budget generous enough for research and travel, and a captive audience of postgraduate students. Behind his back, because rumour of his past employment had spread, his students called him by the unflattering name of Beria. They indeed

20

regarded him as an old fart, but he flattered himself that they still found him amusing. There were seldom empty seats at his weekly lecture.

'President Putin takes tea from Her Majesty's best crockery at Buckingham Palace, dines with Chirac and Schroeder, and is a barbecue guest of Bush, but that does not mean friendship. Under the ageing and boozed-up Boris Yeltsin, the Russian intelligence-gathering agencies were in freefall. No longer. Putin came to power on the back of a promise to resurrect Russia's status as a world power. He is a man of those agencies and dedicated to giving them a degree of authority in modern Russia, today, that might be greater than they have ever known – even in the horrendous days of the Purges. Nuclear missiles are deployed again in *oblasts* from which they had been withdrawn, the testing of those missiles, which are designed to carry warheads of mass destruction, has been resumed. The President has spoken publicly of the need to boost Russia's nuclear potential. Physical and verbal freedom for the mass of citizens is diminishing, as more and more positions of influence at the heart of power are doled out to his old chums in the FSB, the Federal Security Bureau, that is the successor to the Second Directorate of the KGB – different name, same mind-set. Our own Security Service employs some two thousand personnel, the FSB has seventy-six thousand, and that excludes security and support staff. Our Secret Intelligence Service runs to some two thousand two hundred men and women, their SVR is twelve thousand strong. The FAPSI, electronic espionage and security, has a staff of fifty-four thousand, while our GCHQ has fewer than a tenth of that number. How many are thought necessary to guard the leaders of Putin's regime and strategic facilities? Another twenty-three thousand. Add to that the twelve thousand responsible for military intelligence, the GRU, and you are nudging close to two hundred thousand persons charged with the responsibility of protecting the Russian motherland . . . I ask, where do they think the threat will emanate from? From here? From you? From me? They seek to control, and Putin demands this of them, those free spirits that we regard as having an integral place in our society. Do not, in Russia today, seek to be an environmentalist, or an investigative journalist,

21

or a powerful but independent-thinking industrialist, or a local-government officer with his own mind. In Putin's new fiefdom a man challenges the status quo at his peril.'

He paused and drank again, and when he had set down his glass he used his palm to sweep back his silver hair.

'Do we care? Is it our business how Russia is governed? If the brave and the few who have the courage to stand up to be counted go off to a new generation of camps, have their careers wrecked and their lives destroyed, who are we to shout? We can be Pharisees ... But, *but*, there is, and it cannot be ignored, a kleptomaniac psychology about the new Russian government. They steal. They cannot keep their hands in their pockets. If we have it, they want it. They don't steal the know-how and blueprints in order to put more fridges and dishwashers in their people's ghastly, inadequate housing, or more cars on the road. They thieve so that they can make their submarines faster and more silent, their attack aircraft more efficient, their tanks more resilient to counter-measures. They are the jackdaws of espionage. Remember the names of Walker, Ames, Hanssen – all Americans, and I thank God for it – recruited to feed an insatiable appetite for military knowledge. You would be foolish if you believed that the handshakes and deals between our governments and the Russians over this current Afghanistan adventure were anything more than window-dressing. Everything in Putin's Russia is subservient to military power, before the World Trade Center and after it ... Gentlemen, and ladies, thank you for offering your time to this old fart. May I leave you with this thought? If we were to drop our shield, our guard, then we will suffer.'

As he stepped back from the lectern there was a small, underwhelming stutter of applause, soon drowned by the scrape of the chairs. The spotlight beamed on him and he smiled ... It was twenty-eight weeks, half a year and a finger-count of days, since he had left the Service and, God, he missed it. The reason he smiled was that the good, faithful, loyal George would be on the final approach to Heathrow at this moment with a briefcase chained to his wrist, and there would be a package in it. The dead-drop collection was made on that day of each second month and that calendar pattern was always with him.

Ferret was his man, the crowning pride of Rupert Mowbray's life.

*   *   *

It had not been good.

Not good, not even indifferent: it had been lousy sex.

Locke lay on his back on his bed. He stared at the ceiling. They had had the ceiling light on above them. It was the baby oil that had made it lousy. The baby oil, for both of them, was as regular as having the light on. She'd had her shower when he was doing his duty and pressing the flesh at the ambassador's residence, then anointed herself with it, and he'd come in, rushed, stripped down and lain on the bed, and she'd crouched over him, shaken the bottle and he had been ready for a little rivulet of the oil to run on to his stomach, which she would have massaged into his skin. The oil had come in a gush, had splurged on to him and on to the bedspread, which was ruined. He'd cursed. In the middle of it, her on top of him and slithering over him, their bodies glistening under the ceiling light, he had actually asked her if she knew of a good laundry in the city, close and convenient, where he could take the bedspread. She'd tried, at first, to make it work, then gone into automatic mode with a few grunts that he'd known were pretence. Then she'd rolled off him, lain on her belly and turned her head away from him. It was another of their habits that the curtains of his bedroom were never drawn when they had sex, and usually that seemed to add keen tension to their loving. He'd looked at other windows across the street, seen people moving in them and the flickers of their televisions, the big tower blocks on the far side of the river, and he'd said sharply to her that if she didn't know of a laundry then could she, please, ring round in the morning and locate one. But she hadn't turned and hadn't spoken.

'Can you move, please? If you hadn't noticed, it's all over the sheets now.'

Couldn't help himself, he was petulant and annoyed. He had met Danuta in Warsaw two months earlier. Their first dates had taken place where they had met, in an Internet café, before they graduated to his bed or hers. Her English was fluent and his Polish was passable. She was from outside the cocoon of embassy life, and she had travelled. Her parents had emigrated from Poland to Australia nineteen years ago and she spoke with the accent of a town up the coast from Perth. She was one of the new generation of young Poles who had come home, and he'd found her warm, vibrant and fun, a blessed relief from the tedium of being the junior in an isolated corner of the embassy's second floor. He knew he'd destroyed the relationship, and he knew that when she left that evening she would not return, but the anger in him made for his persistence.

She rolled off the bed, didn't seem to care that the curtains weren't drawn, and moved slowly in front of him, bending from place to place to pick up her clothes. Then she stood, framed by the window, and began very slowly to dress.

Danuta was Locke's first girlfriend in the last thirty months. There had been no woman in his life while he was stationed in Zagreb, and none before Danuta after he had been abruptly transferred to Warsaw. There had been a girl from Library at Vauxhall Bridge Cross after he'd passed his probationer period, but she'd been looking for a ring and had wanted him to visit her parents. Before that there had been a girl from the physics department at Lancaster, but she'd slipped away from him at an end-of-term booze binge, and he'd found her on the floor with the hero of the university's lacrosse team. Everybody said he was good-looking and a catch, so the ambassador's wife had told him and Libby Weedon, but whatever it was he searched for had eluded him.

As she dressed, she paraded herself in front of the window.

Did the bloody bedspread, the bloody sheets and the bloody pillowcases matter?

He had screwed up and didn't care enough to rescue himself. In the morning he would tell his Station chief, trying to be casual and offhand, that his relationship with a Polish national was over.

Danuta never spoke. She looked around her, as if she had forgotten something, then went briskly to the dressing table, picked up the small wood photograph frame, slid out the photograph of herself, tore it into small pieces and let them flutter on to the carpet. He heard her quietly close the apartment's front door. In any of those long moments after she'd risen from the bed he could have called her back and apologized. He could have said that he'd had a bloody awful day, but he hadn't. He was left alone in the silence of the room.

It was the fault of Ferret. A dead drop had not been serviced.

After he had showered and stripped the bed, he lay on it again and tried to sleep. He did not have the experience to know what older men and women in the Service could have told him, that crises rarely broke with a thunderclap demanding attention. The veterans would have said that crises dribbled into the consciousness of the officers of the Service, came hesitantly and without prior notice, then incubated at leisure like a tumour. He tossed but could not find sleep.

'I've come for the package – from Warsaw Station.'

The older man behind the desk blinked, as if woken by her arrival. Behind him was a closed steel door and behind the door were the racks on which were laid the packages brought to the building by couriers from abroad.

She showed her ID card, the one she had used to swipe her way through the security check on the main door. Because she thought he had been asleep and needed it spelled out, she said, 'Alice North, 48 RD 21. There'll be a package for me, out of Warsaw.'

The clerk at this small unit off the wide atrium lobby area on the ground floor balefully shook his head. 'I've had nothing.'

'From Warsaw, George would have brought it in. It'll have my name on it.'

'George hasn't been—'

She interrupted, 'George would have brought it in two hours ago, could have been two and a half hours. Were you on supper break?'

'Just had sandwiches. Of course I know George. I've been here all evening, not seen George, he's not called by. Fact is, I haven't seen George for five days. Can't help you, Miss North.'

'Look, I don't want to make a fuss, *but* George flew this morning to Warsaw where he will have collected a package addressed to me, and he will have delivered it, at least an hour and a half ago.'

'He's not been here.'

'George has to have been here, and left a package, addressed to me.'

The clerk grinned comfortingly. 'Perhaps, Miss North, George's flight's late. The new security, you know.'

'I checked on my mobile, the flight was on time. Could you, please, go and look? I'm sure you'll find it.'

25

First the clerk pushed his ledger book towards her, then turned it so that she could read the open page. There was no entry that was relevant to her. George's name was not listed. But the clerk pushed himself up heavily from his chair, sighed as if it were his fate to be the victim of bullying young women, and shuffled to the steel door. He opened it and disappeared inside. Alice eased her weight from left foot to right foot, then reversed it. If this had not been a dead-drop date at Malbork Castle, she would still have been down at Fort Monkton: the rest of them on the refresher course had stayed the night and would not reappear until mid-morning the following day. On the three-day course, with eleven others, she had done sessions with the instructors to refresh her memory of the techniques of property entry, anti-terrorist ambush-driving tactics, and self-defence – from which her hips and the bones at the base of her spine still ached. She had been on Ferret since the start, and had collected every dead-drop communication received since that day. She knew him . . .

The clerk emerged. 'Like I told you – but you wouldn't listen, Miss North – there's no package come in here from Warsaw tonight. I've nothing for you.'

She clattered away on her low shoes, and took a lift to the fourth floor. In a corner of East European Controllerate was her cubbyhole, adjacent to the ever-diminishing team doing Russia Desk. She'd been insinuated into that hole eight years earlier after the move from Century House to the magnificence of the present building, when Russia Desk was still the priority focus of the Service. She thought it was now little more than the equivalent of a once-patronized seaside resort where few with ambition wished to holiday. It was near to midnight. She sat in front of her computer for a full two minutes before switching it on. Alice North was a gentle girl. In the thirty-four years of her life she had never been confronted with the need to practise the violence of either the driving course or the self-defence training. She had a premonition and it frightened her. Rupert Mowbray was no longer in place to soothe the fear. She tapped in her password and entered the ATHS labyrinth. She was cleared for access to that part of the Automatic Telegram Handling System which covered the agent whose package she had come back to London to open. She rocked on her low swivel chair.

As she drove home across London, through the City and out into the Docklands developments, Alice told herself each of twenty reasons why the dead drop had not been met. Her maisonette overlooked the dark Thames waters but reflections played on the eddies. To Alice, it was normally secure, comfortable and warm. She thought of him, why he had not travelled to Malbork, and she felt a chill she could not escape. Her fingers found the pendant stone, polished amber, that hung at her neck from a light gold chain. She held it.

In his bed, hearing the chimes of the hours passing from the tower of the cathedral in the old town, unable to sleep, Gabriel Locke made a note in his mind that first thing at the embassy he must cancel his journey to Krakow for the conference of the security police. In a week's time he would not be in Krakow but on the road to the north-east again and going to Braniewo's street-market, which was the fall-back dead drop if Malbork Castle failed.

He lay alone and cold on the bare mattress of the bed.

2

Q. Which Russian military base is a front-line fortress confronting NATO?

A. Kaliningrad.

From the window of his office, on a clear day, it was possible to see the spire of the Holy Cross cathedral across the lagoon at Braniewo. The window was in the highest office building of the naval base, once German, once Soviet, now Russian, outside Kaliningrad. The Soviets and Russians had erased the German name, Pillau, and called the base Baltiysk, and it was home to the Baltic Fleet. The buildings had been reconstructed in old German style after being flattened by artillery and air attack. They were spaciously laid out, and that window overlooked a wide parade-ground. Beyond the building were the quays, dry docks and moorings of the fleet's warships. Standing at the window with his binoculars, made in Leipzig and with 10×42 power, he could close that gap of thirty-seven kilometres and note the brick texture of the spire. But the thirty-seven kilometres from his office to the spire that dominated the street-market in Braniewo was a delusion, a distance that mocked him. Only a gull could have travelled there directly from his office in the naval base at Baltiysk in the Kaliningrad *oblast*. He could not. The shallow lagoon was covered by military radar, patrolled by fast craft, under constant and vigorous observation.

His journey, from his office to Braniewo, would cover 121 kilometres. Between him and the street-market under the cathedral's spire was the border post, and at the border post, on his side, were fences, dogs, guns and suspicion.

He had seen the tower from his office window, and had made his apologies to the fleet commander, Admiral Falkovsky, whose man he was, and said what time he would be returning, and had been reminded to bring tobacco. He had driven out from the base and had started the detour demanded by the lagoon. It was a long drive on a rutted road from the base to Kaliningrad, then south-east on the secondary route with the lagoon to the west of him. The city behind him, the Pregel river crossed, he drove his small Lada through the fishing village of Usakovo and the camping resort of Laduskin, then the road was clear ahead to Pjatidoroznoe and on to Mamonovo where life was suckled by the border. It was flat ground, leading on his right side to the reed banks of the lagoon; on his left were the wet, harvested, lifeless fields. A kilometre short of the village of Pjatidoroznoe, where there was a school, a shop and a church built a century before by the Germans that was now used as a community centre.

He slowed to confirm what he knew, what he had seen a week earlier.

A Polish lorry hooted at him, then swung out to overtake. His mirrors were clear and showed the view back down the poplar-lined road. A hundred metres behind him was a red saloon, behind that was a dirty silver one, and behind that a black van. He had fine eyesight, and he had cleaned the mirrors before leaving the base. The black van had a smoked dark windscreen. The red saloon, the silver one and the black van had slowed. He eased his weight on to the brake pedal and lightly turned the wheel. His near-side wheels slid off the Tarmac and on to the soft mud of the verge. It was what he had done a week earlier. The red saloon had stopped. The silver vehicle seemed about to ram the bumper in front of it, then also stopped, but the black van powered past the cars, covered the empty road at speed and came alongside him. The passenger window, too, was darkened. He saw the dull flicker of a lit cigarette, but could not make out the faces hidden in the interior cab.

He was not an innocent. He had a working knowledge of surveillance. His friends, in the three face-to-face meetings, had told him what to look for but that had been hurried and there had been so much else to talk of – no more than an hour's tuition to save his life. His safety, the talk of it, always came at the end of the meetings, when he'd been leached dry of tactical and technical detail. But they had talked of it, and sheets of hotel notepaper had been used to scrawl the evasion procedures he should utilize . . . And in the last four years since he had walked into the skipper's cabin of a trawler tied up to the quay at Murmansk, he had never lost an opportunity to make conversation with the security men at the Northern Fleet headquarters and now at the Baltic Fleet headquarters. Gently and carefully, he had pumped, probed and joked, over vodka and beer, at picnics and receptions, with those men so that he might learn how they worked. Alone in his quarters, in his chair with the radio playing, in his bed in the darkness, the images of the surveillance teams and what he knew of them had played in his mind. They never left him.

A week ago it had only been a suspicion, but that suspicion had been sufficient for him to turn back.

A bead of sweat ran down his neck and into the small of his back. A week ago, when he had known the first rise of the sweat through his pores, and the trembling in his hands, he had not been certain. His handlers had told him that it was always better to use the quiet road beside the lagoon than the main highway that was away to the east of his route. It was a rarely used road, with little traffic on it, which gave him a better chance to identify surveillance. His mind raced. He had the radio on in the Lada, but he seemed not to hear the shrieking announcer and the American music on the speakers. The black van had now stopped a hundred or so metres ahead of him. A tractor coming from behind him filled his interior and wing mirrors. Mud flew from its wheels and exhaust fumes from its stack. A week before it had seemed sensible to turn back, although the risk was not confirmed. The tractor pulled a trailer of high-heaped beet past him and spattered the side windows and the body of the Lada, and a man waved to him. He did not wave back because his attention was now on the red and silver cars stationary 150 metres behind him. Gold autumn leaves wafted down on them. There was no doubt of it. He could not wriggle away from it, as he had last week, and tell himself that this was only a sensible precaution to take. The message from what he saw beat hammer blows in his skull. If they stopped ahead and behind him, they did not care whether or not he was aware of them. Perhaps they wanted him to run, drive at speed towards Mamonovo, and then the border post, wanted to shepherd him towards the fences, the dogs and the guns. There they would spill him out of the car, the handcuffs would go on his wrists and they would smile broadly because his running had confirmed the guilt. Or they would radio ahead, and there would be men waiting for him, men of the Federalnaya Pogranichnaya Sluzhba, with guns and dogs to track and hunt him down long before he reached the fence. He was trapped.

He eased the Lada into gear and drove forward. The package was wedged under his seat and in his jacket pocket was the unused, unopened strip of chewing-gum. He passed the black van and saw the red saloon and the silver car pull out. Then, in his mirror, he saw the black van pull off the verge and join the little convoy behind him. He thought, on this day and on the day a week before, that they did not have evidence of his treachery but suspicion of it. If he ran, if the package were found, their suspicion would turn to certainty. On his right side was a turning to Veseloe, and he swung into it. But he did not travel down that road to the small fishing village where the men caught trout, carp and pike in the lagoon for sale in Kaliningrad's fish market. He stopped, turned his wheel and reversed, then eased the Lada into the direction of Pjatidoroznoe, Laduskin and Usakovo. A gull might reach Braniewo, but he could not. If the package were found his reward would be a dawn shuffle into a prison yard and death. It would take him a little more than two and a half hours to drive back to the base at Baltiysk and his office. He should not panic. It was panic that they wanted from him. He should not help them. He did not look at the two cars as he went by them. He drove carefully and slowly, and it was only the thought of his friends that enabled him to keep steady hands on the wheel.

For the second week he had aborted his journey to the dead drop.

He was a captain, second rank, of the Russian navy, Viktor Alexander Archenko.

The sentries on the main gate saluted him if they only carried sidearms on their webbing belts but came to attention and the present if they had rifles. He received the salutes and the rigid 'present arms' because his photograph was in the guardhouse, and all of the conscript sentries knew that he was a man of influence and power. The barrier was raised for him, then dropped behind his Lada.

Viktor was young for his rank.

Aged thirty-six, his power and influence were guaranteed because he served as chief of staff to Admiral Alexei Falkovsky, commander of the Baltic Fleet. It was said, in the guardhouse, that the admiral did not take a shit unless he had first consulted Viktor Archenko, and did not wipe his backside unless he had first asked Viktor Archenko which hand to use. But for all his authority and his closeness to the admiral's ear, he was well liked by the young men far from home who manned the guardhouse. They said he was fair, and there were few officers of whom that was believed.

He acknowledged the salutes with a brief, shallow wave and drove on.

In his mirrors he noted that his trio of watchers had parked up back from the gate and saw men climb out of the vehicles and light their cigarettes. One of them, from the black van, spoke into the sleeve of his padded coat.

With the package secured under his coat he walked away from his car and towards the block where senior officers without families were housed. If his heart pumped and his legs were weak, and if the package held tight under his coat seemed to be a lead weight gouging into his belly, he did not show it. He walked with a good stride. He was 1.85 metres tall, with fine blond hair that blew to a tangle in the wind off the sea, blue-grey eyes, and his nose was prominent. His cheekbones were strong, and his chin stronger. His skin was pale, as if he was used to spending his days in closed rooms and behind desks, not exposed to the Baltic weather. The impression his features gave was of a Germanic origin, something far from the ethnic Russian background listed on his file – his parents, on the file, were Pyotr and Irina Archenko. Only he and his friends, far away, knew the secret of the nationality of his grandmother and the story of his heritage. He was an impressive man, one who in a crowd would be immediately noticed, and there seemed an authority and decisiveness about him. Among the conscripts at the gate, and the fellow officers on the admiral's staff, it would be hard to believe of him that

32

he lived a lie. A captain, third rank, who organized fleet exercises, was in the doorway he approached and laughed a greeting to him, then held out his hand for shaking, but Viktor could not reciprocate because the hand he would have used held the evidence of his betrayal. He smiled and hurried past.

When he went into his room, the warnings that had been given him by his friends at the meetings – when they had snatched the minutes for talk about his security – governed his movements. If he were under surveillance he must also assume that his room had been entered, that microphones and cameras had been installed. All of the previous week, since he had turned back from the journey to Malbork Castle, he had made the point of laying single hairs across the tops of the drawers in his desk, which fronted on to the window, and had always done it when he lifted from the drawers a clean shirt, underwear or socks. If his room had been searched, if they had gone through the room of a favoured officer on the admiral's staff, he would know they were confident of proving his guilt. When he took a handkerchief from the middle drawer he saw the hair that fell to his carpet. From that one hair, not more than two centimetres in length, he knew that his arrest was not imminent.

Was that a comfort?

His father had said, when the leukaemia rotted him, after there was no hope, it was better to finish life quickly and rush towards death. He had been dead a week later, had not fought the inevitable.

For Viktor Archenko, it would be long, slow, because the investigation would be thorough and patient. He stripped off and went into the small bathroom annexe, taking the package in its waterproof bag with him. He ran the shower and closed the opaque curtain round him. He removed a tile at the level of his ankles and laid the package in the cavity behind it, then replaced the tile, which was fastened at the corners with gum. It was the best place he knew of in his quarters.

When he dressed again it was in his formal uniform – what he wore in the outer office at his desk that faced the door to the admiral's suite. He felt calm now, but he knew that was a fraud. It would be bad in the night – it had been bad in the night for a week. He thought of his handlers and that helped to calm him, but when night came he would be tossed into the company of the men in the cars and the van, and he would see a pistol, hear it cocked, and feel the cold of the barrel against the skin of his neck.

Outside his block, a platoon of conscripts from Naval Infantry doubled towards him. In the second rank was the spindly wan-cheeked youth with the cavern chest and the concave belly from which his camouflage trousers sagged; wisps of almost silver hair curled from under his askew beret. He was bent under the weight of an NSV heavy machine-gun and was swathed in belts of ammunition that seemed to drag him further down. The conscript, burdened with the weapon, could not salute as the others did and their NCO, but grinned at him and Viktor nodded to him with friendship and correctness . . . In a few hours his handlers would know and that would be the test of their promises. There was a spit of rain in the air, and the wind carrying it was from the west and came off the sea. He smelt the tang of oil, debris and seaweed, and headed for the dock area where he could walk undisturbed, where he could think how to save himself, because he did not know if the promises were true.

Behind him, the NCO shouted for the platoon of conscripts to hold their formation.

The machine-gun was the dearest thing in Igor Vasiliev's life.

Until he had been given the 12.7mm heavy machine-gun, nothing in his life had been kind to him.

His father, in Volgograd, had been a skilled sheet-metal worker in the steel factory, but it was now closed, and he drove a taxi. His mother had worked in the secretariat of the factory, and now sold flowers on the street. As old Russia, familiar and safe, crumbled, the family's fortunes had plummeted. They did not have the resources to be a part of the new Russia that the leaders said was vibrant and exciting. Poverty now stalked the family, and with it came a sense of shame and diffidence that was passed down to their son. He had been conscripted into the Naval Infantry. His thin body, girlish hair, long, delicate fingers and shyness had made him a regular target for the bullies – other conscripts and non-commissioned officers. He was a victim of the cult of *dedovshchina*. He did not know that the practice of brutality by conscripts and their fellows, by non-commissioned officers on their juniors, was encouraged by some senior officers: it was an escape valve, those officers considered, for the privations of the men, the irregular payment of their wages, their hunger through lack of food, their cold in winter because the military could not afford heating oil. He had not been hospitalized and he had not been subject to homo-sexual rape. But because his appearance was thought effeminate his kit had been trashed, he had been beaten and kicked, the skin on his back and below his stark ribcage had been burned with cigarettes.

At the time when the last spring had come hesitantly to Kaliningrad, and the ice on the lagoon had melted, his life had changed.

The base is built on the peninsula of sand that runs south-west from the mainland. Entry to the naval docks from the Baltic Sea is by a canal, 200 metres wide and regularly dredged to allow merchant shipping access to the port section of Kaliningrad city, via the Pregel river. West of the canal the sandspit runs on to the Polish border fifteen kilometres away. Those fifteen kilometres are the regular training ground for the naval infantry who share the 1000-metre-wide spit with the artillery and the missile units. There was once a Luftwaffe field there, but the buildings are now used for close-quarters infantry combat firing and the land beyond is a scrubby waste cratered by shells and mortar bombs. Rising above the yellowed moonscape are the gaunt batteries of the air defence and ground-to-ground tactical missiles, and beyond are the pine forests, the fence with the watchtowers, and Poland. Past the old airfield and the ground used by the artillery and for the missile launchings is a firing range for infantry weapons. The furthest point on the range between the target butts and the firing ditches is 2000 metres – the maximum distance at which the 12.7mm heavy machine-gun is effective.

On an April day of that year, the platoon had been on the range. The bullies had fired first, and Igor Vasiliev had huddled down in the depths of the trench with his hands over his ears. He had not been able to see the two-metre-high targets and had not known that each of the bullies had failed to register a hit. An officer had appeared and stood tall, erect, with his hands authoritatively clasped behind his back. He had watched for a few minutes as the messages came back from those below the targets that the firing was high, wide or short. Igor Vasiliev, the target of the bullies, had not been ordered forward by the senior NCO in charge of the platoon. Then the officer had asked if each man in the platoon had fired, whether they were all equally as incompetent as those he had seen shoot. The NCO, who was under the withering gaze of the captain, second rank, had called forward the twenty-one-year-old. Has he been instructed on the use of the weapon? the captain, second rank, had asked. And the NCO had stammered that this particular conscript had not yet fired the heavy machine-gun but would have heard the instructions given to others. The NCO had pushed the conscript into position, on his haunches with his knees raised, behind the weapon, and had gabbled through the theory of wind deflection and bullet drop. From the officer's dominating stature, it had been clear to every youth in the platoon, and to the NCOs, that if Igor Vasiliev failed all of them would shoot until their shoulders were bruised and until their uniforms stank from the cordite emissions.

He had settled behind the heavy machine-gun, ground his haunches into the wet and cold of the sandy ground. A corporal lay on his stomach beside him to feed the belt, and the senior NCO had reached forward to check the sight and see it had not been moved. Let him do it, the captain, second rank, had said, let him make any adjustments that are necessary. It was late morning in spring, and the wind came from the east and flew the cone at full stretch from the mast. The wind strength would have been at a minimum of thirty kilometres. The conscript had looked at the cone, at the wave of the grasses, at a distant plastic rubbish bag that careered across the range . . . and he had fired.

Thunder blasted in his unprotected ears. He had to use his full strength to hold the machine-gun steady on its low tripod. Ten rounds in three bursts, then quiet had rested over the trench. They had all waited for the screech of the radio from the distant target butts. Five hits in a target that was two metres high and 1.5 metres wide.

'The boy has a natural talent,' the captain, second rank, had said. 'See that it is encouraged.'

36

After the officer had walked to his jeep and been driven away, the NCO had allowed him to fire again, another belt of ten shots. In those few minutes the wind had dropped, and he needed to allow for the reduction in its strength. He had fired, and the watchers had reported six hits out of ten shots.

That spring morning Igor Vasiliev had insisted that he should carry the heavy machine-gun back to the lorry. The body of the weapon was 25 kilos, plus 9.2 kilos for the barrel, the tripod was 16 kilos, and the ammunition was 7.7 kilos. As he had struggled to lift 57.9 kilos, the full weight of the assembled weapon and its ammunition, on to the lorry's tail, he had asked one panted question of the senior NCO: 'Who was that officer?'

'The chief of staff to the fleet admiral,' the NCO had answered sourly. 'Captain, second rank, Viktor Archenko.'

From that day on, Igor Vasiliev always fired the heavy machine-gun on the range. He had shot in the summer for his platoon in the inter-brigade championships, and had won, and next year – the last of his conscripted service – it was expected that he would shoot in the inter-divisional championships for a silver cup awarded by the general of Naval Infantry. And when Captain Archenko needed a driver to take him to military headquarters in Kaliningrad city, it was Igor Vasiliev who was sometimes assigned, and they talked of the science of target shooting.

After twenty-one wasted years, his life had started that April day on the firing range. Everything that made him proud, and the purpose of his life, was due to that day's intervention by Captain Archenko. The time spent with him and the knowledge gained from it provided the keenest pleasure he knew. And the heavy machine-gun was his.

Doubling away from the officer, hemmed in by the ranks of the platoon, and with the weight of the heavy machine-gun across his shoulders, Igor Vasiliev wondered if Captain Archenko had a head cold, a bad one . . . perhaps even an attack of the influenza virus. He had not seen him, before, so pale and so distracted.

Every building, with one exception, in the naval base had been destroyed in 1945. Because it had offered the final escape chance for the tens of thousands of German civilians and military, the bombing by the Soviet air force, and the artillery barrage, had been merciless and effective.

The one building that had survived had been the two-centuries-old castle fortress built by Gustav Adolph von Schweden. Viktor walked there now. The ramparts were faced with heavy stone and topped by uncut grass, and they had withstood the rain of high explosive. It was where his grandmother might have come for final shelter. She had not found a place on the boats making the last evacuations. The town that surrounded the castle, and was flanked by the canal and the dockyards, had held out for a full two weeks after the surrender of the city of Kaliningrad, after the last boat had gone. His grandmother would have been the luckier if she had found a place on the liner *Wilhelm Gustloff* because then her fate would have been fast and she would have drowned with seven thousand others when the torpedo struck, and luckier also if she had been on the *General Steuben* or the *Goya* when eleven thousand more souls had gone, struggling against death, into the Baltic when the submarines attacked. His grandmother might have been here, cowering, when the resistance had finally collapsed and the Red Army had probed over the bridge that crossed the moat and into the castle. Her death had been slow, humiliating, filled with shame . . . and that was the prospect beckoning to him.

If he turned away from the sea, where patterns of buoys marked the approach channel to the canal and more buoys and lights gave warning of the wrecks, the extremities of old minefields and the probable location of long-ago dumped explosives, if he turned away from the limitless, white-capped sheet of water, his view would be over the canal, the shooting range and the lagoon. Viktor did not turn, did not look behind him. Had he done so, on this crisp afternoon with good visibility, he would have seen the wheeling gulls above the lagoon, and his eyeline would have drifted towards its far shore and to the needlepoint spire of the Holy Cross at Braniewo. By now the courier would be there, searching and failing to find the reason for his journey in the stinking toilets beside the street-market.

Viktor Archenko did not know how the suspicion had settled on him. Had he made the mistake or had it been made in London, or on the Polish side of the border fence? He remembered what his friends had said to him: 'You must be constantly on your guard. It is difficult for us to determine what is dangerous to you and what is not.' At another meeting, his friends had said, 'God has protected you this far, but there is a limit to the chances you can take. Be careful, because God does not protect fools.' However hard he scratched in his mind he could not think of a conversation in which he had betrayed himself. At the third meeting, his friends had said, 'We want you to realize that the most basic consideration we have for you is humanitarian, irrespective of how important you are as an information source.' At each meeting it had been stressed to him that he should exercise the utmost care and not try to send out too much too quickly. He was, his friends always said, an asset for the long-term. Fine words, but not for a man who could not run.

The castle, with its five angled bastions projecting out into the moat, had been repaired from the devastation of the bombing, not lovingly and in the way the Poles had rebuilt Malbork Castle, but crudely sufficient to make the interior a home for naval cadets. There were prefabricated huts in the courtyard and flat-roofed brick blocks, but he could see the old archways and the narrow windows that Gustav Adolph von Schweden had designed, and it was in one of those that his grandmother might have sheltered when the enemy came.

The story of his grandmother, her life and death, had been one of the two reasons that had driven him towards betrayal. On the rampart of the castle, he thought that he walked with his grandmother. She gave him strength.

He did not look back to Braniewo's skyline, where the courier would have been, would have searched, would have left.

With a brisk stride he walked out of the castle and back in the direction of his office. He saw Piatkin near to the Sailors' Club, and walked by him as if the political officer did not exist. They were on opposite sides of the street, and neither seemed to notice the other. But on that day, Piatkin, the *zampolit*, was the most important person in Viktor Archenko's life.

* * *

Every waking hour of Vladdy Piatkin's life was taken now by concern at the movements of Captain, second rank, Archenko. It ranked high enough for him to have used his mobile early that morning to cancel the visit to the base, through a back entrance, of the import-export dealer, Boris Chelbia. Chelbia imported new Mercedes cars, exported heroin from Turkestan and weapons from Kaliningrad. Through his contacts across the *oblast*, Piatkin could offer the full protection of the counter-intelligence spider's web that was the FSB, the Federalnaya Sluzhba Bezopasnosi, and in return he was paid, cash, five thousand American dollars a month. The weapons came out of the armoury, a few at a time, and the paperwork was doctored to account for the missing automatic rifles. Only a matter of the gravest importance would have led Piatkin to cancel a visit from the prime organized crime racketeer in the city.

And this was a matter of the gravest importance.

A little thing had started it, a trifle.

Trying to light a cigarette, a month back, on the naval harbour quay, failing and using the last match, then turning to the officer next to him, and being given a pretty, decorated book of matches with a hotel's name on them, lighting his cigarette at the second attempt, seeing the hotel's name and the city, passing them back to the officer who was responsible for fleet-munitions storage. Asking, with a smile, how the officer had obtained the matches. Being told. 'From Archenko – I think he stayed there when he was last in Poland, the visit to the shipyard, the dry-dock contract. Archenko gave them to me.' Being suspicious because it was his job, knowing that Archenko and the delegation had been booked rooms in the Mercure Hotel, not the Excelsior, which was on the other side of the old town district of Gdansk, and wondering. His cousin was married to the FSB officer stationed in the consulate in Gdansk but came over the border and into Kaliningrad every two weeks to report, and it was natural that his cousin's husband should be given the spare room in Piatkin's apartment.

The last visit had been twelve days earlier. Over beer and sliced peaches from the fridge, Piatkin had asked, 'The visits of the fleet delegation to Gdansk, the matter of the dry dock's availability, I am correct, they stayed at the Mercure Hotel?' That had been confirmed.

Piatkin had then asked, 'Did the delegation visit the Excelsior Hotel on ul Szafarnia?' They had not. 'Could any of the delegation have gone to the Excelsior Hotel for a meal, a drink or a meeting?' None of the four-man delegation, of two naval officers and two civilians from the defence ministry, had visited the hotel. His cousin's husband had escorted the delegation from early morning until late evening, he could vouch that the hotel had not been visited, and Piatkin was told that the prices charged at the Excelsior Hotel put it beyond the reach of the delegation's *per diem* expenses. He had asked, 'Who uses that hotel?' Foreigners – Germans, Swedes, Americans. A worm had crawled into Piatkin's mind, and after his cousin's husband had gone back to Gdansk the next morning, he had spent the whole day drafting a report for his seniors. He had agonized over it because of the extreme sensitivity of his naming a captain, second rank, who enjoyed the patronage and protection of the fleet commander.

Four days later, eight days ago, the signal had come back from the Lubyanka in Moscow that discreet surveillance should be mounted on Viktor Archenko, chief of staff to Admiral Falkovsky. The next day, a week back, with full authorization for his journey to Malbork Castle, Archenko had driven towards the border but had unaccountably turned back fifteen kilometres short of the checkpoint. The team, travelling in two cars and a command van, had been adamant they had not shown out ... And that day the same team in two different cars but using the command vehicle had reported Archenko's second abort. Piatkin could not know where the worm's tracks would lead, and it was inconceivable that an officer of such seniority should be under suspicion.

The response from Headquarters to his report on that morning's abort came as a moment of great relief to Piatkin. It was now out of his hands, a matter for Moscow. By the Sailors' Club, as he had passed Archenko, he could not bring himself to shout a warm greeting to him, but he had noticed what seemed severe strain on Archenko's features. It was now for Moscow to take it further.

Viktor passed the towering statue of Lenin, fashioned in grey stone. There were few enough of them left, but in the naval base in Kaliningrad *oblast*, one had survived. The great man was sombre

41

and his eyes, gouged forward in the granite stone, seemed to peer at Viktor and strip him of the lie he lived. His friends were far from him. He went up the steps to the fleet headquarters building. In the hallway the sentries saluted him and the clerks snapped to stand behind their desks as he passed. His friends were beyond reach. He did not know how to counter the suspicion arraigned against him, or who would be thrown against him to turn suspicion into proof.

He was a man of little stature, but his reputation went before him. His shoulders were slight, his body was lightweight, his dark hair was tousled into untidy curls, and his walk was without the loose, flowing stride of an athlete. The smoothness of his cheeks under a two-day stubble made him seem too young for the rank displayed by the faded cloth insignia on his shoulders. It was his eyes that upheld his reputation. They were slate grey and the light seemed to burn keenly from them. They had a peace about them that came only from his supreme confidence in his ability: they were those of a hawk, a predator.

He had many homes, but none was important because he had laid down no roots. His upbringing had been in the city of Gorno-Altaysk, capital of the Altay region far to the south, his postings had been to Moscow, Novosibirsk and Kursk, where he had left the family he never saw, never wrote to and never heard from. There was a desk in Moscow, in the Lubyanka, that was nominally his, and a one-roomed apartment four streets away where two suitcases of clothes lay under the bed, but home now was the principal barracks in Grozny, some 1450 kilometres to the south-east of his few possessions.

He had flown in from Moscow the day before, had been briefed through the night, and now the helicopter awaited him. He ambled across the Tarmac, a general beside him and four men laden with weapons behind. The engine of the Mi-8 transport helicopter whined towards full power and the rotors made a sweet, clear-cut circle above it. He walked easily and there was a calm about him, but the general's face was puckered with anxiety and the four men, whose eyes shone through the slits in their face masks, betrayed a hint of fear in their gait.

He wore heavy boots of brown leather, not military, and the laces were only loosely tied. His thick hiking socks were around the ankles of his heavy jeans, and protecting his chest from the weather was a grey T-shirt, a maroon wool jersey, a blue fleece coat and the military tunic. At his waist was a belt from which hung a holster and an automatic pistol and in the small of his back, on the belt, a personal first-aid kit.

The general fussed beside him as the engine whine grew. 'You'll do what you can.'

'Of course I will.' The voice was soft, almost gentle.

'He's one of my oldest colleagues, valued.'

'They're all equally important, to someone.'

The general persisted, raising his voice against the engine. 'We were in Afghanistan together, two tours – Jalalabad and Herat. We were in the last brigade out. It's the third time we've been here, this shit-hole.'

He paused, a little frown cut his brow, then he reached up to his shoulders and peeled off his colonel's rank insignia and gave them to the general. A fast grin opened his face. 'I doubt they'll help me.'

'That bastard,' the general spat. 'Take his balls off.'

'I'll do what I think necessary.'

It was complicated. It would be a business of delicacy and danger. The general's colleague was a brigadier in mechanized infantry and had been captured with three escorts, the rest dead, near the Argun gorge. The bastard was Ibn ul Attab, the warlord who held the eastern sector of the gorge. In the follow-up search for the brigadier, by good fortune, a six-man patrol of the special forces Black Berets had taken Attab and his son and had them trussed in a cave high over the gorge, but the location where the brigadier and his escort were held was not known, and the weather had changed. A blanket of cloud had settled on the forested rock faces, and the helicopters were grounded. If the brigadier was to be saved, and his escorts, then the warlord must tell where he was, in which cleft of rocks, in which fissure.

Yuri Bikov, thirty-eight years old, no longer wearing his colonel's badges, was the interrogator with the reputation.

'We depend on you,' the general said hoarsely.

43

He shrugged, laid his hand lightly on the general's arm, then turned towards the helicopter's hatch. From a low-altitude landing strip, they would go forward in armoured vehicles, before trekking towards the location beacon of the Black Beret patrol, then . . . There were conscripts and grizzled ground crew all around him. He saw it in their faces: he was their icon, they had faith in him because his reputation as an interrogator went ahead of him . . . His briefings had told him that the Black Berets had already beaten Ibn ul Attab half senseless and that he had said nothing. Time was now critical if the lives of the brigadier and his escorts were to be preserved.

He climbed up to the hatch and one of the aircrew helped him heave through.

Bikov settled into a canvas cot seat against the cockpit bulkhead, and when his four men were in with him, machine-gunners took their places at the hatches and armed the weapons. As they lifted off, and he looked around him, he saw the bloodstains on the cabin's floor. There was a piece of white bone near his feet. On the interior of the fuselage were plastic adhesive strips that covered incoming bullet strikes. His reputation said that he alone among the counter-intelligence interrogators of the FSB was, perhaps, capable of extracting the information required to save a brigadier and his escort.

Soon, inside the rattling hulk of the helicopter, he dozed. He had no time for the porthole views of artillery-ravaged villages, or for the mountains ahead where the clouds shrouded the slopes. He did not open his eyes as the machine-gunners loosed off a few rounds to check the efficiency of their weapons. If the responsibility given him was a burden he showed no sign of it as his head lolled forward, his chin settled on his chest.

Viktor Archenko had never been to Chechnya and had never heard of Colonel Yuri Bikov.

'What is there that it would be impolite to talk of? What is their disaster area now?' Viktor was settled in the back of the car, the admiral beside him.

'Cheeky boy . . .' The admiral growled his trademark low chuckle. 'You gossip too much.'

Viktor was the admiral's man. He was his eyes and ears. He was expected to prise confidences from fellow trusted men of the other fleets, the army and the air force. What he learned went not only to the dead drop at Malbork Castle for collection by the courier, but also was whispered to the Baltic Fleet commander. Knowledge was power. If Admiral Alexei Falkovsky knew the detail of another commander's problems, or what further funds and resources had been made available to others, then he had the native cunning to turn the knowledge to his own advantage. If the Northern Fleet was short of fuel for operational sailing then Falkovsky would feed into the high echelons of the ministry that he, at Kaliningrad, had managed to conserve sufficient diesel, and his star would shine. He thrived on the gossip that Viktor brought him.

'And how was your day among the ruins, Viko?'

'I didn't go,' Viktor said calmly.

A peremptory question. 'Didn't go? Missed out?'

'Actually, I didn't go. Idiotic of me, I was on my way and then I remembered that Stanislaw – that is, the curator of works – was going to be on leave. I turned back.'

He looked sharply at his admiral in the car's interior gloom. He had learned over many years that this bluff, powerful, boisterous man had the innate cunning of a she-cat. But the admiral had his eyes barely open and his head was back against the seat. The questions had not been barbed probes but had been fashioned out of politeness. Viktor told himself that here, with his protector beside him, he was safe. If this physically huge and mentally muscled man had known that suspicion now rested on his *protégé* he would not have carried him in his car. They still searched for evidence, and without evidence they would not dare to approach a man of the authority of the commander of the Baltic Fleet and make their denunciation. But he did not know how much time he had, how fast the sand would run through the funnelled shape of the glass.

Except when he was ill, and the doctors had summoned the courage to issue an order to him, Admiral Alexei Falkovsky never took a day away from his work. All of his career, and more particularly now that he commanded a fleet of warships, he had been obsessed with the levels of control of the navy his adult life had given him. He had no holidays and he took no leave. His wife enjoyed vacations alone or with her female friends. If they took a week in a Black Sea resort, his wife was abandoned while he spent his days visiting other commands, and in the evenings they went to service dinners. But he accepted, with wry amusement, that his chief of staff should be allowed, under humorous and grudging sufferance, an occasional away-day to visit and study Malbork Castle, over the border in Poland. Why a naval officer of seniority should embark on a love affair with a medieval castle, and become an expert in its history and construction, get to the point of obsession, was to Admiral Falkovsky – as Viktor knew – strange to the limit of eccentricity. Viktor talked of the castle to him, lectured him on its magnificence till his eyes turned away and he feigned boredom. He would cry to be spared. Yet the dockets Viktor needed to cross the frontier and visit Malbork were always signed with a gruff snort – but they were signed.

'So you have not brought back my cigarettes – how may I survive without my cigarettes?' The admiral struck Viktor's arm. The blow hurt. 'I will die without my cigarettes.'

The admiral smoked up to two packets of Camel, no filter, a day. Each time Viktor travelled to Malbork he brought back ten cartons or more, a minimum of two thousand Camel cigarettes. There was always tension in the admiral's office when supplies were dwindling and the next visit to Malbork was more than a week away. In Kaliningrad, at a price, it was always possible to buy Marlboro, Lucky Strike or Winston off the street stalls, but packets of Camel were hard to find.

'As soon as I can "escape", Admiral, I will go and work for a day with the archaeological team, scrape old stones, excavate decaying bones, and buy your cigarettes.'

'If I am not dead . . .' Falkovsky's voice softened. In the front of the car that flew the fleet banner on the bonnet was the driver and the admiral's personal uniformed bodyguard. He murmured, 'Tonight there will be present all of the air-force people. Are they going to get the new aircraft, MFI, or are they not? Are they, the pigs, ahead of us at the trough? I would hate to think so. I need to know. Also present tonight is that buffoon, Gorin, from Missile Defence,

46

and I hear they spend every day and half of every night lobbying for money, money, *money*, and what they get is not available to me . . . I don't want you talking to them about fucking castles.'

They grinned together, like old friends, and then the interior of the car was filled with the admiral's low chuckle.

Admiral Falkovsky and his wife had produced two daughters. One taught small children in Moscow and the other sat at a reception desk in a St Petersburg hospital. They were both, equally, a disappointment to him. Both were frightened of water, turned pale at the sight of a good sea freshening, and each in her own way had made it clear to their father that his adoration of all things nautical made him a sad, remote and distant figure. They had no sympathy for his life, and he none for theirs, and they came to see him at Kaliningrad only once a year. He would have said, to himself but not to his wife, that the absence of a son in his life was negated when he had first cast his hard and experienced eye on the young Viktor Archenko. He was now aged fifty-six, but then he had been forty-two, and the young man who had caught that eye was twenty-two years old. At that time he commanded the destroyer and frigate flotillas sailing out of Severomorsk. His reputation for brutal commitment to the navy had been made thirteen years before their first meeting and came from suppression of mutiny. In 1975, as a part of the celebrations for the anniversary of the Bolshevik revolution, the Krivak-class destroyer, the *Storozhevoy*, was in the Baltic port of Riga, capital city of the satellite state of Latvia, when the political officer and the second officer recognized that the proximity of Swedish territorial waters represented a once-in-a-lifetime chance of escape from the Soviet camp. With most of the crew and the captain locked below decks, the political officer and the second officer, with the bare minimum of the crew who were co-conspirators to help them, sailed from Riga. The flight was not at first noticed, but a member of the crew who either doubted the wisdom of what they attempted or had chickened out, radioed the shore and alerted the command.

Chaos would have reigned, and confusion, when the message came in. The then captain lieutenant, Falkovsky, had pushed aside superiors who dithered and had given the orders. None had dared disobey him. The air force had bombed and strafed the defenceless vessel and had stopped it in the water a mere forty-eight kilometres from the Swedish sanctuary. Falkovsky had led the boarding party that had brought back the political officer, the second officer and the crewmen. The political officer had been summarily executed. Falkovsky had said, to any who would listen to him, that he was proud of what he had done, and he had further explained that his motive was not to protect the sanctity of the revolution's celebration, but to safeguard the good name of the navy. None had dared doubt his argument. He would show short shrift, no sympathy, for traitors. The message of Riga and the *Storozhevoy* was known wherever Alexei Falkovsky's name was spoken, and the reasoning behind his actions.

Thirteen years later he had met the junior lieutenant. The day they had first set eyes on each other had sealed the relationship. The Kanin-class guided missile destroyer, *Gnevnyy*, had been due to sail on a day in early July 1988 from Severomorsk to join a Northern Fleet anti-submarine exercise, and had not left harbour. The crew had been paraded, and Captain, first rank, Falkovsky had stamped on board and delivered a peroration of ferocious bile at the inefficiency of the *Gnevnyy*'s officers, NCOs and able seamen, and of Junior Lieutenant Archenko. They were a 'disgrace', their 'underpreparedness shamed the navy', they were not fit to clean 'the latrines of the fleet's dry docks', and all their shore leave for twelve months was cancelled. In the face of Falkovsky's tirade, the *Gnevnyy*'s captain had hung his head and studied his boots and had known that his navy life was ended. As Captain, first rank, Falkovsky had stared at the crew, stabbing at them with the glower of his eyes, Archenko had spoken up. He had been in the fourth rank and there had been – Falkovsky could still remember the detail of it – a forward thrust of his chin, his eyes had stared directly forward, and his voice had been firm and without fear. He spoke when no one else had the courage to do so: 'Sir, the *Gnevnyy* did not sail because it has no fuel. Although the crew have not been paid for three months, although there was only enough food stored on board for one week's basic meals and the exercise is due to last for nineteen days, those were not the reasons we did not put to sea. The fuel should have been loaded the day before we should have sailed. It was not. It has been sold on the black-market. Our captain was told this by an officer in Administration at Northern Fleet when he went ashore to plead for the diesel. He was told the storage tanks were empty because the last of the fuel had been corruptly sold to *mafiya* criminals living in Leningrad. When the captain, first rank, provides us with fuel we will be ready to sail and will strive to fulfil our mission.' He had been the only one with the bravery to speak . . .

In the morning fuel had been found, and rations, and the ship had sailed, and three officers in Administration had gone to the camps, and a *mafiya* king from Leningrad had died in a road accident. Two years later, when Archenko's duty, closely monitored to see whether he was a barrack lawyer or a duty-driven officer, on the *Gnevnyy* was completed, Falkovsky had sent him a terse two-line note inviting him on to his personal staff. Two years later, Falkovsky had been posted to the defence ministry in Moscow and had pulled the strings to obtain a place for the young man at the Grechko Academy for Staff Officers in the capital.

In 1997, Falkovsky had achieved admiral's rank and left the ministry to take over command of the entire surface complement of the Northern Fleet, and young Archenko had been posted with him. There was a fondness for Viktor, but also an admiration for the workload the man took on his shoulders. Total reliability, the honesty he yearned for from subordinates, and trust were the bricks on which their relationship was built. Viktor was his proxy son. Two years later, May 1999, they had gone to Kaliningrad together: Admiral of the Fleet and chief of staff. In the last twelve months, many young officers had jacked in the navy and retreated into civilian life, so few of those who remained were reliable. This man was a jewel. It was Falkovsky's opinion that he could not have fulfilled his duty without the ever-present and ever-dependable Viktor Archenko. And it was Falkovsky's hope that he would inherit the position of top dog, Admiral of the Fleet of the Russian Federation, when he had finished at Kaliningrad, and that Viktor would be with him, securing his outer office.

They arrived at air-force headquarters. Falkovsky said, 'Don't take any shit from them.'

'Sorry, Admiral . . . Oh, yes, would I ever?' the quiet voice replied.

Again, he punched the younger man's arm. He thought Viktor subdued, distant . . . and then he was out of his car and marching past a small honour guard and hearing the reassuring bite of Viktor's shoes on the gravel behind him.

It was the sort of evening that Viktor fed from.

His admiral and the generals were at the far end of the room, circling each other for advantage like rutting boars, playing with words and seeking to disguise their mutual jealousies. Viktor was at the bar with those who made up the second echelon of authority, where the food was. Although at the bar and close to the steward, it was his skill that he drank little on such occasions – the visit from Moscow of an air-force general in charge of design and development – while making certain that others around him consumed copiously and dangerously. He was inside the web of a network where total trust existed, where men spoke freely.

The chief of staff to the visiting general told Viktor, 'If we don't have it soon we might as well go home and grow potatoes. Without it we're fucked. At a ratio of two to one we need the lightweight fighter and the heavy bomber, must have them. What we're going to get is different, the compromise – one aircraft, with NTOW of seventeen tonnes – but the range, it's promised us, will exceed four thousand five hundred kilometres, and they'll go for the two engines, the AL-41F turbofan, which is thrust of 175kN. It's not what we want but it's what we're going to get. MFI is what they guarantee us. What's the manoeuvrability? we ask. They say it's better than the American next generation, and they tell us the radar will be better, the NO14 system that has a +/–130–150 azimuth, with tail radar for the rest, and they say the payload will be all the current air-to-air and air-to-ground payload. But, but, where is it, the prototype? The 1–44 is stuck in a Zhukovsky hangar, undergoing what they call "ground adjustments", which means it's crap – the word is "high-degree static instability". They're waiting on the test pilot having the balls to go up in it, poor bastard. It's what we're going to get, and the money's there, from last week, if it ever flies . . . And, how are things with the navy?'

Viktor talked for a few moments about the condition of the Baltic Fleet, but his concentration was on memorizing what had been said. MFI was the Mikoyan Multifunction Tactical Fighter. NTOW was Normal Take-off Weight . . . it would be the successor to the SU-27 and MiG-29 fourth-generation fighters, and was designed to confront the Americans' Lockheed Martin F-22 Raptor. Viktor gestured discreetly at his admiral across the length of the room and muttered that 'the fat man' would appreciate an up-to-date paper on MFI and where the programme was going, for 'his eyes only', and was told such a paper would be sent.

Viktor moved on.

At that time, across the border, away to the south-west in the Polish city of Warsaw, on the embassy's second floor, behind a steel door, a signal was being encyphered.

Viktor reached his second target of the evening, a colonel in Early Warning Defence, who with his general was on a three-day assessment-of-capability visit to the Kaliningrad base. Viktor had noted that the colonel's glass was empty and brought a double replacement.

'It's hopeless, worse than ever. I've been in EWD for nineteen years. It's like our knickers have dropped to our ankles, the elastic's gone. You don't believe me? You should. The big word is deterioration. We follow the principle of "hair-trigger" reaction to threat, but that is based on comprehensive satellite surveillance of where the launch might come from, and we haven't replaced the satellites. They've passed their useful lifespan. And not only are my knickers down, I'm blindfolded. There should be nine satellites up if we're to follow "hair trigger", but we have only three. *Three.* We cannot monitor firings from the Tridents out in the Pacific, where they'd launch from. Because it's a high elliptical satellite system there are times when we have no cover for an eight-hour period. *Eight.* And we've lost ground radar – like the one in Latvia. They could shoot from Alaska and we wouldn't know we were under attack until the air burst. We have no shield, not any more. We scream for more satellites, and they are deaf to us. It's bloody freezing with your knickers at your ankles, I tell you.'

Viktor drifted away. He estimated that his admiral would be bored by now with the occasion. He left behind him two men who had each poured out a cupful of heartache about a new air-force programme and an early-warning shield that was a myth.

An encyphered signal would now be in London.

In the staff car he told the admiral what he had learned and won a steady succession of grunted expletives in return . . . He had not noticed them on the outward journey, but on the return leg there were vehicle lights behind them that kept pace with the admiral's driver.

By now the signal would have been read. Were his friends true to him? Was there anything his friends could do for him? Did they care? . . . The signal his friends would read would say: FERRET: NO SHOW.

3

Q. In which Russian city in 1998 was a state of emergency declared
because the majority of the population were in a medical condition of starvation?

A. Kaliningrad.

Every morning when he did not have a breakfast meeting, Viktor
Archenko ran on the beach north of the base. He left the harbour,
the castle, the barracks blocks and office buildings behind him, and
Lenin's statue, which dominated the complex in stature and past
authority, and the guarded gates. He had been tense as he had jogged
past the sentries ... The moment when his freedom would end?
Would he be turned back? But the conscripts with their rifles on the
barrier had saluted him, and he had made himself acknowledge
them. The black van and the silver saloon had been parked outside
the gates and when he was a hundred metres beyond them he'd
heard, against the drumming of his feet, their engines start up. He
hadn't looked back.

In the night he had lain on his narrow bed and he had cursed
himself for the mistake he had made on the road to the border and
Braniewo. The U-turn into and out of the side road had been a major
error of judgement, and it would not be repeated. The run along the
beach was his final throw to save himself. He had talked about it with
his friends in the late-evening and early-morning sessions in the
Excelsior Hotel and it had been stressed to him that he must make a
habit of the morning run. At his age it was entirely understandable
that he should seek to maintain his athleticism, so he ran on the
beach every morning that he was free to do so, and the sentries on
the gate were familiar with it, and so was Piatkin, the *zampolit*, and

so would be the men who sat in the black van and the silver saloon. His friends had told him to make the habit familiar to anyone who watched him so that, when and if it mattered, the run did not create suspicion.

He wore heavy trainer running shoes and thick socks so that his feet would not blister, and light-weight shorts and an athletics vest that had the emblem of the Baltic Fleet front and back, and a red bandanna was knotted tight on his forehead so that the sweat did not dribble into his eyes. In the pocket of his shorts was a small piece of white chalk, no bigger than his thumbnail. His friends had told him he must always have the chalk there, however long he had no need of it.

The only approach road to Baltiysk, and the base, was along the spit from the north. At the town of Primorsk, the land mass shrank to a narrow finger peninsula, and the road ran beside a railtrack that served the fleet. The canal at Baltiysk cut across the peninsula that stretched south across the firing range and the missile batteries, then the frontier, where high wire and watchtowers guard the approach to Poland.

His trainers stamped on the dry sand above the tideline, and the give in it made for hard running. His target, that dawn and every dawn that he ran on the beach, was a watertower built on the upper point of the peninsula, its foundations some thirty metres above the levels of the sea and the lagoon. Running fast, like an automaton, he was soon clear of the base with nothing ahead of him except the sea, the beach and the tall pine trees that hid the road and the railtrack. His stride kicked up little clouds of sand, and sometimes he crunched on the amber pebbles that were washed on to the beach by the fiercer storms. In his dulled mind, he wondered if his grandmother had walked on this beach, in panic, had tramped on the same brittle sand and had carried the suitcase in which were all of her possessions. If she had she would have gazed out over the sea, far beyond the waves breaking on the sand and the little pieces of amber, and she might have seen the disappearing outlines on the horizon of the low, over-loaded *Wilhelm Gustloff*, the *General Steuben* and the *Goya*, and she might have wept because she was not on one of them.

Slowly, as he willed himself faster, the watertower grew closer. The road was now close to the beach, but the trees shielded it. Often he heard the thunder of the lorries coming to the base or leaving it, but that morning he could only hear the lesser purr of the black van and the silver saloon tracking him.

High on the sand, below the watertower, was the wreck of a fishing-boat. It would have been seven metres long and two wide, and half a century before it would have held thirty or forty escapers. It had been caught on the beach by a strafing aircraft, and cannon shells had holed it. Perhaps his grandmother had been close, hiding in the pine trees and pressed down on the needle-strewn ground when the aircraft had come over on its low pass and destroyed her final hope. Viktor always ran as far as the wreck on the sand, and never further. There he would rest for three minutes, timed on the stop-watch dial of his wristwatch, a routine set in stone.

It was his cry for help. In the face of the wind his back rested against the old plank timbers of the fishing-boat. From the dunes, as they smoked their cigarettes, his watchers might see the top of his head. If he had been in the lee of the wind, sheltered, they would have been able to see him, and what he did. He reached into the pocket of his shorts and took out the piece of chalk. Near to the bow, where once the name of the boat and its number would have been painted, close to a shell-hole, he made two short crosses, and underneath the crosses he wrote the letters Y and F. He did not know how his friends would answer his cry. He pushed himself up, his three minutes gone.

He was a traitor. He imagined the unpitying, feral eyes of the men on the dunes before they turned to scurry back to the van and the saloon car.

He was a traitor for two reasons. The learning of the life and death of his father and of his grandmother had tipped him into the chasm and down in freefall to treachery. If he had been told only of his father he might not have taken the big step, crossed that line. Within a few months of his mother telling him of his grandmother's life and death, Viktor had walked the trawler's gangplank in Murmansk. It was fitting he should now be posted to Kaliningrad.

His grandmother was Helga Schmidt, the daughter of Wilhelm and Anneliese, who had had a prosperous pre-war grain-export business in the east Prussian city of Königsberg. Wilhelm died in the

55

air raids of August 1944 when the old town and his warehouses were bombed with incendiaries.

Helga and Anneliese had not believed until it was too late that the Reich could disintegrate. Then, daughter and mother had fled in a final crocodile of refugees from Königsberg the day before the Red Army surrounded the city. They had reached Pillau, walked there, but the last ships had gone. The army garrison at Pillau had fought on for two weeks after the final surrender of Königsberg by General Otto Lasch.

Pillau had fallen when no ammunition remained to defend it, and the women had stood behind white flags and faced the Red Army.

Anneliese had been bayoneted. She had not survived long enough to see what happened to her daughter – which was God's small mercy.

The victorious troops were from Central Asia, but their officers were ethnic Russians. The officers chose the prettiest, and Helga was among them.

Helga Schmidt was raped by a battalion's officer, then by the NCOs, then by those of the troops still able to achieve erections – it was what happened in dark days at the end of a war of brutality. When they were all flaccid, spent, satiated, she was left.

The girl, impregnated, was shipped back to the city, now called Kaliningrad, and existed there as a gypsy waif. She kept herself alive through her love for an unborn child.

Starved, half frozen, living in the bomb ruins, Helga survived her pregnancy, but was too weak to feed her boy baby, born on 25 January 1946.

Helga Schmidt wrote down what had happened to her, wrapped her son in the thickest rags she could find, with the paper that told her history, and left him on a snow-covered step at a side door to the city orphanage.

The same day she had given up her baby, she hanged herself from a beam in the cathedral's ruins, having used the torn strips of her skirt as a noose.

The baby, adopted by a Russian family, was named Pyotr. The family, farmers from the east and resettled on formerly German property in Kaliningrad, had the name of Archenko.

Pyotr Archenko was only twenty years old when he married his childhood sweetheart, Irina, whose stomach bulged at the ceremony. Their only son was given the name of Viktor.

On her deathbed, Irina's mother-in-law had shown her the faded, creased sheet of paper on which Helga Schmidt had written her testament. In turn, on her own deathbed, Irina had allowed Viktor to read it, then had taken it back from him and had held it over a candle until it had burned and her fingers had blistered.

The story, and that of the death of his father, had bred betrayal.

Viktor had done what his handlers had told him to, and he ran back along the beach. The gloom of the dawn had gone and the sun now edged over the tips of the pine trees. On the return leg he ran more loosely. He never looked at the dunes to see whether the men watched him. That he lived was because of his grandmother's strength and that was a small but solid comfort to him . . . Would they hear his cry, and would they answer it? He did not know.

In the night the battery on the alarm clock had failed. The bleeper hadn't sounded.

Locke woke, glanced at the clock's digital face, was turning over to go back to sleep when he saw the first glimmer of daylight through the thin curtains. He looked at his watch and surged out of his cold bed.

For a week now the bed had harboured an icy chill in Danuta's absence. He shaved in the shower and dressed while he was still wet. A best shirt and a best tie, his best suit and his best shoes were snatched from the wardrobe and from the drawers and he dripped pools of water on to the carpet. As he closed his front door for the charge down the stairwell, the lights were still blazing behind him, but he didn't have time to go back and switch them off.

He ran for his car. He had not filled the tank since yesterday's drive to and from Braniewo and the needle flickered in the red segment of the dial. He prayed he had enough petrol to get him to Okecie. If he was caught in the city's early rush-hour gridlocks he would miss the flight. He had the protection of diplomatic plates but they would not stop a policeman, for amusement, waving him down with a luminous baton. He was still on the wide Al Jerozolimskie, had not yet reached the Zawisky roundabout, when he made his first clear-cut decision of the day. He would drive straight past any policeman who tried to stop him – and bugger the consequences. An hour after sending the signal, and a quarter of an hour after he had come back to the apartment after sitting with a coffee for twenty minutes at the Sklep z Kawq Pozegnanie z Afrykq – she hadn't been there – his mobile had rung. Libby Weedon. He was summoned to London, first flight in the morning with LOT, the national carrier. 'Don't miss it, you're in with the big girls,' and she'd hung up. Libby Weedon, clever lady, had distanced herself from Ferret, and left him, the young man on his first Service posting abroad, to do the driving and the collection from the dead drops. What could he bloody well tell the 'big girls'? No detail was more telling than the three words of his signal: FERRET: NO SHOW.

He broke most of Poland's traffic laws on the way to Okecie, and beat the early traffic . . . He was close to the airport when he remembered that he was due to meet a speech writer of the KPN party for lunch. He fumbled with his mobile and left a message on Libby Weedon's voicemail asking for the duty secretary to ring with apologies. The needle banged on the dial's 'empty' segment, but the tank held out and he made it to the airport. He was last on to the flight.

Gabriel Locke's upbringing had been on the southern tip of west Wales. His parents still ran a 150-acre dairy farm on fields that were edged by cliffs that fell to violent seas. It was a harsh place and made for a hard and uncertain existence. Their lives were dominated by the extremes of weather, the coldness of the impersonal banks, the milk quotas, the per-litre price, the ever-increasing call-out fee charged by veterinary surgeons, and most recently by the scourge of foot-and-mouth disease. They survived on the edge of poverty, reduced to hoarding pounds, squirrelling away the silver coins, putting the pence in jars before collecting enough to dump them on the counter of the village shop and the post office. He had wanted none of it. He was one of the few from his comprehensive-school class who had *bettered* himself and broken free. He had thought he would never suffer as he believed they did. He rarely phoned home, only sent anodyne messages on occasional postcards. He wanted structure and certainty to his life and it was ridiculous to him – in this new millennium – that a storm, or a Whitehall bureaucrat's decision, or a virus could tip the difference between minimal financial survival and bankruptcy. Yet for the first time in his adult life, going down the pier and seeing the force of the wind scudding across the Tarmac, he felt unsure as to what the future held.

There was turbulence ahead. They lifted off and the aircraft shook as it gathered height. It would be a foul flight. The uncertainty festered in his mind. The cream of the Service's new intake, his contemporaries on the IONEC course, were now scattered round the Gulf, in Islamabad, Tashkent and Tehran, in Damascus and Tel Aviv, in Beirut, Cairo and Khartoum, and the prize bitch among them was in Kabul. They were at the sharp end of the Service's work, and Gabriel Locke was in Warsaw where less than fuck-all relevant work was done . . . and he was being summoned back to London because two dead drops – procedures as antiquated and outdated as the plumbing of his parents' milking parlour – had failed. The sourness engulfed him as the plane ducked through the choppy air. His annoyance, for want of a better target, focused on the outmoded system that had produced Ferret in the first place.

GL: It's ridiculous – in this day and age, with the electronic capability we have – for us to be dependent on drops where we have no control of the situation. I don't know what's going on, and it doesn't seem anybody else does. Anyway, if he's in difficulty, this Codename Ferret, I cannot see that anything can be done for him.

Alice North was at the far end of the conference room where she would hardly have been noticed with her back to the window. The bright sunlight that was thrown over her shoulder cast a shadow on her face. Her legs were crossed and on her upper thigh was the notepad in which she wrote her shorthand, with sharpened pencil. She was only there to take the record of the meeting, not to contribute. She had met Gabriel Locke once, at Rupert Mowbray's retirement party, and from the first sight of him she had disliked the young man. Not tall, a nice head, fine dark hair, well-cut features, but humourless, cold and without humanity.

Before the meeting had settled, Alice had written at the top of the first page of the foolscap pad,

Codename Ferret.
(Classification/Top Secret)
Meeting at VBX, 21 September 2002. Present:
Albert Ponsford (AP) Russia Desk, Peter Giles (PG) Dep. Director Covert Ops, Gabriel Locke (GL) Warsaw station, Maj. William Courtney (WC) Special Air Service/Liaison, Lt Cdr Geoffrey Snow (GS) Naval Intelligence – Alice North.

Her face, without makeup, was a mask. She was not expected to speak. Of all of them in the room she knew the most of Codename Ferret.

PG: We have a good reputation, deservedly so, for providing help and succour to those who are in need of it. But there are two limitations on what we can do – first, what is possible in the circumstances, second, what is desirable in the current political, diplomatic mood.

Peter Giles had always been a snake in the grass. And Alice had scant respect for Ponsford either, a time-server with a knapsack of pomposity since the last New Year Honours and his OBE award.

AP: I don't want to pour cold water on this – I'm as keen as the next man to do the right thing by an agent, but there are very serious areas that we must look most closely at. HM Government policy is now towards rapprochement with our Russian neighbours. Nobody suggested, of course they didn't, that in the light of the rapprochement we should wind down what we were running inside their territories, but we most certainly do not shove two fingers up in their faces . . . I would assume that ministers would expect, should our man be arrested, that events should be allowed to take their course.
PG: Minimize the damage – for heaven's sake, we now have collaboration committees meeting monthly, and Afghanistan

couldn't have been attempted without that exercise in good relations, because we were the conduit between them and the Americans. Ride it out, let the storm blow over. We couldn't dream of jeopardizing the new relationship for one man. He's only a junior naval officer, isn't he?

Alice glanced up from the notepad and saw the naval intelligence man wince. All the faces were turned towards him. She thought him not a man to put his head unnecessarily on the block. He coughed. The delay he put into the hack deep in his throat, then the shovelling in his pocket for a handkerchief seemed to her to be in the hope that someone else might speak up. There was no escape.

GS: It's difficult to quantify his value. It's not state-of-the-art research and development, but it's all useful. All right, occasionally we get something that's hot, but most frequently we get what is relevant. How I'd summarize, we're being given a rather unique insight into the modern Russian navy. From him we have confirmation of much that we believed but were not certain of, and he's surprised us with detail on submarine depths, hull coatings, engine noise, missile-preparedness and range. What is also clear is that the quality of the material has reached a higher level than we received in that first package. His access is good – now, I don't know who he works for, but I have to assume he's close to a senior admiral. I suppose the possibility is that the admiral will go right to the top, and take his man, our man, with him. Conclusions: because of him we feel comfortable about the Russian navy. Then there's the air-force insights, which colleagues appreciate. But if we lost him, would it matter? No, the world wouldn't stop – I don't think we'd miss him.

Again, Alice looked up and saw heads nod agreement.

Others now took their cue from the navy's man. She scribbled busily.

AP: It's all about embarrassment – formally we'd deny all knowledge of him . . .

PG: Never seek to justify, never look to apologize – anyway, when they walk in, these people, they must have a pretty clear idea of the risk being undertaken. What would he get – ten years, a bit more?
AP: Something a little more drastic than that.

Her face was down and close to the notepad, her pencil moved silently, but her coverage of the word 'drastic' was emphatic, and if she had pressed harder the lead might have snapped.

PG: I thought they'd abolished capital punishment in the Federation . . .
AP: Well, they'd find a way round that little obstacle – but it's not our problem. Our problem is our ministers and how they'd regard the fallout from an arrest. Deniability is indeed the name of the game . . . It was good stuff about the redeployment of the Tochka missiles into Kaliningrad, and good fun the kicking we were able to give them over it, even if it did have to be sourced as satellite photography.
GL: Cut him adrift, forget him. Not worth the hassle. At our station we have excellent relations with the Russians, and it's two-way traffic. They're getting techno-know-how, and we're getting decent stuff on organized crime. It would hurt if we lost that . . . What's the worst, they expel a couple of ours, we expel a couple of theirs, then it's history? What we should not do is exacerbate a situation, turn a clean cut into something that's infected.
PG: He was, wasn't he, Rupert's man?
AP: Rupert's gone – sadly missed. [Irony] Don't know how we manage without him, a wonder the building still stands.

She heard the little ripple of laughter around the table.

He'd waited for his moment. In the past two years she'd twice met William Courtney. He'd be a few years older than herself, might be thirty-eight, and she thought that the best years of his soldiering were behind him. His reward, for ageing, was a transfer from Hereford to liaison work with the Service. It was a part of the Service's glory legacy that a troop was permanently on standby down at Hereford for the rougher end of the Service's work. He wore his grey-flecked hair long on his shoulders, and she thought a ponytail would have been smarter, but it was apparent to her that smartness did not fit the hippie/traveller image he cultivated. No jacket, a thick sweater that looked to have been worn that week in a sheep-pen on the Brecons and had unravelling wool in the elbows and at the cuffs, and jeans that were clean but had not been pressed after an obligatory run through a launderette. He had on trainers that were faded but had probably shared space in the same wash as the jeans.

WC: What's the ex-filtration plan?

Alice knew Ferret's file backwards. She could turn up any page without going to the index. She had never seen an ex-filtration plan, only an 'alert' procedure of chalk signs on a beach. Her pencil was poised. Her eyes rose and she saw Ponsford look away, and Giles stared down at the blank paper in front of him then reached for his glass of water. A smile, fading towards impertinence, wreathed the Special Air Service major's mouth.

WC: Sorry, am I being dim? There is a plan to lift him out, take Ferret out – or isn't there?
PG: Actually written down? No, there isn't.
AP: Never seemed necessary – or Rupert never got round to it.
WC: No plan? No recce been done, no dry run, right? Starting from scratch, yes? Time not on our side? I read up on Kaliningrad last night, briefed myself. It's a bloody fortress. Naval infantry, marines, mechanized regular army. Other parts of good old Russia might have had the capability degraded, not this place. Quite frankly, and it's my job to ensure there are no misunderstandings, I don't think my people would be that keen on a trip in there, not to Kaliningrad.
GL: These people make their own beds, and then they have to lie on them.
AP: Sad, it goes without saying, but that's the life of an agent – Gabriel has put it bluntly but quite fairly – and there is no room for sentiment in these affairs, and it's the death of an agent.

Alice said softly, 'Bertie, your last remark, is that for the record?'

A flush of colour to the man's cheeks, blood running in the surface veins. 'No, I don't think anything of my last little contribution was made for posterity – just thinking aloud. Thank you, Alice.'

None of that speech would be erased with her india-rubber, none of it would be crossed out. When she typed up the record it would be there, and she'd make damn sure it went to the top-floor suite where the director general held court. And then she had gone back into her corner shadow. It was to be Alice's only intervention. No one around the table would have seen it, but her eyes watered. They didn't know him, didn't want to, didn't care what he went through – stress, strain, pressure – to provide the damn detail on hull coating, diving depths, propeller noise. Alice knew . . . She flipped the page over and wrote on.

AP: We're not quite at doom-and-destruction mode. God knows, Rupert's notes were thin enough – I don't think he trusted any of us, you know – but there is a final dead drop available to Ferret, were he to believe himself under surveillance. What I'm suggesting for now is that Gabriel takes on a role as 'factotum' . . .

Alice knew her medieval Latin. '*Fac*' was 'do', '*totus*' (adj.) was 'all'. She looked at him and thought he weighed whether this was good for his career's future, or whether he might be damaged by it.

. . . pulls the committee's decisions together and gives teeth to them. First things first, the last dead drop. Stay behind, would you, Gabriel, please?

Alice put her notepad and pencils into her bag. As she walked to the door she heard Courtney, the Hereford officer, saying conversationally to Giles, 'Don't get me wrong – Who Dares Wins and all that crap – but I meant what I said. We're hardly going to volunteer to go into that rat's nest, Kaliningrad. Don't even think about it – count us right out.'

Ponsford said, 'Like everything else in this life, it was good while it lasted . . . I have to say it, if an agent misses two dead drops, and has never missed before, then he's in trouble. Poor bastard . . . but that's the way it goes.'

As she went out through the door she heard the naval intelligence man ask Giles, 'What would be the form on their side?'

And she heard Giles say, 'They'd call up an interrogator, a very high-quality man . . .'

She closed the door, and thought none of them saw her leave.

Guided by a flare of red smoke, the helicopter put down in a field close to a burned-out farmhouse. The thrash of its rotors lifted up what was left of the farmhouse's roof and tossed aside the corrugated-iron sheets, like paper flaking over a bonfire.

A reception committee of men and officers stared at Bikov and his escort as they jumped down from the hatch. He looked around him. A half-dozen armoured personnel carriers were drawn up in a line surrounded by the treadmarks of their tyres where they had manoeuvred to make the line. They were blank and expressionless faces, the faces of men who fought a war they had realized long ago lacked the possibility of victory. He understood why the helicopter could not take him further forward – the cloud ceiling was low. Only the base of the hills was visible to the south. The snow fell lightly on his shoulders as he walked forward to meet the men who waited for him. If it had not been for the officer and the men who were captured and held in the high ground that was covered by the cloud's fall, and if it had not been for the patrol of Black Berets who were hidden in a cave with their prisoners and, most importantly, if it had not been for the reputation that travelled fast ahead of Yuri Bikov, then no man – sane or lunatic – would have gone up into the killing ground around the Argun gorge.

He was briefed. He took a mug of lukewarm coffee, looked at the maps on which the snow fell, and said little. The four men charged with the immediate protection of his life were from the Vympel unit, controlled by Directorate V of the FSB's Special Operations Centre, and they said less. While he went over the maps and the pitifully small amount of recent intelligence, they checked their gear, weapons and medical equipment . . . Bikov had not been given their names, and if he'd asked for them he would not have been told. He couldn't read their faces because they had masks over them through which only their eyes were revealed, but their breath came through the cotton and he sensed that they, too, thought this an idiot place to be. But he trusted them, as he had to. He was put with his men in the third of the six carriers, and he fastened the studs of the bulletproof jacket, felt the warmth of its weight, and was given a helmet, which he wore.

They had driven for eighty-seven minutes, were already high in the dense clouds and on a hairpin track of slushy ice and snow, when the first RPG-7 shell hit the carrier in front.

An arm snatched him and threw him down on to the steel-plate floor. The second RPG-7 shell took off the forward wheel, right side, and his carrier lurched then slid into a ditch at the track's side.

One of the Vympel men was over his legs and another lay on Bikov's head. The two others crouched on the crazily angled floor at either side of him. He was deafened. The machine-gun blasts, with the anti-tank weapons firing over open sights, and the grenades were from the ambushed carriers. The incoming fire was from the RPG-7 launchers, and mortars, and machine-guns, and rifles, and . . . The sound crashed around him, and men screamed – a soldier fell on the body covering his head and he felt the warmth of blood. The Vympel men never shouted, spoke, or fired their weapons. They protected him: his was a chosen life.

He heard the screams and the pounding of the gunfire. They were like vermin in a darkened pit, and Bikov was choking on the smoke of burned tyres, flesh and fuel. He had been in combat situations before in Chechnya, but nothing as terrifying as this contact. He had crouched at the corner of buildings in Grozny city when small-arms fire had come from an apartment block, and tanks and artillery had pounded the suspected firing position, and he had not felt endangered. The side of the carrier took the full weight of an RPG blast and the interior sang with the shrapnel. He did not know how it was possible that he had not been hit. He moved his toes, his fingers, opened his eyes in the acrid gloom, then ran his hands down his stomach and motioned his spine forward and down, as if he were fucking, and knew he had not been hit – it was hard to believe. But the smoke would kill them.

Who would care enough to come to his funeral if his body was extracted and brought home? Not his parents because he hadn't listed them as next-of-kin on his file, and they wouldn't hear of his death unless it made a paragraph in a newspaper they might read before they lit the paper in the grates of their separate fires. Not his wife, because it was twelve years since the divorce. Not Natasha, who was now fifteen, because her mother had poisoned the child's mind against him. Maybe a few at the Lubyanka would come with flowers as an excuse to get away from their desks for a couple of hours . . . The brigadier would care. Yuri Bikov was the lifeline of the brigadier.

He shouted, 'Let's get the fuck out of here.'

Maybe there was a poorer chance outside, but better to die there than like rats in a darkening hole. The smoke fumes were choking him.

He couldn't read their eyes, expressionless in the slits. One moment he was on the floor of the carrier. The next, he was being dragged its length like a dead-weight sack of potatoes. He 'snagged against a body, had time to see that its left leg was severed free at the groin. As he was pulled out into the daylight, the loose leg came with him. They went into the ditch and their fall broke the ice covering. He went under, then was pulled up. He spat wet mud from his mouth. Among the rocks and scrub bushes, and in the trees above the track, men fought for survival. In the carriers the troops blasted into the murk of the cloud and prayed they might live.

The Vympel men took him down a slope, a rush between each rock then a stop and a murmur between them, then another rush. They used sign language to communicate, and never fired. The convoy of carriers, and its fate, was not their concern: he was. Only for a reputation such as Yuri Bikov's would such an operation, with the risk of such casualties, have been mounted.

They left the firefight and the killing behind them. Bikov knew enough of the war in Chechnya to understand that if the convoy's troops were overrun the men would have saved a last grenade or a last bullet for themselves. The brigadier and his escort had either not been able to, or not had that moment of courage, which was why he and the Vympel men were huddled between the rocks or bent and running.

They went down the slope for more than a kilometre, then took cover in trees. After checking him over to see that he was not hurt, they used their maps and a handheld GPS system to plot their position and work out their route.

For a long time they heard the shooting and the explosions, but Bikov could not tell whether the attack was being driven off or whether the men would need the last grenade or bullet.

The cloud's mist was tight around them as they climbed and Bikov struggled to keep the pace set for him.

He hadn't painted that afternoon but had been on the roof of his hut hammering in the nails left for him on the far side of the loch by the postwoman, beating down on their heads to secure the sheet-iron sections. There had been bad gales the previous winter and this was work Billy Smith should have accomplished in the spring or the summer, but he had left it, and now the autumn was with him and time was against him. All day he had been on the roof, not coming down for a sandwich or a mug of coffee, and it was his penance. When he'd started he'd believed that he'd finish in time to get in three hours of painting, not up the mountain behind the hut but down on the shore where the ducks were preparing restlessly to go south for the winter. His painting was abandoned for the day, and he regretted that. Other than when he used his full strength to thump down the six-inch nails, and the sounds echoed back from the cliff slopes and the gullies, there was a limitless quiet around him.

When the room had cleared, Albert Ponsford poured the dregs of the coffee into his cup and Locke's, and then said, 'I don't think, speaking frankly, it's going to go anywhere, but it's important we move by the form book. The last dead drop of course has to be visited, and we go through the motions of ex-filtration. I'd like you to handle all that, Gabriel.'

'Be very pleased to, Bertie.' Gabriel Locke was well enough versed in the Service culture to appreciate that a request made by a senior man with elaborate politeness was in fact an instruction. Willing hands were always welcomed hands at headquarters.

'Rupert left so little for us . . . There's a rumour abroad that he spent his last morning here shredding material on Ferret. Extraordinary behaviour, and so insulting to colleagues. It's a minor miracle he deigned to provide us with the details of this last drop procedure. He did – and I don't think time is on our side . . . I noted your hostility to Ferret.'

Locke said abruptly, 'It's not personal, no . . . just that there's nothing to be done. I'd call it a pragmatic approach, the real world against a bygone age of sentiment and emotion.'

Ponsford smiled, always the enigma when one to one with juniors, and handed the young man a single sheet of typed paper. Locke thought he had said the right thing but could not be sure.

'You'll take care of it, send the signal, yes?'

'Consider it done – as you say, Bertie, that's the form book. By the way, I came without a bag. I'll need some clothes . . .'

'Can't have you wandering around like the great unwashed. Buy them and bill us.'

It took him a full fifteen minutes to find Alice North. Upstairs, down in the elevator, along corridors, and finally he located her, tucked away on the fourth floor, in East European Controllerate, tapping her keyboard, transcribing her shorthand. She was quite pretty, not beautiful like Danuta, not stylish, but she had good colour in her cheeks, and her dark auburn hair was cut short – he thought that was for convenience not effect. The only jewellery she wore was a half-hidden amber pendant hanging from a gold neck-chain. He hovered behind her. She went on typing. He read on her screen his own initials, then: *'Cut him adrift, forget him. Not worth the hassle. In our station we have excellent relations with the Russians, and . . .'* Of course, she knew he was there. He coughed. She continued typing.

'Excuse me, Alice, but I've a signal to send, and I've got no clothes other than what I'm standing in. I've cleared it with Bertie. Could you, please, slip over to the Strand and get me two or three pairs of socks, for size-nine shoe, two Y-fronts and singlets for a medium fit, and a couple of shirts that are pretty neutral, fifteen-and-a-half collar, a pair of pyjamas, one of those little packs of plastic razors, and some soap? A hundred from petty cash should do it. Thank you.'

She gave no indication that it was not her job to do his shopping for him. She ignored him as she closed down her screen, went through the laid-down procedures for storage, then locked her note-pad in her personal safe. She had her coat on and was gone.

Locke thought her sad ... He grinned to himself. He liked the word he'd used – 'pragmatic' – to Bertie Ponsford. It had set his stall out. He was of the new generation and unburdened by old baggage. When he had been on the IONEC course, the young probationer, the intake's lecture room had been visited by the director general. On his entry they'd all stood until the man, close to retirement, had motioned them to sit. He'd said, 'Russia remains and will remain a potent military threat. Though their military intentions may no longer be belligerent, their capability remains. The unpredictability and instability of the regime could make them all the more danger-ous. This Service will have an important role for many years to come in warning this country of danger signs on their long road to democ-racy.' Then, he'd turned on his heel and gone. The students had discussed what had been said to them. Locke's contribution to the seminar had been, 'What we heard was the leaden weight of the old Service, all the stuff that should be consigned to history books. I, for one, intend to move on and fight the real battles that mean some-thing to GB's security – organized crime, Mid-East terrorism, Islamic fundamentalism, proliferation of weapons of mass destruc-tion in the third world. We all know where the real threats lie.' The tutor had not contradicted him. That director general was now out to grass and the old guard's message should have been dead, buried. Ferret was history.

He took the workstation next to Alice's and typed the signal into the automatic telegram handling system and pressed the 'send' code to move it on its way. Then he waited for her to return with his new clothes.

He sat in a small dank cell. The custody officer had taken his tie and belt but had left him with his shoelaces, and the detectives had kept hold of his wallet. Up to that afternoon Ham Protheroe had always been ahead, but he'd stayed the extra day: he'd reckoned there was one more killing to be made from the woman's credit cards, and that

70

had been his last mistake. His bag was packed in the hotel room and he'd planned to slip out a little after midnight, having sent the night porter away from Reception to get him a drink from the closed bar. The detectives had been waiting for him when he'd come back from the cashpoint. She must have checked her accounts by phone, then rung the police. He wouldn't have targeted her if he'd thought there was the remotest chance that she'd have the face to turn him in. He sat in the cell and felt the harshness of the light burn down on him.

It was problematic but achievable for a general-service officer to be promoted on merit to the rank of officer in the Service. Those who beaver away at clerical and administration duties can, if dedicated, ambitious and able, win such promotion. Daphne Sullivan had the dedication, ambition and ability. Upon the arrival of Gabriel Locke's signal to the Service's quarters at the embassy in Berlin, after its decyphering, it was passed to her. She made no comment but took it to her desk and made three phone calls for guidance, then took from her safe a German passport that carried her photo, heaved on her coat, knotted her scarf round her throat and left the building on Wilhelmstrasse. One call had been to the local colleagues in the Office for the Protection of the State, a second had been to a particular named official in the Association of Travel Agents, a third was to a travel company in the far west of the city, close to its outer limits.

She drove herself to the Marzahn housing complex, where sixty thousand ratbox apartments had been built in ten years under the Communist regime, the pride of Honecker's government. Among a mix of rectangular garden allotments with wood huts for summer weekends, and a moonscape of wasteground, she found a parking space by the S-bahn station, in the Allee der Kosmonauten.

The travel agency she sought had been brightly fitted, was warm, comfortable and had the reputation for extreme efficiency. Its prosperity was based on the owners' sharp appreciation of a growing market niche. Werner Weigel had been a middle-ranking officer in the formerly supreme secret police and his wife, Brigitte, had been a manager in the Ministry of the Interior before the Wall had come down. Their past had disappeared during the last days of Communist rule into the overworked shredders. They were now respected and reliable tour operators. They arranged visits by elder citizens to the old homelands of east Prussia, in particular to the city that had been Königsberg and was now called Kaliningrad. A compelling whiff of nostalgia drew that dying generation back to the region of their childhood, a last visit to scratch in their memories of youth.

Daphne needed a visa to enter that Russian territory.

Under normal circumstances it took the bureaucracy at the Russian embassy five working days to issue such a visa for a visit to Kaliningrad.

It would be about money. The one-time Stasi officer and his wife had done well after reunification in their business venture, and they intended to do better. Euros were passed discreetly over a table in the back room. Daphne Sullivan had been stationed in Berlin long enough to know that, in the new Germany, money had a loud voice. Every day of the week a Mercedes-built luxury coach took a party of elder citizens to Kaliningrad. One would leave the next afternoon. Money bought the co-operation of Herr and Frau Weigel . . . Fräulein Magda Krause, who had intended to travel to Kaliningrad to search for her grandparents' heritage, had planned to take the tour in November, but her holiday had been cancelled and she could only travel that week, in late September. Money ensured that her German passport would be taken by hand to the Russian embassy on Unter den Linden, and more money paid to a clerk would guarantee that the necessary visa was in place in time for the coach pick-up the next day at the car park of the Am Zoo station. Daphne's fluency in German was sufficient for the Weigels, who did not question her story, and the palmed euro notes were slid with effortless ease into the drawer behind the desk. The couple might have wondered why this young woman, who gave an address in the northern district of Pankow, was so anxious to travel so quickly, but their curiosity was mitigated by the generosity of the payment in cash.

The Weigels' was the new world. They would not inform the Russian embassy of any suspicion they might harbour. They had received a telephone message an hour earlier from an official at the Association of Travel Agents. They floated in a sea of mutual favours. Frau Weigel herself would be at the Am Zoo pick-up point with Fräulein Krause's passport and the stapled visa.

72

Daphne drove back to the embassy, reported on her visa application, then went in search of a historian at the Humboldt University who would provide her with background cover. She would spend the rest of the afternoon with him.

His papers called him Peter Flint but all of his teenage and adult life he had only answered to the name of Lofty. He raked the dry brown leaves from around the headstones in the Tyne Cot cemetery. They'd fallen thickly that day because there had been a bitter wind, and away in a far corner, near to the old German pill-boxes, he had a good bonfire going for them. He picked up the leaves and barrowed them to the fire – he could not keep pace with the speed of their fall. It was the time of year he disliked most: impossible for him to keep the little squares of hoed earth in front of the stones and the short-cut grass corridors between them as neat as they should be. He would work that afternoon and evening as long as there was light for him to see the leaves. To Lofty it was a duty.

On his third whisky, and still nursing his temper, Rupert Mowbray heard the bell ring. Late that afternoon he had been ambushed. The ambush had ridiculed him. He assumed it had been planned the previous evening in the bar of the Students' Union. He had been made to look foolish, which hurt, and antiquated, which hurt more severely. He had come home, slammed the front door behind him, and it had taken him his third whisky before he could bring himself to explain to Felicity the wound he had suffered.

'I was well launched, on my feet for ten minutes, and had the total attention of the front row. I'd captured them all – well, all of them who were sat in front of my students. I was on to Putin and democracy and the premise that we're cosying too quickly with a demagogue . . . and I saw those bloody students move. It was concerted, planned. They held up a banner – "Mowbray is a Cold War warrior." They'd done cardboard sheets, "Mowbray the fossil from the Ice Age" and "Mowbray, fight your wars someplace else." One was on his feet, cupped his hands and shouted through them, "You're a disgrace, Mowbray, because all you preach is hatred." Then they were gone. Every row behind the front just emptied, out they went.

73

It was humiliating . . . I went on, I finished, damned if I was going to be beaten by them. It was as if those kids didn't know, didn't care, what I've done with my life, where I've been, what I've achieved – all my experience and the bedrock of my knowledge, just pissed on . . .'

Now Felicity murmured that she wasn't expecting anyone and went to answer the door. Rupert Mowbray, his pride chastised, sat in his chair with both fists clamped around his crystal tumbler. He heard the murmur of voices in the hall, too indistinct to learn the identity of his visitor. He had served his country, from his desk in the Secret Intelligence Service, for close to forty years. That country, while breeding its ignorant, ungrateful youth, had posted him to Aden, Berlin, Bonn in western Germany, Berlin again, South Africa, Berlin once more, and Warsaw. In all, twelve director generals had overseen his work. He had survived the butchery of personnel numbers in '90, the Christmas massacre of '93, the staff cull of '98 – Rupert Mowbray was, dammit, a man who should have been listened to, and into his mind leaped the image of the empty rows in the lecture room.

His wife was in the sitting-room's doorway: 'It's Alice, she's popped by to see you, Rupert.'

Then she stepped back, made space so that she could be passed, and Alice North was walking hesitantly across the carpet towards him. She still wore it, the amber pendant, as she had the last time he'd seen her. He struggled to stand.

'Don't get up, please. It's an awful intrusion, I know. It was just that I had to speak to somebody, somebody who . . .'

Her voice died. To Rupert Mowbray, his one-time clerical assistant, then secretary, then Girl Friday, looked washed out, exhausted. She was pale and the colour had gone from her cheeks. He thought she might have been crying earlier: her eyes were puffy, but dry, and a fierce fire burned in them. She had worked for him for ten years and one month, up to the day of his leaving party. Instinctively he looked at her ears, for the quiet flash of the studs, pearls in a diamond setting. They had been his present to her at the party where he had received the crystal decanter and glasses from the director general. She wasn't wearing them, only the pendant. He hadn't bought the ear studs himself, Felicity had. He knew she lived in Docklands. She had travelled a long way to see him.

He held out his arms, took her as he would have welcomed a favourite niece.

'. . . somebody who cared.'

Rupert Mowbray did not need to be told. It was about Ferret. Ferret had been his . . . and Alice North's. The verbatim transcript of a meeting chaired by Bertie Ponsford, of Russia Desk, was handed to him and he read it.

He was doing the late shift. The other porters queued to hang their heads and plead with him to swap duties, every one of them loathed the midnight start, and 'Wickso' Wicks seldom disappointed them. Ten minutes after he'd started, as he hung around with his trolley at the entrance to the hospital's A&E department, a man suffering the extremes of a heart-attack was rushed by his wife to the swing doors, she hadn't waited for an ambulance. He knew what to do, and that seconds were critical; a colleague ran inside to call the coronary team. The man had stopped breathing, and he had him out on the pavement, away from the car, and he was kneeling over him when the first nurse had sprinted through the doors. She elbowed him aside. 'For Christ's sake, get back. You're only a bloody porter. Leave him alone. Who do you think you are?' The nurse was young enough to be his daughter, and knew nothing of his past. He didn't fight his corner, never did, just waited till the rest of the team were there and the patient was on the trolley, then wheeled it at speed to the coronary unit.

Alone in his room, the darkness around him, sleep did not come easily to Captain, second rank, Viktor Archenko. Dancing before his eyes was a thread – and he thought he hung from it, and below him was the abyss. When he could endure no longer the sight of the frayed thread he swung off the bed, which was sweat-soaked, and made himself a beaker of coffee.

4

Q. Where does 90 per cent of the world's amber originate from?
A. Kaliningrad.

The mist merged with the sea and painted grey walls that blocked off the beach on either side of Daphne Sullivan.

She had used her time well. On the coach from Berlin she had been at her cheerful and chatty best. In the twelve hours of the journey, including the comfort stops at Szczecin and Elblag, she had sifted through the histories of her forty-one fellow passengers on the coach. All of them had welcomed the kindly, interested conversation of this younger woman, and she had made them laugh and had listened to their stories.

Effortlessly she had become an integral part of the visit to Kaliningrad. It had been near to two in the morning when they had pulled up outside the hotel and surly porters had offloaded the suitcases. Even when the coach juddered to a halt Dieter Stangl's frail head still slept noisily on her shoulder. He had been sitting alone after the coach left Elblag, and a moment after she had made a quiet request to sit beside him she had realized why. His breath stank of his pipe and his tobacco, and the ham sandwiches his daughters in Frankfurt had made for him, laced with garlic and gherkins. From Elblag to the border, she had sucked the tale of Dieter's life from him and had decided before he sagged into sleep with his head lolled on her shoulder that his company was what she needed. On arrival at the hotel he had tottered into the hotel lobby and she had seen that his bags were brought to Reception, where she had made it her personal business to ensure that they were quickly taken upstairs as soon as his key was issued to him. In the morning, at breakfast, he had been looking for her as she had come through the glass doors: he had stood for her at his table with old-world courtesy and dragged back a chair for her to join him.

She stood on the dunes close to a place where there were the imprints of two men's shoes and beside a couple of recently ground-out cigarette filters.

She had learned that Dieter Stangl was seventy-one years old, that his father had been a crane-operator manager in the Kaliningrad docks, that the family had lived at what was now Primorsk on the lagoon to the west of the city, and that they had fled on the last train from Königsberg to Berlin four months before the ultimate catastrophe. It was a pilgrimage for the old man: there would be a house at Primorsk which he hoped to be able to visit, and a cemetery, perhaps even access to the docks where new cranes would have replaced those his father had managed. If she had been bored by him on the coach and was bored by him at breakfast, she showed no sign of it. She told Dieter Stangl that her own family were from Povarovka, which was north up the coast from the coach destination that morning, but a great-aunt had lived further south along the beach and her late mother had often talked of that place. The coach wouldn't have time for such a detour, she'd said, but she'd hired a driver and she *insisted* that Herr Stangl, Dieter, should accompany her in the car and they could *share* the opportunity for mutual convenience and memory-making. He had jumped at the opportunity of her company and her transport.

Behind her was the watertower. In front of her, down on the beach, was a wrecked ribbed carcass of a fishing-boat.

She'd told the driver, a scowling, shaven-headed brute with a special-forces emblem tattooed on his throat between his earlobe and his windpipe, where she wanted to go and had warbled conversation about her family and about Dieter Stangl's. It was good cover, perfect, if eyes watched the place.

'I don't remember it here,' the old German muttered.

'Oh, yes, you do,' Daphne Sullivan said crisply. She gave the old man from Frankfurt a sharp push and propelled him down towards the beach and the wrecked boat. As her driver had turned off the road she had seen fresh wheelmarks, and then she had found the footprints and the cigarette ends. The driver was behind them, puffing on a cheroot. She took Dieter's arm to be certain he would not fall and their shoes slipped on the gentle incline of the dunes. She could not see the base down the beach to the south and the fog had closed in on them, but she knew from the maps in Berlin that she was four kilometres to the north of the exclusion zone around Baltiysk. She held tight to his arm and gave an impersonation of those tourists who came to bathe in nostalgia for the past, often seen meandering on the beach to suck up images of childhood: the professor of history at the Humboldt had briefed her well. He shivered and told her again that he could not remember being at this place, but she told him that he should light his pipe. The fumes from his tobacco wafted to her nostrils. She left him on the upper beach – she had done enough to avoid attention. She came to the wreck.

'Do we have to be here long?' Dieter Stangl's voice was guttural behind her.

A metre above the sand, where the boat's name might once have been painted, were two crosses in white chalk and the letters Y and F. The signal sent to Berlin had been most specific. From her coat pocket she took an inch-long length of orange chalk and bent as if a particular shell had attracted her attention. Her own shoes had settled into the indentations left by a man's trainers. She did not know the significance of the chalk crosses and the letters, but she understood the importance of what she had been asked to do. She made two fresh crosses with her orange chalk under the white crosses – then picked up a nothing-special shell and called loudly back to him, 'Do you remember this place now?'

Through the smoke pall of his pipe, Dieter Stangl shook his head. She went quickly to him. She needed to be away from the beach, the wreck and the chalk marks, and took a firm grip on his arm to lead him back up the slope and on to the dunes. They walked together back to the car. The driver eyed them. She told the driver that it was where her grandparents would have taken her parents to swim, and that it was where Herr Stangl had played as a child. The driver pulled away. They would catch up with the tour party in time for the afternoon concert of the Kaliningrad Philharmonic Orchestra, but they would still have time to visit Primorsk. She anticipated that Dieter Stangl would stand rheumy-eyed in front of an old brick house and prattle on about his Fascist, Hitler *jugend* childhood, and after the concert the schedule dictated they would go to the bunker from which the German surrender had been given and then the Oceanography Museum.

On the road, Dieter Stangl complained, 'I do not remember that place.'

Smiling sweetly, Daphne Sullivan said, 'It'll all come back to you. Terrible thing, memory loss.'

She'd ditch him, of course, with his foul breath and awful pipe, before the concert. It had gone well. She'd take credit from it.

The torch beam edged to the rear of the cave.

The roof, back from the entrance, was too low for Yuri Bikov to stand. The beam flickered on the stones of the fissure down which water dripped and icicles hung. On his hands and knees, behind the narrow throw of the light, he crawled forward. At the entrance were the Black Berets, who had taken the prisoner and his son, and his own team of the Vympel men. He and they had struggled for two days to cross the high ground above the gorge on their journey to the cave. No fires for warmth or hot food. No tents to shelter in, or sleeping-bags to wriggle into. On the last afternoon a blizzard had come on but they had not had to worry about leaving tracks because the wind-whipped drive of the snow had obliterated their footprints within moments. Without the GPS to guide them they would never have found the cave and the men who guarded the prisoner and his child. They had been within ten metres of the cave's entrance and as near as two metres from the nearest Black Beret when the challenge had been made. Bikov's heart had pounded – rifles and submachine-guns, on hair triggers, were aimed at him. A swig of vodka was the only refreshment offered him and he'd listened to the story of the prisoner's capture with his son.

The Black Berets had their prisoner and the sullen-faced, defiant child – and they could not extricate themselves. First the cloud and rain had blocked the helicopter flights, now it was the snow. The six Black Beret men were marooned, and the forecast was that the weather would not change for five days . . . It was not thought likely that the brigadier and his escorts, held in a similar cave, farm byre or woodcutter's shelter, would survive five more days. It was a war, Yuri Bikov knew, of excessive brutality.

His journey might be wasted effort. If the decision were taken by the 'bandits' to kill the brigadier then it would be with a knife, eyes out, stomach disembowelled, penis and testicles off, throat slit at the end of life. But the work of an interrogator was not fast work, not in a police cell, not in a forward army command post and not in a mountain cave. The work was for a patient man. He had told them at the cave's entrance that he was not to be disturbed, not to be interrupted, however long he was at the back of the cave, and they would have seen his torch beam slip away from them and go deep into the crack between the great boulders. His stomach growled with hunger, his clothes were soaked wet from the snow, and the cold seemed to gnaw into his bones. He had left his personal weapon with the Black Berets and the Vympel men.

The torch found little specks of white on the cave's floor as he crawled forward.

He took his damp rag handkerchief from his trouser pocket and his cold fingers were numb as he picked up the teeth and laid them in the handkerchief. He raised the torch. If it had not been for the eyes, a man's and a child's, he might not have seen them. Ibn ul Attab, scion of a family of wealth and influence in Riyadh, had inserted his body into the furthest recess at the back of the cave. Bikov shone the torch full into the man's face and saw the black mat of the beard, the blood at the nose and mouth, and the hate. The Saudi man, wiry thin, was on his side and, peeping over his hip, was the head of the child, whose smooth skin was cracked by the same lines of hatred. Ibn ul Attab's hands were hidden, manacled or trussed behind his back, and his ankles were fastened with plastic stays. Bikov smelt him, faeces and urine.

Bikov said, a gentle voice in the Arabic taught him at the training college, 'I am going to ask you, Ibn ul Attab, to roll on to your stomach and then I am going to unfasten your arms. Then I shall free your legs, because it is not right that your son should see his father in such condition . . . I have no gun and no knife. Should you overpower me and try to reach the cave entrance the Black Berets have orders to kill you – but not to kill your son. You will be dead and your son will be at their mercy, and it will go badly for him. Not only are you a fighter for freedom but you are also a man of intelligence. I don't ask for your word, I ask only that you conduct yourself with good sense.'

The eyes of the warlord flashed with loathing and did not blink in the brightness of the torch beam. He did not roll on to his stomach, and through the gaps where his teeth had been he spat phlegm at Bikov.

The length of the flight from Moscow and far into the night he had spent in Grozny, Bikov had studied the fat file on Ibn ul Attab. The man killed with cruelty but was also rated by the few staff officers bold enough to write unvarnished reports as a commander of outstanding ability, and to be fearless. The child was the way to him. It was the skill of an interrogator to recognize the smallest signs of weakness. The child cowered behind his father's hip. Bikov was a well-read man, but he had never been as far as Greece. He knew the story of Achilles, the hero who was the son of Peleus and the sea-goddess known as Thetis. If the Black Berets had been allowed to they would have taken Ibn ul Attab down the mountain to the vehicle track in the gorge and would have lashed a leg to the back of a personnel carrier and dragged him down to the command post. His body would have been split on the rocks, and the death of the brigadier would have been inevitable.

He moved very close to the prone man and opened his handkerchief to show the teeth lying in its folds. 'That should not have been done. I regret it. I am returning your teeth to you.'

Ibn ul Attab's boots lashed at him. Bikov took the force of them on his shoulder. The sudden movement dislodged the child, who cried out in fear. Bikov did not think Ibn ul Attab would care again to frighten his child. He rode the blow of the boots. A full minute they stared at each other, prisoner and captor, then Bikov turned and shouted towards the entrance of the cave that he wanted a bar of chocolate and that it should not be brought but thrown to him. He knew that the Vympel men had chocolate with them, that its possession would be important to them, and they would curse him for asking it of them. The chocolate was heaved down the length of the cave. It was a small bar, two hundred grams, but for Bikov its value was greater than if it had been a gold ingot. He unwrapped it so that the chocolate was exposed and the child could see it, then laid it on the stone of the cave floor. For two minutes they watched each other and the man made no move, but the child whimpered and stared at the chocolate.

Bikov broke the silence. 'Because I respect you as a freedom fighter, Ibn ul Attab, I apologize to you. The war my government wages against the Chechen people and their faith is indefensible. My apology is sincere and from my heart.'

No other Russian officer that Bikov had ever met would have apologized to Ibn ul Attab. After his teeth had been beaten from his mouth, after he had been kicked with steel-shod boots – if he had still not talked – every other Russian officer would have sent for a length of fuse cord and a detonator, would have tied the cord around Ibn ul Attab's penis, with the detonator, laid out the cord's length and lit it so that he saw the sparking fire come close to the detonator, and they would have shouted their questions. And what would they have done when the detonator had fired and the blood had spattered? They would have done it to the child and made Ibn ul Attab watch the child's terror. And there would be two more martyrs and no answers to the questions. It was not the way of Yuri Bikov. He talked for two hours and was never rewarded with a response, but the chocolate was in front of the child. He spoke of Saudi Arabia and its food, of his daughter whom he missed and who did not write to him, of sunsets over the Black Sea and the dawn light spreading on the Siberian tundra, of the majesty of nature, and the glory of God . . . and the child's eyes never left the chocolate. He had an inexhaustible reservoir of patience, and it was only the beginning.

Wages were not paid, the military did not have the fuel to mount exercises, privation in Kaliningrad was widespread, the hospitals were not supplied with sufficient quantities of drugs, the water in the city was not drinkable, but the Federalnaya Sluzhba Bezopasnosi had not gone short. On the flat roof of their headquarters in the city, backing on to the Pregel river, was a mass of aerials and dishes. The listeners in the FSB complex would not have been able to decypher a scrambled signal from Daphne Sullivan, but they would have picked up the high speed and encoded transmission had she made it, and that would have alerted them to the fact that an intelligence operative was loose in the territory. The instructions she had received in Berlin had been explicit that she was to carry nothing sophisticated on her person.

A sudden and violent stomach pain crippled her as she left the concert. The courier was sympathetic. Nobody in their right mind would volunteer for Russian medical attention in Kaliningrad, the courier opined. Was the lady well enough to get to Poland or, better, to Germany? Her face apparently creased in pain, and her back bent from the spasms, Daphne Sullivan said she was. She was booked a single cabin on the night sleeper train from the southern station. She carried on to the train with her a note in the Russian language that would explain to the border authorities why she was breaking away from her tour. When the train rumbled, late at night, into Braniewo she was sufficiently recovered to make a guarded telephone call to Berlin.

Deep into the night, in the cave, Yuri Bikov kept the torch beam on the chocolate bar.

The child, Ibn ul Attab's son, peered at it with longing and tears ran down the smooth cheeks. He was not a soldier. He yearned for the sweetness of the chocolate, but could not reach forward for it because his father's body blocked him.

Everything Yuri Bikov did was planned ahead. He did not know where the child's mother, Ibn ul Attab's wife was. She might have been in one of the remote farming villages on the level ground below the gorge. Perhaps she had fought her man when he had taken her son to the mountains, perhaps the child had been torn from her grip. He did not think the wife would have been in Saudi Arabia with her family, or left in a safe village in the Yemeni valleys. She would be close, and Ibn ul Attab would be thinking of her.

The torch beam was failing and the chocolate bar was harder to see; the light was dying on the silver tin foil that wrapped it. Bikov talked in his soft and measured voice – not about the war and not about Islam – of the beauty of the mountains, the majesty of the deer and the wild goats, the bears and the eagles that soared above the gorge. He won no response, but that did not concern him because his greatest virtue was his patience, and in his mind the strategy of his attack was mapped.

As the light slipped from the torch, Bikov eased his weight forward, picked up the chocolate and broke it into small pieces, then laid it back on the cave's floor exactly where it had been before, within the child's reach.

'I said, Ibn ul Attab, you are a fighter I respect. I also want to respect you as a father. Whatever the differences between you and me, two men thrown against each other by your God and my government, your son is not a part of that. I ask you to allow him to eat. And it is not right that your son should see you trussed, a chicken waiting for its throat to be slit. Your son should see you free. I don't know his name, but he looks to me a fine boy and proud of you. I request that you give me the chance to remove what is round your wrists – and to let your son eat.'

He switched off the torch and the darkness cloaked them.

The luminous dial of his watch told him that half an hour had passed. Then . . . the weight of Ibn ul Attab's body shifted slightly, and he heard the rustle of the tinfoil, then a small mouth chewing, and then there was more movement. Bikov knew that the father had rolled from his side to his stomach. He groped forward and crawled closer to the stinking shape of the man he could not see. His hands clawed over Ibn ul Attab's shoulders and reached down to the pit of his spine. The previous evening, this man would have killed him and thought nothing of it. He found the wrists and the damp cord that bound them, and with his fingernails he began to unpick the knots.

He ran on the beach. The fog of the previous day had lifted in the night.

At a distance everything seemed the same, unchanged. He knew every stride he made across the dry sand. The buoys rocked on their anchorages, where there were minefields, sunken ships and explosives dumps, the watertower dominated the dunes, and ahead of him was the wrecked fishing-boat. Nothing was different. For two days he had stayed away from the beach because that was what his friends

84

had told him he should do. Now he pounded on the beach towards the wreck. And in the distance, against the wind and the rumble of the sea breaking on the shoreline, was the murmur of vehicles driven slowly on the road in the trees.

Viktor came to the fishing-boat.

As he slumped down he saw the neat footprints of a woman's shoe close to the resting place in the sand of the keel. He could see the rubber tread left in the sand made moist under the shelter of the planks. For a moment his eyes were closed and his back was against the coarse wood of the boat's hull. His heart was a drumbeat. He saw them, two orange chalk crosses. He reached up and used the heel of his hand to erase the chalk marks. They had come.

He took the full three minutes then levered himself up and began to run back.

He had been heard. At first, as he ran into the wind, he believed himself saved.

Later, as he became tired and his legs hurt and his lungs ached, and he was nearing the base, the elation and the relief seeped from him. What could they do? The vehicles were on the road that was hidden in the pines, shadowing him. He still saw the distant figures on the dunes, and the whiff of their cigarette smoke curled over their heads. His legs might as well have been in the teeth of a man-trap. The border fence was guarded, he was followed, the sea stretching to the far horizon was raked by the beams of radar and patrolled by fast ships; he was watched inside the base and outside it. He could not see what his friends could do for him. They had heard his cry, but they had given him no answer. Their fine words echoed in his mind: *We'd go to our graves rather than hang you out to dry, Viktor. You're the best we have. It would be shameful for us to abandon you. You're one of us.* Words were easy . . . He knew what would happen to him if his treachery were proven, if his friends could not answer his cry.

The grey light crept into the cave's entrance. Bikov sat with his legs crossed and his arms around his chest, watching Ibn ul Attab, who held his son tight against his body. The interrogator, the child and the warlord shivered together and their bodies shook in unison . . . Bikov talked.

'I don't have a name for him. You know that, I have no name for your son. How many times have I asked you his name? A dozen times, twenty times? You have not told me his name. If you do not give me his name, Ibn ul Attab, then I have to give a name to him. I will call him Sayyed. Do you think that is a good name, or do you have a better name for him? I think Sayyed is good because it has the note of sensitivity. I believe that "Sayyed", if he is allowed to, will grow to be a fine man, a man of culture, who will be revered, but he must be allowed to grow.'

The voice of Yuri Bikov was a croak. He had talked through the evening, and the night, and now the day had come. The cold was in his skin and his bones, and the damp from his clothes prevented any warmth on his body. All the time he talked he asked questions that were not answered and made statements that invited response but the opportunities were not taken. Of all the Chechen warlords this was the one most feared by the conscript soldiers of the Interior units, the one most hated by the Black Beret patrols, with the highest price in roubles on his head, the most brutal. More loathed, more highly priced, more cruel than Gelayev, Basyev and Bekayev. It was Ibn ul Attab who had led the attack on the Special Designation Police convoy – ninety-eight dead – and on the 6th Paratroop Company of the 104th Parachute Regiment – as many as seventy-five dead. His men could move more than forty kilometres, on foot, in a day or a night, and carry with them mines, mortars, machine-guns, anti-tank missiles and rocket-propelled grenades. Among the men of the 42nd Division and the 205th Motor-Rifle Brigade, Ibn ul Attab was a leader held in awe, talked of in whispers, and feared. Videos of attacks and captured conscripts, their torture and killing, were available in the souks, bazaars and mosques of the Gulf cities for the raising of money and the recruitment of volunteers. But some of the videos were left in plain envelopes at the gates of the Interior troops' barracks in the knowledge that they would be watched and that the fear would spread. It was rumoured in Moscow, at the Lubyanka, that increasing numbers of FSB military counter-intelligence officers now refused to serve in Grozny, preferring to face disciplinary demotions or dismissal than come to this killing ground. Yet Bikov was here, and had freed the hands that might strangle the life from him.

His voice was fainter.

'I think you will allow "Sayyed" to be a man. A child, such as he is, can only promise fulfilment. It is why we have children, yes? I think you will ensure that he has a chance, not to be only a statistic of death but to become a hero in his own right. I can feel your child's breath on me and I know he had his father's love and his father's protection. Am I right? "Sayyed" is not a soldier? That does not make him a lesser child. He could go to the university in Cairo, Damascus or Sana'a, and I think he could become a teacher. Not a warrior like his father, but a teacher of science, or of music, or of the great heritage of Islamic architecture. On all his family, long after this war is finished, "Sayyed" could bring distinction. There are too many soldiers and not enough teachers. It is in your hands, Ibn ul Attab, what future you give to "Sayyed".'

'He is called Ahmed. My son's name is Ahmed.'

Bikov heard the thin voice, weak from hunger and thirst, and knew that success was close.

'What would they do to him?' She had leaned across to Rupert Mowbray and had whispered her question.

'I think, Alice, that you already know the answer to that.'

The airliner rolled at increasing speed down the runway at Gdansk on the short-haul flight back to Warsaw.

'Already know and need to have it confirmed.'

It was after their second debrief at the Excelsior Hotel.

'On the chin?'

'I don't want cosmetics – yes, on the chin.'

He'd left in the small hours of the morning, before dawn, gone back to his hotel where the others in the delegation stayed. Later he would have another meeting at the dry dock then return over the border. The plane had lifted off and Rupert Mowbray had stared straight ahead at the cockpit door and spoken so softly that she had had to strain to hear him.

'Colonel Pyotr Popov was fed, alive, into the central-heating furnace in the Lubyanka basement in front of all of his colleagues, and his agony was filmed.'

'That was a long time ago.'

'Perhaps, but the mentality will not have changed. Penkovsky was taken out at dawn and shot in the yard of the Butyrki gaol.'

'Again, Rupert, a long time ago.'

'The men betrayed by Aldrich Ames – that's only yesterday in this game – were tried in secret and executed.'

'Today – what would they do today?'

'Today is Robert Hanssen, another American arrested fourteen months ago – is that recent enough? You don't have to be told, Alice.'

'But tell me.'

'Named by Hanssen, *in camera* court, shot in the back of the neck. They're the same men, different uniforms and names, but the history is in their blood-streams. There's only one penalty, Alice, for a man of such importance. It's a dirty business, but it's what keeps the roof over our heads.'

'But we'd help him . . . ?'

'What I said to Ferret, Alice, was "We'd go to our graves rather than hang you out to dry." I meant it, my dear. But from the moment he walked in he placed himself under sentence of death . . . Why don't you try to doze?'

She hadn't slept on that flight. The whole length of it, she had fidgeted and fiddled with the new gift of the amber pendant. Her fingers had never been away from it. She had promised herself then that she would wear it always.

It was wet in London that morning as Alice North laid out the places for the meeting in the fifth-floor conference room. Half a dozen sheets of paper for each of those attending and two sharpened pencils, cups and saucers. She plugged in the percolator, filled a little bowl with sugar cubes and laid a silver spoon on them. Last she moved a chair to the corner, where she would sit, where she would not be noticed.

She'd read the signal, sent from Braniewo and relayed on by Berlin.

His voice had found a decisive strength. Bikov fought the tiredness as he told the warlord what he wanted and what would be given in return.

* * *

88

Clattering his cup down on to his saucer, for emphasis, Locke said, 'We now have a truer picture but that doesn't take us an inch further forward. One cross would have been "surveillance", right? Two crosses is "close surveillance", correct? Codename Ferret is under close surveillance. I'm not a rocket scientist but I can see that means he is beyond reach. Surely it's bring-down-the-curtain time.'

Never lifting his head, Bertie Ponsford remarked quietly, 'Thank you, Gabriel, most concise – Peter, what would be the position of Covert Ops? How does this run past you?'

Sighing as if the weight of the world rested on him, Peter Giles launched in: 'Well, we have to make a decision, don't we? Do we recommend ex-filtration, with all that such a course of action entails, or don't we? I mean, thank God, ultimately it's not our call, but masters and ministers will expect guidance from us. The difficulty I'm in is that, put simply, we don't do this sort of thing any more – it went out with the Ark. We've not attempted it since the Wall came down. And reading the files that Rupert left us – and they're thin, so thin – I can't find a specific guarantee that was given by us to Ferret. That's important. We're not under a formal debt of honour, or any such nonsense . . . I can't see what we can do, not if it's "close surveillance" . . .'

His fingers running up and down the length of his pencil, Bertie Ponsford turned in his chair. 'Succinct Peter, and I'm grateful . . . Geoff, if we were to go for broke and successfully lift out Ferret, what would be our rewards?'

The officer of Naval Intelligence shrugged. 'Hardly a sack of Christmas presents. I'd say we'd sit down with him for a month, but by the second week we'd be struggling. His value has been in the paperwork he's sent over and most of it is not the material that a man holds in his head. It's been very precise blueprints – submarines' speed, depth, counter-radar, hull specifications and so on . . . We need detail. Take the pressure hulls' outer coating, what is the mix of glass, ceramics and plastics? Generalizations don't help us. We need the paperwork and then we can develop the necessary radar counter-measures. It's exact work, I can't imagine he'd have it in his head.'

Laying down his pencil and reaching for the coffee, Bertie Ponsford smiled, then grimaced. 'I'm hearing a profound lack of excitement. You were downbeat at our last session, Bill, has anything changed Hereford's mind?'

The special-forces officer shook his head. He wore the same sweater and jeans as before. 'No enthusiasm from our crowd. The guidance I have can't go as far as refusal, but we'd lay tripwires and difficulties in the way. Bluntly, we could start talking about planning time, recce time, up-to-speed time, we could spin it out, and then we could say, after we've wasted a couple of weeks, there's the good old ocean involved, miles of Baltic coastline, and it's probably better handled by the "Boaters". I wouldn't recommend that you rely on us.'

The scratch of a pencil on a notepad was behind him. It never entered Ponsford's mind that he should ask Alice North's opinion. 'Well, I don't want anyone to gain the impression that I'm about to wash my hands of Ferret, but I have noted the positions taken by colleagues. My assessment: at the moment the FSB will be engaged rather frantically in collecting what evidence they can, and they will then make it available to a most skilled interrogator. They like things clear-cut over there, a detailed confession with ribbons on it will be what they seek, and it will be the interrogator's job to get it. Right now, the agent is boxed in by "close surveillance", stressed and close to panic, but were he to make a run for it he will merely play into their hands, give them the evidence that will kill him . . . We may have a few days to play with, but only a few. I note Hereford's hesitations and their suggestion that a possible, not probable, ex-filtration of Ferret would be best tasked to the Special Boat Squadron . . . I'm going to ask Gabriel to go directly to Poole and sound them out. Then, I hope, we will be in a position to recommend to the DG a future course of action. I have to say, and I hope fervently I am wrong, that I see no light at the end of this particular tunnel . . . Of course, it's Rupert's baby but he's not here to rock the cradle.'

The meeting was concluded. Gabriel Locke hurried down to the car pool.

In the late afternoon, Bikov crawled on his hands and knees to the cave's entrance and asked the Black Berets and the Vympel men what food they could spare for himself, the prisoner and the prisoner's child. A collection was made of dried, frozen lentils, one apple, some rice and what remained of a Meal Ready to Eat. There was so little food between all of them and they gave it grudgingly. If it had not been for Yuri Bikov's reputation, and his authority, they would have given nothing. They could light no fire, they would have been more cold and more soaked at the entrance to the cave than he was in its interior. He had been in the depths of the cave for more than twenty-four hours and they would have heard the murmur of his voice as they had dozed between watches. They knew that Ibn ul Attab's men would be searching for them. When they had given him the food they could spare, he passed to the senior sergeant a small piece of bright metal, rounded to the shape of a screw's head and four millimetres in diameter and said what he wanted done with it. Then, with the food, he disappeared back into the depths of the cave.

Outside the barracks' gates, as the light failed, Gabriel Locke sat in his car, wired in the secure system, and pressed the digits of his mobile phone. Behind the gates and the fences topped with razor-wire he had been treated as a piece of junior garbage. They'd had fun with him. A sentry strolled with the arrogance of a Royal Marine towards him. The number rang. The sentry slipped a hand from his rifle stock and rapped on the window. Locke lowered it.

'Excuse me, *sir*, but this is a place for parking cars, not for sitting in them. If you want to sit in your car, please, *sir*, go do it someplace else.'

Locke, audibly, told him to go piss himself. The moment of astonishment on the sentry's face was his one small victory from the visit to the Special Boat Squadron's barracks at Poole. He hated this Dorset town and all who sailed in her. But a rifle was a rifle, and a Marine was a Marine, and there were more of them in the guardhouse . . . He turned on the ignition, put the car into reverse and backed away. He saw the smirk on the sentry's face.

He couldn't raise Bertie Ponsford. He tried Peter Giles, deputy director of Covert Operations, but the assistant said her man was out of the building and she didn't know when, if, he was returning. Was it important? Locke rang Alice North's number.

'Yes?'

'Alice, it's Gabriel . . .'

'Who?'

'Gabriel Locke.'

'Oh, right. How can I help?'

'I can't get Bertie, and Peter's gone walkabout. I—'

'Mr Ponsford's granddaughter is in the school concert, that's where he is, in Holland Park. Mr Giles is at his club with Mr Dandridge of Personnel.'

'I need to report on my session at SBS.'

The distant voice, a tinny resonance to it from the scrambler, replied, 'Well, you'd better tell me, then, hadn't you?'

'Yes, yes . . .' Locke had expected that Bertie and Peter would be beside their telephones, waiting for him to call. The scrambler seemed to him to give her voice a mocking tinkle.

'I'm waiting.'

'I suppose it's all right. You'll see they get it? Look, knock this into shape . . . I wouldn't say my welcome was overwhelming – anyway, the place was like a ghost town. They raked up the squadron's adjutant, a lieutenant and two sergeants. I don't know where the proper people were, swanning about in the Hindu Kush or writing synopses for their Afghan memoirs, I suppose. I told them it was Kaliningrad and they found a chart, then they all started falling about, like I was doing a comic turn. It's the chart for the naval base, the navigational approach to Baltiysk, and the Kaliningradsky Moskoy Kanal. Then they patched up on the computer the military force based on Kaliningrad – how many tanks, how many APCs, how many artillery regiments, how many naval infantry were there, and what air-force squadrons. I was supposed to be quizzing them . . . fat chance. The lieutenant said, quote, "We always ask three questions. One, where is he? Two, what's he doing? Three, will it work? Three answers. Answer one, he's in the middle of a protected Russian naval base. Answer two, he's mooching about under close surveillance. Answer three, can pigs fly?" A sergeant said, quote, "Fourth question, is he worth it?" I didn't see any point in taking it further . . . They didn't want to know . . . Are we up to it, what is basically an act of war? The fat lady's singing, isn't she? I mean, it's over, isn't it? I took on board

92

everything they said, and agreed with it, but they didn't have to be so bloody superior. Is he worth it? That's what it boils down to. We're intelligence people, aren't we, not bloody cowboys? You'll see that Bertie and Peter get that?'

'I'll let them know.'

He cut the call. In his mirror, he saw a ministry policeman advancing on him reaching into a breast pocket for a notebook. Locke thought he was about to be booked for parking on the double yellow line. He identified the rainwater puddle nearest the policeman, swerved into it as he passed the man and saw that he'd splattered the uniformed legs. What annoyed him most was that the SBS men had thought the idiotic proposal to go starting wars was his idea. That annoyed Gabriel Locke badly.

Bikov led them out of the cave. The deal was made, freedom for freedom – the freedom of a warlord and his son for the freedom of a brigadier and his escort.

There had been no symbolic handshake. Between two such men as Bikov and Ibn ul Attab the gesture was not necessary.

At the cave's entrance he offered his arm for the other man to use as a crutch to lift himself upright. The blood had drained from Ibn ul Attab's legs and feet, such had been the tightness of the thongs on his ankles, and the warlord staggered when he first stood. Then his weight went on to the low shoulder of his son and that was sufficient a prop to steady him. Bikov asked for the rifle to be given him. There would have been savagery in the eyes behind the ski-masks that the Black Berets and the Vympel men wore. He could not see them in the darkness but one of the men gathered spittle in his mouth and spat it noisily towards the warlord's boots. The barrel of the weapon brushed his sleeve and Bikov took it. He did not have to make a speech about the nakedness of a warrior without his weapon: it was implicit. Bikov heard Ibn ul Attab check the weapon's magazine, then cock the rifle, driving a bullet into the breech. And they were gone.

Bikov remembered the days he had fished as a child in the reservoir on the edge of the city of Gorno-Altaysk when he and his friends had caught large carp by the reservoir's dam, on worm baits. If they had not needed to take a carp home for a family's meal, they would release it. For a moment they would see the fish drifting for the depths, then lose sight of it.

He told them they would stay at the cave for the night then make their descent in the morning.

His voice was hoarse, little more than a murmur. 'You can judge me, and it is your right to do so. All I can ask of you is that you suspend your final judgement until the end of this business. When it is over you will be entitled to make whatever judgement of me you wish.'

He crawled back into the cave. He was so tired, so cold, and the hunger lit a fire in his stomach. Only the child had eaten. He found his handkerchief but the teeth were not in it. Then he curled in a corner, and slept. He slept without a dream.

There was not another interrogator in the ranks of the military counter-intelligence officers of the Federalnaya Sluzhba Bezopasnosi who could have achieved what he had. His quiet snoring filled the cave.

Like an owl in the night, watching and waiting, Rupert Mowbray hovered for four full minutes at the outer gate of Vauxhall Bridge Cross. It was never right to be early. Precisely at the moment he was due in the building, as Parliament's clock chimed the late hour, he presented himself at the security check.

'Hello, Mr Mowbray, funny old time to come visiting. How are you keeping, sir?'

'Not too bad, Clarence, mustn't complain. And you're looking well, very ship-shape. The director general's expecting me.'

5

Q. What is the birthplace of Max Colpet, the Jewish composer, who wrote 'Where Have All The Flowers Gone' for Marlene Dietrich?
A. Kaliningrad.

He used the status gained in a lifetime with the Service shamelessly. 'If you abandon the agent, Codename Ferret, then you might as well pin up a scribbled message on the front door that says, "Don't risk your lives for us, we're not concerned what happens to you." You could broadcast on the BBC's World Service that every agent we run is left bare-arsed and on his own . . .'

He was formidable. Rupert Mowbray stood at his full height while the others sat and flinched, and his voice carried the resonance of certainty. The meeting was in an ante-room off the ground-floor atrium. His audience was the director general, Bertie Ponsford, Peter Giles, and the youngster Locke, and by the door on a hard chair was Alice North. He had not been in the building at Vauxhall Bridge since his retirement party. It was exceptional for a former employee to be allowed access past the front-door security checks, but for him the rules had been violated and the room made available. It was because of the respect that had been awarded the old warrior that the director general had cancelled a dinner engagement after taking Mowbray's call, and Ponsford and Giles had been summoned.

'I ask, does the life of a spy matter? We use him, bleed him, keep him in place even when the alarm bells are ringing, and – of course – we make a few idle promises about going down to the line to save him if the going's rough, but are we prepared to be bold? We should be . . . Not for emotion, but for the reputation of our Service.'

Mowbray centred his argument on the director general. Every word, dramatic pause and glowering glance was directed at the DG. He had never had time for the man who had been his immediate junior during the Bonn posting twenty years before. The director general had ambition, though, had mastered the network of the administrative departments of the Service, and had never stayed long enough in any of them for his shortcomings to be exposed. He had a knighthood, the ear of the Prime Minister, travelled with the head of government on all foreign visits, and he was weak. Mowbray despised him, despised him enough to make an argument for the glory of the Service. He reckoned he had fifteen minutes to make his pitch.

'We go in. We take him out of Kaliningrad, and we let the message be filtered around the world that the British Service looks out for those who risk their lives on our behalf. It would be a powerful message. It would be heard in Asia and on the sub-continent, in the Middle East and throughout Europe. It would be a magnet for the disaffected who are the very men on whom we rely. I urge you to send such a message.'

None of the men around the table met his eye. They fiddled with their handkerchiefs, locked their fingers and cracked them, studied the ceiling, the far walls and the shining table's surface. Ponsford he thought to be a journeyman who would wait on his director general's opinion and would then endorse it. Giles had the guts of a neutered family cat, and the imagination to go with such a spoiled beast. But Mowbray was now armed with the transcripts of two meetings. He had rifled through the second meeting's typescript, given him to glance at by Alice as they had loitered in the corridor before being called in. He needed an additional target. The director general would have read the same transcripts. He broke his walk, which had carried him back and forth in front of the director general, and now stayed, poised as a cobra would be, behind the young man. A smile of contempt played at his mouth and he took his hands from behind his spine, rested them easily on the back of Locke's chair.

'I accept that we should not be governed by raw emotion, but loyalty should dictate our actions. A powerful word, maybe fashioned for the lexicons of old men, but *loyalty* gives us the right to stand with dignity, to walk with honour. It would be a sad day, not just for me but for all of us, if dignity and honour were discarded for a misplaced creed of pragmatism. Show me a pragmatist and I will show you a coward.'

He saw the back of Locke's neck reddening. It was a ruthless demolition and one over which he had no qualms. He had met the rookie once, at his retirement party, after he had been delivered the set of decanter and glasses, and he had tried to sober himself sufficiently so that he could talk for some brief minutes of the value of Ferret, but he had seen the young man's blatant lack of interest as he had muttered through the tradecraft of the dead drops. He mocked Locke, then resumed his pacing walk.

'If you tell me that the Service I left, with such pride after a lifetime of endeavour, is now run by cowards then I will be saddened – I don't believe it. The history of the Service demands better rewards. If the nerves are in your veins then leave the business to those who are not frightened – *me*, and a team I will put together and head. I will deliver.'

He spoke with confidence and certainty. He had no plan for ex-filtrating an agent from Kaliningrad . . . It was what the old Service would have done, in the sixties and seventies. As clearly as if it were yesterday, he could remember the little moments of excitement that had winnowed through the corridors at Broadway, then at Century House, as rumour of triumphs spread in the corridors, canteens and bars. And he could remember also the *frisson* of helpless despair that had moved in the same corridors, canteens, bars, when the news had reached them that the life of the agent, Colonel Oleg Penkovsky of the GRU, Codename Hero, had been ended by a bullet in a prison yard. A secretary who had worked on that handling team had wept openly over her typewriter, and his debriefers had gone to the pub at lunchtime and not returned in the afternoon. The triumphs he could recall had never matched the sadness of the day the big man, Penkovsky, had been reported dead. Mowbray had never forgotten that mood of shame. Nothing had been done to save the agent, Codename Hero. He focused again on the director general.

'Not that it matters, not to the pragmatists, but Ferret is as brave a man as I know of. For four years, day after day, he has hazarded his life, looked execution in the face. For what? For his belief in us as men of our word. It is difficult to imagine the terrifying burden that rests on his shoulders . . . but that's not important, only incidental. What is important is that we show the world that we look after our people, we reach out to protect them.'

Easing up his cuff, Mowbray glimpsed the face of his watch. Never go on too long, he had learned. Never bore an audience. He spoke with a new quietness so that his audience leaned forward, all except Locke, to hear him.

'So, is it to be the day of the fainthearts? Impossible. To lift out Ferret would be, in the old vernacular, a "piece of cake". If we do nothing, allow events to run their course and wait for the echo of that bullet or sit on hands until it is reported that a young man has been thrown out of a helicopter or has "died in a road accident", then all of you, gentlemen, might as well draw your pensions and eke out your lives in retirement. Would the Service have a future – other than feeding from the crumbs dropped off the Americans' table? I doubt it . . . I expect you'd like me to withdraw?'

With a grand gesture, as if he could do no more, he spun on his heel, went to the door and slipped from the room.

Twelve minutes later, Mowbray was called back in.

The director general said, 'The loyalty bit did it, Rupert.'

They had come down off the mountains above the gorge and reached the command post. The other passengers were already there, as Bikov had known they would be, and the helicopter pilot was anxious to be off and up because the snow was settling on the rotors and fuselage of his machine. They had flown low, on instruments, above the rooftops and skimmed the power cables hung between pylons; the war's devastation had been laid out beneath them.

Yuri Bikov was not a man to milk a moment of triumph. When they landed at Grozny military airfield he stayed in his canvas seat with the restraining harness still buckled over his shoulders and across his chest. He could see the welcoming party, headed by the general, but he kept back. The brigadier was down the steps first, needing to be helped because he had received four days of beatings, followed by his three escorts who were young conscripts and who had the fear still implanted in their faces along with the scars and abrasions from their own torture. They had been a full load on the helicopter. Next out were the six Black Berets, who would have achieved near hero status among their colleagues because they had tracked, trapped and held Ibn ul Attab and his son, then the four Vympel men, who could reasonably expect high decorations for the skill with which they had crossed the bandits' country on foot.

He watched through the porthole window. The brigadier was held and kissed by the general, then passed to the care of medical orderlies. The hands of the conscripts, whose faces had the pallor of the young who have been close to death, were shaken with vigour. They had the wet of tears in their eyes. Bikov watched. He saw others of the Black Beret unit, ground-crew technicians and troops gather close to the survivors who had been on the journey to hell and who had, against all the wisdom of experience, returned from it. There was a short impromptu speech from the general, then guttering applause from the men who had pressed close to be part of the celebration.

He was still frozen when he lowered himself gingerly down the rickety steps from the fuselage hatch and his clothes clung, still soaked, to his body. He staggered the few steps away from the dying swing of the rotors as the engine was shut down. The brigadier turned away from the fussing orderlies, lurched to Bikov and clung to him, but the interrogator eased him away politely. He arched his back, stretched himself, and the pains and aches in his limbs were made more acute. The general came to him and saluted flamboyantly, but Bikov barely had the strength to raise his arm in response. The Vympel men had half dragged and half carried him down the long descent from the high ground to the farmhouse where the helicopter waited. He looked around him. Standing as a beacon in the first spread of dawn, bright among the uniform-softened shapes of the camouflage-painted bunkers and aircraft was an executive jet. It had a shining silver underbelly, its superstructure was a brilliant white and its wings and tail carried the markings of the air force. Its navigation lights, green and red, flickered in the early light. It was the transport of an officer of stature. The general took his arm. 'You have my gratitude . . .'

99

'Thank you. I did what I thought necessary.'

'But it came, Bikov, at a price.'

'I was asked to bring him home, your colleague, and I did that.'

'You made a deal with Ibn ul Attab, Bikov. You gave him dignity.'

'I bought their freedom, theirs for his.'

'At a price . . . You let the beast go free . . . How many more men will die because you made a deal that saved the life of my colleague? You did what was asked of you – I do not criticize – but it was a harsh price we have paid.'

The general was turning away. It was not that Bikov had chosen the moment for maximum effect, not his nature. It was more that the moment was appropriate. It had been his intention to deliver the information quietly to the resident team of military counter-intelligence, over a coffee and a beer.

'The price is cheap, general.'

'He walked free. You gave him back his rifle. That is cheap?'

Bikov said quietly, 'I gave him back his rifle. In the shoulder stock there is now a homing bug, set behind the cleaning rod. It has a range of five kilometres and the power of the battery is enough for what I recommend should happen. I would not like it said that I reneged on an honest deal between Ibn ul Attab and myself. I request that you leave it for a week then go and search for the bug's signal. I would guarantee to you that, after what has happened to him, his rifle will not be more than a metre from him, night or day. In a week, search for the signal then bomb the fuck out of him. Use bombs and rockets and kill him, with his child. That, General, is the price of the deal.'

The general's face creased in astonishment. Bikov eased back the shape of his wristwatch. Under it, preserved, written in indelible ink, was a set of scrawled digits. His face was impassive. He reached out and lifted a pen from the front pocket of the general's tunic, then took the senior officer's hand, peeled off the leather glove and wrote the numbers on the clean palm. Then he returned the pen to the pocket.

'That is the frequency of the homing bug, General. One week, then help him to the Garden of Paradise.'

Bikov walked past the general, and heard the crescendo of

laughter behind him. All he wanted was coffee or soup, straight from the stove, and then sleep. But the general had run after him and had snatched the material of his tunic. 'They have sent a plane for you, to take you to Moscow. Everyone wants you, you are a man of that importance. I could almost feel sorry for the next wretch that faces you. Almost . . .'

Fifteen minutes later, Yuri Bikov was airborne. Swathed in warm blankets, naked under them, he sat in the cabin, the only passenger. His clothing was in a leaking plastic bag in the aisle. Before they had cleared Chechen air space, he was asleep.

Two hours later, the early light seeped in the mist over Kaliningrad.

Captain, second rank, Victor Archenko, was in the back seat beside Admiral, Commander of the Baltic Fleet, Alexei Falkovsky.

'I was reading last night, reading history . . .'

Viktor was not expected to reply. He gazed through the side window. Had he turned and twisted in his seat and looked out of the rear window, stared back at the traffic respectfully following the staff car that flew the admiral's pennant, he would have seen the black van and the red saloon. He did not turn and twist.

'The battle of Tsushima. I had gone back to the history book for it, because all our ills come from it. You agree, Viktor?'

He nodded. At least five times a year, Viktor was required to listen as the admiral regurgitated what he had read of the war at sea in the Far East. The battle had been fought on 27 May 1905, combat between the Imperial Japanese Navy and the Imperial Russian Navy, Baltic Fleet. Ahead of them was the regular monthly meeting in the headquarters building in Kaliningrad city of the commanders of the army, the missile forces, the air force and the navy. The admiral used only one book of naval history and Viktor could have recited the text that had been read the previous night. At Tsushima, 4830 Russian sailors had been killed or had drowned, some seven thousand had been taken prisoner, 1862 had reached neutral territory and had been interned, and all the capital ships had been lost. Two or three times a year, Viktor and the admiral re-enacted the battle with models. Viktor took the role of Admiral Togo and Falkovsky took the identity of Admiral Rozhdestvensky, and they would pore for an evening and half into the night over their charts and models while Falkovsky cursed the incompetence of his Baltic Fleet predecessor, then made the decisions that broke history's mould and won the battle. To Viktor, the sessions were a pointless waste of time. They drove into the city, and the admiral's pennant ensured they were not delayed.

'We still suffer because of the incompetence of Rozhdestvensky. The Russian navy, because of his stupidity, has never recovered. From the start . . . They sail from the Baltic, they break out into the North Sea – they are half the world's circumference from Japanese waters – they are at the Dogger Bank off the coast of Great Britain when they see small craft and open fire, believing they are about to be attacked by Japanese torpedo boats. What does Rozhdestvensky think Japanese torpedo boats are doing in the waters of Great Britain? They sink four British trawlers and consider they have won a great victory over the Japanese navy . . . and they sail on and it will get worse.'

The car lurched in a pothole. Viktor had jerked his head up. They were on Prospekt Mira and had passed the Kosmonaut monument. Under his breath the driver swore. Big blocks of rabbit warren apartments flanked the road, the concrete was stained by the rust from the metal window frames and they had a mildew of decay about them. The driver swerved again, to avoid an addict shambling across the street. There was more heroin on the streets of the city this year than last. The base senior medical officer had told Viktor that. He watched the addict collapse on to the pavement as they swept by. He was as trapped in the city as the addict, now insensible in his own filth.

'At last, the fleet approaches the Straits of Tsushima, six months after leaving the Baltic. They come as if for a fleet review, as if the Tsar inspects them. They make no effort to sink the Japanese scout ships that monitor them. Togo knows where they are and where they are going, and Rozhdestvensky is blind to where the Japanese are and their intentions. The man was a fool. He has the finest battleships – *Kniaz, Suvorov, Imperator Alexander III, Borodino* and *Orel* – of the Baltic Fleet, but he has allowed their gunnery to become so poor that they cannot achieve hits even when they have closed to five thousand five hundred metres. It was good that Rozhdestvensky died on the *Suvorov*. If he had survived he should have been hanged.'

The sign for the zoo was behind them. They drove on Leninsky Prospekt towards the Bunker Museum, the Investbank and the big hotel where it was too expensive for a captain, second rank, to use the bar. They went by the House of Soviets: two great concrete blocks linked with two horizontal walkways, known as the Monster. It had sixteen storeys, and beneath it were 1100 sunken pillars of concrete hammered down into the marshland. Beside it were the ruins of the old German fortress of Königsberg. That building had survived for seven centuries before the bombing brought it down, but the Monster had never lived. It sagged, was not safe to occupy, and the money had run out before electricity or heating were installed. Each time Viktor went past the House of Soviets he saw it as the symbol of the state he betrayed. Alone, far from safety, Viktor needed symbols.

'The *Suvorov* is sunk, the *Alexander* capsizes, the *Borodino* explodes, the *Orel* surrenders – the rest are left to be massacred. He was very lucky – Rozhdestvensky was exceptionally lucky – to have died of his wounds. It was the last time we had a great fleet, and it was thrown away. With it went the future of our navy.'

On the other side, some men fished in a canal running into the Pregel river. Viktor knew that Kaliningrad was regarded as a polluting cesspit by its Baltic neighbours. Dawn, and men already fished. He could not imagine what species survived there in its rank water. They would not catch anything, they would stare at a float stationary on the oily surface and hope they could forget what was around them. Abruptly he tossed back his head so that he no longer saw the canal . . . He was a fish. A rusted hook was in the gristle of his mouth. He felt the pressure of the rod and line. He tried to run and could not find the open water, tried to dive and failed, and the pressure on him grew . . . They were at army headquarters. Now, Viktor looked back. He saw the black van slowing in the traffic behind, while the red car came past and stopped beyond the main gate. And he saw Piatkin, the *zampolit*, in the front passenger seat. He clasped his hands to stop their trembling, as their car turned in past smart sentries and came to a stop in front of the main doors. An aide strode forward to open the admiral's door, but the driver waved him away because his admiral still talked.

'The reason why the importance of the navy is not recognized is because of Tsushima, and the humiliation of the Baltic Fleet. Lenin knew of Tsushima, and Stalin. The army and air force poisoned Khrushchev's opinion of us by telling him of Tsushima, and Brezhnev's. Gorbachev and Yeltsin would have been similarly affected by the toxin of Tsushima, and today it is no different. Half a day and half a night of incredible ineptitude has cost us, Russia's sailors, our rightful position. I read of Tsushima last night so as to be better prepared to meet these shits today. Even now we are not considered equals. I tell you, if they had their way, our aircraft would go under air-force command, our submarines would go to the missile forces, our amphibious capability would go to the army . . . I see no future because ninety-seven years ago an idiot threw away a great fleet at Tsushima . . . You don't respond, Viktor. What is wrong?'

'I agree with everything you say, Admiral.'

'You all right? You look like death.' Falkovsky stared hard at him.

He did not know how soon it would be before Admiral Alexei Falkovsky was informed that his chief of staff was to be arrested on a charge of treason. He thought that then the admiral – his patron – would stand in a line and queue with others for the chance to strangle him, bare-handed.

'No problems,' Viktor said.

'Let's hit these bastards – and we give them *nothing*, nothing. Fucking parasites.'

A pace behind, in his respectful place, Viktor followed his admiral into the building.

With his target safely inside army headquarters for a minimum of two hours, Piatkin walked away from the red saloon, down to the canal's towpath, away from the few fishermen, and there he made a call on his mobile to Boris Chelbia. He was full of apologies for the cancellation of the meeting the week before. Because of the cash in foreign currencies paid him by Chelbia, the apologies were abject. Piatkin confirmed at what time in the night the lorry, supplied by Chelbia, would have access to the base, how the necessary pass for its driver would be handled, and the load that the lorry would carry out. Again he apologized for inconvenience caused by the delay. He rang off. He did not feel himself trapped, but he was. The officer of the FSB, Vladdy Piatkin, was owned by Boris Chelbia. He was a servant of the racketeer. He wrapped his coat tight around him as proof against the dawn's cold.

An hour after dawn came to the Baltic, the same light fell on the Bay of Biscay. The *Princess Rose* was out of sight of the Spanish coast and rode the swell on low power. She pitched like an awkward, cussed mule, fell into the troughs, climbed the peaks, and rolled.

With a mug of slopping coffee, and the message received on the radio rolled and slipped behind his ear, the mate headed for the master's cabin. The heritage of Tihomir Zaklan was far from the sea. He had been sick in the night, was always sick in a storm. He was from the Croatian town of Karlovac, eighty kilometres from the sea at Senj on the Adriatic. His training had been at war, not at a university. He had fought the Serbs to save his city, then worked the bars of Split to raise the money to travel to Hamburg for a seamanship diploma. The sea had been his escape from the war. On receiving his diploma he had applied for sixty-eight mate's positions, had written to every shipping agent in the Mediterranean, and for a year he had languished back home in Karlovac and had heard nothing or had received the posted rejections. At the end of that year, 1997, with his savings down to the last few *kunar*, his prayer had been answered. He had flown to Naples, had seen the ship that was to be his home tied up at the end of the quay and had immediately called her, to himself, the Sea Rat.

He put the mug of coffee down beside the bed, and the dog growled softly at him from the floor. He shook the master's shoulder, took the signal from behind his ear and left it beside the mug. He scrambled up the bucking staircase to the bridge.

The signal, from the *Princess Rose*'s owners, he had left for the master perplexed him. Why, if they were ordered to Gdansk to take on fertilizer for the Latvian port of Riga, were they directed first to a position off the south-west British coast for transfer on board of a cargo of less than one tonne?

Tihomir Zaklan was in turn confused and grateful – especially grateful. If there was work for her at least the *Princess Rose* stayed afloat and alive, and he had a home.

One hour after it had nestled over the Bay of Biscay, the first light of day simpered on Central London.

Not that it was a dawn worth waiting for. The rain came down hard on the few street-sweepers who were already out and on the lorries that removed the bagged rubbish from the pavements. The streets ran with little streams and the high gutters were over-whelmed by the downpour. It cascaded on to the windows of a building north of Leicester Square, on the fringe of Covent Garden. At street level the rain beat on the wide plate-glass window of a pizzeria and on the narrow doorway beside it. The doorway led to a staircase and on the first floor, identified by a bell and a slip of card, was a theatrical-artists agency. The second floor housed a mail-order firm specializing in novelty party toys, while the third was occupied by a small firm of accountants, whose trade was limited to clients employed in the clothing market. The top floor was the most exposed to the rain. Set under a shallow, sloping roof, its windows caught the full blast of the weather. The top floor was marked at the front door only by a bell and a grilled intercom with no name attached. That early morning, it was the only floor where a light burned behind slatted blinds.

Alice North had the electric kettle boiling. Mowbray slept on a canvas bed that sagged under his weight.

Locke had left an hour ago. Mowbray had been in the bathroom when he'd gone. 'It's absolute madness, you know that,' Locke had said to Alice. 'It'll end in tears and rightly so.' He would be in the air from RAF Northolt by now.

The managing director of Security Shield Ltd, Wilberforce, had been gone more than two hours. He was a man in his forties who seemed permanently to wear an uncreased suit, a clean shirt and a tight-knotted tie, and always to be close-shaven. Alice had met him before. Security Shield Ltd provided freelancers for the Service. Bodyguards, burglars and surveillance people were on their books. Those who needed employment after coming out of the special-forces units and who had the skill of close protection, clandestine entry or the placing of audio and visual bugs came to their discreet Mayfair office and were enrolled. Wilberforce had arrived at this building at two o'clock in the morning, had taken off his drenched raincoat and was immaculate underneath, as if attending a ten a.m. meeting. He'd brought a briefcase of files, studied the maps, then sifted through a list of names before settling on four files. He'd left at four o'clock. Last thing before going, he had gestured then to the files left on the table and had said briskly to Rupert Mowbray, 'If the regulars don't want to know – and, God, they're getting choosy these days – these are as good as you'll get. They left the Boat crowd under something of a shadow, something where they were together. I doubt they've seen each other since, but at least they've worked in harness. They'll be better than chucking together four strangers. What I can't say, of course, is how much persuading they'll take to go where you want them to. Anyway, if they do agree to take your shilling, my usual commission, please, and up front before they travel . . . They're the best I can do.'

Locke had leafed through the files before dumping them in his briefcase. He'd had a deep frown of distaste on his forehead, but Mowbray had told him sharply not to play dumb insolent and to contribute only when he had something positive to communicate. Alice had been pleased when Locke had left for Northolt with the files.

The kettle whistled breezily.

Later she'd ring her neighbour, who had a key to her apartment and knew how to disengage the alarm, and ask that she let herself in and clear the post off the mat while she was away . . . Alice North was the only daughter of Albert and Roz. Ten years before, her parents had sold their chain of Ford dealerships in Hertfordshire, Essex and Kent. They were hugely rich and shared that comfort with an enduring pride in their sole child. After a convent education at Weybridge in Surrey, the teenage Alice had walked away from the path taken by most of her school-friends, which veered between early marriage and a financial career. She had no interest in marriage, where she felt she would have quickly become an accessory to her parents' lives, breeding grandchildren for them to dote on, and less interest in making money. She had no need for the money: she was protected by a trust fund that the stockmarket downturns had not dented. Albert and Ros North had bought the Docklands apartment and used it as a London base on their thankfully rare trips from the villa on the Algarve. She was thirty-four years old now, and on her visits her mother made a habit of asking when she was going to find a 'nice young man'. Her mother knew so little.

She stirred the instant coffee.

Alice was closer to Rupert Mowbray than to her father. Her worst day in the Service had ended when he had left Vauxhall Bridge Cross, a little unsteady on his feet, and she had carried the box with the decanter and the glasses to the taxi. On the canvas bed, he lay on his back and grunted in his sleep. His tie was loosened and his collar was grimy from the previous day. The bristle was strong on his cheeks . . . From the cupboard above the microwave she took sweeteners and dropped two into the coffee. She carried the mug to the bed, knelt beside it, and kissed his forehead.

He had recruited her. Rupert Mowbray had given her the chance to escape the dead-hand clutch of her parents. She worked in a world where her father couldn't manage her and where she had the perfect excuse not to gossip with her mother: 'Sorry, Mums, can't talk about my day – that's the way it is.' They knew she had been in Poland, but did not know she had travelled three times from Warsaw to Gdansk; nor did they know she had four times visited Murmansk for the collection of dead drops with Mowbray, and they did not know she had wept on the night he had retired, and again when the signal had come through from Braniewo, FERRET: NO SHOW.

He stirred. Right eye first, then left, opened languidly. 'You're very sweet, my dear. What time is it?'

'Six o'clock, still raining. It's going to be a foul day.'

'Oh, I don't know, Alice – could be rather fun.' Mowbray grimaced. He had a spark of mischief.

She had been recruited in February 1992. A late-night train journey from central London to stay with a friend, from her convent-school days, in Thames Ditton and a shopping binge arranged for the next morning. An austere older man with silver hair sitting opposite her reading papers from his briefcase. The train jolting to a halt at Teddington. Him dropping papers on the carriage floor and not realizing it, hurrying to open the door, and gone into the night after he'd slammed it shut. Seeing the papers. Picking them up. The papers were stamped 'secret'. Opening the carriage door as the train started to ease away, stumbling on to the platform, whistles blowing, station staff yelling. Ignoring them. Running to the barrier and seeing the man lowering himself into a car driven by a woman, and it driving away from the station forecourt. Jumping the queue forming for a taxi, telling the driver to follow the car ahead, clutching the classified papers. Losing the car, then finding it after fifteen minutes of kerb crawling. It had been parked outside a semi-detached yellow brick house in a side-street. Ringing the bell. A woman opening the door. Thrusting the papers at her, and showing the stamped 'secret' on the top of the pages, explaining. 'You'd better come in,' the woman had said, then had called out, a stentorian voice, 'Rupert, you're a bloody fool, but – not that you deserve it – the good Lord has smiled on you. Come here, Rupert.' Being sat down, given a large whisky, being a witness to Rupert Mowbray's gratitude. Hearing the woman say, 'They'd have hanged you, Rupert, cut you down, drawn out your bowels and burned them in your face, then chopped you into quarters. Your head would have been on a pike-staff at Century House.' She'd missed the last train to Thames Ditton and the woman had insisted she stay the night, and they'd fussed round her. At breakfast the next morning, Rupert Mowbray had asked for her address, before Felicity Mowbray had driven them to the station. She'd waved him off on the London train and he'd held up his briefcase in the carriage window, tapped it and smiled sheepishly. The application form had arrived at her apartment five days later. The Service suited her.

Alice kissed his forehead again.

He sipped his coffee. 'It's not my birthday, Alice – but still appreciated.'

It was to express her gratitude. 'You did well last night – for Viktor.'

He was grinning. 'Well, I've put my head on the block . . .'

She wandered into the next room, a tiny box under the sloped eaves with a single bed that would be hers if ever she had a chance to use it. She opened the wardrobe. She hadn't checked it in the night, had been too busy with the calls to the shipping agent that the Service used, and those that had brought Wilberforce to Covent Garden, and then the interminable arrangements for Locke's flight schedule from RAF Northolt. In the wardrobe was a rack of men's and women's clothes, assorted styles and sizes. She took what she needed for herself, and what he would need. The top-floor rooms were a frequently used safe house for the Service. She hadn't told Locke about the wardrobe: he could buy himself whatever else he was short of. She came back into the big room.

'You've only an hour.'

Mowbray sat up, rubbing his eyes. 'I think I'd prefer to walk.'

'Then you ought to be up.'

Mowbray beamed his smile. 'Head on the block, as I said . . . It'll be a fine show, worthy of the best traditions of the Service – or I have to hope the blade's sharp. Do you know, my dear, when the unlamented Duke of Monmouth was beheaded the axeman took fourteen chops? Wouldn't want him . . . Right, the last hurdle.'

He crawled off the bed.

The last hurdle was the politician.

'This is the real battleground, not playing at "Bash the Taleban" or having a game of "Kill the Tribesmen up the Khyber", this is the territory that matters. It's what we do well, an operation calling for verve, expertise and clear-minded thinking.'

Political sanction was necessary. The Secretary of State, who had nominal and tolerated responsibility for the Service, was a tired man after a late-night dinner at The Hague, and a flight back in the small hours. His office had been told by the director general that a decision on this matter was necessary and urgent – and the Prime Minister was holidaying. The Secretary of State was alone and vulnerable. Caught in the headlights, he sat behind his wide desk, and the director general lolled in an easy chair close to him, near enough to be a comforting presence.

Mowbray continued, 'I wouldn't want you to think, sir, that we are advocating a mission high on risk. Far from it. We are talking about a surgical lift carried out by trained personnel, men with a first-class record. One minute our agent will be there, the next his surveillance team will be scratching their heads and wondering where the hell he's gone. We're very good at this sort of thing. In and out, without fuss or fanfare . . . but we have to move at speed. Each hour that goes by, so, such an operation attracts difficulties. Give us the green light now, and the risk is minimal.'

A civil servant had opened the door, stood in the Secretary of State's eyeline, and gestured to his watch.

'Let's do it. Go for it. I'll look forward to meeting him when you've brought him over.' The Secretary of State laughed shrilly. ' "The risk is minimal." You said that, Mr Mowbray?'

'You heard me clearly, sir. You've made a very wise decision, thank you. You won't regret it.'

It had been one of the great bravura performances of Rupert Mowbray's life. It went without saying that the support of the director general was critical to his success. In turn, he had entrapped them both. The difference: the Secretary of State had not recognized that a gladiator's net was thrown over him. When he stood he received a little bob of respect from Mowbray. The politician would clatter down the stairs of the Foreign and Commonwealth Office building, but Mowbray and the director general would follow at a more dignified pace. By the time they stood on the step, each under his own umbrella, the official car was pulling out through the archway with a tail vehicle in pursuit.

'Have I ever told you about Betty's aunt, Rupert?'

'I don't think you've ever discussed your wife's family with me.' Mowbray's eyebrow flicked upwards.

'She's a grand maiden lady, now in her eighty-second year, and Betty's her favourite niece. She always comes to us at Christmas, it's an arrangement set in stone. One of our boys goes up to Euston and meets the train from the West Midlands, where this delightful old lady lives, then escorts her down into the Underground and on to the Northern Line. They travel to Waterloo main terminus, emerge above ground and take a train to Wimbledon where Betty and I are waiting. Pretty straightforward, yes? You made it sound, Rupert – lifting Agent Ferret out of Kaliningrad – as simple as seeing Betty's aunt safely between Euston and Wimbledon. And I almost believe you.'

'A good plan and good men, that's the key to a good result,' Mowbray said. 'You'll go down in the history of the Service as the man who gave it back its dignity.'

'Go carefully. There aren't too many naval-infantry battalions between Euston and Waterloo. Don't embarrass me.'

Mowbray walked out into the rain.

Locke's plane and its pilots had a punishing schedule to meet. They landed at Inverness, where an RAF helicopter waited. When the helicopter returned him to Inverness, he would be flown on to an airstrip west of Wolverhampton. After Wolverhampton he would be taken cross-Channel to Bruges in Belgium. From Belgium the plane would go west and follow the southern English coastline to a runway at Torbay used by a flying school. The schedule was tight, but the pilots said it was possible.

For Viktor, back from his meeting at headquarters, the day flickered by. He scarcely saw the papers placed in front of him by the secretariat. In his own big office, Admiral Falkovsky catnapped and did not need him. Was his cry for help heard? Was it acted on? Viktor did not know. There was nothing to tell him that the noose tightened on him. Around him was normality, but he felt that he was slowly, steadily, being crushed.

The shelducks, black-throated divers and mergansers usually gathered in the day on the shallow waters of the loch's edge close to his hut, where it was his habit to feed them, but they had been scattered in terror by the helicopter's landing on the shingle beach, and had not returned.

William Smith, former sergeant in the Special Boat Service – what he called the Squadron – known to the few close to him as Billy, prepared to leave. Dusk had gathered over the water. Where the cloud was broken, along towards the forested spur under Beinn Resipol and the cliff of Rubha Leathan, towards Acharacle, defined pools of gold light had settled. Only a military helicopter, and one flying in emergency conditions, would have landed in the early grey texture of the day on the gradual slope of the beach. He was called back. He felt no satisfaction at it, but he had not refused. He hammered planks across the windows on either side of the hut door. The outside wood of the hut was faded creosote and the windows were well built, except that the putty holding the panes had been loosened by the pine martens that chewed it; he had thought it best to nail the planks across the windows. The young man, off the helicopter, had said he would be back within ten days. 'It's just a quick one, Mr Smith, in and out.' But Billy had seen the evasion in the young man's eyes and he thought it right to make the hut secure against the winter. Beside him, as he swung the hammer, was his filled rucksack, and his dog lay close to it. He had finished inside the hut. Most of his day, since the morning when the helicopter had left, had been spent inside tidying. Out at the back the fire of his rubbish smoked in an oil drum, nearly dead. He had packed away his paintings in his old trunk; it had been with him in both his marine commando and his Squadron days.

Old ways died hard with Billy. He had folded his bedding neatly and piled it on the exposed mattress. To leave the refuge that was his home, beside the loch and under the high mountains, wrenched him to the guts, but he had not considered refusing the work offered. Across the water, the headlights of the post van flashed. The young man had made the arrangement on his mobile phone. Billy Smith padlocked the hut door. He lifted his rucksack, called the dog to heel and went down to the shore, his boots scattering the shingle. The dog jumped into the boat, where its basket and a supply of food were already stored, and Billy launched it. He began to row across the smooth loch waters towards the far side and the waiting post van, his hut diminishing as he pulled strongly away until it was lost beneath the height of Beinn Odhar Mhor. He had not thought of refusing the offer of work because the guilt still weighed heavy on him, and the escape to the hut and his watercolour painting had failed at the ultimate test to rid him of it.

Billy Smith had been the sergeant, the patrol's leader. The others had followed him. He rowed across the loch. Twelve years before, on a night in early summer, he had led the patrol on the east side of Carlingford Lough, between Causeway Bridge and Duggans Point. He had felt no guilt then, but time had changed that . . . He beached the boat and the dog ran to the postwoman. He didn't look back. Ahead of him was the night train from Fort William and the journey south.

There was a fight in A&E. Usually they came later, when the pubs chucked out into the night. This scrap, men and women, was from a lunchtime birthday session. They were all in their finery, best suits and blouses, and it had started in the bar and moved on to the car park, then followed the ambulance to the waiting area of A&E.

Colin 'Wickso' Wicks, ex-marine commando and Squadron member, finished his shift. Other porters moaned rotten about having first the night shift then the quick changeover to day duties, prattled on about the strain of it. It didn't bother him. He was wide awake. He'd discarded his green overalls, dressed in his civilian clothes and come to the waiting area in search of his supervisor. In his lunch break, eating a pie and chips in the canteen, he'd been called out into the corridor where a young man was waiting for him. They'd spoken. He was told he was wanted. When he'd left the Squadron he'd gone on to the books of Security Shield Ltd, as they all had, and he'd endured two years of escorting businessmen to Kazakhstan, Albania and Colombia; he had been an élite man of arms, not a valet, a servant, a door-opener, and he'd cited the boredom when he'd begun to refuse further work offers. He was trained as a battlefield medic but nursing jobs required references and he didn't want any employer going back to Poole and sifting through his records. References didn't matter, weren't important, for a trolley-pusher. He ignored the fight and rolled forward on the balls of his feet towards the door, looking for the glow of his supervisor's cigarette in the evening darkness. He stayed fit because he ran the streets every night when he was on day shift and every morning when he was on nights. Last year, a nurse had persuaded him to run in Wolverhampton's half-marathon, and Wickso had won by a clear hundred metres, but he hadn't stayed around to collect his prize because he might have been photographed. It was an obsession to him that his picture should not appear in any newspaper – the chance of his parents seeing his photograph in a Midlands evening paper was nil, they lived in west London under the flight paths of

Heathrow. The last time he had been home, after his discharge, he had seen the shrine they kept in the front room to their hero, special-forces son, photographs, cups, medals, and he'd left early because what had happened to him was like a bad and painful wound to them. The idolized young man had become a pariah and their dreams were broken.

His supervisor came back through the door, and coughed hard. Wickso told him that he would be away for a few days, at least two weeks, but it could be longer. Overseas . . . 'Well, don't expect any favours from us, sunshine, if you're just pissing off, leaving us in the lurch, and us short-handed enough. Don't come to us begging.' Wickso had never begged anything of anyone. He didn't rise to the bait, just walked on and out through the door, then ran loosely the mile to his bedsit. The young man in the corridor had told him where he should be, and at what time, the next morning. He lived with the shame of what had happened on the early-summer night on Carlingford Lough, near to Duggans Point. The patrol's target had been Sean O'Connell, Provo quartermaster, and from their lie-up bivouac they'd seen the man ease a boat on to the shore and lift a weighted sack from it. It was where Intelligence expected O'Connell to run guns from the South to the North. Billy had whispered they'd have the bastard, not shoot him, but see him shit himself. They'd gone for him. There was a struggle. Billy and Lofty in the water with him, and the thrashing fight as they'd tried to hold his head under so's the spunk would go from him. Wickso had had a torch on them and he'd seen the man's throat as it came up from under the water, and the throat was clean of distinguishing marks. Sean O'Connell, the briefing said, had a mole on his throat, but Wickso hadn't shouted, hadn't intervened. He ran easily back to his bedsit, and there he'd pack what little he owned, grab a couple of hours' sleep, and catch an early train.

It was when the ghosts came out and sat around and smoked and brewed tea and talked of girls and home at the end of the evening and the start of the night. There were still enough leaves in the poplar trees at the bottom of the cemetery by the pillboxes for the wind to rustle there. The ghosts came from their sleeping places of square-cut Portland stone.

At the end of many days, 'Lofty' Flint – one time of the Marines and former member of the Squadron – sat with them and spoke with them. The rest of the gardeners employed by the Commonwealth War Graves Commission at Tyne Cot reckoned Lofty had 'grave fever', but his work could not be faulted and each year his contract was extended, and he did no harm. In the dark, with the cloud heavy over him and the wind on his face, he could no longer see where he raked. The young man had come in the late afternoon, by taxi. Lofty had never looked up from his raking, had made the young man stoop with him, walk with him and stand with him as he fed the leaves on to the bonfire.

He put away his tools and his barrow. There were only the ghosts to see him go. He turned on his bicycle light and it threw a stuttered beam ahead of him. At first he had told the young man that it was quite impossible for him to leave Tyne Cot for two weeks, or even two days, because the Remembrance Day services were only two months away, when the leaves must all be cleared and the graves must be cleaned . . . The young man had said, without sympathy, 'After what you did, after the disgrace of it, I'd have thought you'd be ready for a chance to make amends. These men, here, they served their country – aren't you up to that?'

He cycled on the straight, flat road towards the farmhouse in Passchendaele where he lodged, away from the only place where he knew he belonged, and he heard the singing of the ghosts as he went. He had only done one job for Security Shield Ltd – as driver/escort/handyman for the recently retired commander of 39 Brigade in Northern Ireland, a man thought to be at risk from reprisal terrorism. For six years at the brigadier's Wiltshire home, it had been an idyll for a man severely psychologically troubled. The brigadier's retirement hobby had been a fund-raising committee for the Commonwealth War Graves Commission. Lofty had twice driven him to Belgium to visit the cemeteries at Hop Store, Essex Farm, Spanbroekmolen and Bedford House, and twice they had visited Tyne Cot. The brigadier had died, the house in Wiltshire had been sold, the widow had written a letter to the CWGC commending Lofty for work as a gardener/labourer, as he'd requested. He hoped to live out his life there because, with his rake, hoe, shears and digging fork, it was the one place where he could exorcize the demons.

The chief target of the patrol had been Sean O'Connell, quartermaster. Lofty Flint, who was tall, rangy and strong, lived in the shadow of Billy, his sergeant. He followed Billy where Billy led. Into the water with the target, after Ham had yelped from the kick in the privates and the bite on his hand, and when the Irishman had weakened it had been Lofty who held him down till the bubbles ceased to rise. They had dragged the body to the shore, and then Ham had opened the sack to find not rifles but a confusion of wriggling, writhing crabs. The wallet in the breast pocket of the denim jacket had identified Huey Kelly, sometime inshore fisherman. He would have cracked, when the investigation started, if it had not been for Billy, Wickso and Ham, would have confessed. Tyne Cot was his escape and his penance. He pedalled towards his lodgings. He would tell Marie that he was leaving immediately, and that he did not know when, or if, he would be back. He would pack his bag and cycle in the night to Bruges, would leave his bicycle at the station and take a train to Brussels, then the first Eurostar connection to London. There had been something in the eyes of the young man – doubt or uncertainty – that made Lofty think he would not be back.

Dim light spilled through the open cell door. The prisoners were bedded down, the addicts moaned, the drunks snored and a woman screamed that her baby needed her.

Sitting on the bed with its concrete base, his shoes up on the blanket, Hamilton Protheroe surveyed them. In the Marines he had been 'Ham', given the name by a warrant officer; it had stuck. The WO2 had said he was lippy, with an attitude problem, but he'd passed the physical tests for entry to the Squadron with room to spare, and the tests for aptitude. At the door were the arresting constables, the interview detectives, the custody officer, and a young man. He'd been dozing, near to sleep, when he'd heard the brush of feet in the corridor and the jangle of the keys, and the young man had been put in with him. They hadn't locked the door behind him, had left it open, and he'd known then he was going to walk. The young man had looked dead tired, out on his feet, and perhaps he'd forgotten whatever grand speech had been written for him. He'd been found via his solicitor. 'Well, it's your lucky day, me pitching up,' the young man had said. 'She's retracted her evidence, the woman who's accusing you. I'm taking you out, two weeks abroad, then we cut you loose.' There were papers to be signed and evidence statements to be binned. The detectives glanced at him with malevolence, as if they despised him. What was in it for him, he'd asked the young man, and he'd been told, and he'd nodded and said that was acceptable. That day, why he looked beaten in, the young man had met the other three – had actually met up with the rest of the team, Billy, Wickso and Lofty. One run, one good pay-day, piece of crap. He'd lain on the bed, back cushioned by the pillow, head against the wall. 'Yes, I'll do that. No problem, I'll go to Kaliningrad.' Ham Protheroe's Russian had been categorized as first grade. Not something he'd ever lose. He'd grinned, at the confusion caused by his Russian, then negotiated with the little creep. 'Half up-front, and the rest on return, cash. OK?' It was the money. He felt no guilt about Carlingford Lough. They'd all have been in gaol still, if Ham hadn't thought on his feet. Chucked the body back into the water so's the tide would carry it on. Thanked Christ they hadn't radioed in for a contact signal. All legged it one mile up the coast and away from Duggans Point, beyond Greencastle, on to Cranfield Bay. Ham was the communications man. Had called in. 'Alpha Four Kilo: nothing to report.' Had called in an hour later, near Greencastle. 'Alpha Four Kilo: patrol proceeding.' Had called in a last time, now four miles from where Huey Kelly floated on the tide. 'Alpha Four Kilo: nothing to report. Returning to base.' He'd held the team together when the provost marshal had met them at the gate the next night, and had escorted them to the interview with the Crime Squad detectives. 'They'll position it on the boat. There was no boat when we went by. We saw nothing. We were on Cranfield Bay,' he'd whispered. 'Stick with it.' He'd done one assignment for Security Shield Ltd, after the inevitable invitation to resign. Done bodyguard to a singer in London, but the money was shit, and he'd borrowed from her. And hadn't been home in nine years, because he'd taken a loan from his father while the parents were away on holiday and he'd had the run of the Cheshire house. He had nobody. His home was the hotels of the south coast, his family were widows and divorcees, and now the police cell. The custody sergeant gave him a plastic bag with his watch, his wallet, loose coins, belt and tie, and Ham signed for them flamboyantly, then swung his feet off the blanket. There was no mirror in the cell but he tidied his hair as best he could, knotted the tie and hitched the belt round his waist. The crowd stood back, made room for him, and he wished them well. He followed the young man out into the car park. He was told where they'd be staying for the rest of the night, and he said he hoped it was three-star because that was what he was used to. He never thanked the young man for coming with an offer of work . . . but he'd take it. A beggar could not be a chooser . . . and he was a beggar, and he reckoned that Billy, Wickso and Lofty were beggars also.

6

Q. What part of Russia is described as the 'corridor of crime'?
A. Kaliningrad.

'He is a very senior man,' Bikov murmured, and the squinting of his eyes betrayed surprise at what he was told.

'Wherever you dig you will find moral decay, probably the degeneracy of alcohol abuse,' the general rapped at him.

Bikov doubted it, but did not contradict. He guarded himself. 'There are many reasons for a man to turn to treachery.'

'Vanity and vainglory . . .'

'He will have an ego, I agree.' He seldom reacted to what he was told. He preferred to depend on what he found for himself.

'. . . malicious and distorted self-pride. Dissatisfaction with his work, the yearning for the material trinkets he will have been given.'

'Perhaps, though, some reasons will be deep in the psyche of the man.'

'There is no place on this earth for a soldier who has sold his Motherland. Greed will have led him to the path of the criminal.'

'It will be far in his past – far, far back in the life of Viktor Archenko,' Bikov mused. 'It might go to childhood. It is a puzzle to be unpicked.'

'Unpicked with delicacy, with extreme care . . .' The general leaned forward, dropped his voice.

'Of course.'

'Exceptional delicacy and care . . . Archenko is an officer of seniority and with a distinguished record. He has the patronage of an officer who is listened to, is heard in the highest places. A mistake, and we are fallen men. A mistake, and you – *I* – we have no future, we're on the street.'

'I understand what you say.' Bikov smiled coolly.

It was a challenge that Yuri Bikov relished. He cared little for the reputation that had gathered on his back. He was a predator who pitted himself against a prey. He sought challenges that were worthy of him, but the praise that came with success left him indifferent. Other predators relied on teeth or claws, or a rifle, but Bikov's weapon was his mind. He had never hurt, physically harmed, a man he had interrogated. It was simply crude to use the pentathol truth drugs, cruder to extract fingernails and to rely on the rubber truncheons or the electrodes. He read books on psychology and when he had time, in Moscow, he visited the offices of professors of that discipline, perched on a hard chair and invited them to talk with him. His reputation said that Yuri Bikov had never been bested by a man across a bare table from him. What happened to the prey afterwards . . . it was outside his responsibility.

The youngest lieutenant colonel in the FSB's military counter-intelligence section had arrived in Moscow in darkness. His shoebox apartment was sublet and unavailable. Bikov, instead, had gone to the residential complex used by the FSB in the capital and been allocated a tiny, cold room. The file had been delivered to him by messenger and he had read it through the night, going back and forward over the few pages it contained. The file had been divided into two sections. The first section comprised the naval career of Archenko and read as a success story for a man protected by a fleet commander.

There had been a photograph with that section. He had lifted it out of the file and laid it on the bed where he'd sat, and all the time he'd turned the pages he had kept vigil with the photograph of an open-faced man with the jaw of a decision-taker, a friendly face, and one of calm and authority . . . Father, now dead, a commended air-force flier, reared in the military community, naval entry and quality marks as a cadet, a hobby listed as 'medieval military archaeology', the staff of Admiral Falkovsky, the four unremarkable years at the Grechko staff officers' academy where there had been no complaints, a transfer back to the Northern Fleet, and the Kaliningrad posting, a regime of personal fitness from beach running . . . No relationship was listed. There was no woman. He had written a note of that on the outside of the first file, and then he'd looked again at the photograph. A handsome man with prospects, who would be chased, but no woman was listed. In his own life, Yuri Bikov's, there was a wife (divorced) and a child now aged fifteen years (estranged). It was joked of him that he was married to his work. He slept occasionally with other officers' wives who were bored or itchy, but never for more than two or three nights.

He had underlined what he had written. The second file was thinner. A book of matches was stapled in a plastic sack to the inside of the cover. The matches were from a hotel in the Polish city of Gdansk where a delegation, including Archenko, had visited a new dry dock. But the *zampolit* at the Baltiysk naval base, Piatkin, had questioned the other men on the delegation and they had sworn that the delegation had not visited that hotel. The most recent pages in the second file dealt with that hotel's residents on the three dates Archenko had visited the dry dock in Gdansk. Various nationalities featured: Swedish, German, American and Norwegian had been resident in the hotel on one of the three dates. A British pair had been in the hotel during each of the three dates that Archenko had gone to the dry dock, and Roderick Walton and Elizabeth Beresford had not been in that hotel on any other date. The information had been gained by FSB officers travelling from Warsaw the previous week – with the aid of a donation to the night porter's retirement fund – but the address boxes in the hotel's registration cards had not been filled in. It was interesting but not conclusive. More conclusive were the two most recent sheets added to the file. They detailed the surveillance, carried out by Piatkin on the order of the general in the Lubyanka. Twice the admiral's chief of staff had had proper authorization to visit the castle at Malbork and the church of the Holy Cross at Braniewo, in pursuit of his listed hobby, and the first time he had *possibly* identified the tail vehicles and the second time he had *probably* identified them, and each time the journey over the border had been aborted. The files had given him food to feed off, but he thought them not conclusive evidence of guilt.

He would die – Archenko would be executed inside or outside the law if he were guilty. When or where was a matter of no importance to Yuri Bikov. The gaining of a confession was a matter of importance, was the challenge confronting him.

A nervousness shimmered in the general. He stood at the window and his hands fidgeted behind his back. 'We have to walk on eggs, because he is protected. I rely on you . . . Look, come here, look down there. He is still alive, incredible. Come . . .'

Bikov rose from his chair and went to the window He was beside the general, and followed the line of the general's jabbing finger. A man shuffled on the far side of the square. He was ancient, bent, wore a heavy greatcoat and a woollen cap from which faint wisps of white hair were visible; a grey, straggling moustache hung round his mouth. His appearance was that of a long-retired schoolmaster. He used a stick to steady himself and carried a small plastic bag weighted with shopping. Carpet slippers were on his feet as he crossed the Tarmac, and the stick was raised defiantly to halt the traffic he walked between. Now the general seemed to Bikov to cringe.

'I thought he was dead. You know him? He must be ninety years old. He worked here . . . That is Ivan Grigoreyev . . . They say even the dogs did not dare to go close to him. Stalin's man and Beria's. He was the executioner. He succeeded the executioner Maggo. The forties was his time, this was his place. For ten years he killed, always with a revolver, here, under us. It was said of him: "He has a serious attitude to his work." No firing squads, just him. He was so close that he was spattered. Generals, professors, doctors, intellectuals, officials, they all knelt before him. I was told he stank of blood. He worked with two buckets beside him. One had eau-de-Cologne to hide the smell and the other was filled with vodka. All he stopped for on a busy day was to reload his pistol and to drink the vodka. They say he is deaf in his right ear . . . He was here, his last year, when I first came to work in the Lubyanka. I thought he was dead.'

The general shook his head and turned away. His visage had whitened. Somewhere in the bowels of the building, in a room off a side corridor, was the now underemployed successor to Ivan Grigoreyev. There was a yard off the back of the building with a door to the cell block . . . When he had his confession, Bikov would bring Captain, second rank, Viktor Archenko to this building, to that cell block, and would leave him within a few paces of the yard.

'There is a plane waiting for me. Please excuse me.'

'Nail him, just nail the shit.'

Mowbray and Alice arrived after lunch. He hadn't wanted a pool chauffeur, and she'd driven. They'd stopped for an early sandwich in a pub to break the journey from London.

'God, they've let the place go.'

'It'll be the cutbacks,' Alice said. 'The handyman's gone, only Maggie's here now.'

The large gaunt house of dulled red brick had been built with a brewer's profits a century ago, requisitioned for the military in the Second World War and never returned to after the cessation of hostilities. It had been passed to the Foreign Office for training courses in the fifties and sixties, then given to the Service in the seventies. It was rarely used now. The paint peeled on the window frames and the Virginia creeper was rampant. A pane was broken in an upper window and a gutter above the front-door porch dripped. It was listed as having fifteen bedrooms, of which six were habitable, and twelve acres of grounds. The grass hadn't been cut for a month, and Alice muttered something about Crown Maintenance being a bit behind. Wet sycamore leaves coated the drive and clogged the drains. A dog, marking their arrival, barked hoarsely inside.

'It used to be rather a useful accommodation.'

'I'm sure it'll be fine,' Alice said briskly.

She took his bag, and hers, from the back seat and followed him to the door. They were deep in rolling Surrey countryside, near to Chiddingfold. Mowbray yanked down the bell pull. The ring pealed inside and the dog's barking came to a frenzy. He scowled until the door opened, and Maggie – mid-forties, her waist bulging – reached up, took his head, kissed him wetly on each cheek. Then he grinned.

'So pleased to see you, Mr Mowbray. It'll be just like the old days. You're so welcome.' She arched her eyebrows and asked softly, coyly, 'Seems like it's a big one.'

He winked at her. 'All in place, are they?'

'In the lounge. I lit the fire. Hasn't been one in there this year, might smoke a bit. Mr Locke is in his room.'

'Is he?' Mowbray looked up the stairs. The carpet was threadbare and one of the rails on the lower flight had come loose from its fitting. He shouted, 'Mr Locke – Gabriel Locke – your presence is required.'

Locke appeared on the upper landing, a grim look on his face. He was coming down the stairs and his speech rattled. 'Is that dog shut away? Should be shot, it's savage. It's quite unacceptable having a wild dog.'

'They have arrived, I understand.'

'The schedule was ridiculous. I had no sleep, no chance for a break.'

'And what are they doing now?'

'I'm not their bloody keeper, I've no idea.'

Alice said, 'I'll take the bags into the dining room . . . Oh, and I'll ring Jerry, tell him to expect you.' She'd learned never to push herself forward, and he appreciated that. Later, he thought, she'd help Maggie prepare a meal, and then they'd leave, all of them, but him first. The house was a transit point, out of sight and out of mind.

At the end of a darkened corridor was a closed door and behind it a murmur of conversation. Locke pushed forward, then spun and blocked Mowbray. 'Do I have permission to say what I think?'

'If it's relevant . . .'

'Actually, I can't believe this is happening,' Locke hissed.

'. . . and time is pushing on.'

'The whole thing is pathetic and doomed.'

'It has the sanction of the director general and ministers.' It was said lightly, intentionally so. He sought to belittle Locke.

'It'll fail.'

Mowbray thought this was Locke's big throw. No doubt that it had been rehearsed. His smile was avuncular. 'A faint heart never won a fair lady. *I* don't fail.'

'It's a world, yours, with cobwebs on it. You're deluded.'

'You want to walk away, young man, then walk. See if I miss you.'

'But I can't, I fucking can't. Those men in there . . .' Locke's arm was flung back and gestured to the door. '. . . you should have been with me, to see where I dragged them out from. Weirdos, drop-outs, fourth rate . . .'

'They'll be adequate, they'll be perfectly adequate. Worried about how it will play on your curriculum vitae?' His voice hardened. 'Walk away and see how that plays, young man. If you've finished . . .'

'Adequate? They're deadbeats – one of them's even a goddamn criminal. Is that your idea of adequate?'

'For what we're asking of them – and now please stop the whine – more than adequate. May I come past?'

Locke stepped back. For a moment Mowbray paused. He took a comb from an inside pocket and slipped it through his hair. He gave his tie knot a little straightening tug, then flicked a single dandruff speck from his shoulder. He opened the door. First impressions always mattered. He breathed hard. Confidence and authority were demanded from the beginning. He strode into the room. The interior was gloomy, the curtains had not been drawn back, the easy chairs were shielded by dustcovers, and he smelt the mustiness that the open fire had not cleared. The four men, sitting round a table playing cards, looked up.

Mowbray beamed. 'Welcome, gentlemen – what a tip of a place. Sorry about that. My name's Mowbray and I seldom, as those who know me will tell you, deal in untruths. Like yourselves, I'm retired, pensioned-off, but I've been called back for this one operation because the present generation of heroes don't want to risk dirtying their hands. It's never been a problem for me, dirty hands. Why are you here? You're here because those fine courageous people from Hereford say they're not too "keen on a trip in there". "There" is Kaliningrad, a shit-heap, the Russian enclave between Poland and Lithuania. The equally fine people at Poole, whom you'd know rather better than me, said that they didn't want to know and asked, "Is he worth it?" "He" is a naval officer at the Baltic Fleet headquarters, and has been my asset for the last four years. He is now under close surveillance and near to arrest, and if he is arrested his ultimate fate will be a bullet in the back of the neck. He is one of the finest men I have been privileged to know, and I – and you – are going to save his life. If any of you wishes to leave, now would be the correct moment.'

He looked into each of their unshaven faces. They wore a uniform of trainers, jeans and sweatshirts. None of them moved. None of the chairs scraped back on the parquet. Mowbray heard Locke's sharpened breathing behind him.

'We begin our journey tonight. There's rather too much to cram in, but we'll manage. We'll start with the maps – Kaliningrad, its borders, the naval base and so on. You all come recommended, you're the best and you will achieve the best result and we'll leave the fainthearts with their scrubbed hands in awe of us.'

They started on the maps, and pored over them until the helicopter came for Rupert Mowbray.

There was shooting further up the beach.

The wind had turned and came from the north, otherwise the fisherman would not have heard the staccato bursts. Roman often heard shooting on the range far behind the fence that separated the Polish stretch of the beach from the dunes on the spit where the Russian troops exercised and practised. He worked at repairing his nets. It was most likely that rubbish had been thrown overboard from a passing freighter that week and had drifted then gone to the bottom. He would have said, and so would all the other fishermen who worked from the village of Piaski, that he knew where every obstruction lay in the shallow waters where he fished. Roman was the expert and always brought home the best catches of dab, flounder and plaice. His fingers moved fast, with a whipping motion, as he made good the tears in his net. If it had been early summer he would not have stayed out on the beach to repair the rents, he would have gone to the café in Piaski, drunk beer with the other fishermen and put off the work until the morning. But autumn had come, and soon winter would be hurrying after it. In two more weeks, or three at the most, and Roman was as expert on the weather as on the fishing grounds, storms would lash the beach most days and it would not be possible to launch the boats. The fishing would be over until spring. Then there was no money to be earned and Roman and his family, and the other families of Piaski, would have to scrape, scrimp, for survival. Each day that he was able to fish before the storms was valued. There were a dozen boats pulled up on the sand, white-painted planks with a yellow-painted gunwale, all numbered but the crews from the rest of them, and the colleagues who sailed with him, were long gone to the village café. The border was two kilometres down the beach. If he looked up, away from the nets on which he concentrated -- and he was blessed with eyes as sharp as the cormorants' who competed with the gulls to feast on the heads and carcasses that were thrown over his shoulder when he gutted and filleted his catch -- he could see the empty Polish watchtower and beyond it the Russian watchtower, which was always manned. If he squinted he could see the border's fence, which ran from the spit's pine forest and down on to the beach to the low-water tideline. Beyond were the exercise areas, the missile launching pads and the ranges. He knew the sounds of the different weapons the Russians used. Thirty-one years before, he had been a conscript in the Polish army and he remembered well the sounds of tanks firing, mortars and machine-guns. But he had not heard that day the familiar thunder, carried on the wind, of the 12.7mm heavy machine-gun.

Riding on her anchor, the *Princess Rose* pitched in a swell made worse by the wind that strained the cable and tried to drive her towards the rocks and the shore.

The engineer watched from the rail. The master and the mate were on the bridge and had brought the boat to within a nautical mile of what the map called Mew Stone. He could see the lights up the estuary of the town of Dartmouth, and the white waves thrown back into the darkness by the rapid approach of the dinghy. He was from Rostock, the old principal port of eastern Germany on the Baltic. He had worked in the shipyards until his life had crashed around him and he had been sacked as a casualty of the new grail of capitalism. Reunification had cost him his safe job and the security of cradle-to-grave certainties. His wife and daughters were in Rostock and the coaster would sail north of the port where the ship-yards were now silent, but he would not have a chance to stop off and visit. He was a heavily built man, with a shaven head, and next week he would celebrate, with the master and the mate, his forty-eighth birthday. His life on the *Princess Rose* involved eating, watching wildlife films on video, and keeping the diesel engine alive. It was near to death; without the tender, nursing care Johannes Richter gave it, it would have failed long ago. He liked to say the engine was 'temperamental – like a woman', and he did not allow the master or the mate near it. It was in his care, and he gave it love. When the *Princess Rose* had reached the Mew Stone, as the anchor was dropped, the master had radioed the coastguard and Customs – Richter had heard him do it – on shore and they had been cleared immediately to take a small cargo on board. Richter did not understand how there should be so little interest from the authorities in their coming close to land, at night, and taking on a cargo.

The dinghy came alongside them and pitched under the hull. He threw down a rope-ladder and saw that its crew wore naval berets, but their bodies were in black wetsuits. The master had ordered the Filipinos below deck, the able seamen and the cook, as if the loading of the cargo was not their business. They had no integral crane on the *Princess Rose*, but two of the dinghy's crew scrambled up the rope-ladder and the two left in the dinghy passed up four heavily weighted black canvas bags, then four big cardboard boxes that were more than a metre long and a half-metre deep and wide, then a deflated dinghy and an outboard motor. The last man on the dinghy, rocking below on the swell, was not a sailor. He wore an oiled weatherproof coat, had polished shoes and a mane of silver hair that the wind tangled. When the bags and boxes were on board, and the deflated craft and the outboard, this older man was helped up the rope-ladder with one of the dinghy crew clutching his coat collar from above and one finding the rungs for his feet from underneath. The man showed no fear as he climbed up from the tossing black waters splashing between the hull and the dinghy. The master had come down from the bridge. Richter saw the man pass a thick brown envelope to him, and he watched as the master was given a receipt to sign. He thought the man had come to supervise the loading personally, as if he did not trust others to do his work. It impressed Richter, and confused him, that an obviously senior man bothered to board the *Princess Rose* to see the stowing of a cargo of less than a tonne weight.

Richter was joined by the mate and they started to transfer the bags and boxes, the craft and the outboard off the deck, and he had no more time to be impressed or confused. He did not see the man and the dinghy's crew leave. When the last box was in the mess, the master came to him and said that he should bring the ship to power. He went down into the bowels of the *Princess Rose*.

Within fifteen minutes Richter had coaxed thrust from the diesel engine, heard the clanking grind of the anchor's cable being winched up, and felt the motion of the ship as she ploughed out into the Channel's wind. If he achieved the maximum from his engine, it would take them four days to reach the Polish port of Gdansk.

He came without fanfare, like a wraith in the dark evening.

There had been delays in Moscow because a warning light, governing the undercarriage of the aircraft, had played up. Yuri Bikov should have been into Kaliningrad Military in the late afternoon. The problems of maintenance were more acute with each passing day. It suited him better to land in darkness. He had ordered a signal to be sent ahead that forbade any welcoming party. He wanted neither senior officials from the city's headquarters of the Federalnaya Sluzhba Bezopasnosi nor the FSB resident at the Baltiysk naval base to meet him. One car and one driver were all that he required. He did not wish to draw attention to himself, was determined that his arrival should not be announced.

When his aircraft had taxied to a remote corner of the apron, the two men who had travelled with him were out first and down the steps, which bucked under their weight. They were his major and his sergeant. The major's expertise was in the areas of office organization, and his sergeant's was in the area of personal protection. They had been with him before and the respect between him and them was mutual. The major wore the executive suit of a young, successful businessman, and the sergeant wore a bulky jacket – sufficient to hide the Makharov pistol in his shoulder holster and the submachine-gun with the folding stock that rested in the jacket's inner pocket. Bikov followed them.

As was intended, the ground crew would have thought that the major was the man of enough importance to be flown from Moscow by military jet. Bikov was not noticed. A heavily filled duffel bag was hitched on his shoulder. He wore the boots that had been hosed but had not lost all of the Chechen mud that clung to the stitching and the laces, and the jeans he had had there, which had been washed but not pressed. There was a small fraying tear in the right knee. He had shaved the night before, the first time since going to Chechnya, enough for his audience with the general at the Lubyanka, and he would not shave again until he left Kaliningrad with his prisoner and his prisoner's confession; the stubble was already on his cheeks and chin.

They were driven away on the outer perimeter road, past a silent, darkened battery of surface-to-air missiles, avoiding the lights of the civilian terminal. They headed for the city and a hotel used by tourists from Germany, which military staff officers would be unlikely to visit. There they would dump their bags. Later, they would go to the back entrance of the city's FSB headquarters.

If any had known of the reputation of Lieutenant Colonel Yuri Bikov, they would have felt the aggravated chill of the north wind that blew on the Kaliningrad *oblast*. They would have recognized a man who was formidable, dangerous, who did not travel on business of slight importance. He was relaxed and at ease. Bikov asked no more of life than that challenges should be served up to him. He was sandwiched on the back seat between his sergeant and his major. His sergeant told the driver to switch off the car's heating, and his major wound down the window; neither needed to be told what he wanted. He sniffed the air, and on the chill of the wind was the sea's tang.

He was smiling.

Crow's flight, 475 kilometres away from Kaliningrad, another military aircraft landed. A C-130 Hercules, of transport command, out of the RAF base at Lyneham, landed at Templehof, the airport to the west of central Berlin.

Gabriel Locke had tried as they'd boarded to distance himself from the rest of Mowbray's army – and Mowbray, who still smelt of salt spray after his helicopter ride – but the loadmaster had refused him the seat forward and on the far side to the rest of the group. He was with them, was a part of them. When they'd stacked and circled over Templehof, he'd heard Mowbray launch into a description of the Airlift, as if what happened in the summer of 1948 was

131

important today. Locke had tried not to listen, and Smith, Protheroe, Flint and Wicks had made no pretence and had slept. The woman had worked hard at her nails with a file. In the dimmed light of the transport plane, where their leg movement was constricted by the cargo of wood crates on pallets destined for the embassy's military attaché, only Locke had been Mowbray's unwilling audience. On Mowbray's voice was a whiff of excitement – as if he had come home, as if he valued the city spread out below them in myriad pinpricks of light.

They came down feather sweetly.

Mowbray had shrugged out of his restraining harness before the aircraft had come to a halt, before the loadmaster had given him permission to disentangle himself, with the eagerness of a child about to play a favourite game. When the Hercules finally lurched to its stop, Mowbray had to reach out to steady himself, and Alice caught his arm. It was all pitiful to Gabriel Locke. The rear hatch ground down on its hydraulics to reveal a forklift waiting to lift down the cargo. Mowbray was first off. Locke wondered if the older man was going to do a papal job and kneel to kiss the oil-smeared Tarmac. He didn't. He made a little jump to get from the hatch to the ground and then stood, his hands locked behind his back, and seemed to smell the air. Locke wondered why Mowbray should feel such blatant affinity with Berlin . . . The team filed off. They were quiet. Alice followed them, carrying Mowbray's briefcase and his bag, and her own briefcase and suitcase; she was loaded like a hotel porter. Locke followed.

The loadmaster was already busy with the forklift and had started to supervise the movement of the crates. Three cars waited for them with the engines ticking, spewing fumes. A woman came forward.

Locke heard her say, 'Welcome to Berlin, Mr Mowbray. I'm Daphne, Daphne Sullivan.'

He heard Mowbray say, 'You did well, Daphne. I congratulate you – first-class tradecraft.'

Daphne Sullivan was introducing them to a German civilian, who had brought a passport stamp with him. Mowbray's passport, false name, then Alice North's with her bogus identity. Locke seethed. His passport was genuine, in his own name. Why was he not considered sufficiently important to have been given a new passport with a new name? The team stood back once their passports had been stamped, then began to follow Mowbray to the cars. Alice was close to the greeter, Daphne Sullivan. Locke heard her low voice: 'But he'd been there?'

'The chalk was fresh. The footprints were very clear. I could see that he'd run along the beach. Yes, he'd been there.'

'There were two crosses and Y and F?'

A woman was queried and a woman scratched back. Locke heard Daphne Sullivan say sharply, 'That's what I wrote in my report. Is it a state secret? The Y and the F, that was important?'

Locke thought there was a fractional choke in Alice North's voice, and wouldn't have noted it if he hadn't been close. 'His first communication with us, when he'd walked in, he signed off as "Your Friend" – YF – and in his last line of the letter he'd written, "Protect me." Thank you for having gone there.'

Locke might have registered more, but he was tired as a dog, and his ears still hammered with the engine noise of the transport aircraft – and Alice was scampering with her briefcases and bags, towards the cars, and Mowbray was waving imperiously for him to hurry.

He murmured, 'How was it in there?'

'Foul,' Daphne Sullivan said curtly. 'It's an armed camp ... I don't know what boys' capers you're going to indulge yourselves with, and don't want to know. I'm glad I'm not a part of it.'

Locke took the last place in the third car. Why had Alice North craned to listen when told about bloody footprints in the sand on a beach? They drove out of the airport. Why had Alice North thanked an officer from the Berlin station for merely doing her job? They took the fast lane in the late-night traffic.

Under the bright light of a spotlamp, Yuri Bikov read the files that were brought to him. His major had chosen the room and Bikov approved the choice. The room's door led on to a corridor, and at the end of the corridor were the fire-escape steps leading directly to the rear car park behind the building. While Bikov read, the sergeant was at work with a heavy screw-driver, changing the lock on the door. His major was setting up the new telephone system that would carry scrambled calls to the Lubyanka in Moscow.

Already, by midnight, a photocopier had run off a four-times-life-size copy of a picture of Captain, second rank, Viktor Archenko, which was now fastened with adhesive strips to the wall behind the door. Neither man interrupted Bikov. He would work through till dawn, until the light came up on the windows across which the blinds were drawn. He read and pondered and let the thoughts swim, then looked up at the face that stared back down at him. He circled the man, and searched for weakness . . . It was always in the files, it would be there if he could recognize it.

'Land or sea – that's the first thing to be worked out. What do we want, land or sea?' Billy asked them.

'Do we have the choice?' Lofty shrugged.

'Course we do.' Ham snorted. 'That's why we're here, the experts – God help them. Go in by land or go in by sea . . . We tell Rupert God Almighty what we want.'

'Land. Land's better,' Wickso said. 'Go in by land, come out by land – last bit is cross-country. Better than by sea.'

Locke listened. The hotel on Hardenbergstrasse was big and anonymous, and they hadn't roused a second glance from the harassed girls behind the desk. Rupert Mowbray wasn't with them, was elsewhere, and Alice had told Locke that 'Mr' Mowbray had gone round the corner to a *pension* he always used in the 'old days'. Locke had repeated 'old days' to her sneeringly, but she hadn't responded. As soon as she'd taken her key, Alice had gone to the room allocated to her rather than stay with him for a drink. Locke had had two beers in the bar, then gone up to the corridor, fifth floor, where their rooms were. The TV had been on in Smith's room and he'd knocked at the door, too awake to sleep. Maps were out on the bed. He was sat down by the TV, on which an overweight singer performed in short trousers and braces. They ignored him.

'We don't have the time to piss about. If it's "land" what do we need?' Billy asked.

'Get off the road, go cross-country, cut the fence,' Wickso said. 'Me and Ham either side of the fence in the tree line.'

'Lofty's the driver, got the class act,' Billy said. 'So God Almighty's got to get us a car on the far side, and a driver – we can't, not on the way in. Lofty drives on the way out.'

'What does "close surveillance" mean?' Lofty asked.

'Means you got to drive like there's a bayonet, a sharp one, adjacent to your arse, when we've done the pick-up.'

'What do we call him?' Ham spoke.

'He's Ferret, so we call him Ferret.'

'He's got to be at the pick-up, that's Ferret's problem,' Wickso said.

Locke noticed that the one called Lofty had tilted his head back as if that might help him to understand a difficulty. His eyes were narrowed and gazed at the ceiling light and a frown creased his forehead. To Locke, Lofty was the slowest of the four and the one who had been hardest to recruit. The idea of any man wanting, volunteering, to spend his days at Tyne Cot was beyond his comprehension; it was an awful place, seriously awful. The conversation died, and Billy was folding away the maps of Kaliningrad, coastal and land. The singer belted on.

Lofty said, all the time shaking his head, 'What bugs me – why us?'

Ham grinned, without charity. 'You stupid, Lofty, more stupid than usual?'

'Why not the Regiment or the Squadron?'

Wickso said, 'Because, Lofty, we don't exist . . .'

Billy said, 'Because, old cocker, we're deniable.'

Locke slipped out into the corridor, and none of them seemed to notice his going. He walked past Alice North's door . . . He was outside the loop, and he'd bloody well change that.

He saw the cluster of men gathered at the wharf's edge.

Viktor walked aimlessly. As the admiral's eyes and ears in the base it was known that he often prowled late at night to have the feel of the fleet's headquarters, to be able to report on moods and conditions. He was going towards berth number fifty-eight of basin number one in the naval harbour. It was past two in the morning. The floodlights shone down on the cranes above the berth and on the superstructures of the destroyers. All the fleet destroyers were in basin number one, and the frigates of the Krivak class, and would stay there through the winter because there was no fuel for them to go to sea. In basin number two were the submarines, one of the Kilo class, five of the Tango class and one of the Foxtrot class . . . It was something that concerned him. Since the first meeting in Gdansk at the Excelsior Hotel he had started to alter in his mind Russian class designations for warships to those of NATO. Sometimes a submarine was Kilo class and sometimes it was Vashavyanka class – and it was the little thing that could kill him. Shadows spilled between the light pools thrown down by the arc-lights. He walked because each night, now, it was harder to sleep alone in the silence of his room. If he walked he did not toss in his bed and kick against the cold around him. Sometimes he heard the following feet of the men who trailed him. He did not know how it would end, or when or where. He was close to basin number one, and to berth fifty-eight where the destroyer, empty and dark, was moored, and he heard the cry.

It came like the shriek of a gull. At the cry the cluster of men seemed to dance in a frenzy on a one-metre square of concrete.

He stopped, was dragged from his dulled thoughts of survival. The nearest of the arc-lights did not reach the group, but he could see the silhouette shapes of the men. His mind cleared and he gasped. The feet did not dance, they kicked. The cluster moved. It edged, as if that was the discipline of the music controlling the dance, towards the quayside and the black gap between the concrete and the hull of the destroyer moored there. There was a low moan, and he heard the sounds of the boots or shoes of the men as they thudded into what might have been a grain sack. In the middle was a shape and it moved without the energy of hope, slow and lethargic. The cluster of men, five or six, closed round it, kicked it towards the quayside's edge. He forgot himself, his own pain. Five or six men propelled another man, by kicking, towards the darkness under the destroyer's hull. He started to run.

Viktor tried to shout but his voice died in his throat.

He heard the last scream, and the dulled splash. He ran as if his own life were at stake. There was laughter as the cluster peered down into the darkness. Now they heard him. As one, they spun. Viktor ran under a light pool. They would have seen an officer in best dress for dining in the senior officers' mess sprinting towards them. They scattered. Two or three went right, towards berth number fifty-eight, and two or three went left and round the corner of the basin, towards berth number sixty. He saw the flashes on their arms that marked them as senior NCOs, but he did not see their faces, and he had no more thought of them. The edge of the quay was empty. He heard the thud of their feet. Viktor tore at the buttons, and when his tunic flapped away from his body he shook it off him. He was at the quay, level with the forward pod of missile launchers; and the boat above him was darkened. He yelled into the night, but there was no answer. A thickened black ink was below him and his eyes could not see into it. The answer to his yell was a faint thrashed movement under him.

Viktor went in.

He jumped, feet first, down into the void. For a moment he was clear, free, falling ten metres, then the water met him. He went under. The sensation was of the numbing cold. He groped. His fingers caught loose material, then an arm, but he lost them. The oil was in his nose and the water in his mouth. He surfaced. Viktor trod water, reached in front and behind and to each side, and his hands did not find the man. He spluttered then breathed hard, trapped the air in his lungs and jackknifed his body so that he dived. He went deep. His eyes could not help him. The air dribbled from his lungs, the pain broke in his chest. It was at the end, the final gasps of air in him, that his outstretched fingers caught a plunging leg in the total darkness. He hung on to it, then kicked upwards. There was a moment when death seemed inevitable, then he broke the surface and he still held the leg. The man he gripped no longer struggled. On his back, holding the man's body on his stomach and chest, Viktor paddled the dozen strokes towards the quay.

A torch shone down and blinded his eyes where the oil made fires of agony.

He wondered, another drowning man's moment, if he were about to be shot. A boat-hook stabbed at his shoulder and tore his neck, but he was able to hold it with one hand while he still clung to the man he had gone down into the sea to save. His eyes cleared but the pain came sharper and the ache in his lungs. Instead of the boat-hook, hands now held him. He could see the face, young and pale, of Igor Vasiliev, the conscript boy. Rescuers were on the iron ladder flush against the quay's wall and they held him vice-like, and more hands reached to take the weight of the boy from him.

He saw love and gratitude in the eyes of the conscript.

They were pulled, together and coupled, up the ladder. Alone, Viktor would not have had the strength to climb the ten metres of the ladder with the weight of Igor Vasiliev. They were at the top and Viktor doubled on his knees and coughed, retched, spat out the water and the oil in it, and men were over the conscript and hammered at his chest until he coughed up what had lain in his lungs. Viktor knelt beside him. He shouted his name and rank to the men who had lifted him up the ladder and he ordered them back. There was a fury in his voice that none dare disobey. They made a circle around him. Far in the distance was the wail of an approaching ambulance. He crouched and bent his head so that he spoke into the conscript's ear.

'I have to know, who did this to you?'

No answer, only the fear in the eyes of Igor Vasiliev.

'Don't fuck with me. Who did this to you?' He strained to hear the whined response.

'My sergeant.'

'And who? Your sergeant and who?'

'Corporals.'

'Why did your sergeant and the corporals try to kill you, drown you?'

'I said I was going to report them.'

'To whom were you going to report your sergeant and corporals?'

'To you, Captain Archenko.'

He held Vasiliev's hand. 'Why were you going to report them?'

'Because they sold . . .' The boy's breath came in gasps.

'What? What did they sell?'

'With Major Piatkin, they sold from the armoury.'

Viktor soothed him. 'All right, they stole weapons from the armoury for Major Piatkin to sell on. I hear you. What weapons?'

'Rifles, mortars, ammunition and grenades – and all of the NSVs.'

'Tell me.'

It was the supreme effort of Igor Vasiliev. He tried to sit up. The ambulance was close. He clutched at Viktor's hand. 'All of the NSV heavy machine-guns. The one I fire with, and all the others. I could not shoot today, it was gone. The sergeant said it was sold. I found him tonight, I told him I was going to report to you, unless my machine-gun was returned. They were going to put me into the water. They said that because I was going into the water – and would not be able to report to you – they would tell me . . . They had loaded the weapons on to lorries at the direction of Major Piatkin. The weapons were for a man they called Chelbia. They all get a share from the sale, from Chelbia. It was my machine-gun, and they had sold it. They called him Boris Chelbia – they said he was more important than Captain Archenko, and even more important than Admiral Falkovsky . . . They sold my machine-gun.'

Viktor stood. The water dripped from him. He waved the stretcher team forward.

When the ambulance had gone he walked back to his quarters. His feet squelched in the sea-water. He accepted neither help nor a blanket nor a lift in a vehicle, merely picked up his discarded jacket. A blinding anger consumed him. There was little enough of the night left, and in the morning he would act. He would not count the cost of it – he was doomed. What was the importance of the cost? He wondered where Alice was, where she slept, whether she thought of him and what she wore at her neck.

He walked past the dormitory blocks of the conscripts, and the fleet commander's headquarters, and across the parade area and past the armoury from which all of the NSV heavy machine-guns had been taken for sale. He said Alice's name quietly and no one was there to hear him.

7

Q. Of what Russian city did a European Union report state, 'Organized crime has a pervasive negative effect on the business and investment climate'?
A. Kaliningrad.

The team moved, but not quickly. Its speed was dictated by the number of nautical miles covered each hour by the coastal cargo ship, the *Princess Rose*.

She cleared the Kiel canal, emerged from the lock gates separating it from the Baltic, and gathered what power she could muster for the initial journey between the German mainland and the Danish islands. She made good progress away from the canal's mouth and there was a south-westerly behind her that helped push her along.

When the industrial chimneys of Kiel were behind them they were some 279 nautical miles from their destination. If the engine did not play tricks with them they would be in the channel approaching that destination within twenty-four hours. The mate was on the bridge. The master had faith in the Croatian, though Tihomir Zaklan was twenty-one years younger than himself. The master had more faith in his engineer, Johannes Richter, far down below in the sweat-making engine room. He fed his dog, Feliks, on the cabin floor. When the bowl was licked clean, the master called on the internal telephone down to the engine room and requested the presence of the engineer, in five minutes, on the bridge.

The master was Andreas Yaxis, fifty-two years old he had been at sea for thirty-six of them. He had found time, on shore leave, to marry, but the union with Maria had not been blessed with children. She lived near to the home port from which he had first sailed as a teenage boy, Korinthos. In her letters and when he rang her from a faraway port, she didn't seem to miss him as he missed her. Only the dog seemed to pine when he was off the ship and it was left behind for a few hours. He was away from his wife for months at a time, and now he wanted an end to it. He wanted money in the bank and a grove of olive trees, and another of lemon trees, and occasional work skippering the inter-island ferries when a regular master was sick or on leave. He yearned to feel the warmth of the sun on his walnut tanned face as he sat on a lounger on a villa's terrace. He nearly had the money in the bank, in an interest-bearing deposit account, to fulfil his dream but he could not *quite* afford to make the break. In the safe was, perhaps, the difference between a dream and reality. Andreas Yaxis was a loner, a man who did not seek out friends, but those who did business with him – owners, agents and officers from the building in which Rupert Mowbray had worked – would all have said that the taciturn Greek was a man of his word. For money, for the chance to fulfil his dream, he would take the risks that were asked of him. He allowed no moralities to interfere with his quest for cash. In his day he had ferried narcotics out of Palermo and cigarettes from Brindisi and had brought a host of refugees from Istanbul to Venice. He also carried 'materials' for men such as Rupert Mowbray. He did not own a conscience, so the account at his investment bank was almost filled. Time was running short. The next year the *Princess Rose* would need to pass a rigorous test of sea-worthiness, the Special Survey for Classification. If she failed she was dead and set for the breakers, and her owners would not find another command for him.

He took the brown envelope from his safe. It held ten thousand pounds in fifty- and twenty-pound notes. He counted out two thousand five hundred pounds, put that sum back into the safe, spat on the gum of the envelope and resealed it on the rest of the money.

They were waiting for him on the bridge.

He had a grating voice, as if it were rarely used and then only on a matter of importance. 'You, Johannes, are paid a monkey's wage by our owners. You, Tihomir, are treated worse. I am an old man who is not treated with the respect a lifetime at sea deserves . . . Occasionally a chance comes to make good our owners' parsimony. For a British agency we are carrying materials to Gdansk for offloading before we take on our fertilizer cargo and sail for Riga. When we leave Gdansk another man, perhaps two, will be on board. They will be described as representatives of the owners, and it may be necessary, off the coast of Kaliningrad and in Russian territorial waters, for the engine temporarily to fail. Such matters come with rewards.'

When the *Princess Rose* trafficked in narcotics, cigarettes or people, there were always similar rewards, but there had been none recently. Andreas Yaxis made the big gesture and ripped open the sealed envelope. He laid the bundle of banknotes on the ledge in front of the bridge window. He counted it into three piles, note for note, so that each had an equal share. The master saw their faces glow as the piles of banknotes grew.

'We are equal in the eyes of God, and in each other's eyes . . . I don't think what is asked of us is dangerous. We will be well offshore, if the engine problem is required of us, and safe . . . This is half what is offered us, the rest we receive in Riga when we offload the fertilizer.'

Tihomir Zaklan put his money into the breast pocket of his jacket, and the oil-grimed hands of Johannes Richter slid his into the hip pocket of his engineer's overalls. Andreas Yaxis asked his mate to send the radio signal from the *Princess Rose*, call sign 9HAJ6, to the port of Gdansk that would confirm their arrival in twenty-four hours, and to request the services of a pilot. He went below.

It was about the past, and the dignity of the past, and about the self-esteem that he nurtured for himself.

As a good meal could settle his stomach, so the view of the Glienicker bridge settled the mind of Rupert Mowbray. It spanned the narrow point of the Wannsee lakes and carried the main road from old western Berlin to Potsdam. It had two traffic lanes, two cycle lanes and a pavement for pedestrians on either side. Built on two sunken concrete sets of supports, the gently arched steel girders that took its weight were painted a pallid green.

He had slept well because he was, at last, back on familiar territory in the Charlottenberg *pension* where they knew his name and treated him as a guest of importance, one whose return was welcomed. He had showered, shaved, had eaten a good breakfast of fresh baked rolls, ham and fruit, and then he had set out from the Zoo station, taken the train to Wannsee, and then the bus to the bridge. At the bridge's head he lingered by the gardens of the hunting lodge, the Glienicker Schloss. The bridge was a part of his history: it was a small symbol that had fuelled his determination to see Viktor Archenko, his man, successfully ex-filtrated and not left to die.

Already, though it was still early, the boys were out with their fishing-rods on the banks beside the lake. He barely noticed them. He stared at the bridge and the hump in the middle of the traffic lanes. The highest point in the hump had been, for half a century, the line dividing East from West, a crossing-point between the American zone and Russian-controlled territory for the clandestine business of intelligence officers. He had not been at the Glienicker bridge in 1962, his first year with the Service, when the pilot, Gary Powers, had walked towards the hump in the centre and had passed without a glance the spy, Colonel Rudolph Abel. Nor had he been there when the dissident Anatol Scharansky had gone past Karl and Hana Koecher and into the care of their respective officers; he had been in South Africa. Other occasions, not documented and left unreported, had brought Rupert Mowbray to the bridge, at the invitation of Agency colleagues. The Americans liked to do it, for a favoured few Britons, as if it were corporate hospitality at a golf tournament – a good view from a crouched grandstand behind the bushes of the Glienicker Schloss park, then a good breakfast in a restaurant. He had never tired of watching small figures come at dawn towards the hump and walk at the same rehearsed speed as the man or woman released from the opposite end. He had never seen these early-morning shadowed figures exchange a word or a grimace as they passed, each to their own version of freedom. There had been a crossing-point, a footbridge, in the British sector where he had been more often but that place, to Rupert Mowbray, had never had the same spine-tingling emotion as the Glienicker bridge. The code of loyalty was built into the fabric of the bridge, loyalty for an agent who had been a good servant.

He soaked up the atmosphere and memories of the place, then stepped briskly on to the pavement, crossed the span, and didn't consider that the world had changed.

Rupert Mowbray went in search of Jerry the Pole.

He walked past the Custom House on the far side, now boarded up and decaying. In the days of his memories the exchanges had been watched from the upper windows behind the planks by East German troops and by Russians of the KGB, the enemy, the reason for his working life. Many of the villas on Königstrasse, the road to Potsdam, had now been found, he noticed, by the present breed of property developers; they had been empty in his day, when he had stared down that road from the far side of the bridge. Children played in the gardens and washing hung in the backyards. He wondered if the recent owners of the properties knew of the history of that small corner of Europe; he doubted if they cared because that was the way of the modern world, and he despised it. The developments, the signs said, were *exclusif*. He went past Timmerman's Café, a single-storey building, little more than a hut, and he thought it was where the Russian men, of the Third Directorate of the KGB – his opponents, his enemies – might have gathered for their own celebration while he and the Americans ate and drank at the restaurant in the Glienicker Schloss. He checked the numbers as he walked, and Alice North had done her work well.

The building was more than five hundred metres back from the bridge. The developers had not yet reached it. The small wrought-iron balconies leading from the full-length windows were held up, on the first, second and third floors, by timber props, and the walls were daubed with spray-paint graffiti. The name at the bell was a scrawl, as if written by a hand from which hope had long gone . . . but he needed the man. Jerry the Pole was as much a part of his life as the Glienicker bridge and the *pension* in Charlottenberg. He rang the bell, pressed long and hard on it. Whether he wanted him there or not, Jerzy Kwasniewski was in Rupert Mowbray's life and in his blood.

The door creaked open. The man's eyes lit with a rheumy wetness. Perhaps he had not quite believed it when Alice North had telephoned him. He wore carpet slippers and shapeless trousers held up by braces, a vest with buttons to the neck, and a small blue scarf loosely knotted at his spare throat . . . No, he had not believed that Rupert Mowbray was coming . . . He straightened. Behind him, the hall was dark. A scrawny hand was extended. Mowbray smelt the sewers. When the hand was taken, Jerry the Pole's head ducked in respect.

It was the old world, one long gone, their world – master and man, employer and servant.

On the second floor was a single living and sleeping room that smelt of stale sweat, with a kitchen annexe, and a bathroom that Mowbray deduced was shared. It overlooked a back garden where the grass and the bushes were jungle high. The light was not on and only a single bar of the fire burned. Mowbray counted money from his wallet, enough for a week, and because he had seen the respect, he estimated the minimum that would be acceptable. He thought Jerry the Pole would have taken a bag of boiled sweets and been grateful. When the Wall had come down the Service officers had abandoned the Olympic Stadium and the men who drove them, cleaned for them, translated for them, ran messages for them were discarded. In the days of the Wall, when the quarters at the Olympic Stadium bulged with activity, Jerry the Pole had lived in a decent two-bedroomed apartment in Wannsee village. The last time they had met, eighteen months after the Wall's collapse, Jerry the Pole had moved to a cheaper block nearer the bridge. Now he had moved on again. Money would be harder, work scarcer – he had been forgotten and Alice had had to search in the files, hard and long, to trace him.

'I think that is better, Mr Mowbray . . .'

Jerry the Pole now wore a suit that was too large for his shrunken frame, a suit to be buried in. He had put on a nearly clean shirt and had shaved. He was combing his thin pepper-coloured hair.

'If you come back to me, Mr Mowbray, search out someone you can depend upon, then I know it is going to be a big operation.'

'As big as the biggest,' Mowbray said. He told Jerry the Pole what would be required of him. The man's thin lips dribbled with pleasure. Mowbray paid him and saw a little flicker of disappointment as the money was counted. After it had been placed in a small empty tin under the bed, he asked Jerry the Pole to sign a receipt for it. Then he gave him more money, for the hire of a car, and asked him to sign for that also.

Mowbray beamed his smile of confidence. 'Bigger than the biggest.'

A commander, reading from his notes, said, 'I have to say, Admiral, that the position of the supply of potatoes is critical. We are down to three weeks of potatoes, which is a serious shortage. To buy potatoes on the open market is twenty-two per cent more expensive than using the contracted supplier, but the contractor does not have more potatoes to sell. In addition, at this time of year, the potatoes available on the open market are of poor quality, and I would estimate that a minimum of fifteen per cent would be unfit for consumption. It is difficult – we must have potatoes, but to buy them we must have further budgetary sources . . . Without potatoes, the fleet goes hungry.'

Viktor sat in on the meeting in Admiral Falkovsky's office. Half of his attention was in the smoke-filled room, and half was far away. He still shivered from his plunge into the dock water the previous night. He hadn't run that morning on the beach, not because of the cold in his body but because of the chill from knowing he would be watched from the moment he left his quarters. With care, and trying not to arouse further suspicion of guilt, he had now searched his sleeping quarters three times. He had not found a pin-head microphone or a fish-eye lens, but he could not tear the room apart because that would give them a hint of the evidence they hunted for. It was about nerve: if his nerve broke he was beaten; and if he was beaten, he was dead. There were seven men around the table, the admiral at the head, his favoured chief of staff in the honoured position to his immediate right, and furthest to the left was Piatkin, the *zampolit*, who watched and did not contribute.

'Buy them – we cannot be without them,' the admiral growled, ground out a cigarette, coughed and lit another. 'Next item – what is next on the agenda?'

A second commander spoke up. 'It is early, but decisions have to be taken on the spring exercise. At the present time we plan an amphibious landing between Pionerskij and Zelonogradsk, with one regiment going ashore, that is agreed. Will we deploy a mine

146

clearance capability? Can we reasonably predict we will have the resources to put mine-sweepers to sea along with the assault fleet? I remind you that the minesweepers have not exercised for two years, and their efficiency quotient is highly limited. But the crews cannot be taught minesweeping in the classroom or on a vessel that is permanently tied up. Do we have the resources?'

Admiral Falkovsky's head twisted to his right. 'Viktor, what do we do?'

His head jolted up. He blurted, 'We have no choice. We buy the potatoes.'

There was a moment of silence. Viktor saw the astonishment around the table, then Piatkin's keen gaze, and the commander to Viktor's right broke the silence with an involuntary titter. The laughter was taken up. It rolled around the table. He did not know what he had said that had provoked it. He was the admiral's chosen man, he was given deference because he had the admiral's ear – and they laughed at him. Viktor turned to his protector and saw Admiral Falkovsky's anger.

The admiral said, 'We have discussed potatoes, we are now talking about minesweeping. If we don't interest you, Viktor, I suggest you leave us . . . *now.*'

He stood, gathering his papers together. He was dismissed. It had never happened before. He ducked his head to the admiral and walked round the table to the door. He had learned never to argue, plead, dispute with Admiral Falkovsky. He saw the sneering satisfaction creep on to Piatkin's mouth. He had dreamed, and the dream had cost him protection.

He closed the door behind him. From the dream came a sudden, surging impulse. He stamped to his desk in the outer office and threw down his papers. The staff looked away. He snatched up the telephone and dialled the number of the chief of police for the *oblast* of Kaliningrad.

'This is Captain, second rank, Viktor Archenko, chief of staff to the fleet commander, Admiral Falkovsky. Please, the address of the residence of Boris Chelbia. It is a matter of security, I want it immediately.'

When he had written it down, Viktor went to the armoury. He was light-headed, gripped with a rare recklessness. He did not care that he was followed, watched.

The *Princess Rose* sailed on. Twelve hours out from Gdansk, the master again radioed ahead to the harbour authorities, and again gave an estimated time of arrival. She was now using the main traffic lane that took her south of the Renne Bank and the Danish island of Bornholm. Even the engineer admitted that the diesel engine was performing to the best of its capability. Below the bridge, where the master kept watch and studied relentlessly the radar screen, was a storeroom. On a level below the principal cabins and behind the crews' quarters, it was above the forward section of the engine room. By unscrewing a section of plate metal lining the wall of the storeroom a dead area could be reached. Here, narcotics, cigarettes and people had been housed. Now four weighted black canvas bags and four large cardboard boxes were packed into that space. With galley supplies and pieces of machinery piled up in front of the section of plate metal, the covert hiding-place would survive any search not as determined as a full-scale Customs rummage. A sharp, brilliantly white bow wave peeled away from the progress of the *Princess Rose*.

'Did you know him?' The question had been a long time forming but, like an air pocket in the ocean, it had eventually burst to the surface.

'Of course I knew him,' Alice said.

'Did you meet him?'

'I knew him and I met him.' There was an intransigence in her voice, a challenge, as if he intruded.

Gabriel Locke persisted, didn't know where it would lead him. 'Why is he special?'

She seemed for a moment to ponder. She looked out through the car's windscreen. They were parked up on hardcore at a farm gateway. Behind them was the main road to the town of Braniewo and ahead was the border crossing point. The second car was half hidden in a clump of hazel and birch in front of them. It was three hours since the team had gone, and while they'd waited Locke had said barely a word to Alice North. The questions had seeped into his mind until they filled it.

She shook her head, as if a fly irritated her. 'You wouldn't understand . . .'

'It would help if I understood. We mount an operation, something out of the history books, some sort of vanity trip for a has-been – that's Mowbray – which ignores every paragraph in the rule book of the modern Service, and when I try to find out why, *why*, I'm brushed off, like a piece of shit on a boot. What's so special?'

She climbed out of the car. They had left the hotel in Berlin before dawn, before that city had woken, and had been well into Poland before full daylight, hammering the old roads through forests and past flat, sodden fields and by reeded boglands. Buzzards and kites had been cruising over the pastures and the marshes, hunting, and twice they had seen grazing deer. They had driven through a great emptiness, and he'd thought they crossed the no man's land between the German civilization and the Russian wilderness. It was not what Gabriel Locke had joined for. He had pressed his recruitment in order to be a part of a modern, forward-looking organization, working at the sharp end of intellect, in defence of the realm. They had stopped briefly at the castle, at Malbork – and she'd walked away from him and he'd hung back, and she'd sat for a half-minute, no more, on the bench by the knights' bronze statues . . . Now they were in a farm gateway, two miles from the Kaliningrad border. Gabriel Locke had been once to Hereford, and he'd been told there – often enough so that it itched in him – that reconnaissance was paramount. Time spent on reconnaissance was never wasted, they'd said. The car lurched as her weight settled on the bonnet.

Gabriel Locke's temper cracked. 'I've the bloody right to know what this is all about.'

She didn't turn. Her voice came faintly into the car. 'What I said, you wouldn't understand.'

He shouted, 'When this has fucked up, and it will, I'm going to put a report in – see if I don't. I've my career to think of.'

Her voice came to him, calm, as if he didn't trouble her. 'You wouldn't understand, Gabriel. Just enjoy the view.'

There was an old and dilapidated farmhouse at the end of a lane a quarter of a mile away, with barns without roofs, and clumps of ragged trees from which the wind had shredded the leaves, yellow fields, some cows with their calves, and a distant forest line. The sun threw long shadows . . . She was an attractive girl, but he hardly noticed it. When the operation went wrong, and it would, his career would be among the casualties, would be in the front line and a prime target. He'd fight, whatever it took, to save himself. He could not see into the forest line, and he waited.

Wickso heard the whistle, like a screech owl's, and then the engine. It was the same engine that he'd heard twice before in the last hour, and six times since he'd taken his position in the cavity made by the tree-trunk's roots, and he'd memorized how often the jeep came along the forest track. He made the return call, also the screech owl's, so that Billy and Lofty would hear him and be warned off. The jeep's engine was using poor fuel because each time it came by the smell of the diesel hung on the path between the close-set pines. It was a good position he'd found. The tree had been toppled in a gale, could have been two years or more back, and he'd camouflaged the cavity with dead branches; there was no chance that he'd be seen from the track. The jeep went by. It was open, two men in it, and the soldier in the passenger seat, Wickso's side, had an automatic rifle across his legs. It was twelve years since Wickso had had to find a 'basher' and lie up in it. When the jeep had gone away down the track, he made the owl's call, and waited for them to reach him. The jeep had been regular but there had also been a foot patrol, six men and a dog. The dog had bothered him more than the jeep. It had been in the middle of the group, not out ahead where it would have had the chance of picking up the scent of Billy and Lofty, or of pointing to him in his basher. They came across the track fast. No talking, only hand signs. Wickso crawled out of the basher, and left it covered with old branches so that the chance of its discovery before it was needed next time, the real time, was minimal. It was three hundred metres to the wire, where Ham waited at the hole they'd cut. Wickso didn't look back and a few times he heard Billy's and Lofty's feet on the forest floor, but that was seldom. They moved well, like it wasn't twelve years since they'd crossed opposition ground. When he could see the hole, Wickso did the owl screech and Ham answered it. A drainage ditch, six inches of water stagnant in it, was the route away from the forest and through the fields. Then it was a crawl on their stomachs through an old beet-field. They were muddied damp urchins when they reached the cars.

They were peeling off the overalls. The girl didn't say anything, like she knew better than to talk, but the guy, Locke, piped, like he needed to piss and couldn't hold himself. 'How was it? Everything all right? What did you find?'

Billy said, 'Found a nice pub, doing real ale.'

'For Christ's sake, can you not be serious?'

Billy said, 'We went three kilometres in. There's a farm barn just outside the village of Lipovka, on the Vituska river. It's by a road – it's a good enough drop point. Right now I'm looking for a bath – you got a better idea, Mr Locke?'

The girl hadn't spoken. She helped Lofty and Ham out of their overalls and held a plastic bag for them. Wickso liked her. The best of the nurses at Wolverhampton kept their mouths shut when talking helped nobody.

He had been summoned.

A flurry of messages had alerted Yuri Bikov. Captain, second rank, Viktor Archenko had left a meeting at fleet headquarters early, he had gone to the armoury and had drawn a service pistol with two clips of ammunition and four hand grenades. Then he had driven out of the base and was headed for Kaliningrad.

The messages from Piatkin came by radio, were fielded by Bikov's major. Piatkin reported that additional patrols were on the frontier and that the crossing point was alerted. At first, as the messages were given him, Bikov felt a sense of nagging disappointment, as if he might be cheated. Was Archenko making a run for the border? It would fail . . . fail in blood and vulgar capture, and his journey to this dead shit-heap of a place would have been wasted. Then the tone of the messages had changed to a note of bewilderment from Piatkin, and an address was given on the north side of the city.

When he arrived at the pleasant street, different from anything else in the city he had seen, Bikov saw a staff car parked outside high gates that were flanked by high walls. A dog bayed. There were properties like that, with high gates and high walls, in Moscow. He knew the trade of men who were protected by gates, walls and dogs. Short of the staff car, half on the grass and under the trees, were a silver saloon and a black van with smoked windows. He went to the saloon and spoke sharply to Piatkin: 'Whose home is this?'

'It is the home of Boris Chelbia.'

'Who is Boris Chelbia?'

Piatkin flushed. 'A local businessman.'

'A *mafiya* businessman?'

'I would not know.'

'Does Archenko know him?'

Piatkin stumbled, 'I have no record they have ever met.'

'But you know Boris Chelbia?'

'I have met him, yes, socially . . .' Piatkin squirmed, and Bikov saw it.

'Would Boris Chelbia, *mafiya* businessman, wish to buy one service pistol with two clips of ammunition and four hand grenades, from your "social" knowledge of him?'

'I don't know why Archenko is here.'

Bikov walked back to his car, settled on the back seat, and waited.

Viktor was offered a chair but declined it.

The home of Boris Chelbia was in the old city, the part that had survived the bombing and had been outside the defensive perimeter line of strong points built by General Lasch. These streets had not been fought over: the hand-to-hand, building-to-building combat had bypassed them. The old merchants' houses had survived and had become the homes of the new élite. The largest home in this tree-lined street, running off Borzova, north of the city, had high iron gates that were screened with plate metal, and there had been the barking of big dogs when he pulled up outside. Men, shaven-headed and leather-jacketed, had let him walk through the gates. Because he had been at the admiral's meeting he wore his best dress uniform with the bright gold braid at the shoulders and on the sleeves, his medal ribbons were on his chest, and he had carried his naval greatcoat over his arm. A man of such status, a man alone, was not searched by the minders at the gate. He had walked up the swept drive, the loaded service pistol under his tunic and the grenades in the pockets of his greatcoat. Nothing of what he was about to do had been thought through: it came from instinct bred by anger.

'You took delivery of weapons from the base at Baltiysk. The weapons were sold to you. Your purchase of the weapons is a theft from the state. Among the weapons were five NSV 12.7mm heavy machineguns, and ammunition for them. One of those machine-guns has on the shoulder stock the carved initials IV. The machine-gun is used by a conscript, Igor Vasiliev. I want it back, that machine-gun, and all the ammunition of that calibre.'

He spoke in the short sharp sentences so beloved by his master, the admiral, when authority was to be built. Chelbia lounged in a low, soft chair, and a minder watched from the door with tattooed arms folded over his chest. No response. Viktor thought his grandmother might have fled from such a house or such a street. The furniture was old, German and heavy, the pictures on the walls were lushly romantic and showed sea views with women in long muslin skirts paddling on the shore. The brocade wallpaper alone would have cost a half-year of a captain, second rank's salary. In a quick movement, Viktor took two of the RGO fragmentation grenades from his greatcoat pocket, laid them on the tray in the middle of the walnut-veneered table and let them roll in their awkward, lurching pineapple shape as far as the tray's rim would permit. With his second quick movement – too fast for the minder at the door – he held a third grenade in his hand. He pulled out the pin, held the lever tight in his right hand, below his overcoat, then tossed the pin over the carpet and on to Chelbia's lap. The killing radius of the grenade was listed as twenty metres. Inside its casing were ninety grams of A-1X-1 explosive. If his hand released the lever, he would die – as would Chelbia. The pin lay across the fly of Chelbia's trousers.

'It is all I want. I will leave here with that one NSV machine-gun and its ammunition. Please, make whatever arrangements are necessary.'

He thought the man, Chelbia, was a street-fighter and from the gutter, and would have been hardened by time in the *gulag* camps.

There was no flicker of fear on Chelbia's face, and his hands did not fidget. His voice was calm. 'Only that weapon?'

'The machine-gun with the initials IV cut with a knife on the shoulder stock, and the ammunition.'

'And the rest?'

'Not important to me – one day your friend Piatkin will tell you what is important to me.'

'And you have a steady hand?'

'You have to hope my hand is steady.'

The slightest gesture: Chelbia bobbed his head. His eyes were focused beyond Viktor, and the grenade in Viktor's hand, aimed at the minder by the door. The door opened and closed behind him.

'Your conscript's weapon is coming. We should do business, Captain Archenko, mutually profitable business. Whisky, gin, vodka, brandy, will you take a drink – one-handed?'

Viktor said, 'I would like to take two cartons of Camel cigarettes, if that were possible, if you have them.'

He walked across the carpet, bent over the low, soft chair and reached down to Chelbia's trousers. He lifted the pin and, holding the lever down tight, replaced the pin in its socket.

'Would you have done it, Captain Archenko?' Chelbia chuckled. 'Killed yourself and me for a conscript's machine-gun?'

'Can you not, Mr Mowbray, do something about my pension? Is that a big matter to ask? I . . .' the voice wheedled.

'Just keep your eyes on the road, Jerry, watch the traffic, and look for a parking place.'

For Rupert Mowbray it was a pilgrimage. But the voice bleated at him, 'I have no pension. There are German people, they have pensions, and they were not as useful to you, your colleagues, as I. I do not understand why I have no pension.'

'I think you can get in there.' Mowbray leaned forward in the back seat of the Mercedes, one hand resting on the shoulder of Jerry the Pole's suit jacket, the other pointing expansively to the slot between parked cars on Friedrichstrasse. He had never visited Berlin, before the Wall had come down or afterwards, without travelling as a pilgrim to this place. He was the true believer. The car came awkwardly to a halt.

Jerry the Pole turned to him. 'What I am asking, Mr Mowbray, is to be treated fairly, to be awarded a fair pension.'

'Just wait here, Jerry, just wait with the car.'

He slipped out, shut the door behind him and looked around. Checkpoint Charlie was a place of worship to Mowbray. His eyes raked the new scene and a little curl of disgust played at his mouth. There was a token sangar of sandbags in the centre of the street, a large, hanging colour photograph of an American GI, and a modern museum; scaffolding disguised the façade of the Café Adler. Mowbray, on his '69–'73 tour in Berlin and on his '78–'82 posting to Bonn, when he'd often come to Berlin, had always preferred Checkpoint Charlie as an inner-city crossing-point for agents, rated it as better than anywhere in the British sector. The Americans of the Agency had been kind to him. He'd sat in the Café Adler so many hours with the Agency's Marty, Dwight and Alvin, had sipped coffee, drained beer bottles and waited. He'd waited, and all the time looked out of the café windows and down towards the floodlit empty street in front of the crossing-point. And further down the street, in another café, would have been the opponents, the enemy, with their coffee and their beer. God, it had been a world of certainties, and a place of brave men. He thought of himself as the flag-bearer for those agents coming in the dark to the checkpoint. Old Americans in veterans' caps were having their photographs taken by the sangar, and Japanese tourists were painting the place with their digital video cameras. Sometimes, on the bad nights and far back behind the floodlights, there would be a rasp of brittle gunfire, and sometimes on the worst nights they would see the agent walk to the final check and then the Volkspolizei would pounce. Many nights he had waited in the window seats of the Café Adler and had not left until dawn.

He told Jerry the Pole where he wanted to be driven.

'Can I rely on you, Mr Mowbray, to settle for me a pension – not a great sum, but what reflects my value?'

'I'll look into it, Jerry.'

'Times are very hard for me, Mr Mowbray. I have written to London six times . . .'

It was the last stretch of the Wall to have been left by the city's authorities. He saw the street sign: Niederkirchnerstrasse. The Wall was painted with pop-art. Mowbray would have said it had been defaced. The Wall had been so precious to him. He had spent hours each day, each week and each month staring at it as if it had secrets that only constant observation might unlock. The length of this section was around two hundred metres. Well, the bloody authorities didn't want *history*, did they? History was uncomfortable. History made heroes and cowards. Without the weight of history, an agent could be abandoned, surplus to bloody requirements. Behind the wall, hidden from him as he sat upright on the back seat of the Mercedes, was the bombsite of what had been the Gestapo headquarters, and on the raised pile of rubble, where the offices and the torture chambers and the holding cells had been, was the old viewing platform where Rupert Mowbray had stood with binoculars. On the platform he had believed he communed with the agents he ran on the far side of the Wall. It was the least he could do, because he could not walk with them where they were, separated from his protection by the guards, automatic guns, dogs and mines. He had been obligated to stand there, as if that way he could share their danger . . . That day the danger lay as a shadow on Viktor Archenko.

They were at the last stop of his pilgrimage. He would have liked to bring flowers but that would have been ostentatious. He walked from the Mercedes through the wide entrance and into a wide cobbled courtyard. Around it were the windows of what had been, more than a half-century before, the war ministry of the Third Reich, its pulse point. In the exact centre of the courtyard was a statue in bronze, two metres high, of a naked man, commemorating the life and death of Count Claus von Stauffenberg, who had laid the bomb in the briefing room of the Wolf's Lair. A plaque marked where he had stood and faced his firing squad. The man had given his life . . . Mowbray thought him noble and bowed his head in reverence in front of the statue. Nobody watched him. Germans rarely came here. A traitor confused the ignorant. Nothing, they parroted, was owed to a traitor . . . They were bloody wrong: Viktor Archenko was a traitor. He walked out of the courtyard.

'I am very glad, Mr Mowbray, that you will look into the matter of my pension.'

'I think it better that we let the matter rest, Jerry.'

'Because with the winter coming, and the cold – you know the cold of a Berlin winter, Mr Mowbray – and the influenza and bronchitis, it is important to have heating. To heat myself I must have a pension . . .'

'As I've said, I'll see what I can do.'

'Heh, Mr Mowbray, you chose old Jerry the Pole for an operation that you say is "bigger than the biggest". I have that importance. Surely I am worth money each month, a pension?'

'Depend on me, Jerry.'

They called at the embassy. The building was heavily guarded by troops of the Bundesgrenzschutz, who carried machine-guns and peered officiously at the passenger from the Mercedes. Mowbray saw Daphne Sullivan, who relayed to him that his people had arrived safely in Gdansk and gave him the position of the *Princess Rose*. He dictated a short, bland, confident progress report for transmission to London. Dusk fell on the city.

Six and a half hours' driving time, Jerry the Pole said. The Mercedes was at least ten years old and it had in excess of two hundred thousand kilometres on the clock, but it was warm and comfortable, and he would doze in the back. And if he slept he would not have to listen to the wretch's drip-moan about his bloody pension. By the time Mowbray reached his bed he would be, fancifully, within spitting distance of Kaliningrad.

If he were not too late. For what he had done, he would be consigned to hell if he were too late.

The master had the charts of the approach spread out. He watched his instruments closely to be certain that the course he took bisected the areas marked on the chart as dumping grounds for explosives (disused) and minefields (cleared). Andreas Yaxis did not trust the Polish navy, under Communism or democracy, to have made safe the charted positions of mines or explosives dumps. When he was within a sea mile of the rocking light buoy at the head of the inshore traffic zone, he relaxed. He cleared away the chart, ordered the engine room to cut power, and felt the throb of the *Princess Rose* die, as if sleep took it. He strained to see through his binoculars, and was

157

rewarded. The pilot's cutter powered towards him, and in the distance were the lights of Gdansk.

Viktor elbowed open the door to the darkened dormitory. The weight crushed him. He sagged against the wall, wriggled his back until he felt the light switch, and the dormitory flooded with light. He staggered down the aisle between the beds. White, staring faces watched him. The audience were upright, rubbing the sleep from their eyes. Viktor looked for the conscript's bed. At the bed, Vasiliev's, he dumped it. The machine-gun dropped to the floor, and the clap of noise reverberated through the dormitory. He straightened, arched, then peeled the belts of 12.7mm ammunition off his shoulders and let them fall, clanging, on to the concrete. In Vasiliev's face, he saw disbelief turn to gratitude. He gasped, then pointed down to the machine-gun's stock where the light caught the carved initials.

He said, 'Set it up. Load it.'

Wearing only a tatty singlet and pants, Vasiliev crawled off the bed, then crouched beside the weapon. With sure hands he extended the tripod's legs, locked them. He worked open the breech and used the singlet's hem to wipe the chamber. No one spoke. The clatter of the movements destroyed the silence. He loaded a belt, lowered the breech flap on to the bullets and looked up. He would have seen a trace of madness on Viktor's face. Above where Viktor stood was the single light that lit the dormitory, with a Bakelite shade over it.

Viktor pointed to the light, and ordered, 'Shoot it out.'

The safety lever rattled. Vasiliev squatted behind the weapon, then elevated the barrel aim, fired. The dormitory crashed into darkness and the fumes of the shots stank in the air. Viktor could no longer see the faces that had watched him. He imagined them pressed against their pillows, holding their hands over their ears.

He shouted, 'Now, go back to sleep.'

The last sound they would have heard of him was the beat of his feet as he strode towards the door. He threw it open, slammed it shut after him, and walked away into the night. It had been an insanity, but for a few minutes it had displaced the nightmare. He went towards his quarters, the insanity was blown out, and the nightmare once again settled on him.

A broad smile dragged across Yuri Bikov's mouth.

Before leaving his mother, his father had said that the teenaged Yuri did not smile enough. His wife had not contradicted him. A smile came rarely to him and was not to be witnessed.

But in the dark he could smile.

When Captain, second rank, Viktor Archenko had emerged from the gates, shown out by two thugs, his features had been hidden by the breech mounting of a heavy machine-gun. Bikov had not been able to see his prey's face. At the barracks, in darkness, Bikov had told the driver, his sergeant, to hold back as Archenko had laboured into the barracks building under the weight of the machine-gun. He had sensed that the man was bowed by the burden of his position and that the machine-gun was the focal point of a throw for self-esteem. The gesture had been glorious. The roof of the building had exploded in gunfire, and then Archenko had emerged.

It was a strong face, it had purpose. Archenko could not have seen him. Bikov was back against a stores building; his sergeant stood in front of him and his major was beside him. He was hidden from Archenko, but he saw the resolution in the face. There were bears in the Gorno-Altaysk region that were tracked and hunted by marksmen who went deep into the mountains and forests after them. A hunter had told him that the best of the bears, as the marksman came close but was still hidden, seemed to sense the danger and would always turn to face it, even when they could not see it. Big animals, and proud, worthy quarries for a hunter. There was a light high above Archenko. Archenko seemed to face him . . . There was, Bikov thanked Archenko, stubborn, obstinate defiance. He could not ask for more.

Then the shadow was on Archenko's face and his body seemed to wilt. Archenko missed a step, tripped, lurched, then regained his stride. Bikov knew it went hard on him. The surveillance tightened, the pressure built. The matter of the machine-gun was to relieve the pressure, but there was no escape. Behind him the watchers kept company with him, from corner to corner, doorway to doorway, shadow to shadow.

No file, however detailed, could tell Yuri Bikov more than the shortened glimpse of a man's face. It was a good face. He gulped the air, scented by the sea, and felt the excitement.

Locke wanted to talk, Mowbray didn't.

Jerry the Pole had been waved away, sent to find a seaman's lodging-house, somewhere down by the Solidarity docks. The car stayed at the Excelsior Hotel.

The night lay heavy on Gdansk.

Locke wanted to talk about the reconnaissance by the team but Mowbray refused, left him in the bar, took his key and his bag, and climbed the stairs heavily. It was rare for him to feel his age, but he did that night. One more call . . . the most important of his day.

He knocked on the door, said his name, and heard the feet padding to it. The door was unlocked, then the chain was loosed.

She wore a simple cotton nightdress, white, with little flower patterns on it, and a wool dressing-gown lay around her shoulders. He saw the amber pendant at her throat.

'Forgive me, I just wanted to see you were all right.'

'I'm all right.'

'The room – did they offer it you? If I am not impertinent, did you ask for it?'

'It's the room they gave me. Don't worry, Rupert, that's all right.'

'Good night, Alice.'

'Good night.'

The room was as he remembered it: same curtains, same furniture, same bed as had been in it the first time he had come to Gdansk with Alice North. The first time they had come to Gdansk to meet face to face with the agent, codenamed Ferret, she had been given that room. The door closed on him and he heard the lock turn, the safety chain engage. He felt old and tired, weary . . . and the guilt sapped him.

In the calm waters of the dredged harbour channel, the master slept and the dog snored at the foot of his bunk. There was no need for Andreas Yaxis to be on the bridge. The pilot brought the *Princess Rose* to her berth by the fertilizer factory and loading beltways. Only when the engine had cut did he rise from his bunk, smooth the blankets, punch the pillow, then shrug into his jacket and slip on his boots. He climbed the steps to the bridge and thanked the pilot formally. When the pilot had gone, and ropes secured them to the quay, he began to prepare the master's declaration, the cargo manifest and the crew declaration for the Gdansk Customs men. It had been a good voyage and the engine had performed well. Over the internal telephone he thanked the engineer for his efforts. But it would not be difficult, if that were necessary, for the engineer with his skills to create 'difficulties' below. He expected Rupert Mowbray to come aboard in the morning.

8

Q. Where was the home of the philosopher Immanuel Kant?
A. Kaliningrad.

She hugged the dressing-gown around her, and the draught of the dawn came in through the opened kitchen door. If Gail Ponsford heard her husband moving downstairs when it was still dark she always left her bed, went to the kitchen and made an early pot of tea. She knew when he was disturbed, fretted. She watched him, out in the garden, fill the songbirds' peanut cage. That was a waste of time: the squirrels would have emptied it before he was off the train, well before he'd walked into Vauxhall Bridge Cross. She waited till he saw her.

'Tea?'

'Be blissful.'

'Couldn't sleep?'

'Bit of a bad one – sorry.'

'Going to talk about it – or "need to know"?'

Bertie, her husband of twenty-eight years, grinned ruefully. Gail Ponsford had been a General Service girl in Century House. The then head of Russia Desk had been their best man and her matron-of-honour had been a dragon from Personnel. She was steeped in the Service, knew the people and the procedures.

'You remember Rupert Mowbray?'

She could play the comedienne. 'Rupert the Professor, Rupert the Pompous, Rupert the Patriarch, Rupert the Principled . . . but he's Rupert the Pensioned now, isn't he?'

She'd put the kettle on the ring, and he'd slumped at the table. 'He came back, did a Lazarus, and preached to the DG. Doesn't matter

162

who he is, where he is – out beyond our back fence, where civilization stops, there's an asset in trouble. Likely to be arrested, might already have been arrested. Rupert used to handle him. Remember Alice North? Of course you do – the little grey spinster. She tipped Rupert off. He's at the outside gate. What do I do? Turn him away? I can't . . . He charmed me, enthused me, made me feel big and tall – he'd sell whale blubber to the Greenlanders – then did the same to the DG . . . and he repeated the dose for a minister. We're going to ex-filtrate the asset. He had us all in the palm of his hand – talked about loyalty and integrity, and making the Service great – you know, admired. He made it seem so easy, and we swallowed it. You know what? It would have sounded wimpish to put the old hand up and query: "What if it all goes wrong?" Nothing ever went wrong in Rupert's day.'

She poured the boiling water into the teapot.

'A few hours ago a ship docked in Gdansk – that means it's all in place.'

'Are we talking, Bertie, about Kaliningrad?'

'Not a fair question.'

'But isn't that a closed military zone?'

'And don't arch your eyebrows like that, please . . . It's all in place. I won't survive if it goes wrong, and I doubt the DG will. We'll go quietly, in a couple of months, but go we will. Only Rupert is ring-fenced. He's retired and we've rubber-stamped him. If it goes right, and we bring our man home, to clarion calls of applause, then the people on their side are on the train to the salt mines. Who's going to be left standing? Someone has to lose. Me, our crowd – them, their Service – who's going to be left standing?'

'Is it today?'

'Tomorrow we are going into Kaliningrad, to lift out our dubious asset, with guns . . . Jesus Christ . . . and I sanctioned it, and the DG did, and the minister.'

Gail Ponsford poured the tea, strong.

'Please, would you pass me the marmalade?'

The dining room of the Excelsior Hotel overlooked the junction of the waterways, the Stara Motlawa and the Nowa Motlawa that sliced through Gdansk. From the window, across the water, was the old town of the Hanseatic port. On his previous visits, Rupert Mowbray had always taken the seat with the panoramic view. He was able to share the majesty of the historic buildings, but was protected from a sight of the harshness of another East European city that struggled to make a living from the post-Communist times. The cranes of the docks – Solidarity territory, where the rotten apple had infected the barrel that was the Communists' territory of satellite regimes – were beyond his vision. What had happened here, the strikes, the lock-outs, the police baton charges and the bloody-minded obstinacy of the dockyard workers, had brought down the whole damned pack of cards . . . and had destroyed the certainties in Rupert Mowbray's life.

Gabriel Locke passed him the marmalade, and returned to his *Herald Tribune*.

'Thank you so much.'

Locke had eaten yoghurt and fruit, Rupert had eaten a full cooked breakfast and was now on toast. Locke, behind his paper, and Rupert, his back to the door, did not see her entry into the dining room. He was smearing butter on to the toast when Alice eased into the chair beside him . . . as she had that first time, after the first long night.

Rupert Mowbray remembered it with the clarity of crystal.

The *evening*: Rupert Mowbray had been with Alice in his hotel room, waiting. The messages had been passed; there was nothing to do but wait. Dead drops before that in Murmansk and Malbork, but never a meeting until that first evening in the hotel in Gdansk. The hesitant knock on the room door and the moment's meeting of his eyes and hers, then she had been on her feet and at the door, unlocking it. He had stared at the door, then seen him. Calling him 'Ferret', him not understanding, Rupert had hugged him, Alice had gravely shaken his hand, and the tension had dripped off Ferret. Such a handsome young man, such dignity, and such painfully obvious stress. Like a blind date, he'd written in his report for London. For a quarter of an hour, not more than fifteen minutes because time did not allow it, they had sparred and made small-talk about the weather, the journey to Gdansk from Kaliningrad and the business of the delegation at the dry dock, then to work . . . Bundles of papers, blue-prints and manuals, work procedures and diagrams outlining chains of command. Then the talking. A tape-recorder turning, and Alice doing the back-up shorthand, her eyes never off him. Intense and exciting, as Ferret had bolted the sandwiches they'd provided and had never stopped talking, as if each minute with them was the last available. Rupert never interrupting the flow . . . it was the best source material, raw and clean, that he had ever handled . . . Ferret sweating, driblets coming down his forehead, shoulders knotted tense and the hands always moving, tie pulled down, jacket slung on the floor. Four hours of it, and Ferret starting to ramble when asked why. His father and his grandmother, and the thread lost because of his tiredness . . . The first time they had put a face to the agent they called Ferret.

The *night*: He hadn't wanted to finish, but the coherence had gone. They had moved past the point of useful communica-tion . . . Ferret was losing concentration. Rupert had done a few minutes on tradecraft, because this man was an innocent. They'd talked personal security, and he'd reached forward from the chair where he sat to the bed where Ferret was propped and held the man's hand, tried to squeeze the shaking from it, as he would have gripped his children's if they had been in crisis. Ferret was his new family, Ferret craved to be admitted to the circle. Easy enough for him, for Rupert Mowbray, in a room at the Excelsior Hotel, with a diplomatic passport in his room safe, to lecture on personal security. He hadn't wanted to go, to walk out into the night and slip away back to the hotel where the rest of his delegation stayed. Rupert had watched the way Ferret gazed, awestruck, at Alice North, little sweet Alice. He'd said, 'I'm a bit tired, not as young as I used to be,' had grimaced, and then had spoken so softly and with such innocence: 'Alice, you've a bottle in your room. What about a nightcap for our friend, a little drink for him – yes, Alice?' The complete performer, he'd yawned wide and rubbed his eyes, then blinked – so natural – and he'd loosed Ferret's hand, and stood. 'Yes, I've a bottle,' Alice had said. He'd hugged Ferret, wished him well and muttered about the next dead drop, how much he looked forward to the next visit of the delegation to sort out the negotiation for the use of the dry dock.

He'd yawned again and seen them out through the door, then moved with a cat's speed to gather up the papers brought for him and whip the spool off the tape-recorder.

The *morning*. He'd been at breakfast when she'd come in and sat down beside him. He'd murmured, 'Good morning', to her. There had been on her face, at her mouth and in her eyes, a meld of defiance and shyness – what he called 'the first-time look'. No cosmetics on the eyes, mouth or cheeks, no little splash of perfume or toilet water at her neck. She'd kept her head down, toyed with a single piece of toast, and hadn't spoken to the waitress who brought her coffee. It was how Rupert Mowbray had hoped she'd be. It was what Ferret had needed. To Rupert Mowbray, the worst that could have come from the first meeting, face to face, in a hotel room was the request by an agent for a defection package, when they caved and wanted out. Then they were useless ... But the best, the best of all, was when the agent left the meeting and walked tall, was enthused, went willingly back behind the fences, the guards, the guns, and dug, stole and eavesdropped for more, went strengthened ... He hadn't supposed that Alice North was a virgin – who was at that age? No woman he knew with a pleasing face was a virgin, certainly neither of his own daughters ... She had looked like a deflowered virgin that morning at breakfast. Not sex for the first time, but love. Emotion, romance, lust – for the first time – he hadn't cared which Alice North had found. He'd said something about the time he'd booked the taxi for, and she'd nodded, distant. Over the weeks and months that had followed he'd watched Alice in Warsaw at the Station, and in London and, he was prepared to bet his shirt on it, no other man had been welcomed where the Ferret had been. He'd seen men try and had seen them summarily dismissed ... The second time, and the third, that they had come to the Excelsior Hotel to debrief Ferret he had, each time, slyly, called a halt to the talk of submarines and missile warheads and the biographies of military commanders, and left them to slip away to her room. And each time, in the morning, she had come to breakfast with the defiance and shyness highlighting her prettiness. He had used her, as he had used Ferret, and the glory that had come to him from it shamed him.

She wore no makeup, but her eyes were reddened and he thought she had cried in the night.

He passed her a sheet of paper from his leather-cased notepad. 'It's the number, the extension and the message. I suggest you use a handkerchief . . . Right, it's going to be a busy morning, so let's get on with it.'

The ship, predictably, had engine trouble. The engineer of the *Princess Rose*, Johannes Richter, told the officials of Customs, the harbourmaster's office and Immigration who trooped on board that it might be in the engine's main drive shaft or perhaps the piston heads. Any who cared to listen were given a full diatribe on the age of the engine and the work it had put in during its nineteen years at sea – but, and Richter emphasized the point by hammering his oil-stained fists together, he was confident that the *Princess Rose* would be able to sail when the cargo of fertilizer was in the holds, on schedule. To back his story, in addition to the master and mate's protestations that the engine would soon be serviceable, a representative of the Cyprus-based owners was on board, and an additional engineer.

Through the morning, parts of the diesel engine were taken off the *Princess Rose* and replacements were carried on board.

There was no reason for the officials of Customs, the harbour master's office and Immigration to be suspicious. The necessary passes were issued for entrance and exit of the dock area on the Motlawa river, and the movement of vessels from Hamburg, Toulouse, Piraeus, Tallinn and Stettin demanded their presence elsewhere. Rupert Mowbray, the owner's man, was on the bridge with the master, and Jerry the Pole played the part of the additional engineer. While Mowbray stayed deep in conversation with the master and worked through the charts of the coast off the *oblast* of Kaliningrad, Jerry the Pole was the courier. By the evening, the time the *Princess Rose* was due to sail on a full tide, she would be laden with nine hundred tonnes of fertilizer in fifty-kilo sacks. Four hand-guns, three stun-grenades, six smoke-grenades and a field medic's kit would have been taken off, and a state-of-the-art communications system would have been brought on board.

At midday, the official from the harbourmaster's office came down the ladder into the engine room for final reassurance. He was confronted with a frightening puzzle of pieces laid out on oily newspaper. Was it definite that the ship would be ready to vacate its berth on the fertilizer dock? 'If I am left alone to work, then it is definite,' Richter growled. A rider was added by the master: even if the work was not completed to his own satisfaction and that of the owner's representative, the ship would have power enough to leave the berth and would tie up further down the Motlawa river – it was a guarantee.

Buried in a bag under grease-coated engine parts, the pistols and grenades were taken out of the docks and driven by Jerry the Pole to the hotel. Then he went to the Excelsior, where he collected from Gabriel Locke the scrambled radio equipment that could receive and transmit encodes and 'burst' high-speed messages, and returned to the *Princess Rose*.

The Immigration men were told that, in order to facilitate the departure on schedule, the representative of the owners would stay on board for the sailing.

'Where am I going to be?' Mowbray asked.

'I promise nothing,' the master said. 'We do not usually carry passengers.'

'You'd better find somewhere . . . and remember it's a full-fare-paying bloody passenger.'

As a young Service officer, Mowbray had been posted to the high commission in the protectorate of Aden and once a month, before the danger had become too great, he had gone up-country and stayed with tribal chiefs. He had acted out the part of the young Lawrence, sleeping on mud floors, cursing the discomfort and the smell . . . He thought this experience would tax his tolerance.

The *Princess Rose* was foul, filthy and uncomfortable, and he had only seen the deck area, the cramped bridge, the engine room, where he had stepped in an oil pool and damn near fallen and could have broken his neck, and the storeroom from which the handguns and grenades had been retrieved. It would be his base, his command and control centre, for a day and a half if his planning played to the optimum. The coffee brought him by the Filipino cook-boy was disgusting. He had seen a leviathan cockroach appear in a corner of the bridge as the mate had eaten a sandwich . . . but it was the nearest he would come again in his lifetime to running an operation across a hostile frontier.

The *Princess Rose*, his new home, rolled on her moorings and he heard the banging down below, a heavy wrench on metal, for the benefit of the man from the harbourmaster's office.

It was a regret that he would not be there when Ferret and Alice were reunited. He would be incarcerated on this heap of rusting scrap when they met again, by his hand. He, the magician who conjured with their lives, was sorry he would not be close to Braniewo the next evening to see it.

The message on the notepad given her by Rupert Mowbray was in front of her.

Alice sat on the bed, legs tucked up, her back against the headboard, and reached into her handbag for a handkerchief. Then she picked up the mobile phone.

Jerry the Pole had bought it early that morning in the streetmarket behind the flower shops on Podwale Staromiejskie. Under the counters there, for sale, were mobile phones from Poland, Germany, Sweden and Kaliningrad. If records existed, and that was doubtful, the number would be registered as from Kaliningrad, and the report of its theft buried.

The second time they'd met, Viktor had given them all the numbers and extensions for the outer office in the admiral's suite. She tapped out the digits for the international code, then the general switchboard of Fleet Headquarters.

A woman answered, sharp and superior.

She held her handkerchief over the mobile's mouthpiece, as Rupert had suggested, spoke in Russian, and gave the extension she wanted, for the clerk who sat at a small desk beside the larger desk of the fleet's armaments officer. By now the number of Viktor's direct line and his extension would be bugged, but there were nine other lines into the outer office.

It was curtly answered. She asked if that was the extension number of Captain Viktor Archenko, and was told it was not. Was Captain Archenko available to come for a moment to this telephone? He was in a meeting. Would he, please, take a message for Captain Archenko?

He would . . . Rupert had always said it was sensible for a Briton speaking Russian, however good the command of the language, to use a handkerchief to blur the speech and cover a failure in the accent. She used a soft voice, a lover's, because Rupert had said the clerk would respond by passing on the message as if it were private, personal. She gagged, was tongue-tied, and the clerk asked her for the message. In her mind, Alice saw him and touched him, felt his fingers on her.

She gave it, read through her handkerchief the message Rupert had written for her, and cut the call.

That morning Viktor had gone back to the beach, had run fast because the pain made him forget the building pressure. He had gone as far as the wrecked fishing-boat: the chalk marks were not visible and the wind had blown away the shape of the woman's foot-prints. He learned nothing and, desolate, had jogged back to the base, showered, changed and gone to work.

He took the cartons of Camel cigarettes and laid them on the admiral's desk. The admiral grinned. The cartons went to a bottom drawer.

'But you haven't been to Malbork, to kick in the ruins . . . Where do they come from?'

'On a street corner.'

'What street corner?'

'Met a general's wife – he commands Armour . . . or might have been Air Force. She wanted me to fuck her on the corner. I'll do anything, I said, for two cartons of Camel cigarettes.'

The belly laugh of the admiral spread across the inner office. 'You know, Viktor, I believe I nearly saw you smile. When did I last see you smile? Have you smiled this last week, two weeks? How long is it since I have seen you smile? Thank you . . . What was that shit about the potatoes?'

Viktor had already apologized twice. He felt an insane desire to share his burden with his protector, the fleet commander, stifled it and cringed that he had even thought of it. 'Don't know what was the matter with me – it will not happen again.'

'They were like wolves round you. You saw how they sneered at you. I do not like my man to be sneered at, to be shown to be asleep.'

Viktor said evenly, 'I can apologize again, if that is required.'

'You want leave, or a woman? You are unwell? What the fuck is the problem, Viktor?'

He could have said that for four years his life had been a deceit and that he was now under close surveillance. He could have taken the admiral to the wide, polished window and shown him the watchers hovering by the front door of the headquarters building and across the parade area. 'Just a bit tired – and I am grateful, sincerely, for your concern.'

He organized Admiral Falkovsky's in-tray, what must be read, what must be signed, and slipped out.

In the outer office, Viktor settled at his desk, picked up his pencil and began to sift the documents and memoranda in front of him. A clerk came to him and handed him a slip of folded paper.

He read. 'We should meet at the zoo, by the hippopotamus pen, at 4 p.m. tomorrow, Wednesday, love, Alicija.'

For a moment Viktor thought he might faint. To steady himself he bit on the end of the pencil, filled his mouth with little wood splinters. He thought of her, Alice, and the touch of her. He crumpled the paper in his hand, and began to read, vacantly, his work for the day. At the first chance he flicked the switch on the shredder beside his desk and fed into it a document on training programmes for two frigate crews, the sheet of notepaper, and a memorandum on the meteorological forecast for the coastal waters of the eastern Baltic for the next week, then turned off the machine. He thought of her smile and her love, and he trembled. An officer, a captain lieutenant, stood in front of him and said there was a deterioration problem in one of the torpedo tubes of a Vashavyanka-class submarine moored in basin number two. Could he come personally and inspect it before a report was written for Admiral Falkovsky's attention?

He went with the captain lieutenant to the naval dockyard. He was often used as a filter before reports were written and submitted. He did not recognize the trick.

'You have an hour,' Piatkin said. 'A clear hour.'

He waved Piatkin away. An hour was sufficient. Yuri Bikov walked to the front entrance of the officers' accommodation block, paused to wipe his feet hard on the outer mat, then checked his boots to see they were free of mud and dirt. The three-storey building was for single men, not officers with families who would have larger units. The doorway was empty, the staircase deserted. Single officers were at their desks or at the training lecture halls – no one saw him enter with his major and his sergeant. He wore the same clothes as those in which he had travelled; had he been seen he would have appeared to be a plumber or an engineer sent to repair one of the quarters' heating systems.

The files were gutted and could tell him nothing more. He waited on news from Gdansk, but that was a long throw. He had seen the face of Archenko, his prey. The room would tell him more of the man than he could find elsewhere: the secrets of a room were always paramount in an investigation. The deterioration of a submarine's torpedo tube would give him the time he needed. His sergeant inserted a master key. The door creaked open and the silence swam in the block.

He knelt in the doorway. He searched the floor for a cotton thread, a blond hair or a sliver of see-through adhesive tape. He did not find them. He stepped into the room. His major followed him, his sergeant closed the door and relocked it.

Bikov went to the centre of the room, and his major and his sergeant stayed back by the door. They would not distract him. He had an hour, he did not need to hurry. A man's room gave insight to his soul. In front of him was a Spartan iron bed, carefully made up, with the sheets and blankets uncreased, the corners exactly folded and the pillow had been punched as if it were new. There was a bedside table on which were a telephone, a notepad and a pencil laid geometrically alongside it, a small alarm clock and a battery radio. Beyond the bedside table was a window with the curtains opened, but the ledge was bare. In front of the window was a bare desk top, with empty drawers, and a small swivel chair.

Bikov made a quarter-turn. On his left was an easy chair covered with frayed material facing a television set. Beside the chair was a low table on which lay a naval magazine, not dropped down but placed exactly against two of the table's corners. Screwed to the wall, above the television set, was a double-shelved bookcase. From where he stood, Bikov could read the titles: naval manuals in Russian, medieval archaeological history in German. Midway between the bookcase and the end of the wall a single framed photograph hung. It was an enlargement and showed a river in the foreground and a castle of red brick whose outer defensive walls, set with battle towers, dominated a riverbank.

He turned again.

The wardrobe's two doors were closed. Next to it was the open entrance to the shower room and toilet, and past it was a hard, upright chair. There were no clothes, uniform or civilian, on the chair, no discarded shoes on the floor. Bikov's own room, wherever he was, was carpeted with dropped clothes, trousers and shirts, underwear and socks. Where there was wall space, beside the wardrobe and the door and above the chair, there was a year's planner chart, a traditional reproduction of a painting of a destroyer flotilla at sea, and nothing else.

He looked into a corner of the room, where the sink unit was. Across the wall was a work surface that reached to a small electric cooker. Under the sink and the work area were cupboards. Above them were hooks for saucepans and racks for plates, bowls and cups. His lips pursed and his tongue ran against his teeth. Every item was washed up and stowed. No used saucepans in the sink, no rinsed plates or cups left to dry on the draining-board.

Now Bikov faced the door.

A greatcoat and a waterproof hung from the hooks on it. There was no furniture against the walls on either side, no more pictures hanging. Bikov spoke. His major and his sergeant knew better than to think he addressed them. He spoke to himself.

'What is remarkable is that the man, Archenko, hides himself. This is his room, where he is alone and in privacy, and it is *clean*. Not clean with a broom, a pan and disinfectant, but clean of character. This is not some sudden gesture, the cleansing has not happened overnight because he believes himself to be under surveillance. All the time that he has been watched, which would have first alerted him, he has not worked through this room and taken from it anything that could betray him. It would have been seen. If he had come down the stairs and out through the back or the front and had carried a bag with materials to be disposed of, it would have been seen. The room, I think, has been like this for months or for years, perhaps from the day he arrived here. It would be a clear decision on his part to minimize the property he owns that sends a message of him. The state of the room is an indication – not evidence – of guilt. It is the room of a man who covers himself, who does not wish anything of himself to be observed. This is not a mania for tidiness, it is beyond that. Where are the photographs? There is no picture of any significant person: a grandmother or a mother or a girl, no pictures of friends and fellow officers, of him today or of him in his youth. Even here, in his own room, he guards against outsiders. The room has been sanitized, and I believe that happened from the start of his occupancy. He is not an emotional eunuch. I consider that everything he does is plotted with care . . . He goes to Malbork Castle inside eastern Poland three or four times a year, and that is permitted because he makes a great play of his near-obsessional interest in medieval castle-building. It is the one interest that his fellow officers and his commander, and the *zampolit* Piatkin, need to know of. So, he has a photograph that I assume is of Malbork Castle, and books to verify the interest – nothing more. He would know that I, or anyone such as I, whom he will inevitably face in interrogation, would look for family as the first point to talk of . . . There is no family. He tries not to make it easy for me, for an interrogator . . . I do not intend to go through the drawers. This is the room of an intelligent man. If we were to dislodge one hair from a drawer top, or from the wardrobe, or the drawers at the kitchen unit, then we arm him, and I do not wish, yet, for him to be alerted. I said that he was intelligent, but I think Viktor Archenko may be, could possibly be, under the delusion that he is clever, cunning, and that would be an error. The room tells me much of him, enough of him.'

On the way out, Bikov knelt and examined the mat and the carpet again. He heard the footsteps coming up the stairs, iron-shod boots on the concrete. He stood and stepped back, and his sergeant pulled the door shut. The footsteps came on up the stairs. His sergeant fumbled with the master key. Bikov faced the door, that his face should not be seen, as did his major and his sergeant. The footsteps went on by, crossed the landing, going easily, and climbed the next flight.

Yuri Bikov did not know of the mistake he had made.

When he had heard them go, the conscript came down from the top landing. He breathed hard. He waited until he heard the snap of the ground-level main entrance door, then followed. Igor Vasiliev thought himself the chosen friend of Captain, second rank, Viktor Archenko. He had been saved from drowning. His machine-gun had been returned to him. He had come to tell his friend, the chief of staff to the fleet commander, when there was next a firing exercise on the range for his platoon, because he hoped his friend would come to see him shoot . . . Men had been at his friend's door, had been closing it and locking it, and had turned away from him as if to preserve the secrecy of their identity . . . He did not know the importance of what he had seen, but it frightened him.

Deep in the water from the weight of her nine hundred tonnes of cargo, the *Princess Rose* edged up the river in an aisle of cranes and moored ships. They were almost level with the Westerplatte monument on the starboard side, and the new ferry wharfs were on the port side. Mowbray caught the tang of the sea, close to open water, and clung to a rail as the ship nudged into the river's mouth.

He climbed the last set of steps to the bridge and worked his way through the narrow door. He wore a clean shirt, the tie of the Parachute Regiment, not that he had ever jumped but it had been presented to him at a mess thrash in Aldershot, his tweed suit, the brogue shoes that had good tread, which Jerry the Pole had polished for him, and a life-jacket. He had insisted upon the life-jacket. In an hour, when they were clear of the harbour and out to sea, and the risks of interception were least, he would send the signal to London, tell Vauxhall Bridge Cross that the operation would run in the morning. He came to the bridge to find the master, whose cabin he had purloined, and vent his annoyance.

'There's a dog in there.'

'Where, Mr Mowbray?'

'In your, my, cabin. There's a bloody dog in there. It scratched the door.'

'It is our dog, it is Feliks.'

'I opened the door, it ran in. Looks flea-infested. It's underneath the bed.'

'The bunk, Mr Mowbray.'

'Underneath the bed, and it growls.'

'We love that dog, it brings us luck.'

'It smells, and we don't need luck. We don't rely on luck, Captain Yaxis, because we are professionals. Get rid of it, please.'

They were now past the Westerplatte monument. He lingered on the bridge to give time for the master to call the mate, and for the mate to remove the dog from the cabin. He looked back at the monument, a hideous, angular mess of carved granite blocks with a thin square column topping the plinth. It had no beauty, but a savage strength, and it marked a point of history. Mowbray was a man of history: it governed him.

She would be there at dawn. He could predict it. Alice would be there, on the high promontory dividing the Motlawa river from the sea, by the monument as the light came . . . She had history there. The *Princess Rose* chugged into the channel and the swell caught her, but then the ship veered to star-board, slowed and approached a disused quay.

The master told him the dog had been taken from the cabin, that he had informed the harbourmaster's office that he was still dissatisfied with the engine's performance, and the pilot had been stood down.

Rupert Mowbray went below to prepare the signal he would send to London.

She had taken charge. Locke could see that the men enjoyed her authority. She gave them each a sheet of paper and a pencil. They were in Billy's room high in the Mercure Hotel and Billy had the easy chair, Wickso and Lofty were squatted on the carpet, and Ham had the straight chair at the desk. He thought it childish.

She read out the questions. 'One: Who was the German commander defending Kaliningrad from the bunker? Two: In what street is the Kosmonaut memorial remembering Leonov and Patzayei, both from Kaliningrad?' Locke had done the detailed briefing, as he had been taught to, with the maps, had seen the barely stifled yawns, and had known that he had not carried his audience. She had usurped him.

Alice had used the same brief and had chatted through it as if she were a tourist guide. Now he thought she pandered to them. 'Got those, boys? Moving on . . . Three: What year did Peter the Great visit what is now Kaliningrad? And four: What was the last church dynamited in Kaliningrad, in 1976, to remove the final traces of German culture? Keep scribbling, boys.' He had talked to them for an hour, then she had intervened, gone over the same ground in thirty-five minutes, and held them. He hadn't.

Locke was ignored. 'Five: What is the name of the restaurant on Sovietsky 19? That's a good easy one.' It was effortless and made them laugh. She held them in her hand, as he could not. 'Six: The cobbles in the streets round Kaliningrad's cathedral were dug up by the Russians – where were they relaid? Didn't you listen to me?' He sat on the bed and thought he had no part to play. She diminished him.

He understood what she did: she bonded with them and relaxed them, made interesting the papers, maps, books they had searched through to learn of Kaliningrad. She made them scratch in their minds for what Locke and she had lectured. They had all been passed over, disgraced, and she wound them back into the family, did not take them for granted, made them feel they were players of importance, and calmed them. 'Keep going, boys. Only another fourteen to do. Seven: Name the ship now moored at the Oceanography Museum that successfully evacuated twenty thousand Germans from Kaliningrad, in several sailings to Denmark? That's the lucky buggers – most weren't. Eight: When Brezhnev wanted to destroy the cathedral, whose tomb saved it? Are we doing all right, boys?'

Locke pushed himself up from the bed. He wanted out, fast, could not accept more of the humiliation. They fed from her fingers and had yawned at him . . . Then, she reached into her handbag and pulled out a boutique's little gift bag. She was smiling at them. From it she took out four small boxes. Her smile switched to mock-solemn and she gave a box to each of them. 'Go on, yes, open it.'

Locke realized that none of them knew what they would find. The lids of the boxes were lifted . . . In each was a pendant of amber stone and a fine gold chain. She blushed. Her fingers were on her own pendant.

'Wear them when you go across – I'd appreciate that.'

Billy came to her. 'I wouldn't let all those slobbering blighters do this, ma'am, but this is from all of us – thanks.'

His coarse hands held her face and he kissed each of her cheeks, and the blush was brighter.

The clasps were too delicate for them. She moved from Billy to Lofty, then to Ham, unfastened the clasps, hooked the chains, then let the pendants swing on their chests. She got to Wickso, and reached behind his neck.

'Don't strangle me, ma'am . . . Oh, and I've a problem,' Wickso said.

'What is it, Wickso?'

'It's the photo we've been shown of him. It's not good enough. It's not sharp and the flash has washed the life out of him . . . What I'm saying, we could walk past him.' Billy was holding up the picture. Ferret lounged in a chair in a room of the Excelsior Hotel, shirt-sleeves and tired. Mowbray had taken it. It was the only picture of Ferret in the file.

'I'm saying the same, ma'am,' Ham said, and Lofty nodded. 'It doesn't do the business.'

Well, that wasn't the fault of Gabriel Locke. None of it was his fault. Better if the photograph had stayed in the file, and the file had stayed in the archive. He was drifting to the door. She reached again into her handbag, took out a small leatherbound clip-over picture-holder, and tossed it towards Billy. He caught it, and prised open the catch. Locke couldn't see the picture. Billy looked at it. Ham shuffled to him; Wickso and Lofty crawled across the carpet. They stared at the picture-holder, soaked it, then returned to their places.

Billy said, as he closed the catch and passed it back to Alice, 'That'll do nicely, ma'am. Nice picture – and we'll be glad to wear them . . . Keep firing, ma'am.'

Locke was at the door. 'I'll see you all in the morning.'

Alice was saying, 'OK, back to work. Where were we? Yes. Nine . . .'

He closed the door, padded off down the corridor, and took the lift, then walked out into the night. They didn't value him. He was not valued because he, alone, stood against the cowboy culture of the operation.

Past midnight, and the hotel slept. The man leaned across the reception desk, took the card sheet from his attaché case and showed it to the night porter. He was married to the cousin of the *zampolit*, Piatkin, a rank lower in the Federalnaya Sluzhba Bezopasnosi than him, but he knew he was spoken well of, and he had commendations. His life in the consulate was dull, his office overlooking Batorego was an empire of tedium, and then, from a clear blue sky, had come the matter of the book of matches and the queries as to who had stayed on three relevant dates at the Excelsior Hotel by the river and the marina. The task entrusted to him was the most sensitive yet given him. He had come the previous evening, late, but a fresh-faced young night porter had been on duty, and the one he trusted had been away from work, out of Gdansk, visiting a sick relative in Torun. The last time he had visited the hotel in the dead of night with senior men from the Warsaw embassy, and had greased the night porter's palm, he had been given the names of Roderick Walton and Elizabeth Beresford, resident when it was relevant, and they had taken away a vague description of the elderly Walton. The card paper he took from his attaché case carried a montage of twenty-four covert photographs of older men. They came from the Lubyanka, had been flown to Warsaw, then couriered to Gdansk. Underneath each photograph was a number. Each one had been taken, long lens, of officers in the British intelligence-gathering service. 'Was Roderick Walton among them?' Had a senior and experienced man of the Service of Great Britain stayed at the Excelsior Hotel each time that Archenko had travelled to the city to negotiate dry-dock facilities? It was why he had joined. They said at the Lubyanka that the war was not finished, was dormant but not over. This was the battleground that mattered, they said in the Lubyanka, not the fucking about in Afghanistan, Chechnya and in the Islamic satellites in the south. The old

179

discipline of ideology might have gone but the suspicion had survived and the lack of trust for those who now came from the West and patronized, slapped backs, stank of talc and lotion and who believed they had ground the Motherland to defeat . . . He showed the photographs; a wad of *zlotys* lay across them. He had been told in the signal sent to him by courier that if a photograph was identified then evidence was found.

Locke came into the hotel. In front of him a man in a long raincoat was bent across the reception desk and the night porter was squinting down at something between them.

The porter looked up, saw Locke, made an ingratiating smile, recognized him and reached for a key.

A low light lit the desk but the rest of the hall was in darkness. Locke took the key. The man's face was away from him. He took a step towards the stairs, then hesitated. Did he want a morning paper? In Gdansk there were the *Gazeta Morska* and the *Dziennik Ballycki*. Ahead of him was a day of hanging around, waiting; he had no book. Should he order a paper? He turned. Both their heads were down as they studied what was between them. He saw a sheet of photographs, on the desk, and the night porter's finger wavered over one, in the left column, and he heard a little scratched gasp of excitement from Raincoat Man. Then his finger, too, tapped the picture. Locke saw the photograph, saw the swept-back silver hair, the hawk's eyes and the proud chin of Rupert Mowbray, and their fingers. He turned away and padded to the dark corner of the lobby.

In Polish, 'Him, each of those dates?'

In Russian, 'Certain?'

The night porter's Polish, 'And here last night and checked out this morning?'

Raincoat Man's Russian, 'Again, last night?'

Raincoat Man pushed the banknotes off the sheet of photographs and the night porter slid them into his hip pocket. His hand was gripped, squeezed. Raincoat Man spun and strode quickly to the door. This was not a training exercise, he was not at Fort Monkton. He was far from his instructors, far from the tradecraft lectures on the hill beside the golf course used by the members of the Gosport and Stokes Bay club, far from having his hand held and orders given him. The sweat ran cold on his neck and his back. He followed blindly. The door swung in his face and he careered through it. He had seen a Russian intelligence officer identify a photograph of Rupert Mowbray. The cold of the air hit him. Raincoat Man was fifty metres in front, going towards a car parked under a light by the marina's pontoon bridge. Nothing moved, only him and Raincoat Man – no cars, no pedestrians. They were alone in the night. Locke started to run.

Raincoat Man's pace quickened. Locke closed the gap, started to sprint, his shoes stamping for speed.

Why? His mind was blurred. What did he intend? He was dazed by what he had seen.

Raincoat Man reached a family Fiat saloon car. Locke saw the bright material of kids' seats in the back. The door was opened, the attaché case was thrown into the back, on to the kids' seats. The shape ducked inside and was reaching out to drag the door shut after him. Locke was beside the car.

What would the instructors have said?

The scenario had never been played out for Locke at Fort Monkton on the IONEC course. Never, on the Intelligence Officers New Entry Course, had they told the rookie recruits what to do when confronting Raincoat Man – of Russian counter-intelligence – beside the marina on the Motlawa river in old Gdansk. They taught the tradecraft of surveillance and anti-surveillance procedures and dead drops and brush contacts and the techniques of short-range agent communication and evasion-driving and self-defence. Nothing that Gabriel Locke had been taught in the lecture rooms and the courtyard of the Fort would help him at that moment. A special-forces man, there for the day, had preached a clear mind and a clear head: *Piss Poor Planning makes Pathetic Performance*. He had no plan. Unarmed-combat training at the fort was gentle, well inside the rules laid down by the Health and Safety Executive, just a few rolls on to the mat off the instructors' shoulders, no pain.

Locke grabbed him. He dragged him up and out of the car. His fist was locked in a crumpled mass of Raincoat Man's coat. He saw the fear, heard the gibbered entreaties. Raincoat Man was terrified, too frightened to scream. So ordinary, like the Russians, the bright young ones, that Locke met on the cocktail circuit in Warsaw, the sort of guy he'd have button-holed at a party. He did not know what he intended, what was the end of the game. He threw the man back against the wall of the Fiat saloon's side and saw him crumple, go down.

The eyes pleaded. Perhaps it was the names of the kids that sat in the back seats, but Locke only heard little squirts of sound from the lips. He swung back his foot and kicked him in the gut, low. And because he had kicked once, he kicked again. He was past his limit of control.

The instructors at the Fort, on self-defence, always yelled for 'control'. He had lost it. No scream, only a whimper below him.

Locke pulled at the flabby weight of the Raincoat Man, lifted him. Held him up. There was no resistance, and pain had dulled the fear in the eyes that stared at him, cried to him. He threw the man away from him, as careless as the dropping of a sack of coal by the back door of the farmhouse in west Wales. The man left his grip and slumped, staggered once, then collapsed. *Piss Poor Planning makes Pathetic Performance*. Raincoat Man's fall took an age. The goal replayed in grinding slow motion. The head going down. The stagger had taken him away from Locke. A bollard of old black metal was set in the quay's edge, half a metre high. The head hit the bollard's rim and jerked as if rubber held it to the body.

Locke knelt beside him. He took the head in his hands and shook it and seemed to cry to the man to react, to speak, but the head lolled in his hands. He laid it down, left it to lie at its strange angle. His hands shook but he felt Raincoat Man's neck, tried to find a pulse and failed. He heard the wind in the riggings in the marina, whistling and rippling, and the creaking heave of the pontoon bridges. He looked around and saw nobody, nothing that moved . . . Across the city, on the junction of Nowe Ogrody and Third Maja, was the police headquarters of Gdansk. Locke had seen the building that morning, tall, austere, formidable. He had also seen that behind the police headquarters was the city's gaol, bleak, dirty and secure with razor-wire topping the walls. He had killed a man, had murdered him with his own hands. If he cried in the night for an ambulance, for help, he would be taken to the police cells, then to a court, and then to those prison cells whose small barred windows he had seen . . . He stood. His father had taken him out once from the house and into the right near corner of the five-acre field and had shot a dog that could no longer work. His father had said it was good for the ten-year-old's character to watch life and death. Together, father and child had dug a grave for the dog. Father had told him to put the animal into the bottom of the pit, but the child could not touch it. His father, with his boot, had pushed the dog in. The child had run, streaming tears, back to the farmhouse, leaving his father to fill the pit. He had often walked close to that corner of the five-acre field, where only nettles grew, had thought of the dog and put primroses there in spring. He had gone there the day he had left home while his mother called for him that his father was in the car and waiting for him.

With the end of his shoe, Locke prodded Raincoat Man past the bollard and over the edge of the quay. There was a sluggish splash, then the marina's debris and the oily water closed on the body. He took the sheet of photographs from the attaché case, closed the car door and went back to the hotel.

In his bathroom, bent over the pan, Gabriel Locke was sick, sick again, and again. Each time he flushed it he vomited another time. When his stomach had no more to throw up he tore the photographs to small pieces, waited for the water to fill the cistern, dropped them into the pan and flushed it finally.

He knew what he had done, not why. He lay on the floor, dressed, curled up like a baby.

Alice was at the memorial. They had been there together on a summer's morning, the sun rising away to the west and breaking the mist. Behind them the taxi engine was purring, the clock still running. It was where they had been together the last time they had met, after they had made love and before he had gone back to the hotel where the delegation was lodged. He had understood her camera, had set the delay action, propped it on the plinth of the monument, run back to her and put his arm around her, his hand against her hip. She had dropped her head against his shoulder, and they had laughed and heard the shutter's click. He had pointed towards the sun, where it broke the mist, and had said that that was where he would be – Kaliningrad.

'You don't have to go,' Alice had said.

He'd kissed her, then smiled rakishly. 'But I'm not finished. I have work to do. There is no danger, I am very clever. I will come over, when it is the right time, when . . .'

He'd run. The taxi had driven away. She'd taken the first bus of the day back to the hotel, and as she had packed her bag before joining Rupert for breakfast she had found a little gift-wrapped package, had torn it apart, and found the pendant of amber stone and its gold chain.

It was dark still. Then it had been light. Now the summer was gone and the autumn was settling. Another taxi waited for her and there was the glow of the interior light as the driver read a magazine. She only heard the wind in the tall trees and the beat of the sea on the beach below the promontory. Alice had asked them to wear a talisman for her, and she had shown the men her photograph so that they would better recognize him at the zoo. Billy, the team leader among them, would have seen a trickle of emotion on her mouth and the flash of wetness in her eyes. He'd spoken for all of them when the meeting had broken, when she'd marked the quiz and given Ham the prize, out of petty cash, fifty *zlotys*, spoken quietly. 'You don't want to lose your beauty sleep, ma'am. We'll bring him out.'

9

Q. In a security emergency, where in the Russian Federation would units of naval infantry patrol a land border?
A. Kaliningrad.

The plan, as dictated by Rupert Mowbray, was simple, straightforward to the point of banality.

Jerry the Pole led the team past Braniewo until they turned off at the farm gateway and parked up to leg it cross-country. He had the papers to go through the frontier post in his old Mercedes. The team would go through the fence where they had holed it, then move on foot to the barn outside the village of Lipovka, by the Vituska river, where Jerry the Pole would pick up three of them, drive for the city of Kaliningrad, the zoo, and the rendezvous point at the hippopotamus pen. The Mercedes, with Ferret aboard, would drive back to the barn and Ferret would be taken over the fields into the forest line, and through the fence, while Jerry the Pole negotiated the frontier post. A simple plan, Rupert Mowbray maintained, was always the best plan.

Locke hadn't slept, had risen at dawn plagued by the notion that what was done could not be undone. He had met Alice at breakfast, they had driven to Braniewo – now they walked the streets.

'So, what the hell's the problem?' Alice was at his shoulder and gripped his coat sleeve. He shook her off. 'If there's a problem, it's better talked through.'

Ahead was the open street-market, the stalls laid out with vegetables and cheap clothes. Among them were older men and their women, and housewives with small children, peering at the produce, tugging at the clothes and looking wistfully at the price tags. Past the open street-market was the concrete block, graffiti-scrawled, of the public lavatories.

'For God's sake, Gabriel, it's the big day – what's the bloody problem?'

When he had risen, and gone out of the hotel – while Alice was at breakfast – he had seen the local men, who hadn't work to go to, sitting, smoking, on the benches overlooking the marina. Others had promenaded past the yachts and launches, had gone by the pontoon bridge to the piers. One had stood close to the bollard, unwrapped a sticky sweet and dropped the paper beside it. Cars hemmed in the Fiat saloon. Everything was as he had remembered it in the night. The man chewing his sweet, cracking it in his teeth, would not have seen the slight blood smear on the bollard, level with his knee, but it was there. Locke had moved on past the benches and had gone near to the car; the men lounging nearby would not have seen that the Fiat was unlocked, the button on the door clearly in the 'up' position, and the open briefcase lying between the kids' seats. He had edged towards the pontoon and the water lapping it. The leg floated under the pontoon's planks among plastic bags, drifting cans and wood spars – Locke had seen it. The sodden dark trouser turn-up, the grey sock and the laced black shoe. He had seen them, then hurried away.

'You want out, don't you?' Alice accused. 'You think this is all beneath you?'

Beyond the lavatory building, above the flapping canvas stall roofs, was the high spire of the church. Two young men – shaven heads, T-shirts, genuine leather jackets – were emptying the boot of a shining Audi 6-series of cartons of American cigarettes and stacking them on a stall.

'It's in your mind that he's a traitor . . .'

He snapped, 'Do me a favour, Alice, don't presume to know what's in my mind.'

'Obvious to a blind deaf mute – he's a traitor, he's not worth bothering with. You have a big, big attitude problem. You know that? How did you get through IONEC? They're supposed to weed out the misfits. A traitor . . . A hundred years ago, army officers wouldn't touch agent intelligence unless they'd gloves on – "Mustn't get our lily-white hands dirty, must we?" When he first walked in there were

186

idiots at VBX who couldn't believe he was genuine, wanted him to do a polygraph. Rupert gave them a good kicking. Our Service is nothing – got me? *nothing* – without agents. Viktor—'

Locke spun, faced her. 'Oh, thank you. Viktor – I've never been trusted with his name.'

For a moment he'd stopped her. She gagged. 'Ferret . . . Ferret has more bravery, more than you'll ever know, more in his fingernail than in your whole bloody body.'

His face was set, cold. 'If you say so, Alice.'

Alice softened. 'Sorry – tell me about the problem.'

Locke said grimly, 'Did I say there was a problem? Did I? Fine, you want a *problem*. Try this. We are asked to take risks. People get hurt when risks are taken. We are sanctioned to hurt people – for a flawed bloody daydream, a lunatic policy. We play as if we are above the law, like morality doesn't count for us. We—'

'Not *we*, Gabriel. We are here, not in Kaliningrad. The people who are trained for it, they're going to Kaliningrad. We're cosseted here – leave the sharp end to people who know what they're doing. Get real.'

He could not tell her. He wondered how long it would be before the body was fished from the marina.

It was like the time between life and death, or the hours when darkness turned to light.

Viktor did not know about religion, and few of his fellow officers were churchgoers because that was still a hindrance to career advancement, but his mother had turned to the Orthodox faith after his father's death. His mother had said that death was not darkness.

Time had to be spent, exhausted, used up. He had barely looked round the room that might be contaminated by the presence of a radio microphone or a fish-eye lens. He must struggle, for the remaining hours, to follow a routine of total predictability. The first decision: whether to run on the beach. He had not. He had dressed in his best, as he would on any day that he went to work in the admiral's outer office, and he had taken breakfast in the senior officers' mess. He had left the cache of papers behind the tile in the shower unit. When he was gone, and his flight was confirmed, that night or the next morning, his quarters would be taken apart with crow-bars and sledge-hammers. By then his new life would have begun. Viktor would have liked to take the picture of Malbork Castle down from the wall and put it into his briefcase, but it was left, as was everything else. Before he had locked the door behind him, he had looked a last time around the room. He had eaten sparingly, because that was his way, and an officer from Personnel – a decent man – had come to his table to talk leave charts; another, from Armaments, had come to mutter of a difficulty with munitions shelf-life. He had dealt with them the way he always did, curtly but not unpleasantly. The route between life and death was the zoo in Kaliningrad. He'd felt a strange peace as he'd sipped coffee and eaten a roll.

He walked from the senior officers' mess across the parade-ground. In front of him were the low dormitories of the conscripts and beyond was the complex of the fleet commander where he would spend those hours . . . Viktor Archenko had been seventeen years old when his father had died at Totskoye. Outside that town, 225 kilometres west of Orenburg, hidden from outsiders by a forest, guarded by fences and patrols, was a closed community of the air force. His father, Pyotr, was a major, a test pilot. The base was dedicated to the preparation of air-launched nuclear weapons. His father's illness had come quickly. As the leukaemia had gripped him, as plans were made for his retirement from the air force, Viktor had watched, in his own unspoken agony, the deterioration. A month before the family were due to move out of the base, already avoided by the neighbouring families living beside them, his father had died. At the funeral, an air-force general had suggested that the young Viktor, with his athleticism and parentage, would easily find a berth as a pilot when he left high school. There was in him – well hidden – a streak of rebellion. He had seen the way his father's colleagues shunned him in illness, and he had volunteered for the navy . . . Fourteen years later, when the same leukaemia had taken his mother – when he had learned on her deathbed of his grandmother – he had been told also the cause of the disease that had taken his father's life.

A test pilot had been ordered up in a veteran Mig-17 fighter that was loaded with measuring instrumentation. He was Major Pyotr

Archenko, and he had told his wife of his fear. The fighter aircraft was aged, at the end of its working life, as was the pilot. His father had said that the order could not be refused, or the charge at a court-martial would be that of treason. A nuclear device was exploded, on stilts and a few metres above ground level. A test pilot was instructed to fly through the spreading mushroom cloud. The generals had cowered in the safety of radiation-proof bunkers. His father had flown through the pitching storm of the explosion. The instrumentation's information had been downloaded, the test pilot had been checked over by doctors cocooned in radiation-protective suits.

Viktor had heard the story, and the story of his grandmother. He had taken the first opportunity. An earlier chance, five weeks before, had been a visit of Archangel convoy veterans from Great Britain who had come to the city to celebrate the bringing of war munitions to the Soviet Union, but he had not been able to get close to them. The first opportunity had been the arrival of a Hull-based trawler to Murmansk. It was in memory of his father and his grandmother, and the hate had burned in him, with the demand for revenge.

He walked briskly, the way he always walked. His name was called, softly and with respect. Workmen were on the top of the second-nearest dormitory building where they were replacing a section of metal roofing, through which machine-gun bullets, 12.7mm calibre, had been fired. He turned, and saw the conscript, Vasiliev.

'May I speak to you?'

'Speak,' Viktor said sharply. It broke the pattern of his everyday life that he should stop for conversation with a conscript. He had not seen the watchers, but assumed they were around him. It was his discipline that he did not look for them.

'I am going to shoot on the range tomorrow.'

'That is good.' Viktor took a part of cruel indifference: it was necessary. He walked on, indicated he did not wish to linger.

But the conscript followed him. 'Because of you – thank you for saving me, for bringing back the NSV machine-gun . . . Captain, I went to your room to give my thanks yesterday.'

'It was not necessary.' Viktor was brusque, as if he sought to brush away an irritation.

'You should know . . .' Vasiliev blurted. 'I went to your room yesterday. Men were coming out, they had been in your room. They hid their faces from me. Three men. They had a key to your room.'

From the side of his mouth, without turning his head, 'Was Piatkin with them? Was the *zampolit* one of them?'

'No, no . . . I had not seen them before. I had never seen them before, with Major Piatkin or not. The one who seemed in charge, controlled them, he was the youngest . . . but he dressed like a derelict, not like an officer . . . I had to tell you.'

'Thank you. I hope you shoot well tomorrow. Go back to your duties.'

He walked on, leaving the conscript behind. The very action of talking to him endangered Vasiliev. A watcher would not have known the bond between a captain, second rank, and a young soldier of Naval Infantry. There would be many who would face danger by association when his flight, and his guilt, were discovered . . . They had come, the new men. They would have come from Moscow . . . Time ran, sand slipped in the glass. Did he have enough time, now that the new men were on the base? The sentries saluted at the entrance to the fleet commander's headquarters building.

Viktor found Admiral Alexei Falkovsky in a mood of noisy good humour.

Jerry the Pole was late.

The frontier checks had been slow, but that was predictable. First the Polish formalities, with a long, stretched queue of cars and lorries: he had allowed for that. Five hundred metres beyond the Polish border post was the first Russian block, and more delays as his papers were examined by the stolid-faced military. Then a further half-kilometre on was Russian Customs and more questions to be answered. Beyond the border, Jerry the Pole had accelerated. Then he had heard the siren.

The speed limit in the Kaliningrad *oblast* was seventy kilometres per hour. Jerry the Pole was used to Germany, where there was no limit on a motorist's speed on an open road.

The siren was behind him, and the police car filled his mirror. He slowed, then pulled over. He sat bolt upright in his seat, and wound down the window as the policeman advanced on him. A fat sloth of a man in dull blue uniform, shapeless and ill-fitting, sauntered to him and, with studied contempt, pulled out a notebook. What to do? Jerry the Pole asked what was the fine for speeding. He was told that for being guilty of speeding it was forty roubles. He paid the fine with a 100-rouble note and gestured that he did not expect change and a receipt. He wondered when the traffic policeman had last been paid, and whether he would have a pension when he retired. There was a large pistol holstered at the traffic policeman's belt. If it were the return journey from the city across the *oblast*, if he had had the three men inside the Mercedes, and the one they had gone to lift, and if a traffic policeman had stopped them, what would they have done? He smiled ingratiatingly and stumbled his apologies. On the road again, he made certain that the speed limit was not exceeded.

When he reached the village of Lipovka he reached into the glove box for the map drawn by Billy. He took a wrong turning because he was not expert in reading a map, and that delayed him further. He'd lost fifteen more minutes before he came to the rendezvous point at the barn. As he turned the car, they emerged from the undergrowth – three of them.

Billy rapped on the window. 'You are fucking late.'

Lofty opened the back door, snatched at it. 'Don't you carry a bloody wristwatch?'

None of them had asked why he was late, had queried if he had had a difficulty and how he had overcome it. When the doors slammed shut on them, the wheels spun in the mud near the barn and he drove away. Beside and behind him they were silent. Jerry the Pole drove towards the main road and at the junction was the signpost to Kaliningrad. Inside the speed limit they would be in the city, and the zoo, in an hour. Billy was in the front, hunched over the map spread across his thighs, and his coat was thrown open. Jerry the Pole could see the pistol butt jutting from his waistband.

Billy Smith was the team leader – why was he there?

He had left behind the tin-roofed, plank-walled hut on the shores of the loch, and his paints and his paper, and the panoramic views that were his inspiration. The owner of the gallery in Glasgow that handled his work had told him that his was a rare talent. He went to Glasgow to deliver his work twice a year; the larger water-colours were priced by the gallery at £3250, and the smaller ones fetched £1195. They were hung in the boardrooms of Glasgow banks, in the waiting rooms of investment brokers, the lobbies of medical consultants, and they were in the homes of the élite of the city. The gallery owner had introduced him to a money man. His takings from his work were in gilts, blue chips and government bonds. He could have lived in a smart apartment in Glasgow, in a warehouse conversion . . . He had no financial need to be bent into an old Mercedes, with a pistol handle gouging his stomach, heading into Kaliningrad. The money man sent a monthly cash package to his wife, Josie, for the upkeep of the children, Tracey and Leanne; he was long divorced and had not seen his children for fourteen years, but he kept them in food and clothes, and paid for the roof over their heads.

Why?

Life, for Billy Smith, was a slow dribble of failure. The refuge on Loch Shiel, under Beinn Odhar Mhor, was an escape, a bolthole. His work, his watercolours, were a flight from the consequences of what he had done. He had taken the life, on the foreshore of Carlingford Lough, of a young man who had gone to lift his pots for lobsters and crabs, and had protected himself and his patrol from prosecution by brazen lies. He had failed himself and, as their sergeant, had failed Ham, Wickso and Lofty. He had failed the Marines and the inner family of the Squadron. He was like a vessel that was dry, like a tube of paint squeezed empty.

He blessed the moment that the big naval helicopter had flut-tered down on to the shingle beside the loch and the young man, so fucking supercilious, had dropped from the hatch . . . There was no mirror beside the sink in the hut. He did not look at himself when he shaved or snipped his beard: he did it by touch . . . He rode towards Kaliningrad and felt it was a chance, the last one that would be offered, of redemption. He could still see, would always harbour the image, of the young man's eyes – staring, drowned, lifeless.

Billy Smith knew redemption did not come easy, came harder than brushing paint on paper. They were driving into the city, going past the tower blocks, towards the bridge.

Because the *Princess Rose* was clear of the wharf, her cargo of fertilizer loaded, the port authorities had lost interest in the movement of the ship, and the problems of its engine. They were tied to the quay under the towering Westerplatte monument. The dog scratched at the door of the master's cabin, but Rupert Mowbray ignored it. The communications were in place, although it was an hour since Locke had come through. What Mowbray knew: it was launched, Jerry the Pole was across the border and had made the rendezvous, the team was heading for Kaliningrad. The last message had come, relayed on; from Locke. He did not believe in unnecessary radio talk. They were now as helpless, useless, as any ground-control team monitoring one of those old moon-shot space-craft from thirty years before when orbit had taken the astronauts to the far side. He must wait . . . as they must wait at Vauxhall Bridge Cross. It would be vindication, a moment of saccharine sweetness, a wonderful ecstasy for Rupert Mowbray when he could send the signal: ferret: onside. He would bask in glory. He sat by the communications equipment, but hurled a shoe at the door to frighten away the mongrel outside.

The wife of the FSB officer, attached to the consulate in Gdansk, had telephoned four times. Her husband had gone out the previous evening in the family car, and had not returned.

The consul had no knowledge of the work practices of his FSB man. He did not have access to his room, to his diary, and knew nothing of the content of the signals from the Lubyanka.

Initially he had done nothing. Although the woman was verging on hysterical, he was loath to interfere in what might be an operation of sensitivity – or a matter of domestic infidelity – so he had sat on what little he knew of a counter-intelligence's officer's disappearance.

After her fourth call, the consul sent an urgent signal to the embassy in Warsaw and asked for guidance. A return signal had come from the senior officer of the Federalnaya Sluzhba Bezopasnosi stationed in the Polish capital ordering him to check around Gdansk's police and hospitals. By the early afternoon the missing man's description was in the hands of the police, but hospitals reported he had not been admitted, and the plates of the Fiat car had been circulated.

The complication was that only the section in the Lubyanka dealing with the probable treachery of Captain, second rank, Viktor Archenko knew of the mission undertaken the previous evening by the officer in the Gdansk consulate . . . Those dealing with the report of the missing man were outside the loop of information.

There was confusion. The wife sat by the phone, held her tearful children, and waited for it to ring, but it did not . . . and the police in the city did not know where to search.

Viktor slipped away from his desk. The last memorandum he initialled concerned the programme for the visit of the fleet commander to the cadet school to watch athletics and present prizes, and he left, uninitialled and unread, at the top of the in-tray a note requesting the fleet commander's inspection of a frigate back from recommissioning in the Far East. Viktor Archenko told the outer office staff that he was going for an early lunch in the senior officers' mess. He had not informed his secretary, his personal assistant or Admiral Falkovsky that he would be driving off-base that afternoon.

As he walked to the parking area, Viktor saw a man in civilian clothes throw down a cigarette and start to follow him. There were many civilian workers on the base, so there was nothing peculiar in a man strolling after him in jeans and a windcheater; another lounged on a car bonnet close to where his own vehicle was parked and read a pocket magazine. He knew he was watched, did not have to turn to confirm it. As he drove out of the base, he was followed by the black van with the smoked windows and the red saloon. If his room had been searched, he thought that his arrest would follow within a day, two days at the most.

He did not look back at the base. He did not see, in his mirror or by twisting his shoulders, the flags of the Federation and the fleet flying from tall poles; nor did he look a last time at the Lenin statue, or the headquarters building, or the façade of the Sailors' Club, or at the castle where his grandmother might have been, or at the high radar scanners perched on the upper masts of the fleet in the dockyard. It was all behind him, and he did not see the van and the car tucked in and close.

He wondered where he would sleep that night . . . where *they* would sleep. He would be with Alice . . . He drove slowly. The needle of the speedometer was within the legal limit, not because of any respect he held for the law, or from a fear of being intercepted by the traffic police, but he knew that to go fast to the zoo would weaken him. Speed demonstrated the intensity of his flight. He went slowly, and that gave him the sense of control. The lights were against him. He braked. Instinct made him glance at the interior mirror.

Immediately behind him, as if joined by a tow-rope, was the black van, which shared his traffic lane. In the outer lane, level with it, was the red saloon.

Viktor eased away from the lights. His fists clamped on the wheel. Within an hour he would be in the hands of trained men sent by his friends; until then his control and discipline were of paramount importance. He was breathing hard.

Bikov was called. He worked on his notes in the room at the back of the FSB's city block, prepared himself for interrogation, and waited for the information to be serviced from Gdansk . . . Archenko was on the move. With his major and his sergeant he hurried down the back fire-escape staircase.

The autumn sunlight settled on the city, fell low over the river.

It was on the big concrete apartment blocks and on the addicts who lay slumped in doorways, and on the abandoned monstrosity of the House of Soviets and on the infected HIV victims who staggered gaunt on the streets, and on the old cathedral where slow renovation had started with German money, and on the whores who guarded their pavement pitches, and on the polluted rubbish-filled canals and on the *mafiya* men who strutted to their BMW vehicles. The low sunlight could not brighten the city, even the zoo park where the shadows lengthened.

The paint on the letters was chipped and had flaked: it was hard for Viktor to read the sign. He had to brake sharply or he would have missed the turn. He gave no warning of the braking and the turning, and when he looked in his mirror he saw the wind-screen of the van was almost against his boot and back bumper. Two men were in the van, vague shapes behind the tinted glass, and they would have known that he saw them, recognized them. He remembered what Rupert Mowbray had said to him, the second of the fast fifteen-minute sessions tacked on after the principal debrief, before he and Alice had sidled from Mowbray's room: 'Russians are *Pavlovian*. They instil psychosis and nervousness to render you inoperative.' He realized that they wanted to be seen, it was the route to psychosis. If he followed it, the nerves would shred him. If he were 'inoperative' the pick-up at the zoo would fail.

He parked the car. Kids on a school tour of the city were peeling out of their bus, their last stop of the day's tour of the *oblast* capital. He saw their teachers, pale and tired, threadbare men and women, struggling to marshal them. The kids were alive, noisy, and surged from the bus as their teachers shouted at them. When he looked at the kids, and past them, Viktor saw the watchers from the black van and the red saloon and they didn't turn away. There was nothing to take from the car other than his coat and he shrugged into it, buttoned it so that the sight of his uniform, with the gold on the sleeves and the medal ribbons on the chest, was hidden. He bought his entry ticket from the *babushka* crone, who scowled at him from the depths of her kiosk, and walked to the gates, a heaviness weighting his legs.

'Has he been here before?'

Bikov stood at the zoo's gate. His office had been alerted by Piatkin, the *zampolit*, and they had careered round corners, tyres screaming, as the directions given by the tail cars had zeroed them on to the target's vehicle. They had jolted to a halt in the parking area and Piatkin had strode to Bikov.

'Not that I know of,' Piatkin said.

'What's here?'

'Very little.'

'Why would he come to see "very little"?'

'I have no idea.' Piatkin shrugged.

'Stay close.' The instruction was quietly spoken. 'He does not come here without a reason . . .'

He waved away Piatkin, let him speak softly into the microphone that protruded from the buttonhole of his coat's lapel. Archenko was a hundred metres in front, going past the zoo's closed café. Bikov watched his man, the target. It was not possible that the target came to this decayed, soulless place without good reason. The target walked behind the flurry of shouting, whooping children. As if he were armed with an antenna, Bikov watched and the suspicion flowed in him, but he could not see the 'good reason' why the target had come here. He could identify each of Piatkin's six watchers, all blended to the surroundings of the pens and cages. Two were behind the target and two were wide but level with him and two had gone ahead and would be controlled, from their moulded earpieces, by Piatkin's button microphone.

He watched the target moving behind the children, saw him glance down at his wristwatch. He looked at his own watch. Five minutes to four o'clock. The best pleasure Yuri Bikov knew was the final minutes of a chase, closing on a prey.

'Delta One from Delta Two . . . I have an eyeball. He's doing dry-cleaning. I have eyeball on Target One. Present speed he's two minutes from the RV. I'm in position to brush him. Wait out, wait out . . . I think he has bandits. Will confirm on bandits. Delta Two out.'

Billy said, 'Get over, Jerry. Get the wheel, Lofty.'

Jerry the Pole was wriggling over the gear-stick, vacating the driver's seat. He snagged the stick and Lofty's fist thumped into his back, pushed him, then Lofty was behind the wheel and rolling his shoulders as if to loosen himself. They were on the far lane of the road from the retaining wall that flanked the side of the zoo. There was a seven-foot drop from the top of the wall to the pavement. Above the wall was a sagging chain-link perimeter fence in which rubbish – paper, wrappings, plastic – was caught.

Billy said to Lofty, 'Ham's got him in sight. He's acting natural, doing it well, less than two minutes till Ham's with him . . .'

'That's great.' The breath sighed between Lofty's teeth.

'. . . and Ham thinks he's got a tail.'

'Oh, shit.' Lofty gunned the engine once, tested its power, then let it fade to idle. Billy took his pistol from his belt, armed it, slipped the safety with his thumb, and laid it down between his thighs, half covered but close to hand.

Viktor followed the children and listened, half aware, to the commentary given them by the eldest of the teachers, a dour woman. She was by a pen where the low concrete wall had crumbled, and the wire above it was holed. Inside was a concrete cave entrance in which weeds grew. A crazily angled sign showed a lion's head.

'There are no lions now. Once this was a very famous zoo, but these are difficult times. It is expensive to keep animals, and it is difficult to justify spending money on animals' food when many people do not have enough to eat. But soon there will be monkeys here, chimpanzees and all the apes. There is going to be a programme of development to return the zoo to its former status, one of the best in Europe. The zoo was opened in 1896, and by 1910 there were 2126 animals in residence, including two Siberian tigers that had been donated by the zoo in Moscow. Look, children, there are deer . . .'

If they'd had the strength, if their ribcages had not been so prominent and the muscles on their hind legs so withered, the five deer in the pen could have leaped out because the wire enclosing them had collapsed. They grazed on mud, not a blade of grass available to them, and they sniffed at old sandwiches and orange peel thrown for them. The television showed antelope and gazelle feeding on the African plains, and Viktor liked those programmes, but these deer were unrecognizable . . . There was a bear in a concrete pit, pacing as if demented, and the children gathered above it and shouted for its attention.

He crossed a canal of stagnant filth, walked over the footbridge, the children tripping and dancing in front of him. He saw the cause of their excitement. Near to the side fence of the zoo park, was another concrete bunker. The old sign said it was the home of the hippopotamus. But the teacher dashed the enthusiasm.

'No, children, I am sorry. There are two hyenas from Africa that we are going to see. There are no elephant and no rhinoceros, and no hippopotamus – soon they will be here, but they have not arrived. Listen to me, children . . . Before the great Patriotic War the zoo was filled with animals, but most were killed and eaten by the German Fascists then living in Kaliningrad before the city was conquered by the Red Army of heroes. Only four animals survived the war – one deer, one fox, one badger and one hippopotamus. When the zoo was taken, our soldiers found the hippopotamus and loved it and tried to save it. It would not eat. It was dying, it had been traumatized by the fighting and by neglect. After many days, as it starved, and the soldiers despaired, the decision was taken to try vodka . . . Yes, *vodka* . . . For two weeks, four times a day, the hippopotamus was given vodka, and it is remarkable but the hippopotamus regained its health. Until it died, it was the best-loved animal in the zoo, and the symbol of the zoo is that great creature . . . It is promised that soon there will be another here. Now, come on, keep together, and we will find the hyenas.'

He could no longer hear her. She led the children away. He looked again at his watch. Four o'clock and two minutes. He had to stop. It would be hard to be natural. If he had had a cigarette to smoke it would have been easier, but he had no cigarettes, and no guidebook to look at. He saw the man on the far side of the hippopotamus pit, and caught his eye. The man stared back at him. He turned, breaking the rule of dry-cleaning, and there were two more men who stood and watched him, not caring that he had identified them. Far at the back, his hair receding and the wind lifting the wisps of it, was Piatkin. They were all around him, within three or four seconds' running of him. He could only wait: it was where he had been told by Alice that he should be. A stocky man, with a little stomach paunch disguised under artisan's overalls, came into his eyeline, and carried with him two filled plastic bags, as if he had been to do shopping. The man was on course to collide with Viktor or to brush against him. The man's head seemed to bob down and for the briefest moment it rested on his collar-bone, and Viktor saw that his lips moved.

* * *

'Delta One from Delta Two. Going in for the brush on Target One. I confirm there are bandits. Stand by, stand by. Delta Two out.'

Billy Smith knew that brush contacts were the hardest, were to be avoided like the plague. In a brush, a message was passed, verbal, or a scrap of paper was palmed. It was bloody difficult . . . His hand rested on the pistol butt between his legs.

The man came on, sauntered towards Viktor.

Viktor looked away from him. He looked to the right, for the contact's approach, and then to the left. It was bad tradecraft but he could not help himself. Where were they? Why did they not come? Around him were the watchers. The man who looked like an artisan came closer, slow and relaxed, and Viktor thought he had taken time from work to shop and now took a shortcut across the zoo park to go back to whatever he did – builder, plumber, engineer, fitter – and Viktor could not see the contact and it was now four minutes after four o'clock. He felt the beat of his heart. He could not see the contact, only the watchers who were twenty, thirty metres from him. He was not trained in counter-surveillance, nor in evasion. Those were not the arts of a chief of staff to a fleet commander. The man, the artisan, came past him, close. He heard the words, at first hardly registered them, in Russian.

'I'm from Alice. Follow me in ten. Go where I go.'

Viktor rocked. The man was past him and walked away, whistled a tune to himself and had no care. His Russian had been flawless, but in the idiom of a classroom, and the accent foreign. He began to count. *One* and *two* and *three* . . . what should he think of as he counted? *Four* and *five* and *six* . . . He thought of the sun sinking on the city and its bright warmth flooding his face, and the early sun of the dawn the last time he had been with Alice. *Seven* and *eight* and *nine* . . . He thought of where the sun never reached, at dawn or dusk or in the middle of the day, and his mind had a picture of a prison yard with a heavy mesh grille over it, and the handcuffs cutting his wrists and the men who held his arms on the walk from the barred door to the yard's centre, where the drain was, and ahead of him, already uncoiled and ready, was the water-pipe leading from the tap. *Ten* . . . His legs were knocked from under him, and he knelt . . . The man was walking away from him, and the speed of his stride quickened.

Viktor followed. He had to kick his feet forward to move. There were no children now to watch, no teacher to listen to. He had spotted the watchers ahead of him, and when he went to the right of the bear pit and could see the demented beast pacing the concrete and scratching at its own shit, another watcher was on the far side of it. They hemmed him in. Another was separated from him by the pen for Arctic foxes. And they would be behind him, tracking him, and at the back – he did not need to turn for the evidence of it – would be Piatkin with his radio. Even with the weight of his legs slowing him, and the shudder of his heart's pulse, he wanted to break and run, to chase the man in front of him . . . It was what they wanted. Then they would close on him. When Viktor stopped, the watchers on either side of him stopped. He started off again, and they did. He veered away from the direct route, the way the lone man in front of him had gone, and went to the left of a solitary caged elk that had a broken horn. It was a choreographed dance, the steps co-ordinated. He could not break the tempo of it.

His eyes misted with tears. The back of the man ahead was blurred. He could see four watchers, beside and in front, as they moved in the dance towards the perimeter fence around the zoo's park, but there could have been ten, or fifty, or an army. They trapped him. Viktor walked in an avenue of overgrown, rubbish-strewn flower-beds, with the watchers. The fence was in front of the man. It was hard for Viktor to see clearly. At the fence, behind a clump of birch trees, off the path, the man hesitated, stopped but did not look back. Viktor stopped. They all watched him, faced him. Viktor realized the skill of the man who had made the contact; they had not seen him, had not noticed him. Viktor blinked to clear the wet from his eyes . . . The man ducked down, and was gone.

Viktor saw the hole in the fence, half masked by the trunks of the birches.

Through the hole was freedom. The point of escape, little more than a hundred metres ahead, beckoned him. He could hear the rumble of traffic behind the hole and the trees, and he saw the upper part of a lorry's cab speed past. He forced himself to step out, punching his feet forward. The pace of the watchers quickened. He started to trot, and they matched him. He sucked the air down into his lungs . . . a few more seconds, a few more metres, and the hole gaped wider. He went faster, a longer stride than when he was on the beach. The watchers ahead, as if marionettes and controlled, as if they had long rehearsed the steps, turned, faced him, and the two watchers on either side of him each cut across the mud and weeds of the flower-beds and a line of them formed and blocked the way to the birch trees and the hole in the fence. Viktor slowed, the sprint to the jog, the jog to the walk. He was a few short metres from them. They gazed back at him; no mercy in their eyes. He heard the clatter of heavy feet behind him.

Viktor looked through the trees, and through the hole gaping in the fence. An old Mercedes was parked against the far kerb. He was blocked.

The watchers stood in his path. The fists of one were clenched in black-leather gloves. The hands of another were buried menacingly in the coat pockets as if they concealed a weapon. One held a Makharov pistol close against his body, poised to raise it and aim. Viktor had no hidden weapon, no protection.

The back door of the Mercedes was held open. The man who had brushed against him, whispered the message, who had given him Alice's name, was framed in the door. Another man was in the back, hardly visible. Two more were in the front. He could see, through the trees and the fence, across the road and into the open door, that the man who had brushed him now jerked his head. *Come . . . come . . . for fuck's sake, come.* They waited for him. In a moment, Viktor knew it, if he gazed any longer at the open door of the car he could not reach, one of the watchers would turn to follow his sight line. So slowly, imperceptibly, Viktor shook his head.

He turned on his heel. He heard behind him a door slam and a car drive away at speed. He walked briskly back towards the hippopotamus pen, the caged elk, the bear's pit and the concrete den of the Arctic foxes. He dropped his entry ticket into an overfilled rubbish-bin, went out through the gates, and unlocked his car.

Viktor would be back in Fleet Headquarters in an hour, back with his telephone and the filled in-tray. The next day or the day after, he thought he would be arrested.

He had cried for help . . . been heard . . . They had come . . . It had failed. He sat in his car and his head rested on his arms. The wheel took the weight of them, and Captain, second rank, Viktor Archenko wept. It had been the one chance and the last chance.

As he lurched in the speeding car, Billy sent the message on the communications gear half out of the glove box in front of him: 'FERRET ABORTED'.

'Don't know whether it'll get through,' Billy said. 'Not with us being down here and all the crap around us . . . You saw his face? Fucking haunted, poor bastard, poor wretched . . .'

Ham mimicked the grate of Billy Smith's East London accent. ' "You don't want to lose your beauty sleep, ma'am. We'll bring him out." Oh, yes.'

Eyes never off the road, taking the turns called by Jerry the Pole, Lofty said, 'Not our fault – we did what we could.'

'But it wasn't good enough,' Billy said, and the bitterness rang through the car.

10

> Q. Where, between 1709 and 1711, did plague claim more than a
>   quarter of a million lives?
> A. Kaliningrad.

Three times Locke had said, with anger in his voice, that they must have fouled up, and that was why the communications had stayed silent, and three times Alice had stubbornly answered him: 'They could have been in a dead hole when they lifted him, and then they're on the road and too busy, and then it's cross-country and they've more to think about.'

Hope died for Alice, and confirmation came for Locke, when the headlights of the old Mercedes picked them out beside the road. They were two miles back from the border, and a mile and a half short of Braniewo. The lights caught them, blinded them, and Alice snapped out of their car and ran to the Mercedes. Locke had the engine running and the rear lights threw a dulled reddened glow on to the wind-screen of the Mercedes when it pulled up behind them. He saw Alice at the driver's window and he saw the explanation from Jerry the Pole – and a helpless shrug. She didn't come back to the car where he sat but paced around him in a circle. Her head was down as she walked at the edge of the darkness. He wasn't going to beg, wasn't going to call across to her: 'Excuse me, if it's not inconvenient, would you mind telling me exactly what has happened?' He didn't have to be told, because Jerry the Pole's shrug was enough to educate an imbecile. It was what Gabriel Locke could have told them a week before, and had done, and had not been listened to: '*There's nothing to be done. I'd call it a pragmatic approach, the real world against a bygone age of sentiment and emotion . . .*' He'd said it. He could hear his own words. He remembered the calm appraisal of the Hereford major. They should have listened. If they hurried, stamped on the accelerator they could be back in Gdansk by mid-evening, across the German border by the small hours and into London by mid-morning. They came out of the ditch.

He counted. From their body shapes, and the slight light available, he counted the four of them. They were peeling off their overalls, the ditchwater running off them. Locke left his car. He had the right to be told, but would not beg. He looked into Billy's face, but the man turned away and worked at pulling the leggings of the overalls down his thighs and shins. Locke went to Ham. He remembered the man in his cell, his arrogance and his Russian: '*Yes, I'll do that. No problem, I'll go to Kaliningrad.*'

Ham said, 'We did what we could, and what we were asked to do. It was slick, it might have worked . . . What happened? OK, I'll tell you. He came into the zoo and we were in place with enough time to do a good recce. We'd spotted this place where there was a gap in the fence and then a drop down on to a fastish main drag. We were there and could have made it away quick. We saw him, he was on time, there on the dot. That zoo is a dump. You'd have to be sad to want to go there. Maybe there are too many sad people in Kaliningrad, but not too many of them were in the zoo. Apart from a few kids it was near empty . . . I saw him, doing what he was told to do, and I saw the tail. You said he would be under "close surveillance", but that didn't tell the half of it. Before I went close for the brush approach, I reckoned there were six of them, with a back marker doing the radio control, and there were more men behind the back marker, but standing off. The ones standing off, I thought they were the head honchos, the big guys – you get to sniff them – especially one of them. Anyway, they moved in a box, classic stuff, except that they didn't seem to make any effort not to show out. It was like intimidation. Like they wanted to be seen, and wanted to pressure him. OK, so that's a tactic – build on him, break him. Any way he looked he would have seen the box. But it wasn't clever. The eyes were on him, not on me . . . I did a really good brush. I went past him, eleven words – that's a touch under four seconds of speech – and I told him what to do. We never had eye-contact, and I was moving all the time.

I did it well, and I know that because the box didn't pick me up . . . I have to say, with that box round him, I'd have been justified in quitting before I brushed him . . . He was in uniform but with a coat covering his tunic, all smart, like he'd just left the office or wherever, just as he should have been, not carrying anything. I didn't see him again, not till I was at the car. I couldn't turn and watch him, not with the box around him. I should have been picked up, but I wasn't, and that was sloppy of them. They only had eyes for him. I went down through this hole, got across the road and to the car. We were all ready to go. From the car, door open, I saw him. He'd have had to fight through those bastards, and at least one had a weapon. We weren't shouting, of course not, we were *willing* him – for fuck's sake, go for it. All of us were. If he had, if he'd broken through, got across the road, if Billy had fired over them and kept their heads down for the necessary seconds, he'd have been in the back of the car, and Lofty would have been doing the business, and we'd have had not a hope in hell, not a snowball, of getting through. He looked, just a moment, at us, and then he turned away. It was sensible and realistic, and it saved us from some real shit. He walked off like we weren't there, like the tail wasn't. That's what happened.'

Locke said, 'It was futile, a waste of everybody's time. Let's get out of here.'

What surprised Gabriel Locke, they didn't hurry themselves. Billy was still bowed and shook the ditch-water out of his boots, and Lofty held tight to Alice. Ham rolled a cigarette and lit it. Wickso produced a metal thermos flask and poured coffee or tea from it into its cap and passed it round, but Locke wasn't offered any.

'Are we going to stay here all night?' Locke demanded. 'It fucked up as it was always going to. What do you want – a tent? Are you intending to bivouac here for the night? I said, let's go.'

But they waited until Billy had dried out his boots, Ham's cigarette was smoked, and Wickso's thermos was finished. Then they were ready. Lofty had his arm round Alice and they went in a tight group towards the old Mercedes. Billy took the front seat and the rest of them squashed into the back, with Alice perched on Lofty's lap.

Before he closed the door, Ham said, 'Mr Locke, one last thing. We came out clean because of him. He had the guts to walk away

206

from us. If you'd seen his face, you wouldn't be talking like such a fucking prat.'

The door slammed.

Locke drove after them, alone, and Ham's venom played in his ears.

The cell had been warm and the mattress in it had been comfortable. If the woman had stood up in court, and he'd gone down, Ham Protheroe could have survived a year banged up in gaol. Not liked it, but survived it . . . She wouldn't have gone to court. She'd have cracked, pulled out, looked to keep her dignity intact. For fourteen years no one had ever come to him, asked something of him, wanted his help.

Not his parents in the Cheshire suburb after he'd 'borrowed' from them. The photographs of him, they'd promised, were out of the frames, shredded and bin-dumped – and he was out of their wills. And he was out of the 'Royals' and out of the Squadron. Russian linguist and communications expert, Ham was thirty-nine years old, and a little boy lost – an evacuee kid on a train going nowhere, but with the label identifying him torn off. There was no love in his life. When the body had been lifted from the water, when the bleak-faced bastards of the local Crime Squad had interrogated him, he had lied and had not broken, but when he had gone out of the interview room they had not hidden their contempt for him. For twelve years, without a family, he had lived off lies.

Why was he there?

Locke – the 'fucking prat' – had taken him out of the police station and given him back his family. It was like he was again in the snow and on the ice, or in the canoe, in the wastes and fjords of northern Norway – and like he was back on the exercises when they climbed the steel ladders of the oil-rigs while the North Sea pounded below, and like he was back on the yomp treks on Exmoor and across the Brecons, like he was back with his pride.

It was, for Ham, a purging, a cleansing, of the stench of that contempt. He had walked the Damascus road. He had allowed himself to be recruited to get the smell of it from his nose.

* * *

Locke parked by the marina, not in the lit yard available to the Excelsior Hotel's guests.

The Fiat was still there. A couple kissed on a bench near to it. Locke walked past the car, past the couple, and towards the pontoon bridge – against common sense and tradecraft's rules. He should not have gone near the car, should not have approached the bridge that led to the moorings. He looked down. There were low lights on the pontoon and on the piers, but brighter light from the high floodlit buildings of the old city on the far side of the river was thrown across the marina, and more light came from the cafés and restaurants. The reflection of the light helped him, and he knew where to look.

He could not see the trousered leg, or a flash of white skin that would have shown between the trouser turn-up and the sock, but he could see the shoe. It was between a bag of white plastic and a floating container that had held lubricating oil before being thrown overboard. All day the shoe had been there and had not been noticed . . . If he had walked out on to the pontoon bridge, stepped along the spaced planks, he might have peered down because he knew where to look and, through a gap in the planks, he might have seen the eyes of the man he had murdered.

Locke drove his car into the hotel's yard. He collected his key at Reception and was asked whether he would be dining in that night. He declined a table, and went to his room. For a full minute he leaned against the closed door, then went to the bathroom and sluiced his face with cold water. While it ran and splashed on his skin, he saw the shoe move in gentle motion beside the pontoon.

He drove to the meeting, and would be late.

'Ah, the estimable Mr Locke . . . We were almost starting to worry about you. It's never a good meeting without its conscience present . . . I'll recap in a moment, for your benefit, so's you're not in the dark. Please excuse me.'

The smile, Locke thought, on Mowbray's face had the chill of a January storm blowing off the cliffs on to his father's farm. The team were packed into the cabin. A cat could not have been swung there. A map was spread over the bed and they were sitting, kneeling, squatting round it; Alice was beside the porthole window with her notebook. Mowbray had taken centre stage, and Jerry the Pole guarded the door in the narrow corridor, stood flush against it, but was the outsider, not on the inside. Jerry the Pole had to knock twice before it had been opened to Locke.

'We're all here, Gabriel, bar the master, who was present for the first half-hour of our meeting but has now left to prepare for sailing . . . It's been a good, productive meeting, but would, I'm sure, have been all the better for your usual valuable contributions. Again, excuse me. So, that's it, gentlemen. I've told London it can work. I never travel with only a single option in my backpack. I have always believed in the inevitability of the unexpected. Proof against the unexpected is a second option. I've told London that it can work if we have reasonable good fortune – which is a fair evaluation, wouldn't you say? But, and it is a huge *but*, it is not I who will be fulfilling this second option, it is you, gentlemen. Twenty years ago I would probably have been with you. I won't be there, you will. I've lost track of the days, happens with age, but however many days back it was, at that revolting place in Surrey, I said to you all, "If any of you wish to leave, now would be the correct moment." Are there any changes of heart?'

In the silence, Locke heard a slight scratching outside the cabin door, then a soft thud, then a dog's yelp, and the silence came again. Alice never looked up from her notepad. Billy's fingers still scratched the hair on his neck thoughtfully, and Lofty used a toothpick aimlessly in his mouth while gazing at Alice. Locke looked at the floor. He would speak when the room was cleared, not in front of them all when he would be ridiculed. He saw his scuffed right shoe where he had tripped as he had come on to the *Princess Rose*, taking the step down from the gangplank. When he looked up and his eyes roved over them, he was drawn to Ham's quiet, incessant tapping with his finger on the map. It was the map he had seen at Poole, the admiralty chart, number 2278, covering the navigational approach to Baltiysk where the Baltic Fleet was based. He saw the flecks of grey in Billy's hair, and Ham's little paunch, and wondered why none of them spoke up.

Mowbray's voice boomed into the void. 'All on board? Thank you, gentlemen. What the great man said: "I see you stand like greyhounds in the slips, Straining upon the start. The game's afoot." Well done.'

'I don't think we know that one, Mr Mowbray,' Wickso said.

'Henry the Fifth, Act Three, scene one.'

They filed out. Ham held a slip of paper and seemed to read it. His lips moved and Locke caught the murmured words, Russian. Alice lingered, her fingers loose on the pendant at her throat; he hadn't looked to see whether the men still wore their gifts. Her face was set, her lips tight, narrow, and a frown cut her forehead, like she carried a burden. Of course she had been upset when it had gone down, when Lofty had held her. It was as though she knew Gabriel Locke was spoiling for the fight. Mowbray glanced at her: he nodded momentarily and his finger pointed to the door. Their eyes met, Mowbray's and Alice's, like they held a mutual secret, and Mowbray smiled at her, as if he had no concerns and neither should she. As she went by him her hand brushed the tweed of his jacket. Locke was on the outside, as cut off as Jerry the Pole, who guarded the door from the corridor. He'd bloody well change that.

They were alone.

Mowbray said, 'A great shame you couldn't make the meeting, Gabriel. Anyway—'

'I think we've exhausted the sarcasm.'

'Anyway, where we are is . . . From the top. The *Princess Rose* sails tonight, but makes slow progress. Shortly after the pilot leaves us – that is the crew, myself and our Dogs of War – when we are off Russian territorial waters, we will again suffer recurring engine trouble. The weather forecast is a blessing, a most welcome bonus. We will drift on a roughening south-westerly towards Kaliningrad. Tomorrow evening, as soon as we have darkness, the Dogs will go ashore by inflatable dinghy, with a landfall on the Baltiskaya Kosa. As members – I correct myself – former members of an élite force they have been trained for this. They will meet Ferret, and will – with him – return to the inflatable and ferry him back to the *Princess Rose*. Our engine trouble will miraculously disappear – and we head off into the great blue yonder, like we're a porpoise with a killer whale up our tail. You, with Alice, will—'

'That's insane,' Locke spat. 'Utter madness.'

'If you had been here, Gabriel, instead of being wherever you were, you would have heard the Dogs' evaluation of acceptable risk. They're on board.'

'Because they're losers. Look at them.' Locke's voice rose, bounced off the cabin walls. 'You should be ashamed – you've manipulated them, you old fool. They're no-hopers. You've lied to London.'

'An "old fool" perhaps, Gabriel, but a bare-knuckle fighter for all that. The lesson of street-corner fighting, as I've learned it, is always get the retaliation in first. You understand me, Gabriel? London's with me . . . Want to find that out for yourself? Give Bertie Ponsford a call. Secure communications here. Try Peter Giles. Don't like the sound of that? Give the director general a ring, have him pick up his blue phone. Got a job in the City lined up, have you? I wouldn't ring, if I were you, Ponsford or Giles or the DG, if I hadn't alternative employment arranged. They're so excited, all of them . . . Just marking your card, Gabriel, and meant kindly.'

'What I think—'

'Do I need to know what you think? You, barely off the training course . . .'

'I think you have deceived London.'

'They are adults, used to making up their own minds. Do you actually believe they will welcome doom and gloom from you, been nowhere and done nothing? Your choice – try it.' Mowbray waved expansively to the communications box that was wired to a laptop on the table across the cabin from the bed.

He could not. He was beaten, was boxed as tight as Codename Ferret had been in the zoo park that afternoon. He could make a report, but *afterwards*. With the operation sanctioned, he could not take a negative tack. Mowbray beamed at him, as if recognizing victory. Locke blistered him.

'You're on the shelf. You've wheedled your way back in, but at a cost. You're living off your ego glands, vanity's your food. You're too conceited to admit the failure of your preposterous plan, so you dig a deeper hole and will drag others down with you. All the bullshit you've peddled will spatter in the fan—'

'You disappoint me, Gabriel.'

'I want out. Damn you, don't you listen? *Out*.' But his head hung. He was beaten, could not tell his part of the story. 'And he's a traitor,' Locke said sullenly. 'He's not worth it.'

For a moment Locke thought he was about to be struck. Mowbray's fist clenched, then caught at the material of his trousers. The voice was quiet, conversational. 'When you get back, Gabriel, to London, I would like you to ask your line manager for permission to take a day in Library. Read about Popov and Penkovsky, read about the agents betrayed by Blake, Ames and Hanssen, read about the men whose names had crossed Philby's desk before they were parachuted into Estonia or Lithuania or Latvia, or sent by fast boat to Albania. Read about the deaths of brave men who were beyond reach. Will you do that, Gabriel?'

He was surly: 'That was decades ago.'

'Always know your history, Gabriel, it's what I teach my students. Without the clothing of history on your back then you will walk naked . . . Now, where were we? Yes, you with Alice, and Jerry the Pole to drive you, will go up the Mierzeja Wislana, the Polish end of the sandspit – before it becomes the Baltiskaya Kosa – right up to the border, and that's where you will get the best communications from the Dogs when they're ashore. You'll be my half-way house, my relay point. You up for that, Gabriel?'

Locke nodded grimly.

'Why don't we have a drink, eh? A good, stiff Scotch, yes?'

Locke said, 'If this goes foul, which it will, I give you fair notice that I will report on every aspect of this piece of lunacy. Any reputation, under the Old Farts Act, which you may now enjoy will be in tatters. I will do what I have to, but I promise you I will not take a single step forward, not even half a step shuffle, beyond what is required of me . . . and I'll see you rot.'

'Don't tell Alice that, there's a good fellow. Scotch straight or with bottled water?'

Locke left him.

A policeman, given its description and its registration number, found the car. He circled the Fiat warily. He could see the briefcase in the back, between the children's seats, and the flap of it hanging open. He noted that the driver's door was unlocked. He called in, radioed his news.

The radio waves were flooded. The consulate in Gdansk called the embassy in Warsaw. The resident at the embassy called the Lubyanka. The necessary officials at the Lubyanka, now alerted, called the consulate in Gdansk and demanded an immediate response: What had been found in the car? Were there indications of where the official had been? A further flurry on the radio waves between the consul and the Lubyanka: Was the briefcase empty? Was the car close to the Excelsior Hotel? The briefcase, as collected by the consul from the Gdansk police headquarters on Nowe Ogrody where the lights burned late, was empty except for the missing man's personal organizer – the car was parked two hundred metres from that hotel. The Lubyanka forbade, in the strongest and most direct language to the consul, that any reference to the man's employment in the ranks of the Federalnaya Sluzhba Bezopasnosi should be made to the local police. An unaccounted-for sheet of photographs of Britons working for the Secret Intelligence Service vexed the Lubyanka's section. More radio messages, coded or scrambled, passed.

Yuri Bikov was informed at the room in the Kaliningrad complex of the FSB where he worked late . . . and Vladdy Piatkin was woken from his bed: 'If we send our own people,' Piatkin was told, 'we admit our work in counter-intelligence activities in Gdansk. In the climate of relations with Poland that is unacceptable.' It would be well after midnight that Piatkin called back with a solution to the delicacy of the problem, and the radio traffic could slow.

There were three policemen now guarding the car while two detectives painstakingly examined it. One of the policemen, bored and cold, reached into his pocket for his cigarette packet. He took out the last cigarette, lit it, saw that he was not watched and threw the empty packet over the quay edge. He dragged on his cigarette and the smoke was carried off by the wind. He shivered and stamped. When he had finished the cigarette and it was down to the filter, he flicked what remained of it into the water. He could still see his packet floating away . . . and then it snagged close to the pontoon. If he had not thrown away the packet after taking from it his last cigarette, the policeman would not have seen the shoe.

The brigadier, intoxicated from the many drinks thrust into his hand, was the star of the Ministry of Defence party thrown in an annexe of the Moscow building. Only favoured foreigners were invited, those who would be impressed that the power of the Russian military reached far enough to pluck a favoured officer from certain death. Again and again, the brigadier told his story to a select few who had been ushered into the inner room off the outer salon. He did not, of course, name the young lieutenant colonel who had saved his life but spoke of him with an almost childlike gratitude.

'And, what is worse, I never had a proper chance to thank him. We met at the helicopter pad after I had been released, after he had come down from the high ground above the Argun gorge, and we immediately took off. It was impossible to speak in the helicopter, with the noise. We landed. I thought then I would have the chance to talk with him, to learn more about him . . . He has the reputation of being the finest interrogator in the whole of FSB, and so young and calm. We landed at Grozny, and an air-force jet was waiting for him. He was gone – another assignment. A matter of national importance. The general told me what he said to the interrogator, my saviour, "I would almost feel sorry for the next wretch that faces you." He is unique, formidable, and because he already targets another "wretch", I could not thank him . . . He is remarkable.'

Among those taken into the inner room was an artillery colonel from the Ukrainian embassy. In the outer salon, as the hospitality flowed, the Ukrainian colonel repeated the story to a Belarus major, who in turn passed it verbatim to a Swedish military attaché, who happened to have a lunch appointment the next day, a long-term commitment in his diary, with the British attaché.

Good stories were rare in Moscow, and were always passed on as barter to lighten the boredom of the posting to the Russian capital. The story of the interrogator's achievement was launched.

*　*　*

Bikov worked in his room at the FSB headquarters. He prepared himself. Papers from Moscow and local files were strewn across his desk. The next day he would strike.

His sergeant brought him coffee. His major was away at the base, making the final necessary preparations.

The message came through, decoded by his sergeant, that a missing FSB officer had been found; a body had been hauled from the river in Gdansk. The drowning of a junior officer in the Polish port city was a setback, but small in the scale of the interrogation for which he readied himself. The next day he would face Captain, second rank, Viktor Archenko across a bare room.

Fast notes were scrawled on his pad as he gutted the files and papers. He consumed them. The challenge lifted him, excited him and drove away his tiredness. He would break his prey by the skill of his questioning, by finding the weak point and then by launching his attack through the crack in the man's defences. The next day the notes would be abandoned and his eyes would never leave those of his prey.

Bikov was calm. He believed he controlled his destiny, and the traitor's.

The window of his hotel room was open to the night, and the traffic was far below. The noise blown through it by the wind would distort his voice and hide his accent.

Billy, Wickso and Lofty sat near him, there to give support to Ham. He was always the confident one. None of them had ever seen Ham as nervous and hesitant, but what was asked of him was harder than anything else he had attempted. He had good linguist's skills, but they were old and untested. He was asked to speak as a native would. Their bags were packed and piled by the door, their bills were paid, and by now Jerry the Pole would be waiting at the front entrance with the old Mercedes. The slip of paper given him by Mowbray was on the bed beside him as he lifted the phone, and dialled.

It rang out. Ham took a deep breath. He waited an age.

'Fleet Headquarters. Yes?'

'Night duty officer, please.'

Another wait, another age.

'Mikoyan, night duty officer.'

'Please, this is Air Force Headquarters, I am the exercise planning officer. I have a message for Captain Archenko, chief of staff to Admiral Falkovsky.' The air expired from Ham's lungs. He thought his accent was crap and his hand shook on the receiver. They were all looking at him, willing him to succeed, like they were family to him.

'Yes, the message?'

Ham breathed again. 'I wish to inform Captain Archenko that we will conduct a low-flying exercise over the Baltiskaya Kosa at 20.00 hours tomorrow, that is Thursday, the fourth of October. The line of the air assault will be east-west at the eight-kilometre-mark point from Rybacij. We invite Captain Archenko to attend.'

Ham heard the distant voice, 'I don't have his diary. I don't know if he is free to attend at this notice.'

Ham had read what Rupert Mowbray had written for him. He was now alone, cut adrift. For an eternity, the words, vowels and consonants gagged in his throat.

'You are there?'

'We believe the exercise would be of exceptional interest to Captain Archenko. It is the general's invitation. Space is severely limited. The invitation is for Captain Archenko alone, not a subordinate. Do you have it written down?'

'I do, but . . . I can transfer you to the senior officers' mess, or to Captain Archenko's quarters.'

Ham grated, 'I am a busy man. Find Captain Archenko, deliver my general's message.'

'Yes, it will be done.'

The phone slipped from Ham's hand. He rocked and the sweat trickled down his neck and his stomach. 'God, don't just sit there. Get me a drink.'

Viktor sat in total darkness.

There was a light and respectful knock at his door.

He had returned from Kaliningrad and had spent an hour in the outer room beyond the admiral's office working methodically through the remaining memoranda and messages in his in-tray.

When he had cleared them, he had gone to his room. He had eaten no lunch and had no hunger for dinner.

The quiet was broken by the rap at his door. He sat on the floor, his back against the foot of the bed. He didn't answer the knock.

He heard a slight scuffle at the base of his door, then the retreat of footsteps down the outside stairs. Although his curtains were drawn, an opaque, dulled light penetrated the room and he saw the folded sheet of paper on the carpet.

Viktor stared at it. Filling his mind was the snapshot image: the man approaching him, brushing against him, whispering the name of Alice, and the instructions. The words came again and again in his mind: *I'm from Alice. Follow me in ten. Go where I go*. And, still clear, the view of the car, the open door and the fence gap. Could he have run? Could he have burst through the line of watchers who blocked him? When he had been there, seen it and faced it, the answer to the moment of dilemma had been obvious. He would have been knocked down, they would have been taken at gunpoint from the car. Now, in his room, the doubt wormed in him. Then, he had been certain about everything; now he was certain about nothing. He crawled towards the door.

A ribbon of light, from the landing and the stairs, seeped under it. Viktor reached the folded sheet of paper. He opened it. He spread the paper on the floor, held it against the door and the light flooded it. A night-flying exercise. A location. A time. An invitation. He was confused. He crumpled the paper and tossed it into a black corner, where his bin would be. He was on his haunches, and the self-pity that was fuelled by fear . . . He yearned to be back in the zoo, to have again the chance to run.

He was jolted. He knew about drownings at sea. A man clung to a single straw if that was all he could reach. On his knees and elbows he crossed the carpet, groping for the crumpled paper. When he found it, Viktor stood, went to his bed and switched on the side-light. He blinked in the brightness. He took his diary from the drawer of the chest beside the bed, flicked the pages until he saw the necessary number, and memorized it.

He left his room, the door wide open, and slipped quickly down the stairs. He went out into the night air and scented the tang of the sea. Crossing the parade-ground, he sensed that watchers observed him, but did not turn to look at them. He could not use his own telephone, the one beside his bed. He strode towards the repair workshops down by basin number two. Only the night-duty sailors and engineers were there. Without explanation, he strode past the table where they sat, smoked and ate sandwiches, to the back of the workshop. There was a wall-mounted telephone.

He dialled the Kaliningrad code and the number.

'Good evening. This is Archenko, chief of staff to Admiral Falkovsky. You are NDO for air-force headquarters? You are, yes? Thank you ... Some confusion here. Do you have a night-flying exercise, low-level simulated bombing across the Baltiskaya Kosa tomorrow evening?'

The voice in his ear was abrupt. 'No, we do not.'

A faint glimmer of hope was born, as if a candle were lit. 'You do not have a night-flying exercise at 20.00 hours tomorrow evening?'

'Absolutely not. Good night, Captain.'

The light of a candle had guttered, now flared brighter.

Locke left the hotel. He had knocked on Alice's door, woken her, called to her, had dropped his bag and laid his note on it. By the time she'd opened the door the corridor was empty but for the bag and the note, and he was on the last flight of stairs, carrying a blanket from his bed and shielding it from the reception desk.

He saw the fierceness of the lights ahead of him, brighter now than when he had come back to the Excelsior. Then there had been spotlights, now there were raised arc-lamps that brought unreal daylight to that part of the quay and the marina.

The note he had left for Alice asked her to pay his bill when she checked out in the morning, bring his bag, and meet him in the fore-court of the railway station after she'd been picked up by Jerry the Pole. He'd given no explanation.

To get to the stone road bridge over the Motlawa, he walked fast past the marina and kept clear of the lights. They were bringing the body from the pontoon. Four policemen laboured under the weight of the stretcher and water drained off it. He saw the scene-of-crime photographer and the flashes from his camera. Detectives stood in knots and watched. The back doors of a hearse were open. Locke had imagined men coming to his door, the same detectives that he now saw, and battering on it, him being confronted with the night porter, and being asked to explain what he had seen when he left the Excelsior Hotel because he had followed the Russian out. What had he seen? If he claimed diplomatic immunity then he identified himself as an intelligence officer, and by now they would know the Russian shared his trade . . . two intelligence officers leaving the same hotel lobby within a minute of each other, and one dead, the other claiming he had seen nothing, heard nothing, knew nothing . . . He would not be believed. Libby Weedon, severe and remote, would be up from Warsaw before the first bloody cock crowed, and legal officers from London would be on the first flight. Would they protect him? Could he rely on them to play the diplomat's card for immunity? Do pigs fly? He had said, himself, with bravado: *Anyway, if he's in difficulty, this Codename Ferret, I cannot see that anything can be done for him.* Heads had nodded when he'd said it. The body went into the hearse. Locke walked head down as the hearse surged past him.

He crossed the historic city, which had been restored with love from the ravage of the world war's firestorm. He was on Mariacka and the clatter of his shoes was the only sound around him. The amber-jewellery stalls and the shops were shuttered, the coffee bars were closed, as were the tourist restaurants; the boutiques were barred. A notice in his hotel had warned of the danger of walking at night, on one's own, through the streets of the old quarter, and had cited the dangers from pickpockets, muggers, addicts, thieves. It was for that danger that he had left behind the warmth of his room. The beat of his own footsteps echoed back at him from the high buildings with ornate gold-painted decoration on their pastel-painted walls.

Locke wanted to run but dared not.

He reached the station. The departures board was empty save for a long-distance train south to Katowice, the straggling passengers milling under it. It was years since Gabriel Locke had been in a mainline terminus so late, with the flotsam who travelled through the night in upright seats. He went into the subway tunnel.

There were little groups of kids in it, some sitting against the tiled walls where the shadows of the shut kiosks darkened them, some already laid out flat on cardboard beds. He looked for a space. Vacant eyes watched him. He went the length of the tunnel and found a corner where the ceiling lights barely reached, the roof dripped and the wind came down the staircase ahead of him. He settled into the grime and wrapped the blanket tight around him. He snuggled under it. Here he felt, at last, safe ... His words laughed at him: *Cut him adrift, forget him. Not worth the hassle.* The train for Katowice rumbled on the track over the tunnel.

He had trouble with the key at the front door. The bulb had gone in the porch and Bertie Ponsford swore because he could not find the keyhole. As he shifted, he dislodged a geranium pot from its metal stand. A light came on upstairs, and that was enough for him to find the keyhole. He righted the stand and put the pot back in place.

Inside his hall, he threw off his coat. She was at the top of the stairs. 'Are you drunk, Bertie?' It was not a criticism.

'No, more's the pity ...'

Gail was coming down the stairs, tying the belt of her dressing-gown.

'... utterly sober, sadly – just couldn't get the key in the bloody lock.'

She sat on the bottom step of the stairs. 'What happened? What's going on?'

Around him everything was familiar and safe. It was a home that he and his wife had built over nearly thirty years of marriage. Paintings, the bric-à-brac of antiques fairs, little ornamental mementoes of foreign and domestic holidays, the wallpaper that they'd hung together two years before. It was all, he believed, threatened. The comfort of the castle was breached.

'Nothing happened.' Ponsford cracked his fingers. His post was on the hall table and he pecked at it, examined the envelopes that would hold bills and circulars, but didn't open them. 'We couldn't do the pick-up. Our man walked away, one direction. Our team drove away in the other.'

'So, it's all gone down?'

'No, no ... Dear Rupert, never underestimate dear old Rupert. The second plan is now in place. Believe me, I am not sneering, but

Rupert always has a second plan, and such a reasonable one. We're sending our team in by sea, can you believe that? We're sending armed men for a covert landing on Russian territory – and I've agreed to it. We all have.'

'You're not being serious, Bertie. What'll happen to us?'

He smiled sparkily. 'Early retirement, a carriage clock and a decanter, time for the garden – but the whiff of failure is banished by Rupert. He doesn't acknowledge the possibility of it. I agree to his pre-posterous idea because that way I show *élan*, and because I know that, ultimately, Peter Giles has to rubber-stamp it. Peter agrees because I have, and anyway it'll go to the DG. The DG agrees because I have, and Peter, and he will seem weak and fussy if he kills it. We're not the men of yesteryear, and we know it. We're not the glory-boys of the past but we crave a little hidden limelight.'

'I can't believe you're saying this, Bertie – if you're not drunk.'

'Did you ever read any of those First World War books, the origins? You know, mobilization, and railway timetables. The Austrians mobilized, so the Russians did. Because the Russians mobilized, the Germans followed. With German mobilization, the French had to start the process, and we were sucked in so as not to be left behind . . . There was an inevitability, once Rupert mobilized. I suppose, then, in 1914, men all around the chancelleries of Europe wondered when they could have acted and stifled the chance of war, but by then it was too late – and it's too bloody late now. We had our chance when Rupert bloody Mowbray turned up, like a bad penny, on the doorstep in the night. I didn't have the balls to send him packing. Ah, well . . .'

'You're doing a whinge, Bertie. Let's go to bed.'

The *Princess Rose* slipped her moorings.

The pilot took her out and towards the lanes of the Inshore Traffic Separation Scheme. Already, Rupert Mowbray had laid the ground; he was a master of disinformation. On his instructions, as the engineer had started up the diesel engine, the master had muttered to the pilot that the engine was sick, the power was uncertain, but he hoped it would last long enough to get the ship across the eastern Baltic with its cargo.

In the master's cabin, now the operational centre for the team, his Dogs, Mowbray stood by the porthole window. They were quiet behind him as they prepared their gear, the kit they would take ashore. Clear of the mouth of the Motlawa river, the sea caught the *Princess Rose* and rocked it, and that, he had been told, was good. They would be boxed up in the confines of the cabin until they were at the extremity of the Inshore Traffic Separation Scheme, until the pilot went down the rope-ladder and jumped for the deck of the boat that would collect him; and they must all be quiet. The pilot should not know more men were on board than was stated in the master's crew declaration.

The pilot took them to port and they skirted the headland. Mowbray wiped the porthole window and stared out. On the headland the monument was lit, a gaunt pillar rising up. He turned.

Their eyes watched him, pierced him, and the *Princess Rose* rode the growing swell.

'I've given, to London, the mission you will undertake a name, a fine name. This is OPERATION HAVOC. All of Locke's communications from the ground to me will include the word "havoc" . . . *"Cry Havoc, and let slip the Dogs of War."* "Havoc" is yours, gentlemen, not mine . . . Forgive me if I show slight emotion – God speed.'

Mowbray stood at the porthole until he could no longer see the floodlit monument, and the *Princess Rose* dipped, fell, rose again and ploughed towards the open water.

II

Q. Where is the distillery that produces the cheapest vodka liqueurs
in Russia?

A. Kaliningrad.

The *Princess Rose* drifted.

In the master's cabin, commandeered by Rupert Mowbray, the dog
had finally won admittance. For the dog, the mate's cabin or the engineer's was not home. Home was on the master's cabin floor by the bed,
and now the dog shared the territory with the weapons and the gear.
Billy had shared out the equipment, had allocated responsibility.

The freshening winds from the south-west pushed the *Princess
Rose* in a jagged north-easterly line up the coast from the exit of the
Inshore Traffic Separation Scheme.

Lofty had the weapons. They had been lugged up the narrow
ladder, through the entry hatch from the engine room and he had
made four heaps of them. They had talked about what they wanted,
what suited them, and what they could best remember from the
long-ago days. They were men not inclined to noisy exuberance, but
the sight of the weapons served further to quieten them. The heaps
made a square around the sleeping dog.

Each time he took a weapon from the black bags, Lofty – the
disciplines were not forgotten – checked the breech to be certain it
was empty then rattled the arming mechanisms and clicked the
firing trigger. He had a respect for weapons, dinned into him by
instructors at the commando training centre on the south coast of
Devon and at the base at Poole. The respect would never be lost.

Lofty had always been big with firearms, at Lympstone, at Poole
and wherever he had served in the happy days. He had been the one

who lingered in armouries, spent time with the men who were the custodians of weapons, and who read the magazines and the books cover to cover. For Billy he had laid out, by the dog's docked tail, a Vikhr SR-3 9mm short assault rifle with a rate of fire on semi-automatic of thirty rounds a minute and on automatic of ninety rounds; it had a maximum effective range of 200 metres. It was the right weapon for a leader who would take them where they were going. He knew that *vikhr* was the Russian word for 'whirlwind', and he judged it right for suppressive, defensive fire. With it were the six magazines he had loaded with the 9mm bullets.

By the sleeping dog's back legs, in the next neat pile, was Ham's firearm: a Model 61 Skorpion 7.65mm machine pistol. From a Czech factory, it was short, had a fold-over stock and was a *mafiya* firearm capable of intense volume of fire but effective only at short range. Lofty had seen the Skorpion fired on a range and would never forget the crashing punch of its power; it was for close quarters, in a building, on a stairwell, a last throw to drive back a superior force. He had loaded six more magazines and left them beside the Skorpion.

By the dog's front paws, Lofty had laid the weapon selected for Wickso, the OTs-02 Kiparis submachine-gun, in service with Russian interior-ministry troops; the range of the Kiparis was little more than 100 metres, but its rate of fire on automatic was higher than that of the Vikhr. It came from Kazakhstan.

At the dog's thrown-back ears, as it snored, was the hardware he'd chosen for himself. Lofty would be back marker when they had done the pick-up, when they moved back towards the dinghy and their beach-head. It was the AK-74 assault rifle with a 40mm mounted grenade-launcher. He had fired it on a range, he knew the procedure of reloading the grenades, four a minute on a bad day and five on the best day. The weapon would buy time if the pack followed them, closed on them. Lofty would be principal fire support: he had loaded ten magazines of ammunition for the rifle and had laid out beside them twenty high-explosive grenades, five more that threw out phosphorous, and six loaded with smoke. If it all went to hell, Lofty with the grenade-launcher was the last best chance they would have . . . Then there was a pistol for each of them, a Makharov and two magazines, useless but Lofty knew it would make them all feel better.

They drifted in the darkness and the navigation of the master was expert. Only rarely did they hear him use the main engine to correct the direction they took.

Ham handled the communications. A headset for each of them, with a bar microphone, plastic ear-pieces, and a control box to be strapped to their belts. His voice murmured as he tested each earpiece and each microphone, from the workbenches of a Bulgarian factory. When he was satisfied, he put the earpiece, microphone and control box on the pile beside the weapons and the ammunition.

The sea caught them, rocked them. It was the best sort of night they could have.

The kit was for Billy. He plundered the boxes. To each pile of weapons, ammunition and communications gear, he added a wetsuit, a pair of flippers, socks, camouflage tunics and trousers, boots from Slovakia, the night-sight goggles, the compasses . . . and the Meals to Eat, dry rations that had not been opened since their capture in the Kuwaiti desert eleven years earlier, which still carried the Russian instructions duplicated in Iraqi Arabic . . . and the condoms for keeping weapons' barrels dry, the webbing for ammunition magazines and stun grenades, the masks to keep the smoke out of their windpipes, toilet paper and clingfilm . . . and bergens, the inflatable waterproof bags, the sealed water canteens, the explosives and detonators . . . Like a housewife, Billy checked each item, and any label not Russian or Russian satellite was snipped off. They were deniable, and each of them had been taught – long ago, brutally – the science of Resistance to Interrogation.

The *Princess Rose* ducked, climbed, and the waves' swell battered them. None of them cursed it.

Wickso added to the piles around the sleeping dog. He had little to offer, but none of them cared to gaze at what he placed on their pile: an olive green package holding a first field dressing, what they called a 'sanitary towel', with the Cyrillic stamped print of the Serbian army, enough for one wound, but Wickso kept four for himself. A morphine syringe for each of them, but five more for Wickso. A single bootlace for each pile, but three more for Wickso, for tourniquets, and an indelible marker pen, which Wickso also retained. The others didn't look at the medical gear Wickso gave them, there was so little of it, and the creed of the Squadron had always been that first aid came second to carrying ammunition.

Billy went out into the night to do a final check on the dinghy that had been brought deflated and trussed to the *Princess Rose* off the Devon coast, the outboard engine and the gas bottles. The others would pack the bergens and the inflatable bags. They would be gone in an hour.

He clawed his way along the deck, above the holds loaded with fertilizer sacks, towards the stowed dinghy. By now they would be over the line on the chart that divided Polish waters from Russian sea space. Where they drifted, rising and falling, with the spray climbing to the deck, was marked on the chart as formerly mined, and they would be marked on the scanners of Kaliningrad radar. Above him, from the mast, behind the bridge and before the funnel, two red lights shone. They would be visible through the whole 360 degrees, and gave notice that the *Princess Rose* was NUC. They were Not Under Command, their engine had failed, they drifted, and he heard the master shouting into the radio that if he did not quickly regain power he would need to anchor. The white wave crests were bloodied where the red lights fell on them. It was the best of weather, enough to confuse the shore's radar. In the 'poppling' water, a dinghy with a low profile would not be seen.

Gabriel Locke slept, his arm around a girl and a youth's arm around him.

Alice looked down on him. The first of the fast-food kiosks in the tunnel were opening, the shutters coming down. The waft of new bread and fresh pastries filled the tunnel and overwhelmed the stench. She would not have known him if she had not recognized the blanket from the hotel. The tunnel was filling with the early rail passengers, and the vagrants, for whom it was a night home, were scattering.

He woke when Alice put her toe against his shin and prodded him.

He blinked at her. He loosed the girl and shook off the youth. The sides of the girl's scalp were shaved. The youth's hair was overgrown and tangled but his beard had only a flimsy strength, and a ring was set in his lower lip. Alice held out her hand and Locke took it. As soon as she felt the clasp of his fist, she jerked him up. He rubbed his eyes.

'I was waiting upstairs, where you were supposed to be,' Alice said. 'I waited ten minutes. I thought you might have come down here for a coffee, or a roll. What the hell are you doing here?'

Locke's eyes flickered nervously. He arched and stretched.

'Well,' Alice said, 'if you can bear to wrench yourself away from your friends, perhaps we can get on with our lives.'

She walked off, fast, towards the far tunnel exit. It was the sort of place, with its stink of shit and urine, that she hated. He must have run to catch her. Her arm was taken. She turned and saw his anger. 'Yes?' She could not break the hold he had on her coat sleeve.

'Don't play the bloody madam with me. Actually, they're rather nice people. I was alone, they talked with me – have you ever bloody talked with me? They wanted to share with me, their lives and their kindness . . .'

'Let's hope the needle was clean,' she said evenly.

He was shrill. 'It's charity. They found me, I was in crisis, they got me through the night. That I came through it is thanks to their charity. From you, Miss Fucking Organized Perfection, I get no charity.'

'Why do you need charity, Gabriel?' she asked, with mock-gentleness.

'Why do I need charity?'

'That's what I asked, Gabriel.'

'I need charity because of you . . . because . . .'

On the steps up from the tunnel, he loosed her arm. They spilled out into the smeared dawn light. Train passengers buffeted them. She walked ahead of him. Across the station's forecourt the head-lights of the old Mercedes flashed them. The wind was up. Leaves and rubbish were blown low and hard across the cobbles and bounced on her shins . . . She realized he had left the blanket for his *charity workers*. He was changed. Locke was different, altered, sculpted in a new way, and he had told her that she was responsible, and Alice did not know what she had done.

She left the back to him, took the front passenger seat.

'Right, Jerry, let's go. Sorry about the little delay. Let's hit the Mierzeja Wislana.'

The dry sand, lifted by the wind, pricked against Roman's clothes and found the folds, the tears in the trousers and the long-used jacket of the fisherman. It stung his eyes, although he had his hand raised to shield them.

The Mierzeja Wislana was his home, his life, his place. The sea, the beach, the pinewoods, and the lagoon behind were his birthplace and would be where he died. He swore a fisherman's oath, which he would not have dared to utter within the hearing of the Father who led the community of Piaski from the new village church. Time was running out and the autumn rushed to engulf them. Very few fishing days remained, and without them his income dried up; the winter's months were long and the strain of providing for his wife and five children, without money, was a burden.

He had risen at five, from habit, and had pretended to himself that he did not hear the wind singing in the electricity cables. His two-bedroom home overlooked the lagoon and was not exposed to the worst of the wind. He had left his wife and children asleep, and had walked through the forest, across the dunes and down on to the beach.

He swore because the weather that morning made fishing impossible. And Roman swore again because all of his fellow fishermen in Piaski village had read the singing cables better than him and had stayed in their beds. The yellow- and white-painted boats were high on the sand, above the tideline, and would remain there that day. His eldest girl, the Father said, was talented at the piano and would benefit from lessons – which cost money. His eldest son, the Father told him, had a brain for science and mathematics and should go abroad to university, perhaps to Canada – which cost more money than a fisherman could earn.

The sand stung him . . . It was impossible for a fisherman to earn the money necessary to pay for piano lessons and to send a student to Canada . . . He squatted down in the lee of his own boat, slipped a first cigarette of the day from the packet and cupped his hands to light it. He dragged on it, and a small spasm of pain fired in his lungs.

The sea thundered on the sand. When there was a big storm, small pieces of rough amber were left on the beach and he, his wife and the children would walk in a line to collect them, as would the families of other fishermen, and what they had collected in a plastic bag was sold to a shopkeeper in Krynica Morska, which was west along the peninsula, but the shopkeeper paid only a few *zlotys*, not enough.

Far out in the darkness and to the east, beyond the dawn's throw, Roman saw two faint lights, red, one above the other. He knew all the laws of the sea. Beyond the surge on the shore, the breaking waves and the white caps, a ship drifted and signalled that it was Not Under Control. It was in Russian waters, close to the old minefield that was said to have been cleared but was not trusted by the Russian fishermen who came out from Kaliningrad. If the growing storm did not soon drop then his boat and the other boats would be hauled higher on the beach for the winter. He would earn no money for five months or more. He laughed.

It amused him that the Russians would panic if a ship, Not Under Command, edged closer to their military shore where the missiles were and their fleet. He laughed until his throat hurt.

In a black 7-series BMW, Boris Chelbia was driven along the dual carriageway and into Gdansk.

At the Russian border posts that straddled the road between Mamonovo and Braniewo, his driver had powered past the waiting queues of vehicles to the front. Word had gone ahead. The inspection of documents was cursory: he was saluted and waved through. Boris Chelbia was a man of the highest importance, the mission entrusted him was of extreme delicacy; he was not Piatkin's man: Piatkin was his.

In the world of the Federalnaya Sluzhba Bezopasnosi, as it had been in the former times of the Komitet Gosudarstvennoi Bezopasnosi, informers ruled. Piatkin might have regarded Chelbia as his informer, and would have deluded himself: the reality was that the racketeer, who now called himself a businessman in import-export, sucked information from the FSB major, just as in the old days he had squeezed it from KGB officers. What he learned he paid for in cash and by carrying out small missions, for which there was great gratitude. The payments to Piatkin, and Piatkin's superiors, guaranteed that the opportunities of rivals were checked and that his own trade flourished. Out of Kaliningrad's docks and through its frontier posts, Chelbia exported narcotics from Afghanistan, refugees from Iraq and Iran, and weapons from the Russian Federation – the same docks and posts were the import point for whisky from Scotland, luxury cars from Germany, newly printed dollar bills from the United States of America and computer software from anywhere. He preferred to pay in cash, from the roll of banknotes that bulged his hip pocket, but occasionally a small task was given him which was in lieu of cash.

The matter entrusted to him was so delicate, of such sensitivity, that counter-intelligence officers of the FSB had not travelled from the Warsaw embassy, the Moscow headquarters or the Kaliningrad out-station . . . and it would cost them a high price. The cost to Piatkin, and Piatkin's people, would be heavy. He had never been involved in the movement of radioactive waste, weapons-grade enriched uranium or plutonium, and he understood there were many buyers. With the increasing gratitude of the internal security agency, that trade would come.

Boris Chelbia had his villa in Kaliningrad and an apartment block on the Côte d'Azur in France and a four-star 300-bed hotel on the Black Sea. He had investment accounts in the City of London, in Nassau and on the Caymans. Cash oozed from every orifice of his body, but he still went after it, with a ruthless drive, because money was as addictive to him as the refined heroin from Afghanistan that he shipped through the docks and over the frontier. Money was his Christ. A naval officer had come to his villa with a grenade in his hand and with the pin pulled. He had taken back a single heavy machine-gun, and ammunition. On the open market, Boris Chelbia would have received a hundred US dollars for the machine-gun, and the ammunition would have rounded its value up to a hundred and twenty-five dollars. But the whole shipment of arms from the base, going out buried beneath a timber cargo from the docks the next week, would fetch him two hundred and ten thousand dollars from the Lebanese. He had not understood the naval officer, had thought him a crazy man, but he had been cheated of a hundred and twenty-five dollars and that stung him. Piatkin had said that if he fulfilled his mission, he would earn the FSB's gratitude and would hurt the naval officer. No man cheated Boris Chelbia lightly . . . yet he had liked the naval officer's boldness, had admired him.

The car wound its way through the old streets of Gdansk. He had allies, associates, affiliates in the city, but this was work for himself. With his jet-black-dyed hair and his black Italian suit, Chelbia came like death's angel over the bridge crossing the Motlawa river.

The car stopped within easy walking distance of the hotel, near to the quayside and close to the marina.

As he stepped from the car, Chelbia saw a young woman bend at a bollard at the edge of the quay. Her hands held a small but bright bunch of flowers. Two children clung to her legs. He glanced at the sight, then turned away. It was of no interest to him. He walked to the hotel.

He was smartly dressed. He was the sort of customer the hotel craved. How could he be helped? Chelbia spoke fluent German to the young woman at reception. He had been a guest at the Excelsior a month before – and she was too polite to admit she did not remember him. The night porter had done a service for him, and had not been paid for it; regretfully he would not be in the city at the time the night porter came back on duty. It was irregular, of course, but could he be given the man's address so that payment and thanks could be made in person?

He was so grateful and his smile was so sweet. Boris Chelbia went to wake the man who had worked all night.

Without glancing at him, they walked past Viktor's desk.

Piatkin, the stoat, led and two men followed. One was middle-aged with his hair carefully combed, wearing a good civilian suit, carrying a briefcase of polished leather. The second man was younger, shabby to the point of scruffiness; stubble carpeted his chin and cheeks and he wore old jeans and a sweater on which strands had snagged and been pulled. There was long-dried mud on his walking-boots.

They passed Viktor's desk, and the communications clerk's, those on either side of the liaison officers and of the headquarters staff's specialists, and went to the final desk that guarded the fleet commander's door.

The second man, the unshaven one, the one who looked as though he had slept in his clothes, had a strong face. He was Viktor's age, not more. He had a hawk's eyes and a jutting, beaked nose, and he walked after Piatkin with supreme confidence. Viktor, involuntarily, shivered. Piatkin spoke, out of earshot, to the fleet commander's guardian – a severe woman, grey hair gathered in a meticulous bun, without humour and without emotion. She had been with the admiral for years before Viktor had become a chosen man. Viktor could not read her face, which was expressionless as she put down her pencil and, for a moment, tidied her desk. Then she was on her feet and knocked quietly at the door she protected. She went in and closed it after her.

He had shivered because he knew.

She came out and stood aside for the two men to go into the admiral's inner office. The door closed on them, and Piatkin stood, arms folded, in front of it.

Eleven o'clock in the morning. Always at eleven o'clock a trolley was pushed into the outer office, and the pretty young girl with the ponytail of blonde hair came with tea, coffee, hot chocolate and biscuits. Mugs and plastic plates for the outer office, bone china for the fleet commander. He had primed himself for his day, but was suffering. Work, the minutiae of it, and the glances at his watch were not filling the time he needed to pass until the late afternoon when he would make the journey to the rendez-vous. Endlessly, that morning and through the last night, he had covered that journey.

Viktor scraped back his chair as the pretty girl put hot chocolate – the drink he had every day – in front of him. He advanced on Piatkin. 'Excuse me, Major. I had not been informed that you had made an appointment to see the fleet commander. I—'

'Captain Archenko. I have no appointment to meet Admiral Falkovsky.'

'You should have told me.' Viktor attempted to stifle the choke in his throat. 'I always sit in on meetings attended by the fleet commander.'

Piatkin smirked. Viktor was a half-metre from him. They were chest to chest, chin to chin. It was Piatkin's grin, that of a stoat, that destroyed him. All eyes were on him. In such a moment, power was transferred. All of them in the outer office would have seen the way Captain, second rank, Viktor Archenko – who had the admiral's ear – deferred authority to a major of the Federalnaya Sluzhba Bezopasnosi. He should have run when he was in the zoo park, should have run when he was last at the castle at Malbork and making the dead drop, should have run when he was with Alice on the promontary by the monument at Westerplatte: he should have run but he had not.

He turned his back on the closed door and went to his desk. He had to hold the mug of hot chocolate with both hands to drink from it.

'I find it very hard to believe – no, impossible to believe . . .' Had there been a mirror in his office, and had he looked into it, Admiral Alexei Falkovsky would have seen the pallor of his face and the shock that widened his eyes. 'If what you say is true, then it is incredible, too incredible for me to comprehend.'

He could not doubt the man. In front of him, held tight in his fists, was a single sheet of paper from the Lubyanka that served to *introduce* Lieutenant Colonel Yuri Bikov of Counter-Intelligence (Military), and to *order* his full co-operation with the FSB officer. He could have blustered, shouted, but it would have achieved little and damaged him more.

'I have treated him like a son, trusted him.'

Damage was the key to it, the limitation of damage was the only sure route to his survival. He had had, throughout his thirty-eight years in the navy, acceptable relations with the men of the Federalnaya Sluzhba Bezopasnosi. He had played the game with them, had never sought to frustrate them. He understood their power, had recognized it when he was young and knew it now. Twice a year in Kaliningrad he met with an FSB general, took lunch with him, and wine, and they would gossip together about subordinates and rivals, the tittle-tattle of who slept with whom, who drank too much, who rifled his garrison of building materials for sale to the *mafiya*, and they would embrace at the end of the lunch. By the time his staff car was half-way back to Baltiysk he would have forgotten what he had said and what he had been told. But the power of the FSB was ever present . . . At each stage of promotion a serving officer would be vetted. If the vetting was negative that officer would not gain access to classified material. Without the access to secret files there would be no possibility of promotion. They did not have to love each other, but to live together as fleas and dogs.

'I don't doubt what you say, Colonel Bikov, but it is hard, *hard*, to accept. I think it would be easier to believe my wife is being fucked by a conscript. The bastard . . .'

Only on one occasion in his life had he deliberately refused an order from the old KGB. After he had taken control and ordered the stopping in the water of the Krivak-class destroyer, the *Storozhevoy*, on its flight to Swedish waters, he had led the boarding party that retook the ship from the nest of traitors, and had brought them back to Riga. Then, he had been ordered to hand his prisoners to the KGB's investigators, and he had refused. He had, himself, brought them down the gangway, taken them to the military prison and thrown them into the cells. Only then had he given the key to the investigators. It was the one time. Not for a moment did he consider that he should defend Viktor Archenko.

'You will find that no obstructions are put in your way by me. You have the freedom of my base, I guarantee it . . . but you understand that I am sick – a knife is in my back.'

A man such as this did not come on a wasted errand. If any other counter-intelligence officer had blundered into his office and laid down vague, unsubstantiated accusations, he would have grabbed his collar, twisted him round, frogmarched him to the door, then pitched him far into the outer office. Not this man, not this Bikov. There was a confidence, a serenity of calm, that spilled across the room. This man, Bikov, could destroy the long career of Alexei Falkovsky. For all of the gold on his shoulders and on his tunic's sleeves, for all of the seven rows of medal ribbons on his chest, he had sensed that his future lay in the hands of this man. Loyalty? Fuck loyalty . . . as Viktor, his *protégé* and proxy son, had fucked him. Already the worm was in his gut. What was his future?

At best – his mind raced – it was to end his life in a miserable tower apartment, with an inadequate pension, in the anarchy of outer Moscow or Murmansk, disgraced because a spy had operated under his nose, and had been given his friendship. At worst – and it chilled him as he offered the guarantee of total co-operation – he would be prosecuted for negligence of duty, locked up among the *zeks*, the criminal scum.

'What do you need to nail the bastard? Whatever you want I give you.'

The answering voice was quiet, matter-of-fact. 'I want evidence. I don't have it yet. I have only impressions of guilt, but not the confirmation of it. I am tasked to find irrefutable evidence. In these times, to arrest a senior officer and charge him with treason, with aiding a foreign power, which I believe to be Great Britain, with leaking every document that crossed his desk – that lay in your locked safe, Admiral – I must have evidence.'

'Where do you get that?'

'From interrogation, from a confession. Always a confession is . . .'

He was hunched over his desk, his voice was hoarse. 'Do you hurt him?'

On the journey of his career in the navy's upper echelons, Viktor had travelled with him. Viktor had sponged away his frustrations, had fixed anything he asked for, had protected and guarded him. He leaned on him, Viktor was his crutch. His ultimate ambition, to end his naval life as commander of the Northern Fleet, was being snatched from him. Fuck . . . fuck . . . but he could not bring himself to hate him.

'No.'

'You don't hurt him?'

'I will talk to him.'

'You *talk* to him . . . and he will condemn himself with talking?'

'Yes.'

'When does it happen, his arrest?'

'I am almost ready.'

His head was in his hands, his fingers masking his eyes. He was drained of life and strength. He was a man feared by those who worked for him. Officers and men stiffened when he glanced at them, were afraid of him. He felt himself shrunken.

'I don't want to see it.'

'Very natural, Admiral Falkovsky. Please do not communicate with him, do not order up any classified files, do not open any safes, do not take any calls, do not leave your office. Your attitude is natural because he was your *friend*.'

The door closed soundlessly on them. From his drawer he took a packet of Camel cigarettes from the carton Viktor had brought him. The tears ran on the old sailor's cheeks.

'I expected more of him – more fight, more argument,' his major said.

On the headquarters building the flags and pennants were whipped by the wind. The sun shone. It was a good autumn day and would have been perfect without the wind's bluster.

'Most men watch their own skin. Skin usually measures the depth of friendship,' Bikov responded.

Ahead of them was a squat concrete block that housed the military police and the offices of the FSB on the base. Only the final preparations remained to be confirmed.

His major persisted: 'I expected him to stand Archenko's corner, but he abandoned his man.'

Outwardly the block gave the same appearance as it would have the previous day, or the previous week. The difference was subtle. Inside the door was a desk and at the desk were two armed military policemen, who had not been there the previous day or week. On the first-floor landing, at the entrance to the FSB's rooms, was a table and, behind it, a third military policeman sat with an assault rifle across his knees. And, though the midday sunshine gave brightness and warmth, the windows of those rooms were covered with sheets of newspaper, the blinds were drawn, and from the smallest of the rooms all furniture had been removed. They surveyed what had been done at the supervision of his sergeant, but his major returned to the theme.

'I expected more from the admiral . . . Archenko is alone.'

'Not quite alone,' Bikov mused. 'He will have me. I will be his friend.'

* * *

The heavy machine-gun, the NSV 12.7mm, chattered on the range. The conscript, Igor Vasiliev, knew every working part in its body. Blindfolded, he could strip the barrel, the breech block, the firing chamber, and reassemble them. It was difficult firing on the open range on the sandspit, with the fierce cross wind, at 2000 metres. Between each burst of five rounds he checked the angle of the range's windsock and looked for rubbish blowing over the range. His hits on the targets were radioed back to the trench from which he fired. The other conscripts of 8 platoon, 3rd company, 81st regiment of Naval Infantry crouched behind him and watched, as did the instructors who had nothing to teach him, and his platoon sergeant. The latter was now cautious, wary, with him. It was midday. When he had finished shooting, and the barrel was hot, Vasiliev pushed himself up from his hunched firing position.

'I would like to shoot again this afternoon, because the championship—'

'This afternoon there is the navigation lecture, then the gymnasium.'

'I would like to shoot after the lecture, instead of the gymnasium.'

Because of the power of Vasiliev's friend, the chief of staff to the admiral, and because of his own guilt, the platoon sergeant buckled to him. 'You may shoot again this afternoon.'

In Moscow, at the table of a quiet restaurant on a street behind the Bolshoi, a place favoured by foreigners, the Swedish military attaché was being entertained by his British colleague. A second bottle had been called for. To repay the quality of the hospitality, the Swede was retelling his choice anecdote.

'Picture it, the interrogator returns to Grozny, to be fêted, to be the hero of a party where their disgusting champagne substitute will flow until the small hours – but he's not there. The star act is gone. Doesn't even have time for a shit, shave and a shower. The Lubyanka's sent a jet for him. He's top of the bill and he's gone ... What everyone wondered, down in Grozny – what's so important that the interrogator isn't allowed his moment in the spotlight? What they were saying last night to the esteemed Ukrainian, who told the valued

Belarussian, who told me, there has to be a scandal on the greatest scale, at the heart of this horrid place, for the interrogator to be called away from his moment of glory.'

'You didn't hear, did you – I don't suppose you did – what section of FSB the interrogator comes from? Did you?'

'Military counter-intelligence.' The Swede beamed. The second cork popped.

'My father was here,' Jerry the Pole said, and he chewed the toothpick.

'I'm sorry.' Alice bowed her head. Locke reckoned she couldn't think of anything better to say. Himself, he said nothing – nothing was appropriate.

Small flashes of sunlight danced on the barbed wire. By the gate, over which there was a platform to support a watchtower, a single cluster of fresh-cut sunflowers was fastened to the strands and their brightness competed cheerfully with the pinpricks on the wire. Locke counted thirteen strands nailed to the vertical creosoted posts, and there were four more off angled struts at the top, set so that a man could not climb the fence and break out.

'My father was here in the war,' Jerry the Pole said.

When they had left Gdansk, Alice in the back and Locke beside the Pole, the question of the pension – its non-payment – had once again been raised. The wheedling query: was there not something they, as decent people, could do? Mr Mowbray could do nothing, was there something they could do? Locke had said curtly, without enthusiasm, that he would look into it, a deflection. The old Mercedes had been on a long, straight road after the junction at Stegna: Jerry the Pole had cracked the silence and started again: he was as good and as loyal a servant as any ever employed at the Olympic Stadium, no work in Berlin was ever avoided by him. Alice had interrupted. Too much coffee at breakfast, she wanted a toilet. They had turned off the road, an avenue of beech trees. Locke hadn't noticed the sign, and they'd pulled into a wide car park, empty but for a solitary coach. Alice had been directed to the toilet, and Jerry the Pole had walked to the camp gate and bought two tickets.

'It is called Stutthof – that is the German name, you have heard of it? No? My father was here for three years.'

Locke looked stonily ahead. He thought an expression of extreme gravity, of stolid seriousness, was appropriate. He had heard of Auschwitz-Birkenau in the south, and Sobibor close to Lublin, and Treblinka, but he had not visited them. Too much work, not enough hours in the day, too much pressure . . . He would have said to Danuta, or when he met young Poles at symposia, that to live in the past was to live in a prison. He had never heard of the Stutthof concentration camp.

'Let's go,' Jerry the Pole said. 'Let's take a walk while she pees.'

'Why not? We'll do that.'

Locke did not know what else he could have said. His agreement was a politeness. The Pole rolled in front of him on weak hips, and Locke followed. They went through the open gate into an oasis of quiet. A teacher at his school, the comprehensive in Haverfordwest, had once said to the class that these were places where the birds did not sing. 'Ridiculous,' the kids had shouted in the stampede along the corridors to maths or Welsh language or economics. How did bloody sparrows know what had happened five decades before? Daft . . . He listened, and heard no birds, but there were layers of birch trees the far side of the wire ahead and at the side, beyond the huts. No birdsong came to him. They left the brick guardhouse behind them. The coach in the car park had brought schoolchildren from Düsseldorf, handsome teenage boys and pretty little Lolita girls: the Pole and Locke played a sort of tag behind them, not catching them, letting them do their tour of each hut and leave it before they went in. They saw the bunk beds, on two levels, and the little guidebook that had come with the tickets said that at the end four men had slept on each bunk on a mattress of compressed straw. They went into the hut that had been the bath-house, where half a dozen circular tubs would each have held six men for the few minutes allowed them to scrape off dirt and pick off fleas and lice. After the children had left it they went into the medical room where there were rusty, grimed trolleys; the book said it was where 'experiments' had been performed.

He fingered the book. Stutthof camp had been the first to open in occupied Poland. It had stayed open for 2,077 days, and 110,000 prisoners had walked through the gates, as Locke had. In the camp, 65,000 men had died from starvation, disease, lethal injections, hangings and gassings. There was dark gloom in the huts but the sunshine warmed his face each time they stepped outside. At the far end of the compound, beyond the wire but in clear view of the huts, was a single gallows, a vertical pole with a horizontal bar supported by a strut; a hook was screwed in under the bar's end. Locke felt sick. There were two more buildings for them to see – he wondered where Alice was, whether she now followed them or stayed by the car. A small brick building, near to which a candle burned in a vase, had a sign: Komory Gasowej. The children were all white-faced as they spilled from it. When they'd gone, Locke went into the gas chamber, stood in the cool chill near to Jerry the Pole and saw the ceiling hole where the crystals would have been shaken down on to heads below. The last block, newly painted on the outside to preserve its timbers from the weather, with a tall brick chimney at the far end, was signed Budynek Krematorium. He went to the door, pushed past Jerry the Pole, and stared in and saw, over the heads of the children from Düsseldorf, the open doors of the twin ovens. He turned away. The final piece of the panorama's jigsaw was two wooden rail wagons on a track that led into the shadowed depth of the birch forest. He strained to hear birdsong, and failed . . . He wondered what had happened to Mr Frobisher, who had taught history to the sixth form, whose words had been derided.

They walked back up the central path between the huts, the watchtowers and the wire.

His question was a long time coming, was crafted and rehearsed and, he hoped, showed sensitivity. 'Your father, Jerry, did he survive or did he die here? Did he die in that chamber or on that gallows, or was he shot? I don't suppose you know.'

'Die? Of course he didn't die,' Jerry said. 'Didn't I tell you? My father was the carpenter, was employed in the camp. He *worked* here.'

Locke stumbled. His knees went, and with them his balance. His hand groped out and caught the Pole's shoulder. He steadied himself. He knew nothing . . . The world around him, silent, was a mass of convex and concave mirrors that distorted. Everything had been

240

certain in the life of Gabriel Locke until the time he had sat on the bench at Malbork Castle, below the gaze of the Knights of the Cross – von Salza, von Feuchtwangen, von Kniprode and Markgraf Albrecht. Until he had reached under the bench's slats to retrieve the dead drop, everything had been clear, easy, simple. The agent was a traitor – clear. Mowbray was a dinosaur, a fossil of the old days – easy. He himself was the new modernist, the new broom, the new thinker – simple. What was Alice North? She was by the gate, her arms were across her chest, and she leaned against the post, as if admiring the sunflowers' bloom.

He hardly heard Jerry the Pole's litany. 'My father, Tomasz, was like every other man, he must work and feed his family. There were several of them, and the commandant needed them, these Poles. They were called "honorary Germans". What did my father do that was wrong? He backed the wrong throw of the dice, the loser's throw. For three years he worked there, and then we moved in 1942 to Krynica Morska on the peninsula – it's where we are going, and I will show you our former house, Mr Locke, and the cemetery where my grandparents lie before we go on to Piaski, and I think you will be very interested. At Krynica Morska my father was a foreman on the project to reclaim land from the lagoon, he supervised the prisoners' work. That was till February of 1945, and I was then eleven years old. We had to go. The Russians were coming. The camp was evacuated, and the "honorary Germans" and their families walked with the prisoners and the Germans to what is now Gdansk. Then there were trains to Rostock, and from Rostock there was a boat to Denmark. It was a great adventure for a small boy. My father settled in Lübeck and again found work as a carpenter. Six years later I went to Berlin, for a future, and five years from then I was employed as a junior interpreter, what your people called a "bottle-washer", at the Olympic Stadium. I learned from my father, Mr Locke. I only work for the winners, for Mr Rupert Mowbray . . . and I believe that you also, Mr Locke, are a winner.'

The mirrors destroyed him. Locke saw the shoe in the water. Death would have been in the drowned eyes as surely as it had been in the eyes of the men in the gas chamber, in the crematorium and below the gallows. The mirrors made the shoe huge.

They were near to the gate, near to Alice.

Jerry the Pole smiled at him. 'I think you enjoyed your tour, Mr Locke, found it interesting. Many of the huts my father built are gone, not because they were poorly built but people from the villages took the wood to burn in cold winters . . . Mr Locke, you are a kind and intelligent gentleman. Please, look into the business of my pension, please. May I depend . . . ?'

'Hear me, Jerzy fucking Kwasniewski, you bloody Fascist. Why not just shut up about your fucking pension?'

He walked past Alice.

She called after him, 'You all right, Gabriel? You look like death.'

He had no answer.

They'd made a basher.

The machine-gun, in the distance, had stopped firing. They'd been late launching off the ship, the outboard had been checked and checked again, but at the last check it had failed to fire. It had needed stripping and they'd drained the fuel then refilled the tank. The dinghy had handled like a pig in the white caps, but it was twelve years since any of them had ridden a dinghy in that sort of sea, in darkness. They'd sunk the dinghy a hundred metres off the beach, in four metres of water, they'd 'cracked the valves', as they called it, and the air had hissed and bubbled out of the dinghy's sides. They'd swum ashore, dragging their inflated bags with them through the surf – and still, just, had the cover of darkness. They'd scuttled over the sand, up on to the dunes, and then had run bent double for the pine-tree line. While the dawn was still black-grey, it had been Lofty's job to take a pine branch down to the water and brush away their footprints in the sand. Then they'd made the basher, and later the machine-gun had started up.

Lofty was there because he was from the dead. He talked with the dead each day, and took back his conversations to the lodging-room in the farmhouse at Passchendaele. The dead were his only friends. They were under the stones from which he scraped lichen, under the little beds of hoed earth that he kept free from weeds. The dead had no guilt . . . Not a day went by on which Lofty Flint did not recall his own guilt when he had worn a uniform. Every day of his working life the guilt seared into him, and the face of the drowned boy screamed at him. If it had not been for the rest of them he would have vomited up his guilt to the Crime Squad detectives, but they had given him the strength to cling to the lie, and it shamed him. All the dead, under their stones and flower-beds and mown grass, at Tyne Cot knew of the killing of the Irish crab fisherman, and they offered him no comfort. Only when he lay with them, when his life was gone, would he be free of the guilt.

He had no fear of the danger, only of the living hell of his existence. Twice, since he had gone to work for the Commonwealth War Graves Commission, Lofty had taken down a length of rope from the gardeners' store shed, and at the end of those two days he had bicycled away into the dusk, had gone off the straight flat road to the village and pedalled along tracks that led to the clusters of poplar trees that had been planted on the old pocked battlefields. He had intended to take his life. Once he had gone as far as throwing the rope up over a branch . . . he had not had the courage to take the coward's way. He had told them all, all the stones, on his last day, why he went, and where.

Lofty was a country boy. His childhood was from the woods and hills around a village close to the Surrey town of Guildford. He had made his own entertainment, played his own games, and knew how to manufacture a secret hiding-place that would only be found if it were stepped on. The basher they built under Lofty's supervision was more expert than any an instructor could have constructed. Where a pine tree had been felled in a gale, its roots lifted from the ground leaving a shallow sandy hole, the basher had been made and its roof was from fronds and dead branches. Around it there was no indication of their presence – no snapped twigs, no disturbed needles, no prints.

The machine-gun had stopped firing. Huddled together, they lay in the darkness and waited for the day to pass.

12

Q. Where in the Russian Federation is the military base that has won seven of the last thirteen nationwide competitions for readiness and excellence?
A. Kaliningrad.

The bow waves streamed back from the hull of the patrol-boat. The yellows and greens of the land's line, the high towers and the cranes of the harbour were clearly defined behind it. Mowbray had it in his binoculars. It headed for them, an arrow. The *Princess Rose* rolled viciously and Mowbray had to cling to the screwed-down table at the back of the bridge. Above him, on the mast, now hung two black balls – the day-light signature for Not Under Command. When they had been under control, and had had power, Mowbray had been able to cope well enough with the ship's pitch, fall and lift, but since they had drifted it had been worse than anything he'd known. He'd refused food and had huddled over the radio. The radio was an excuse. There would be communications silence until the zero hour, 20.00, but staying close to the radio focused a little of his mind away from the ship's motions. The patrol-boat ate up the distance, surged closer.

'Do you know what it is?'

'If it is important, Mr Mowbray, it is a Nanuchka III. It carries six tubes for launching the NATO-named Siren surface-to-surface missiles, range forty sea miles, and – yes, and – it has a single surface-to-air launcher, and one anti-aircraft gun, and if that is not enough it is also armed with a 30mm Gatling. I know because I used to sail Karachi to Bombay, and the Indians had them. It could put us out of the water, or under the water, in two minutes.'

Mowbray growled defiantly, 'There's nothing to worry about. We're clean.'

'Forgive me to correct you – almost clean. We no longer have your Dogs with us, Mr Mowbray, and their kit – but we are inside their territorial waters, are subject to their laws, and we are only *almost* clean because we have you on board. If they were to find you, Mr Mowbray, we would not be clean.'

'You got paid,' he hissed.

'Better you go down, Mr Mowbray. The engineer, good Johannes, will help you.'

When he went below and down to the engine room, he wouldn't know what happened when the *Princess Rose* was boarded by men from the patrol-boat. He would be incarcerated in the space where the kit had been, sealed in against the hull and below the water-line, in darkness. Before the departure from Gdansk, he'd thought he could pose as the owners' representative, but the mate – the Croatian Zaklan – had spoken contemptuously of his complete lack of sea-faring knowledge; he was consigned to the hiding-place, smaller and a deck below where the Dogs' gear, kit and weapons had been stowed.

He glanced a last time at the approaching boat . . . He no longer had control.

'If they come on board, what will you do?'

'Give them your whisky, Mr Mowbray, as much as they wish to drink – and show them the engine room. Go below.'

He struggled down the steep staircase to the accommodation floor, then gingerly lowered himself into the hatch and felt frantically for the steps of the narrow ladder, half falling to the oil-slicked floor of the engine room. The engineer, Richter, eyed him. In the dim light thrown by a single swaying, uncovered bulb, he tripped on the engine's cowling, his hip cannoned into a workbench, and he swore. Richter grinned at him, the same hidden laugh of the master, Yaxis. The sheet of metal plate was removed for him and he stepped into the cavity. There was room for him to stand or crouch, but not to lie down. He wouldn't have lain down because he could feel the cold of the bilge water seeping into his shoes. The metal sheet was replaced. The darkness became blackness. He heard the screws being tight-ened, then the scrape as rubbish was piled back against the sheet.

The sea broke against the hull and threw shivers down his spine. Later, in his priest's hole, he heard the echoing impact, and felt it through every bone in his body, as the fenders hanging from the deck of the patrol-boat were crushed against the hull of the *Princess Rose*. And when he heard the muffled voices through the sheet of metal he barely dared to breathe . . . God, if he came through this, every bloody novice going down to Fort Monkton would know his story.

Boris Chelbia climbed the concrete stairs, followed by his driver. Ahead of him, a flight above, a woman struggled with three small children and her shopping. Every second flight she paused to recoup her strength. Chelbia stopped and waited for her to go on. He had no wish to be noticed.

From the landing windows there was a fine view out over the roofs and church spires of Gdansk and beyond to the docks. The high cranes of the shipyards were a part of his history. Twenty years earlier – not for Jaruzelski's secret police, nor for the Red Army based with their battle tanks at Braniewo, but for the KGB – Boris Chelbia had been an agent. When the yards and their workers had been in ferment, the time of strikes, riots and barricaded lock-ins, he had appeared to be a trusted courier for the Solidarity movement. He had represented – his story went, and it was believed – sympathizers from the docks at adjacent Kaliningrad. One month he would bring to the workers' committee a telex machine, and another it would be money. A third month it would be a lorry-load of basic food supplies. It was all done quietly, but sufficient to create trust, and he had been able to provide a blueprint of the names and functions in the movement of the strikers' principal personalities. The cranes in the shipyards of Gdansk, which could be seen from these windows of the workers' block, had been his launch pad. Then the KGB had controlled him, and the influence they had given him had started Boris Chelbia on the road to fortune. He was the king of Kaliningrad. He understood, and had no squeamish qualms about it, that a king must dirty his hands, must go down in the gutter when necessary. The king could kill as easily now as on the day he had started out on his journey to power. The past had no hold on him.

He did not look from the windows, down at the cranes, as he followed the woman up the flights of stairs.

He heard her gasp with exhaustion. Radios played in the block, blared out music. Graffiti, which he did not read, was daubed on the walls of the stairwell.

His finger closed on a doorbell.

He waited. He assumed that the wife would be at work or out, that any children would be at school or college or gone. It was a long wait before he heard the shuffling feet approach the door, and the faint mutters of impatience as he pressed continuously on the button. The night porter wore only underpants and a vest and stood in the door-way, wiping the sleep out of his face, puzzled to be confronted by a man of obvious wealth, who was smiling as if to greet an old friend.

Without explanation, other than Chelbia's smile, the driver took the night porter's bare arm, then reached with his other hand to pull the door to, and led him up the last two flights to the roof. Perhaps the night porter realized that his door was now shut to him, and that he had no key to re-enter his apartment, and perhaps he realized that to scream was futile, and that, against the grip on his arm, resistance was not possible. He did not struggle. Chelbia was strong. His muscles were tuned on the weights in his villa. He put his shoulder twice against the door to the roof, and it swung open.

The wind ripped at them. If the driver had not held his arm, the night porter would have collapsed into the puddles of rainwater.

Chelbia's cupped hands were against the night porter's ear as he whispered his questions, and after each question he put his own ear against the night porter's lips to hear better the answer – and the wind shrieked in the television aerials. The answers came in a messy confusion. A Russian had come to the hotel, money had passed, photographs were shown and one was identified, but that guest had moved out . . . The guest's colleague and a woman had stayed . . . The colleague, younger, had followed the Russian from the hotel, and he had not seen him again. The woman had stayed the night, had left early after breakfast, had paid up.

'Where did she go, the woman?'

The night porter would have known, because he was in his under-pants and vest and his door was locked on him, that he faced the inevitability of death. He was beyond a point of return, but he answered the questions as best he was able, as if that were his duty. It was the experience of Boris Chelbia that the condemned were most often supine, co-operative.

'I carried her bags out. There was a Pole driving her, a big grey Mercedes, old model. She said, "How long does it take, Jerry, to Mierzeja Wislana, the far end?" It's what she said.'

He was thanked by Chelbia, as if courtesy were appropriate. On the rooftop, among the television aerials and dishes, was a hut of concrete blocks with a wooden door half rotted by rain, snow, gales and sunshine. Nailed to the door, with tacks, was a maintenance sheet of reinforced paper, on which the engineers were obliged to write their signatures confirming work had been carried out on the elevator that served the twenty-four floors of the block. Chelbia put his shoulder to it, but cautiously. The third time he battered it, the door opened, but his instant reaction was to cling to the jambs and prevent himself falling into the chasm. The FSB – once the KGB – employed him because he left behind him no evidence, and dirtied his hands while theirs stayed clean. He stood aside.

The driver took the night porter to the top of the elevator shaft. At the last the man struggled. His shout was carried on the wind towards the idle cranes of the shipyard. Then he was gone, falling and twisting.

'There's a fucking rat in there,' was the first thing Mowbray said, when the last screw in the sheet of metal plate had been removed, and the rubbish hiding it had been manhandled away. 'A big bastard. I felt its fucking tail on my ankle.'

The master gave him his hand, the engineer grinned, and Mowbray lurched clear into the engine room. The lights, only faint, dazzled him. He had been in there more than an hour.

'They were good guys, very considerate of our problem,' the master said. 'It took time because we had to examine the charts to find where it was permitted to anchor. Then we hit your Scotch.'

From inside his hole, he'd heard the echoing drop of the anchor's chain. The roll of the *Princess Rose* was worse at anchor than it had been when she drifted.

248

'You didn't bloody finish it?'

'They wouldn't go till it was finished. At sea, Mr Mowbray, the hospitality of Scotch always creates trust. They were on their way out to sea but they were asked to check us, in spite of what I said to them by radio. Any vessel that is Not Under Command makes suspicion. In spite of the Scotch, Mr Mowbray, they will watch us closely, and I think other boats will be sent to visit us. You will see, I regret, your hiding-place again.'

'And that fucking rat,' Mowbray said dismally.

He was helped up the ladder and through the engine-room hatch. They steadied him as he climbed the stairs to the master's cabin. In it, he reached for his binoculars. He peered at the strip of land and the trees, the gold-white of the beach. Past the trees he saw a red windsock flying horizontally. Then he raked back over two kilometres of open ground until he reached the treeline. The edge was – because he had measured it and the Dogs' leader, Billy, had confirmed it on the map – exactly eight kilometres from a village given the name of Rybacij. He was asked if he wanted lunch, but he shook his head. After he was left alone he stared a long time at the tree line and the distant windsock past which Viktor, his boy, would come as evening turned to night . . . The confidence drained from him. Without control, he was helpless. He could not take his eyes from the magnified vision of the treeline, where they waited for the sun to sink . . . But the sun had far to travel.

Locke stood on the dunes, and the wind caught his clothes, tugged them. As far as he could see, to the north-east and the south-west, the beach was empty save for one man and the cluster of bright-painted fishing-boats pulled up high on the sand. He gazed out over the rough swell of the sea.

Jerry the Pole had driven Alice and Locke into Krynica Morska and had gone off the road and into a car park. The town was a resort and, out of season, desolate. They had business ahead, at the village of Piaski at the end of the road on the peninsula spit, but the driver had shown his obstinacy and had ignored Locke's demand that they should push on and Alice's softer suggestion that they did not have time to waste. They had sat in the car when Jerry the Pole had left them and walked off into the cemetery. Later, he had stopped the car in front of a small, single-storey building with newly painted walls and front door. It had been his home when his father had been a carpenter, and would now be the holiday home of a German family or rich Poles from Warsaw. 'It's not a bloody nostalgia trip, Jerry,' Locke had spat, and Alice had murmured, 'I think we really ought to be getting on, Jerry.' Moving on, he had pointed out a big villa, with developers' scaffolding around it and he'd said – as if they cared – that the mistress of Hitler had stayed there, in that building, when the Führer was at the Wolf's Lair directing the eastern-front fighting . . . Then he had accelerated away as if his point was made.

At Piaski village, eight miles further up the spit from Krynica Morska, Locke had insisted they went first to the beach . . . and he'd walked ahead and out on to the dunes.

A long way out, to the north, his right, was the *Princess Rose*. Locke could see, squinting, the red of her hull. Away from her, the distance slowly growing, he thought he could make out a brilliant bow wave that the sunlight caught. She was still, isolated. His eyes swept away from the lone *Princess Rose* and raked across an empty seascape. Far beyond the one man, the beach stretched away, tranquil, a place for tourist brochures; a place that would have delighted the walkers who tramped the coastal path that bordered his parents' farm. A mile and a half down the beach, jutting up above the trees, was a watch-tower on stilt supports. Beyond it were Mowbray's Dogs, with their guns, holed up. The sunlight bathed him, but he shivered. He had become, against his will, a part of the madness.

The man on the beach threw a weighted, baited line out into the sea and Locke saw the faint splash where it fell into the foam of the waves' crests; the line snickered out from where it had been carefully paid in circles by his feet. Locke understood. The weather conditions were too adverse for the man to launch his boat. He was hunched down and held the line between his fingers. He could not walk away from the seashore so fished with a hand line.

Locke turned away. His shoes sank into the sand and the coarse grass binding it. He walked towards Alice. The wind and the air suited her. Her hair was ripped and the colour flushed into her cheeks. Before, he had barely noticed her: she was the woman who

250

sat in the corner at meetings and never looked up from her short-hand pad; she arranged the transport and the accommodation; she was only General Service, not an officer. She had her hand up and against her forehead, shielding the sun from her eyes, and she stared away down the beach, past the watch-tower, past the end of the tree-line, past the open ground of the spit.

She looked for him. He knew it.

Back in the hotel, she had shown the Dogs her picture of Ferret. Locke hadn't seen it. He, Codename Ferret, was there, where the land and the skyline met.

When he reached her, she was still looking along the beach, her hand was still up, and he thought she kept a vigil, but she said, from the side of her mouth, 'There's a grave over there.'

'A what? A grave?'

'It's what I said, a grave.' With her free hand she pointed behind her.

He walked to where she pointed. Near to the path was a picnic bench in a half-moon of pines. In the third line of the trees, a break in the lush grass, was a bare square of ground with a raised mound in the centre of it. A wooden cross had a wreath of evergreen foliage fastened where the cross spars met; at its foot was a second wreath and some pottery jars, which held long-spent candles. A sheet of laminated paper was tacked to the lower part of the cross. The sun threw shafts on to the grass he walked over to reach the grave. It held eight men's decayed corpses . . . He saw the names of six of them, and their ages, typed on to the laminated paper, but two more were listed as 'Unknown', and the date against the eight was the same: 30 April 1945. They had died in the last hours of the war, been buried in a pit, and only recently had been found; they had been left by those who had discovered them in the resting place beneath the trees; that April, fifty-seven years later, people had come with flowers and a wreath, and had lit little candles. It should have been a place for kids to play and for parents to bring food and beer – but it was a place for the dead. He was tricked. Everything Locke saw deceived him.

He strode back to her. She gazed into that far distance.

Locke asked, with a harsh snap, 'You showed the men a photo-graph – not the file one. May I see it?'

She didn't turn to him but reached into the bag slung from her shoulder. She took out the small leather pouch, unfastened its clasp and gave it to him. It had been taken with a flash, delayed. It was a snap-shot in the night. She stood in her coat, and pride, joy lit her face. He was beside her, his arm was around her shoulder and her head was tilted to rest on his chest; he was comforting her, protecting her, and the broad smile of happiness creased his features. He closed it, fastened it, gave it back to her. 'Right, let's go,' he said.

Jealousy cut him as he walked back up the track, away from the sea, towards where Jerry the Pole waited with the car.

The room was ready.

Before the flair for interrogation of Yuri Bikov had been recognized, when he was posted to the section of the Officer Cadet Training School that fed the Dzerzhinsky division, the lecturers had hammered at the cadets the value of preparation. Only, they said, on the rarest and most exceptional investigations – where time was critical – should preparation be less than thorough. Bikov had now read every file that was available to him on the professional career of his target, and he had had faxed to him the files on the career and death of his target's father. His major had been to an academic at the university for briefing on the importance of the castle at Malbork to archaeologists. Bank accounts had been gutted. Every place he had looked had told Bikov more about his target. The very clothes that he wore – dirty, smelling, mud-spattered – were a part of the preparation.

The room was the final brick in the block he built, and it was ready.

The lecturers had taught him the basic skills and had awakened an interest that he had not known existed. Every matter beyond the basics he had learned for himself – and they were little things, but each was weighed with importance. In the room, the windows were papered over and the blinds were drawn. Every picture, calendar, duty-roster chart, plan and map had been taken down, every hook and nail removed from the walls. The previous evening, under the supervision of his sergeant, the radiators had been switched off, and overnight the windows had been left open. Not until the morning had they been closed, then covered. The rug on the carpet had been taken out, and the carpet had been lifted from its adhesive fastenings, and the underfelt. All furniture, any trace of civilization, had been removed.

He had turned the room into a grey tomb without any focus point that might help his target. There would be nothing in the room but himself, the predator, and his prey, and a single candle. The candle, passed to him by his sergeant, was held upright on a plain plate by congealed wax. His eye roved for the exact centre of the room and when he had found that point he set the plate down on it.

Nothing was to chance.

'He is still at his workplace?'

'Yes.'

'No phone calls and no visitors?'

His sergeant was linked by radio to the admiral's suite. 'None.'

'And Falkovsky?'

'In his room, has cleared his diary, takes no calls.'

Bikov went to the side of the room, leaned against the wall and slid his back down it. When he sat on the concrete floor he drew up his knees and wrapped his arms around them.

'Then we wait another hour, or perhaps two hours – while the anxiety cripples him, until it is an agony for him . . . Until he would, almost, thank us for ending it. Yes . . . yes . . . thank us for taking away his pain.'

He rested his head on his knees and closed his eyes. The next day, or the day after, the electronics housed in the nose-cone of an MI-24 attack helicopter, below the main machine-gun and forward of the rocket pods, would home in on the beacon that was hidden in the stock of an assault rifle, and his head filled with the crescendo of the general's laughter . . . In truth, he liked what he had seen of the man and thought him worthy of the preparations that were made. But it was not important to Yuri Bikov that he had liked what he had seen, or what would happen to the man once his job was done. He dozed.

The conscript, Igor Vasiliev, had boastfully told the corporal in the armoury everything of the difficulties of shooting that morning, the cross-wind's strength, and how he'd hacked it – then had told the corporal of his special permission from his platoon sergeant to return to the range in the late afternoon and shoot again. The corporal said he was 'shit' and 'crazy', if he wanted to go back to the range at dusk when any man of half sense would be getting his arse up close to a stove or a radiator. Anyway, did he know that the forecast was changing to north winds and rain? Vasiliev lodged the NSV heavy machine-gun back in the armoury, initialled the log, then said when he would return for it, and what time in the evening he would check it back in.

The excitement of the shooting still ran within him. He went for his navigation lecture. Afterwards, before going to the armoury, he would hang about outside the headquarters block in the hope that he would see his friend, who should know how well he had shot with the crosswind so strong. He would tell him, if he saw Captain Archenko outside the headquarters.

They had waited now for more than twenty minutes. Bikov's major and his sergeant sat in the car at the bottom of the steps to the main door of the headquarters block, with the engine running and the doors half open.

The in-tray was empty, the out-tray filled. His computer was switched off. Viktor knew it would happen but did not know when ... On any normal day he would have been summoned three times, or four, into the fleet commander's office to wrestle with a planning paper, or the diary, or to act as a sponge while the admiral talked. Since the men had come that day, he had not been called.

The trolley came again, as it always did, in mid-afternoon. The hot chocolate was put on his desk and the girl with the ponytail smiled warmth at him, then went to the guardian's table and put on it the tray with the china cup, saucer and plate. She poured the tea. She waved to them all, her day's work done, and backed her trolley out. None of the other officers or the secretariat would have known what had changed, but all would have known that for the greater part of a working day the chief of staff had not entered the inner office of the fleet commander. The silence clung. They waited for resolution. They would have heard Piatkin's refusal to allow Captain, second rank, Archenko into the admiral's office when strangers had come. In the outer office, men and women made themselves small and unnoticed, and whispered into telephones. None caught his eye. The admiral's guardian took the tray to him. The door was open behind her. Viktor could see the admiral, side on, at his desk, his head down, his shoulders shrunken.

She put the tray on his desk and the admiral seemed not to see it, did not move.

He called out, 'Admiral, is there anything I can do – should we talk about your diary?'

Admiral Falkovsky's chair spun on its pivot, away. Viktor saw his back, the prickled cropped hairs on his neck.

A shout answered him, pebbles in a concrete mixer, 'Go to your quarters. Get out . . . Go.'

The guardian came out, white-faced, and closed the door. Viktor stood. Every head was turned away. His desk was clear, as it had been the day before, when he had not run. He went to the stand by the outer door, lifted down his coat and slipped it loose to hang over his shoulders. He looked up at the clock on the wall. He was expected at the rendezvous on the eight-kilometre stone beyond Rybacij in five hours less twelve minutes. He would run. He straightened his tie, as if that were important, and brushed dust flecks off his epaulettes.

He went down the stairs from the second floor. When he was clear of the building he would cross the base, take the ferry – whether he was followed or not – commandeer the first wheels on the far side, run, and hide up . . . He stamped across the lobby area. The military policeman at the table beside the door stiffened, stood, and waited for him to pass, but did not salute. The military policeman at the door always saluted. Viktor pushed open the door. A car was up close to the steps, and two men jackknifed out of it. The sun was in his face.

The men came fast up the steps, one on each side of him and the car blocked escape. A flash of light on metal in the hand of the man on the left side of him. As he realized that the metal was handcuffs, his arms were grabbed. The click reverberated in his ear, and the pain was in his wrist. He lashed out with his shoe and caught a shin, then flailed with his free fist and hit a throat. One half down and one reeling away. He tried to run. His arm seemed to be wrenched from the socket at his shoulder, as though he dragged a hundred-kilo sack of sand. He stamped his feet to gain speed but could not loose the hold and the handcuff dug deeper into his wrist. The great broad arms of the military policeman encircled him from behind and suffocated his last attempt to run.

In the middle distance, Viktor saw the conscript.

He blustered once, 'What the fuck is – who the fuck do you think – You know who I—'

He could think of nothing more to yell in protest. The man he was handcuffed to had worn the suit and carried the briefcase into the admiral's office.

'Right, Captain Archenko. Unnecessary but understandable. I can put your teeth down your throat, or we can go with dignity. Which?'

He was led the last steps to the car. The man to whom he was handcuffed slid in through the open door, then tugged Viktor after him. The second man retrieved his coat and threw it in after him. The door was slammed shut, and the car eased away.

Viktor did not realize it, could not have analysed it, but a feeling of light-headed relief consumed him. It was over. At a stroke, the double life was gone. He sagged back in the seat. The car went past the conscript, slack-jawed, past the senior officers' mess, the armoury, the non-commissioned officers' club and the workshop complex, past the landscape of his territory. He could see the upper outer walls of the fortress where his grandmother might have waited after the last boat had gone . . . He felt at that moment freer, more liberated, than at any moment since he had gone up the gang-plank on to the trawler tied against the quay at Murmansk. A weight, which had lain there since his mother had told him how his father had been exposed to leukaemia, seemed lifted from his back, and with it went the burden of the last months of his grandmother's life . . . What price now, in the steadily driven car, his hate? When a man was in the waters of the Barents or on the glacier rocks of the Kola peninsula, above the Arctic Circle, they said all he wanted was to sleep, and if he slept he would die . . . He thought Alice North called him.

He jerked up in his seat, and wrenched the handcuff fastening him to the man.

He would fight, would not sleep, he would give them nothing.

The car stopped outside the building that housed the office of the *zampolit*, Piatkin. He was led inside and up the stairs. Viktor tried to walk straight-backed, to set the pace, and made the chain taut between the handcuffs. He was taken through Piatkin's empty office, and in front of a closed door a key was used to unfasten the handcuffs. He rubbed at his wrist. His uniform jacket was pulled off him, his tie was taken, his pockets were emptied. His belt was dragged from his waist, the shoes off his feet, and his watch was snatched. The door was opened. He was pitched through it and it slammed shut behind him. He fell to the concrete floor and the darkness enveloped him.

'Heh, you. Yes, Vasiliev, you . . .'

Vasiliev stood rock still, in shock. He had seen his friend, Captain Archenko, step through the doors and he had taken a half-step towards him. From that moment he had been rooted. The platoon, on their way to the gymnasium, marked time, stamped out the rhythm.

'Vasiliev, what the fuck do you think you are doing?' the sergeant shouted.

Half a step forward and the excitement welling in him – having rehearsed what he would say about his morning's shooting – then frozen as two men had rushed his friend.

'Vasiliev, are you shooting or are you jerking off, or are you doing the gymnasium, like you're supposed to be?'

He had seen a short, bitter little fight. The handcuff had prevented his friend's escape. Then the military policeman had intervened and his arms had smothered the fight. His friend, the chief of staff to the admiral, had saved his life, had brought him back the machine-gun he loved beyond any other possession.

'Vasiliev – shoot, or the gymnasium? Which?'

His friend was arrested, like a criminal would be taken by the *militsiya*, a thief. Other officers had been crossing the parade-ground and had seen nothing, and had gone on. The platoon and the sergeant had not seen it. Only Igor Vasiliev had been the witness.

257

'Vasiliev, what's the matter with you? Are you an idiot? Do you shoot, or don't you shoot?'

The chief of staff to the fleet commander was his friend and protector, was almost a father to him. In his locker, hidden at the back, was a simple chart on which were listed the dates of each month, and every day he crossed out another. That morning, at dawn, after crossing out the day in October he had counted the dates remaining of his three years of conscripted service – ninety-six. The sergeant stared at him. If he disobeyed his sergeant, when Captain, second rank, Archenko was in handcuffs and no longer his protector, father, friend, they could stick on him five more months, or six, in the military gaol.

His voice was strangled, 'Going to shoot, Sergeant.'

'It's the sort of place that screws you up . . . Know what I mean?'

Billy was back. He had been gone a few minutes more than an hour. When he was close to the basher, he'd done the screech-owl call, and Lofty had answered him. He'd crawled into the dark space and there'd been curses as his boots and body took space from them.

He whispered, 'I went out west, about two hundred metres, and then I've done a circle. You know what? This was a battlefield. In the trees there's trenches and bunkers – good trenches in zigzags and good bunkers made with tree-trunks or concrete. They're everywhere. You find a bunker and go forward twenty-five metres and then you find a trench, head on another fifty metres and there's another bunker, then another set of trenches, they're everywhere. There's old wire, I found ammunition cases, and a mortar but no bombs for it. It must have been fought over, yard on yard – and there's craters, bombs and artillery craters . . . and I found a skull. I reckon a fox had dug it up. There must have been poor bastards here with nowhere to go, blocked at each end, and no more ships coming to get them. I don't reckon, however hard you looked, you'd find ammunition. The sods would have used it up, each last round of it, maybe kept one back for themselves, or the last grenade. Don't mind saying it, the skull spooked me. It was just stuck out of the leaves and the rest of him was covered. It still had the helmet on it, and two bullet-holes in it, straight through the eye sockets. He'd have been on his back and looking up at the night or the day, doesn't matter, and the last bloody thing he saw was a barrel aiming down on him. No more ammunition, no more medics, no more evacuation boats – it's a shit of a place.'

He'd quietened them, stilled them. He could hear their breathing.

'OK . . . OK . . . North is the shoreline. The beach is clear. There are signs on it forbidding access. She's way out, the *Princess Rose*, anchored. The tide's down, maybe on the ebb, but the dinghy's fine, you can't see it. I worked from the west side to start with. There's one track and I'd say it's used by patrol vehicles. It's hard-packed so the vehicles using it can go fast. It'll go right up to the border. The forestry's not managed. No bugger's been in it. I don't think they come this far up for exercises. There's bramble and thorn in there. You wouldn't try to run through it, snags and snags, it's slow going. What would worry me, if the place was a battlefield then there'd have been mines. If there were mines put down, it doesn't look as though anyone's ever cared to come back through and clear them, but there's fox tracks and I saw deer prints – not that a fox would set a mine off, but a deer might, so where the deer have gone is our best route . . . I'm not big on mines but I think they'd last from the time this place was a battlefield.'

Lofty murmured that if ordnance was still live from 1915 at Passchendaele, it would be live from 1945 here.

'Just so, Lofty, and you'd bloody know . . . Going south, there's the lagoon. The beach is different. Good ground for running on, but the lagoon side is a waste of time. Bog and reed beds. You wouldn't want to be in there, couldn't move fast or quiet and they've the track to get behind you, if it comes down to that. I'd write off the lagoon . . . Tell you what, though, you remember Braniewo? You can see Braniewo straight across the lagoon, only seven or eight kilometres. You can see the church, but I didn't see any boats on this side. The lagoon's a non-starter for us . . . It has to be the beach.'

It was just like the old times, with Billy as the team leader. Going up the anchor chains to board tankers for anti-terrorist exercises, getting flushed out of a submerged submarine, then paddling to the towering supports of oil-rigs in the North Sea for more exercises, stalking the foreshore of Carlingford Lough when it wasn't play-time, holding the team together in silence in the Crime Squad's interview rooms when it was for real. Like old times . . .

'So, I'm going east, and I can tell you what we didn't know . . . I have the GPS plot on Rybacij, and I can take myself to eight kilometres this side of it, down to the last five metres, the pick-up point. It's marked on the map as forest . . . No, no, too easy. The map's out of date – big surprise. The firing range has been extended. I'd estimate the range used to be for thousand-metre shooting, but it's been extended to two thousand. There was that big machine-gun this morning, the bad bastard, and they've extended the range for that calibre. When I got there some smaller stuff was firing, way back, and the flag was up, but they finished and the flag didn't come down. Maybe they don't bother to lower the flag, maybe there's more shooting scheduled. The big surprise? The eight-kilometre mark is on a hardcore road and is just about bloody adjacent to the targets at two thousand metres. I've found a bivouac where we lie up and we're off that road and headlights won't find us, but there's questions I can't answer: will there be firing at rendezvous time? Will there be spotters at the targets? Just don't know, can't know. I've marked a track back as best I can. Plastic strips from a rubbish bag, what the spotters would have dumped. The GPS says we're five hundred and fifty metres from the eight-kilometre mark . . . If he comes, and if he's got company, too bloody right we're going to squirt them with grenades – up to you, Lofty. I'm not fucking about, not out there. Anything you want to ask, guys?'

Nothing they wanted to ask. He sensed the nerves, felt them himself. Always the same, on exercise or action, there were nerves.

'What's the grub?'

Their meal, the last they'd eat before moving out, was rehydrated chicken casserole in cold water and tack biscuits with a smear of margarine and plum jam squeezed from tubes, and a half a Mars bar for each of them. They ate in silence, close to each other in the basher.

Wickso swallowed the last of his half Mars bar and then, with all the sensitivity of his fingers, felt over his lap for any flakes of chocolate that had fallen on his camouflage trousers or top.

260

He was there for a photograph that was not yet taken. There was a maisonette in West London, under the flight path of Heathrow used when the prevailing wind was from the southwest. It was the home of his father and mother – two bedrooms, a kitchen, a bathroom, a cramped hallway, and a living room. He had not been back there since the day after his discharge from the Squadron, and then there had been a shrine of photographs and cups in the living room. His father, disabled by heart trouble, had sat in his chair to the right side of the shrine and blinked to hold back tears; his mother, who was the earner and who left the maisonette at four thirty a.m. each weekday to clean offices, had gone into the kitchen to make a pot of tea. He had told them that 'something in Ireland went wrong', that he was washed up, finished. The photographs were on a table and the cups were on shelves above it. He'd not stayed long, less than half an hour, and after he'd gone his father had been free to weep and his mother would have brought through the pot of tea from the kitchen. He knew they were alive still because on their birthdays and at Christmas he telephoned the neighbour across the landing and learned what little was new – and in each phone call he asked the same question. Were the photographs and cups still in place? They were, and each call hurt him worse.

He had seen the camera in the drawer by the wheel when the master had opened it to produce a chart. They would stand on the deck of the *Princess Rose* – Billy, Ham, Lofty and himself. They would be wearing their wetsuits or the camouflages, and Mr Mowbray would hold up the camera, and they'd josh him about his focus, his aim, and they would all be laughing, and the pride would be on their faces. Their arms would be round each other . . . The same photograph was in the shrine. They were on the upper superstructure of a rig, or forward on the deck of a tanker, or on a submarine ploughing the Clyde, or in the barracks hut at Ballykinler a month before the last patrol. Four photographs of the team were in the shrine, and there would be a fifth. He would take it back himself. He would collect the enlargement from the chemist, and a frame, and would go back to the dreary redbrick building under the flight path. He could not go back without the photograph. 'Just something we did for government, Dad – all a bit hush-hush, Mum. Good to see you're keeping well.' It was Wickso's dream.

From the doorway of the room she'd chosen, Locke watched Alice unpack. Her back was to him. She took out her washbag and laid it on the bed.

In the village of Piaski there was a church, a café, the homes of fishermen and a caravan site. There had been an arrow pointing to the lagoon shore for campers. Jerry the Pole had driven them through the village, then Locke had ordered him abruptly to stop. He and Alice had quit the car, taken the bags and the gear from the boot, and he had told Jerry the Pole that he should find himself a table in the café and stay there until they came for him; he should not leave the café. They'd walked up the street, on the Tarmac of the one street in Piaski, past the turning to the new church, past dogs rearing and barking behind fences. They'd gone on till the street petered to a dry, sandy track, and kept walking. Where the track ended, became a footpath, there was a pink-painted bungalow, all the windows closed, no washing on the line, no dog throwing itself against the gate. No recent tyre tracks indented the turning up to the gate or the ground inside it. Spent honeysuckle climbed the bungalow walls, but a red rambler rose meandered in the boundary hedge. The bungalow would be dry, and the owners – from Germany or Warsaw – would not miss a few kilowatts of electricity. The gear always received and transmitted better when on mains power. They'd crept through birch trees and scrub on the far side of the bungalow to the village, then slipped over a low fence. A cat, on its stomach, had scowled at them, then fled. They'd taught property entry on the IONEC course at Fort Monkton, but Locke had never before put it into practice. It was a simple lock on the back door, and his credit card did for it. The living room was all closed down for the winter and dust-sheets covered the chairs. It had been a long day, would be a long night, and Locke had suggested Alice might cat-nap for an hour or two while he rigged the gear and ran the aerial into the kitchen, which had a flat roof. The first drops of rain pelted on to it.

Locke had played back the recorded message, transmitted thirty minutes before: 'Delta 2 to Havoc 1 – In place, site recce completed.

Out.' He had sent his own: 'Havoc 1 to Havoc 2 – Delta in place and site recce completed. Out.' The signal from along the peninsula was strong, but the possibility of it being intercepted was minimal. His transmission out to the *Princess Rose* was adequate. Using the dog-leg from the team to Mowbray reduced the interception potential. She'd shown him the picture, and in the picture Ferret's arm was round her.

'Did you sleep with him?'

She turned to face him.

'Slept with him, didn't you? Was it Mowbray's idea? Doing your bit for Rupert bloody Mowbray. Got the nod and wink from Mowbray, did you? "Our boy's stressed up, Alice dear, might crumple, needs a bit of comforting." Couldn't ring down from the room and tell the porter to send up a tart, could he? How did you feel about playing the whore, or was it just *duty*? "Don't think of him as a traitor, Alice dear, think of him as a colleague." But he's not a *colleague*, he's not one of us and never will be – am I right? He's a traitor, and he'll bring us all down. Christ, Alice, you didn't think, did you, that he loved you – you were just getting rid of his fucking stress – you didn't, did you? Alice?'

She no longer looked into his eyes. She took the picture from her handbag, opened its clasp and laid it on the bed beside the washbag. As she bent the pendant hung free from her throat. She smiled at him, a little grin of mischief. It was her answer. She was beyond his reach.

He blundered back to the kitchen.

The room was in Piatkin's palace.

There should have been a pile carpet and furniture. Without his watch, Viktor did not know how long he had been in the room before, at last, he sensed the movement. The darkness was too dense for him to see. It had been a long time, because his mind had throbbed, before he had known he shared the room. A man breathed *somewhere*. Somewhere in the room was another man. His knees scraped the concrete and the palms of his hand were gouged by its roughness. He thought the darkness was like the moment after death.

263

Viktor crawled towards where he thought he might find the man. His head hit the wall. He went right. There should have been chairs and bookcases, filing cabinets and table legs. They had made a cell for him of a room that had been a king's quarters. He came to the wall's end and twisted, felt a power socket but no flex led from it. He had told himself he would fight. He would not cry out. His fingers touched a boot. The fingers worked over its laces and a sock, then skin, then the material of rough jeans. A match was lit. It was cupped in hands and the palms took its light away from the face of the man. Viktor let go of the jeans. The match's light moved to the centre of the room. A candle was lit. Its flame grew in the still air. The man sat cross-legged on the far side of the candle. Viktor saw a face, younger than his own, and he thought it humble, that it showed him respect.

'It's the sort of shit they teach these days at the Lubyanka, Viktor. Disorientation, that sort of crap . . . I am Bikov, and now we can talk – I think we will grow to like each other . . . I sincerely hope so.'

13

Q. What Russian city was occupied by Napoleon for thirty-nine days as a springboard for his advance on Moscow?
A. Kaliningrad.

'I cannot speak for the state, Viktor. I am not responsible for it. What I see of the state, Viktor, makes me ashamed to be its servant: it is a cesspit of corruption. Criminality, organized and spontaneous, is out of control. The state, Viktor, is sick. Any man of sensitivity and of dignity has complete justification in rejecting it. I accept that. If I possessed your courage, I would have done what you have done. I am your supporter, Viktor.'

No tape-recorder's spools turned. No microphone carried Yuri Bikov's words. No note was taken.

'You may trust me, Viktor. I will protect you from the thugs with truncheons, electrodes, drugs, from all the shit people. They would not understand, to them pain is an end. I want to understand and then I want to help. Your friends have abandoned you – but you are fortunate because you have a new *friend*, you have me. I know so little of you, Viktor, but you will help me to know you better. I want to learn about you.'

The bright flame of the candle kept company with them. First Bikov would talk, then he would listen. He would create an atmosphere that he could tap into, then milk. When younger, when he had started to recognize his own skills, he had watched the work of other interrogators in Counter-Intelligence (Military). He had learned their style, then had pitched his own in a directly opposite fashion. Most regarded themselves as an élite and had showered themselves with superiority – most took an attitude that they were the chosen

265

representatives of the highest power, and the suspect was barely worth the time and effort given him.

Imagine an empty bucket and a tap against a wall, and a day of stultifying heat. The need of the interrogator was to have the bucket filled, if he were to drink and cool himself. The tap must be turned, the water must flow and fill it. If the water does not lap at the top of the bucket the interrogator has failed. Hitting the tap with a pickaxe handle would not fill the bucket; the tap's handle must be turned, and gently. Once, in the dog-end days in Afghanistan, in the camp at Herat where the sand blew and the flies bit, when Bikov had been a junior lieutenant he had watched a fellow officer, same rank, hammer the face of a *mujahidin* to a pulp with an iron bar. When the suspect was unconscious, incapable of giving information, Bikov had told the officer he should have been a *plumber*, not an officer: 'If you had chosen employment as a plumber, not as a soldier, and you had cut your finger with a knife you could have beaten your knife with a hammer, and been satisfied.' The officer had not understood him.

'You are a senior officer, Viktor, a man of stature, and I respect you. If a man of your intelligence, your insight, has a grievance then it should be listened to. But fools don't listen. How many times, Viktor, have you voiced concerns, anxieties, worries, and how many times have you been ignored because the system does not have the legitimacy or the confidence to allow itself to be criticized? Don't answer . . . The system is rotten . . . To me you can speak with freedom.'

In Chechnya, his first tour, the bandits had crossed a minefield to attack a camp south of Grozny, had planted explosives and had run back through the minefield, but in the attack's confusion one had been captured by the paratroops based at the camp. Their commander had tied a rope to the ankle of the prisoner and he had been prodded at bayonet point back into the minefield. The paratroops, in hot pursuit, had followed the rope's length behind him, believing he would take them through the mines. The prisoner had killed himself, and the two paratroops who held the end of the rope. Bikov had arrived at the camp two hours later, and had told the commander he was an 'idiot'.

By the candle's light he could see Viktor's face, and his prey could see his. But the light of the candle did not reach to the bare walls of the room, or to its ceiling. He denied his prey the chance to turn his head to a bookcase and memorize the titles on the shelves, to stare at the pattern on a chair or the scratches on a hard seat; there were no window bars for him to gaze at or a heap of files on a desk in which Viktor could escape the questions that would come. They were together, the two of them, alone . . . There was no evidence – Lieutenant Colonel Yuri Bikov worked towards a confession from Captain, second rank, Viktor Archenko. He had time and he had patience, and the confession, when it came, would end the life of his prey.

'We are here to sort out your difficulties, Viktor, as friends do, true friends . . . I respect you, and I believe you will come to respect me . . . Together we break down the difficulties, you and I.'

He spoke quietly. If Viktor were to hear him he would have to strain and concentrate, and that was good. He saw Viktor's head tilt and twist, but there was nothing for his eyes to reach towards, only the darkness, and that was the best . . . The old shabby clothes, an artisan's, and the boots with the dried mud of Chechnya still on them, the stubble on his face and the tangle in his hair were the superficial signs that he was not superior, not in authority, to the man separated from him by the candle's sharp flame. Viktor, if Viktor looked at him and studied him, would read the openness and honesty of his face . . . Everything was planned, prepared. Bikov did not think it would be easy – the prey he stalked had lived a deception for many years and would have survived black-dog days of despair and also the days of elation when he would have believed himself untouchable. Only a man of steeled character could have come through the bad days and the good. He was ready to land the first blow: his soft-spoken words would hit harder than a crow-bar, or a pickaxe handle, or a lead-tipped truncheon.

'We should start at the beginning, Viktor, with *family*. Myself, I have no family. My father divorced my mother twenty-two years ago, I was fourteen. I have not seen my father from that day. My mother is in Gorno-Altaysk, an awful place. I think she is still there, but I don't write. I was married, and divorced, before I was twenty-five; there is a daughter but I have no contact to know if she is the star at school or is indifferent or is poor with her books . . . Money goes from my bank to them, but . . . You were the pride of your father, Viktor, and the joy of your mother. You had family.'

He hit home. The candle's light showed Viktor jolted.

Back to the hole in the hull's lining.

The wind had turned, the clouds blackened, the swell lessened.

A launch had come out. Mowbray was entombed behind the sheet of metal plate. He heard the voices, a cocktail of accents in English – the Russian from the launch, the Greek master and the German engineer. The dispute was over the position of the *Princess Rose*. Did they not realize they were anchored inside a prohibited-entry zone? But only by three nautical miles . . . Were they in need of assistance from a tug out of Kaliningrad? The problem of the engine would be fixed by midnight, and the cost of a tug was too great. What exactly was the problem with the engine? Age, and there had been laughter . . . The voices had gone. Mowbray knew that the harbourmaster's office in Kaliningrad would have contacted the authority in Gdansk and would have been told that the shitty little rust tub had left Polish waters with a recent history of engine problems.

Once more he was released from his prison – this time the rat hadn't visited. The signal was now in London: 'Havoc to VBX. In place, all ready. Out.' They'd be chewing on it, half frightened out of their wits at what they had unleashed, and that brought a limited sardonic smile to Mowbray's mouth. Through the porthole, misted now because of the thickening cloud, was the tree line where his Dogs were, where nothing moved.

'Your father was a hero.'

If he looked at the ceiling, which he could not see, or the walls that were beyond the candle's throw of light, if he stared down at his shoes that had no laces and counted the eyes, if he did not answer he admitted guilt.

'I hardly knew him.' Viktor's voice was as frail as the candle's flame.

'You were seventeen years old, Viktor, when he died – I think you would have known he was a hero . . . A fit, strong man, a pilot of the highest quality, then struck down in his prime, doing his duty – he gave his life for the shit, corrupt, criminal-ridden, rotten state. I doubt he ever complained – heroes don't. How do you remember your father?'

He hesitated and the voice mesmerized him. His friend, Rupert Mowbray, had told him he should never lie when questioned. A good interrogator – and if he were questioned it would be by the best – stored facts given him in his memory and passed on from them, then returned to them an hour later, or a day later, when the lie's statement was forgotten. A lie confirmed guilt . . . The lies in his mind were for the matters of importance . . . What documents had he removed and taken to Poland? None. Had he left the hotel where the delegation stayed in Gdansk to go to meet his handlers? Never. Where were the dead drops or the brush contacts? They did not exist. Was he a spy, a traitor, who betrayed his country? No. Those were the lies of importance, but he was not asked those questions. He had expected to be on a cell's floor with the boots pounding him, then to be dragged to a room where a light dazzled him, then to be hustled to a plane for the flight to Moscow. He had been told his father was a hero.

'I remember little of him.'

'I remember my father, Viktor – not with love because I hated him. Your father was an exceptional, extraordinary man . . . A good father, a good husband, and a respected test pilot at the experimental range at Totskoye. He flew into a nuclear cloud. Did you know that, Viktor?'

'My mother told me.'

'I think, Viktor – but it is difficult for a man to put himself in the mind of another – that I would have felt a bitterness if my father, if I had loved him, had been ordered to fly into a nuclear cloud, with all those risks, and had carried out his orders.'

'I do my duty as an officer. My father did his duty.'

'A good answer, Viktor . . . I do not believe it. For some wasted experimentation your father flew through a nuclear cloud. It killed him. What was the value of it? *Nil*. His life was given away so that

269

scientists could examine data. Was the data ever of real use? I doubt it . . . I would have felt bitter.'

'It hurt . . . yes, it hurt,' Viktor murmured.

No expression crossed the face of Bikov, across the flame from him. He felt a great tiredness and a hunger, and he knew he was lulled. If he looked past the shoulder of Bikov, or away from him, only the darkness bounced back at him. If there were pain, torture, shouting, he could have fought it. The man opposite gave him nothing to fight. He recognized the danger but did not know how to confront its sweet reasonableness . . . the switch.

'Are you German, Viktor?'

He was shaken. 'Why?'

'Am I impertinent? I don't wish to be. I don't stereotype, but you have German features. You are the image of your father, from the pictures I have seen, fair and tall and . . . I have seen also photographs of his parents. They were farmers who had settled in Kaliningrad, but they had come from the east, from the steppes of Kazakh, they were Asiatic. But their son is not sallow, he is blond. He is not short, as they were, he is tall. Explain it to me, Viktor, please.'

He should not lie, Rupert Mowbray had warned him of the risk of falsehoods, unless the questions involved his life and his death. He could not know if Bikov trawled with a net or knew of the hours that he had spent in the archive of the orphanage, and if Bikov had examined the old records of the nuns.

'Is it important?'

'I think so, if I am to know you.'

He saw the humanity . . . designed to win trust. He saw the warmth of the man. For four years he had trusted nobody, had confided in no man, and his loneliness had savaged him.

'My grandmother was German.'

'And your grandfather?' The lips barely moved but the question probed.

'My true grandfather was Russian.'

'Your father's birthplace, Viktor, is given as Kaliningrad . . . You have come home.'

'It is where my grandmother lived.'

270

'And your father was born, Viktor, in January 1946, and if your grandmother had gone full term then the conception would have been in April 1945, the month that the Red Army arrived in Kaliningrad. Was it love, Viktor?'

'What do you mean?'

The voice purred, the face bled sympathy. 'Love, you know – a young soldier and a young girl, from the different sides of the greatest conflict the world had seen, rejecting the politics and finding romance in the ruins of a wonderful city. Romeo and Juliet. Was it?'

'My grandmother was gang-raped. She was probably unconscious when my natural grandfather dropped his trousers.'

A frown of concern cut his forehead and the candle's light caught the sympathy. 'I'm so sorry . . . I didn't know.'

'She bore my father, whom she left on the step of the orphanage before hanging herself. She lies in an unmarked grave.' He could hear the shake in his own voice. Bikov leaned to hear him. 'It was not a love story.'

'I feel for you, Viktor. I lift a veil and I had no right to . . .'

The windsock had dropped.

Over the telephone from the concrete bunker below the targets, the messages came back. 'No hits' or 'Outer only'. Igor Vasiliev, the twenty-one-year-old conscript, had built a reputation on the range. The new inducted arrivals, 2 Platoon of the 4th company of the 81st regiment of naval infantry, had been firing for the first time with assault rifles, and when they had finished the instructors had held them back in the failing light, and had held up Vasiliev as an example they should strive towards. Boys, barely out of the schools' classrooms, were gathered in a half-circle behind him, and they had never seen a weapon as sleek and powerful as the NSV 12.7mm heavy machine-gun. Many times he had fired with spectators pressed close to him, but never before had he fired so poorly.

The fifth time that the calls had come back, 'No hits' and 'Outer only', the instructors called away the platoon, marched them to their lorries, and glowered back at him, as if he had wasted their time.

After they'd gone, and he was alone, he fired again. He lay behind the breech block, legs apart, and the belt was fed from the top of an ammunition box. It was the position he always took. The ear-muffs were clamped tight over his scalp. He squeezed the trigger with the same rhythm as every time . . . but as he fired and felt the shudder of the stock against his shoulder, heard the deadened crack of the firing, he could not concentrate. What he loved, the heavy machine-gun, took second place in his mind.

He had seen Captain, second rank, Viktor Archenko wrestled to submission, handcuffed, taken into custody. He was a simple young man, without education, and as he shot he struggled to look back on what he knew of his protector, and to find a reason for the arrest. His hold on the weapon wavered and he snatched at the trigger bar: he could not hold the cross-hairs of the sight that was calibrated to the maximum effective range of 2000 metres. If there was a fault-line shown him, Vasiliev did not see it . . . All that remained in his mind, distracting him, was a vague feeling that the captain had been detached from the life of the base and was different from other officers . . . Five shots in the burst . . . Talking to the conscript about the beauty of the castle across the frontier . . . Five more shots . . . Never mentioning the politics of Putin and the new understandings with the old enemy . . . Five more . . . Nothing of the shortages of fuel and food, equipment and training days . . . Five . . . The captain was like no other officer: he had gone into the sea to save him and had brought him back his machine-gun.

The belt was finished. The message came back, laconic and bored, 'No hits.'

Vasiliev chewed gum.

They said on the telephone that it was five o'clock, that their duty of target-spotting was finished. He asked them to leave on the sunken lights that lit the targets after dark: he had 120 more rounds to shoot. He hoped in the dusk he would regain his concentration. He eased back from the weapon, did the discipline, slipped the catch to safety. His teeth ground on the gum. He heard the distant sound of the jeep coming. He did not know whether his failures were from his hold on the stock or from his calculations of the changed wind's deflection or from the bedding into the sand-mud of the tripod's legs.

The jeep reached him. The target-spotters laughed at him.

'You're shooting like shit, Vasiliev. You couldn't hit a barn door at a hundred metres. What's your officer going to say when he hears you're fucking crap?'

They drove away. His jaw was set as he threaded the next short belt. Away ahead of him, in the gathering gloom, he could see the faintly lit white targets.

'In Gorno-Altaysk, Viktor, where I was a child, there is not a single building of historic interest. Not one. It's a dump. You know, there is more that's interesting in Grozny, believe me. In Gorno-Altaysk there is a bus station, a post office near to Kommunistichesky Prospekt, a little museum, which is a reconstructed Pazyryk burial site, and one lousy hotel. There is nothing more in Gorno-Altaysk. It's a pile of dog shit.'

There had been tension in his prey's shoulders when he had led him through the deaths of his father and grandmother; now he saw the grin. Bikov smiled back, felt the lines crack his cheeks. The candle was more than a quarter burned down, and the windows must have been ill-fitting because a draught caught the flame. Other than their voices, and the rain's beat on the covered windows, there was no sound in the room. He had instructed that the rooms underneath and above should be cleared. Bikov laughed out loud.

'Maybe there is a cinema now, to show films of Putin leading heroic police charges against the *mafiya* . . . maybe. What is the main sport in Gorno-Altaysk? Planning how to leave, checking the bus timetables . . . There is nothing of substance there unless you go into the forests and shoot bears, nothing . . . You, Viktor, are lucky.'

A cautious hesitation. 'How?'

'Because of your interests, your hobbies . . . I have nothing. I live out of a bag. There is no room in the bag for such interests.'

'What do you mean?'

He laughed again. 'Medieval archaeology, the interest that takes you to Poland for visits to the castle at Malbork. How did that start?'

'When I was a cadet at the Frunze naval college we sailed . . .'

'That is Leningrad?'

'Yes . . . We sailed on the fisheries research ship, the *Ekvator*, to Gydnia, and we were taken by bus to Malbork.'

273

'The castle captivated you?'

'It is magnificent.'

'Tell me.'

Bikov listened. His head was cocked as if he was fascinated by what he was told. The High Castle and the Middle Castle, the Amber Collection, the Grand Master's Palace and the Porcelain Collection, the Great Refectory, the Golden Gate, the Seven-pillared Hall and the Vestibule of the Infirmary. When he had heard enough, he interrupted.

'And I am told, Viktor, that the cathedral at Frombork, nearby, is a masterpiece of architecture from the same period – and the ruins of the Teutonic Knights' castle at Torun are a treasure chest for the archaeologist, and the Great Mill of Gdansk where the first bricks were laid in 1350. Your interests gave you much to see when you had the pass to travel to Poland. You were . . .'

'I only went to Malbork Castle.'

'. . . privileged – I'm sorry. You only went to the castle at Malbork?'

It was all in the eyes. The eyes led him. He looked for them but they evaded him.

'It's filthy. It's a disgrace. What are you, incompetent or idle? Which?'

His visit was unannounced. At the end of the working day, Admiral Alexei Falkovsky had come without warning to the harbour. The commander of the minesweeper flotilla had been called back from his second drink in the senior officers' mess and was lashed by the admiral.

'Rodents, vermin wouldn't use those toilets – there's cockroaches in the galleys and the potatoes are rotten. Fucking incompetent or fucking idle, which do I choose? Pack, go, you are dismissed.'

The admiral left a stunned, quivering officer behind him as he strode away. He had no escort. On any other day, for any other inspection of the fleet, his chief of staff would have hovered at his shoulder. His car followed him at a discreet distance as he strode from basin number one to basin number two. The submarine flotilla was his second target. He was betrayed, and he was frightened.

In basin number two they had already been alerted. A reception line of officers and senior NCOs was waiting. The grapevine would

274

have spread the news faster than he could walk with his pounding stride.

He was greeted. 'Good evening, Admiral, a pleasure to see—'

'I want to inspect every toilet, every galley, every torpedo tube, every weapons storage unit, every bunk in crew quarters. If I find dirt, you go,' he barked.

Men cringed.

His anger was usually held in check by the calming presence of his chief of staff beside him, but he was not there and never would be again. He stamped over the gangway, then hauled himself up the conning tower's ladder.

Few men, if any, frightened him, but the one who had come into his office had shrivelled him. It had been in the man's eyes. Merciless, piercing eyes. The man now held Viktor and interrogated him.

Blind fear consumed him as he began a search for dirt, inefficiency and idleness. The first toilet he inspected in the Vashavyanka-class vessel was blocked with a wedge of sodden paper and faeces. He rounded on the submarine flotilla's commander. 'You clean it yourself. With a bucket and a brush you fucking clean it yourself, then you get off my base.'

The men behind him in the cramped corridor, he knew it, had loved him, had boasted that they served the best fleet commander in the navy, and he saw them reel from his attack. He could not combat the fear.

The candle was burned down half its length, and the wax dribbled off it. It gave no heat. Viktor shivered.

'Heating's off,' Bikov said. 'That's how crap the system is here – no heat for serving officers, or for the NCOs, or for the conscripts. The money for the heating oil will have been pilfered by the likes of the weasel Piatkin. Heating oil and weapons stolen . . . Is the cold bad, Viktor?'

'They took my coat.'

He did not see the trap set for him. All the time, with each line of questioning – his family, the castle at Malbork, his daily work – he looked for the big traps: there were none. Opposite him, beyond the flame, Bikov peeled off his sweater. Bikov wore only a singlet against his chest. The sweater was thrown over the candle and fell beside him.

'I don't need it.'

'Put it on, Viktor.'

'The cold does not affect me.'

'Wear it, Viktor.'

'I can stand cold. If you had been in Murmansk—'

He threw the sweater back, fluttering the flame.

'If you are cold and won't wear my sweater, then I too will be cold.'

Bikov pushed the sweater away from him. Viktor saw his arms, the freshness of the scrapes and scars that covered them.

'What happened to you?' Again he was led and did not know it.

'Last week I was in Chechnya. There was a firefight – the war there is criminal and incompetent. We were ambushed and had to escape across a hill . . . rocks, diving for cover, any place to hide.'

'Why were you there?'

'To save a man's life.'

Viktor stared, big-eyed, at him. 'Did you? Save his life?'

'He is a decent man, worth respect. I saved an officer's life.'

He saw Bikov's scarred and welted arms close around the singlet. They would be cold together; they shared the cold.

'Christ knows if this is going to be readable.'

Ham broke the quiet in the basher, and his laughter tinkled. They'd been sombre when they'd started. The team had withdrawn inside personal corrals having wriggled for space. Lofty, who played quartermaster, had given each a sheet of paper and an envelope. Inside their lockers in the Ballykinler camp there had always been a sealed, addressed letter, and there had been the same at Poole when they had left the base for more dangerous exercises.

'Can't see the paper myself. God knows how anyone's going to read it.'

Billy shifted. 'Who you doing it for, Ham?'

'That's personal, nobody's business.' He was subdued again. 'My mum and dad – if they ever get to read it, if they don't bin it when they see the handwriting.'

276

The machine-gun's firing had finally stopped. It had unsettled them, made them nervy. It was a full ten minutes now since it had last fired.

'What about you, Lofty?'

'Don't care who knows. The place where I lodge in the village. Just to tell them to sell up what I left there, not that it's much, and buy some flowers and put them in the chapel. Even the children of the veterans are pretty ancient – they sit in the chapel, rest up after they've gone to the graves. It's near to that time of the year, when they come. That's where mine's going. My bicycle, a few clothes, some books – should make a couple of bunches of flowers.'

When Lofty had brought out the paper, the envelopes, and the pencil, they'd all taken turns to bollock him. As quartermaster he should have done it on the boat, where they would have had light, space and time to think. They were crushed together in the basher and the rain was coming in in dribbled columns. What were they going to do with the letters? Who was going to have them? If they caught it – why they were writing the bloody letters – when would the letters be *posted*? He'd taken stick, but each of them had bothered to write something on the paper, a name and an address on the envelope.

'Shit,' Ham said.

The machine-gun had started up.

They each licked the flaps, sealed their envelopes and gave them to Lofty.

'What do I do with them?'

Wickso grinned in the darkness. 'When we're all gone, Lofty, and you're lying there and blubbering for your mum, with your last breath, Lofty, as this big *Spetznaz* bastard's lifting his bayonet to finish you, ask him very nicely: "Sir, can you direct me to a postbox?"'

Then Lofty gave them each a strip of adhesive tape. They groped at their throats for the amber pendants and wrapped the tape round the chain and the metal that held the stones so there would be no rattle. They did it because none of them would take off the pendants and dump them.

Billy said they should try to sleep. They would go forward in two hours.

*　*　*

A quarter of the candle remained.

'Admiral Falkovsky . . .'

'The fleet commander.'

'I know, Viktor, that Admiral Falkovsky is the fleet commander. A good man?'

'A very good man.'

'And fair?'

'Very fair. You would not find a single officer at Baltiysk who will not say that the fleet commander is a fair man.'

'Trusting?'

The time for Bikov to listen.

'For his best subordinates he has total trust. If he wishes to he can make you feel special and important. He is not a man of detail. He has the broad vision and he relies on trusted officers, I was one, to do the detail for him. We are very close.'

He saw his prey shiver, so he shivered as a response. 'Go on, Viktor.'

'Every time he has an important meeting to attend, we go through it together first. I tell him, as I see it, what matters will be raised that are detrimental to the navy's position and what matters are advantageous. He hears what I say. His door is open to me. What he reads, I read. I accept that I am junior to him, but we are colleagues.'

Bikov thought it was a combination of cold, arrogance, tiredness, conceit that led Archenko to condemn himself.

'I have a problem and I need your help, Viktor. Two years ago, when Admiral Falkovsky was already fleet commander, it was reported that American intelligence officers had identified the redeployment of the Tochka 22–21 missiles with nuclear warheads at Baltiysk. What was Admiral Falkovsky's reaction to those reports?'

'What could be his reaction? It was true.'

'How did Admiral Falkovsky think the Americans had learned of the redeployment?'

'We talked about it. It was a very serious matter – there was a strain on relations with the United States. I agreed with the admiral's response to Moscow when he was queried on it. I wrote the signal he sent. The Americans have spy satellites over the Kaliningrad *oblast* . . . They must have photographed the transfer of the missiles and the warheads from the ship that brought them, or the transfer to the storage bunkers where warheads are kept . . . It must have been spy satellites.'

Bikov did not allow himself to smile. His sincerity and concern were sculpted to his face. 'Of course, Viktor – what other explanation . . . ?'

Locke sat in the kitchen, his shoes hitched up on to the pine table. Everything around him was German. The pictures on the walls were of views of the Rhine and the calendar on the page for August showed a sketch of the Harz forests.

Where his parents were was prime territory for 'second homes'. Professionals – solicitors, surgeons, surveyors – came from the West Midlands to the Welsh coast, bought up old cottages and made them into weekend boltholes. Their money bled the life out of the local community by driving up property prices. They made their new homes little sanctums of Sutton Coldfield, Solihull and Bromsgrove, and at the end of each summer they scrubbed the rooms clean, emptied the fridge-freezer and were gone for the winter months. They were despised and envied by the community. He hated the owners of the house into which he had broken, and hated himself.

All Locke could find in the kitchen units to eat was a solitary packet of sweet biscuits. To the crime of breaking and entering, he added that of theft. He had wolfed down five biscuits, scattering crumbs on the washed-down table, and they had not alleviated his hunger, or his hate. Beside his shoes, circled by the crumbs, was the radio equipment. The rain beat on the windows but the lights shone brightly on the console's dials. In little more than an hour and a half Mowbray's Dogs would be moving.

She came in, slowly circled him and the table. He'd heard her washing. She had changed into thicker trousers and a heavier sweater. There was a new freshness in Alice North's face, and he had made it. The mischief still sparkled in her as she rounded him and the table. His sneers had brought the light back to her: *Did you sleep with him? You didn't think, did you, that he loved you?* The light in her dazzled him and gave maturity and strength to her; he was unloved and it made him hate her.

'And just what sort of little romantic nest is it you're going to build?'

She stopped, turned, faced him.

'Has Mowbray told you what'll happen? You'll have to quit. You'll be out through the front door in double-quick time. Security risk and all that. Treachery is an infectious disease. He's a traitor, done it once and can do it again. You're out. They'll be grateful enough to buy him a semi-detached in Coulsdon or Croydon, pebble-dash and a bit of mock-Tudor, and there you'll vegetate. All of them, once they've come over, die for nostalgia of the Motherland. At first he'll be useful. You won't see him for three or four months while they gut him of what information he hasn't already passed. Then he's on his own. There's a cheque into the bank every month, not a big one. Does he want to be with you? Does he, hell. He wants to be with the other sad cases who've travelled the same route, wants to talk Russian with them and moan about the politics in Moscow. Nothing to do but complain. He'll get, after the first few months, an occasional trip to Portsmouth or Plymouth to talk about his navy to our navy, but pretty damn soon he's out of date. You'll be as safe, as bored and as pathetic as any other suburban couple. Get to learn tennis, Alice, you'll have plenty of time for it. Ignore what I say if you want to . . . I'm going for a walk.'

His feet swung from the table. Jealousy wounded him, envy cut him. He was at the kitchen door.

She said, 'I don't think you've ever loved, Gabriel, or been loved. I'm sorry for you.'

The first time . . . Alice going down the corridor, leading, taking his hand, feeling the tremor of it, and only loosing it to get her key from her bag, unlocking her door, taking him inside and kicking the door shut behind her. Standing in the centre of the room and the light filtering through the drawn curtains and knowing that time was precious, reaching out for him. He'd come slowly to her as if he did not believe what was offered. His jacket on the floor, and his tie, starting as unspoken duty for Rupert Mowbray, then changed, all changed. The light from the street had shown the desperation, and she had wanted to wipe it from his face. When she had unbuttoned his shirt then stripped it off him, she had taken his hands and brought them to her blouse. So frightened, fumbling with the buttons, and when he'd done it, an age later, she had shaken her blouse off her shoulders, and then she had brought his fingers to her bra clasp, and when that had fallen away she had seen the awe in his eyes. When they were naked, he had ducked down to his jacket and taken the little plastic sachet from his wallet. She'd thanked him and he'd grinned, and they had gone down on to the bed and she had peeled it on to him. Bad, desperate, frantic sex, the first time, but afterwards – as the little bedside clock had spun away the minutes and hours – he had lain with his head on her breast and she had held him, and had known that she had stilled his fear. He'd gone, she'd knotted the condom and flushed it down the toilet. She'd not slept . . . It was not for duty, she had found love.

'You are tired, Viktor?'

'Yes, I am tired.'

'I am enjoying our talk. Every day I work with idiots. It is rare and a pleasure for me to be with a man of integrity and intelligence . . . You can continue?'

'Yes.'

The tiredness came in waves, but each time his eyes closed and his head sagged the light of the candle burned them open, and the humanity of the man opposite held him. He should have feigned sleep, should have slumped.

'That's good, Viktor . . . Viktor, many of the papers that cross your desk, or the admiral's, are confidential – they are state secrets and military secrets. You see them because you are cleared to, have the highest vetting. You also see papers that have come from GRU sources or civilian agencies. Some are from electronic intelligence and some are from human intelligence. When you read them, Viktor – analysis of the American navy, NATO formations, whatever – which do you value more highly? The electronic intelligence from satellites and intercepts or the human intelligence from agents on the ground? Which?'

'HumInt, always HumInt.'

'Very interesting. You see, your insight fascinates me. Explain, please.'

281

'Look at the Americans in Afghanistan, the war against terror. They have no agents but the sophistication of the electronics they employ is their substitute – without success. The picture given by electronics is only bland, it is without substance. HumInt has depth, understanding . . .'

The voice murmured, 'Provided by brave men and women.'

'The bravest. A spy plane or intercepts gives you pictures and sounds, but it is only a fraction of the intelligence a human source can give. If the Americans had agents inside Taleban or al Qaeda, they would capture the principals.'

'Very dangerous work, the agents' work.'

'The most dangerous.' A slip of pride would have shown, but only to the sharpest observer, in Viktor's eyes. He remembered how Rupert Mowbray, in the hotel room in Gdansk, had hung on every word he had spoken, how his hand had been wrung and his body hugged. 'I always tell the admiral that the best information we get from the GRU or the SVR is HumInt, and I tell him how the Americans have failed with their Electronic Intelligence reliance.'

'Go on, Viktor.'

The fisherman, Roman, again heaved his baited line into the surf.

He wore no wristwatch, time did not matter to him, but he estimated the man had come and sat behind him, a couple of paces from him, at least a half-hour before. Roman had not greeted him and the man had not spoken. The man was old and wore a long raincoat and a black beret, and he did not complain about the rain that fell steadily. To Roman, a man who sat on the beach when it rained to watch another who fished was a total fool, not worth speaking to.

Between his fingers the line jerked. Roman struck, swept back his arm. In the half-hour, estimated, that the man had been there he had caught nothing. He felt the tugging fight of the hooked fish, and sensed the man push himself up. Line dropped at Roman's feet as he hauled in the fish. The man was beside him.

'I lived here as a child.'

'Did you?' Over many years, Roman had learned that, when handlining, the best chance of losing a fish was when it was dragged in through the shallow surf. He concentrated on keeping his line taut.

'I am Jerzy Kwasniewski. My parents came from Krynica Morska, but they left a long time ago. My grandparents are buried in the cemetery at Krynica Morska.'

'Are they?' Roman did not know the name and had no interest in the burial of people he had not heard of. He saw the silver flash of the fish in the surf. He dragged it, flapping, over the wet sand and to his boots, bent and unhooked it in one fast movement, then tossed it into his bucket.

'What fish is that?'

'A cod.'

'And what are the others?'

'Mackerel and the flat one is plaice.' Roman had caught two mackerel and one plaice and they were now dead in the bucket beside the gasping cod. It was a poor return for a day on the beach with his handline, but the evenings always fished better, and the evenings after a storm fished best as the tide turned. He was baiting the hook again.

A new voice came softly from behind him.

'Would you mind if I fished?'

Roman turned. He understood a little Russian, and was about to spit, curse, and rid himself of strangers. The man was short, squat, heavy, and had sand sprayed over his shined shoes. Maybe the coat was mohair, maybe it was camel-hair, and Roman would not have known the difference, but he thought the cost of it would have kept him and his family through the winter. The rain ran on the man's forehead and on to a shirt collar of brilliant white. It was a request, *Would you mind if I fished?*, but the body, the physique, and the soft tone of the question did not brook argument. The man grinned and there was a boy's enthusiasm on his face. Roman thought the hands held out for the line could have broken every bone in his arms, his legs.

'I have not fished since I was a child – may I, please?'

Another shrimp was wedged down over the hook's barb. Roman handed the line to the man. His first cast barely reached the sea's edge, but by his fourth the weighted line was well out into the surf. He stood very still with the line tucked in his fingers, as Roman did. The rain fell on the three men now standing on the beach.

'When I was a child I loved to fish.' He turned and faced Jerry the Pole. 'At the café I saw the Mercedes car and they told me its driver had walked in this direction. It is my pleasure to meet you. I am Boris Chelbia . . . we have reason to meet. But, first, I wish to fish.'

Roman gave him the line.

His head bobbed, a little bow, as if the line was a valued gift. 'Thank you, I appreciate your generosity.'

'Would you like something to eat, Viktor?'

'I would, thank you.'

The claps of his hands, three of them, were the signal Bikov had agreed with his sergeant. They gusted the flame, small now, of the candle.

'I hope they can find us something to eat . . . Viktor, you were telling me about the meeting you went to at the headquarters of the missile unit. Please continue.'

Locke walked. The trees were close around him and the light fell.

He had gone towards the beach and seen the track over the dunes blocked by a sleek BMW 7-series, in which a man sat. Caution had taken him into the undergrowth bordering the dunes, away from where Alice had found the grave. He had seen Jerry the Pole with a fisherman and a man in a mohair overcoat on the beach; he had heard little guttural whoops of excitement, and had seen a fish pulled in. He had gone on a path to the east, towards the watchtower.

He walked and his loneliness bruised him. He followed a rough track. It was insignificant when he came to it, and it told him nothing . . . The forest was pine and birch and the grass was a lush carpet. The fence wound down from the higher ground at the centre of the peninsula and straddled the track. Not more than four feet high and of chain-link, it would have proved a hindrance only to rabbits. The fence dipped away between the trees and fell towards the shore. The rain dripped on him. There were no wheel-marks, but the fence was broken across the track by a single red- and white-painted bar – and a sign prohibited him going further. It told him nothing because this was the Polish fence. The main fence, the barricade, would be five hundred metres deeper into the trees, where the watchtower was. He stopped, alone, by the barrier. He heard the spatter of the rain and the call of the songbirds. This was Mowbray's world, not his. Mowbray was a creature of the times when fences cut across Europe, made a curtain from the Baltic to the Mediterranean, but those bloody times were gone – except here. He shuddered. The quiet frightened him.

He began to run, away from the fence. His knees were up and his breath spurted.

Locke came back to the cottage where the roses grew. He burst into the kitchen. She sat beside the radio console and he could barely see her in the gloom. He panted, sweated, supported himself against the sink.

'Where've you been?'

'I went to the fence – the border. I went to the border.'

'What's there?'

'Just a fence.'

'The way you're looking, Gabriel, there might at least have been an infantry division and an armoured brigade.'

'You can't see anything at the fence – what's behind it.'

The mocking was in her voice. 'Would you go through it?'

Her face was turned away from him, but it filled Locke's mind, the prettiness of it on the dunes when the wind had blustered her hair. 'I'm not trained for . . . Why?'

'Would you go through the fence for a man's liberty?'

He snarled, 'For a bloody symbol, a tatty old symbol of yesterday, geriatric's games . . . No.'

'For a man's liberty?'

He thought of the computer codes in the console on the table, the procedures for transmission, the call-signs – any bloody thing. He could not escape her. 'So that Rupert Mowbray can swagger in London? No.'

'For liberty?'

'I'm not trained . . . No.'

The candle's flame hovered above the pool of wax.

A rap on the door. It opened, but the door was beyond the candle's light. He heard the scrape of something pushed inside, then the door closed.

Bikov crawled away.

Viktor could no longer remember what he had said, where he had been led.

Bikov placed a plate of soup and a spoon beside the candle.

'Is it for you or for me?'

'For both of us, Viktor. We are together, we share.'

14

Q. In Communist times where was the largest area of the Soviet Union that was a closed military enclave?

A. Kaliningrad.

There was one bowl and one spoon. Viktor thanked Bikov each time the spoon was passed to him. He took it and crouched, his weight forward, his head lowered, dipped the spoon into the thin stock and fished for meat or potato or a scrap of cabbage leaf, then lifted it to his mouth. His hand shook from the weakness of exhaustion and hunger, and much of the soup spilled from the spoon before reaching his lips. After he had taken what he could, a single dip for the boiled water, the pieces of meat, potato, cabbage, and had sucked it clean, he solemnly passed the spoon back to Bikov, and each time he was thanked with a quiet courtesy. The spoon went backwards and forwards between them and the bowl gradually emptied. His mind now was too confused to realize the game played with him. They were together, they shared, they bonded . . . The candle threw low light over them, still bold but dimming . . . He thought, as his mind addled, that it was kind of Bikov to share a single bowl of stew and a single spoon with him. He felt a growing gratitude to the man on the far side of the candle.

Viktor knew of the *gulag* camps, and of the *zeks* who had inhabited them. They were written about in the modern Russia. There were huts of thin wooden planks deep in the forests rooted in permafrost, surrounded by wire and guards, where the denounced enemies of the old regime had been sent to rot and to die. They would have eaten, shivering, the same bowl of stew that he now shared with Bikov. He had refused Bikov's sweater, and wished he had accepted it. The cold cut into him. Where he had been at school, at a base near Novosibirsk, before the family had moved to the experimental station at Totskoye, there had been an old woman who cleaned the classrooms, the pupils' lavatories and the canteen where they ate. She had had dead eyes and a death pallor below and around them, and it was whispered that she had been in the camps as a young woman, had survived, and the pupils had been frightened to speak to her. What he remembered of her was her savage criticism of any pupil who left food on a plate when she came to lift it off the table . . . Only when he had read of the conditions in the *gulag* had he understood. The water and the scraps rumbled in his stomach, seemed to make his hunger worse, and his head rocked with tiredness.

When there was only tasteless water left, Viktor thought of the plates of meat, potato and cabbage served in the senior officers' mess, piled high, and the beer brought by stewards. It seemed to Viktor that Bikov looked away and into the darkness. He slipped the spoon, a fast but clumsy movement, back into the bowl and dredged it again. He craved to eat, then sleep, and to be warm. The spoon scraped the bottom of the bowl.

'Go on, Viktor, you finish it.'

He crumpled. He did not think he had been seen when he broke the rules of sharing. The voice was kindness. Bikov had made a sacrifice for him, had gone without because his, Viktor's, need was greater . . . The woman who had cleaned in the school and had taken the plates with food left on them from the table of the pupils' canteen would not have shared: she would have scratched the eyes from any woman in the *gulag* who had eaten more than her share.

'It's all right, Viktor, it's for you.'

He dropped the spoon on to the concrete floor. He trembled as he reached, with both hands, for the bowl and lifted it. He tilted it. Lukewarm water ran into his mouth and he felt the remaining meat fibres, the potato pulp and the wafer pieces of cabbage stick between his teeth. He cursed that some of the water dribbled from his mouth and was lost. He licked the bowl. His tongue wiped it, caressed it, cleaned it. He licked it until the bottom of the bowl was bare and the only taste in his mouth was that of the plastic. He knew he had cheapened himself and a wave of regret splashed him.

'Thank you – I am sorry, but . . . thank you.'

'For nothing, Viktor. We are friends.'

There had been other friends, but too long ago. Because of those friends, forgotten, he had run on the beach and had made the chalk marks on the wrecked fishing-boat, and he had seen the friends' answer – and a friend had been in the zoo park, had brushed him, and he had followed the friend, had seen the open door of the waiting car. They were gone. And Mowbray, who had hugged him, was gone . . . and Alice who had loved him. He thanked his *friend* and was humbled because he had cheated him.

'I should not have done that, taken your food. I am ashamed.'

'No cause for shame, Viktor. You are tired and cold and hungry – most of all you are tired and want to sleep. Soon, Viktor, you will sleep . . .'

The candle's flame glistened a reflection on the wax pool.

'A little more, Viktor, and then you sleep.'

The stock pressured on his shoulder as he fired the last bullets of the last belt.

The last bullet was a skimming red dot, tracer, that left the barrel at a velocity of 850 metres a second. He saw it go, his eyes clung to its trajectory. It was on target then seemed to dip late in its flight of two and one-third seconds, and its bright red flame, alive in the rain mist, ducked below the illuminated target. Perhaps the shudder of firing had dug the tripod legs deeper into the mud, perhaps his arm had flicked against the distance dial on the sight mounted over the breech . . . Perhaps his soul was not locked to the concentration required to fire the heavy machine-gun at the maximum of its effective range.

The rain fell on him.

He wiped his forehead. Away in front of him the light was shining up at the target. Without his sight to magnify it, the target was little larger than the red dot that had dropped short . . . He had missed food back at the base, he would get nothing hot. If he was lucky he might successfully plead in the cookhouse for a loaf end, and an apple if he was luckier. He must be back by midnight because that night 8 Platoon, 3rd company – from midnight – was duty platoon.

He stood, stretched, then heaved a tarpaulin over the weapon . . . Igor Vasiliev was young and he was stubborn. Captain Archenko had said to him that if he wanted to achieve excellence he must always be *dedicated*. Vasiliev did not accept that he was stubborn, but the thought of dedication gave him warmth. He could not comprehend the arrest of Captain Archenko, would not have believed it if he had not seen it, but he remembered what he had been told.

Dedication meant that he should walk 2000 metres in the driving rain, to examine the target butts. He should find the pattern of his failed shooting. It was an obligation to him.

He started out on the long trudge along the track beside the range. He had to know the pattern of his failure.

Into a little scooped hole, Ham dropped the four clingfilm-wrapped bundles of faeces, then scraped the earth and pine needles over them.

Billy checked his watch, watched the circling second hand, then peered at each of them to satisfy himself that their faces and hands were well enough smeared with camouflage cream. He felt each buckle in their webbing to satisfy himself that they were wrapped and would not scrape together.

The kit that they would come back for was piled by Lofty at the entrance to the basher, to be collected on the way to the beach.

Wickso's hand, as it had a half-dozen times before, felt against the chest pockets of his tunic as if he needed to reassure himself again that the morphine syringes and the additional field dressings were in place.

They moved out . . . and, thank Christ, the machine-gun had stopped firing.

Lofty made the sign, and they armed their weapons. The sounds of metal on metal seemed to fill the tree canopy above them.

They slipped, ghosts, between the trees. Lofty led. He was the one with the greatest confidence. None of them, back in the days with the Squadron, would have hesitated about going forward in darkness, but that was too long ago. Billy could have done it, but Lofty had pushed himself forward. Lofty didn't need an image-intensifier, preferred to let his eyes acclimatize to the wet murk of the early night, and he went first, Billy was close behind, then Ham, and Wickso was back marker. Lofty had Billy's plastic shreds to guide him. He weighed each footfall as he walked, and he felt with his outstretched hand ahead of him for snags when he crawled. He took them close to the skull in the helmet that Billy had found, and through the network of old trenches and around two bunkers. It was where men had died half a century before, but that did not faze Lofty. He was the right man to lead.

For Lofty, it was like moving between the stones at Tyne Cot cemetery. When he came to each plastic piece, left by Billy at fifty-metre intervals, he stopped and crouched and the team halted behind him, and he listened. He heard nothing beyond the pattering drip of the rain down through the pine branches.

He led the team towards the rendezvous.

Ahead, the trees thinned.

It was not the 'scope sight, not the tripod legs. He could blame no one but himself. The well-used white canvas of the target, three metres high, had former hits covered with white-painted adhesive tape. He had found new holes in the outer area of the target, beyond the largest of the concentric circles, and a few inside the outer ring, and precious few within the inner circles close to the black bull. At least half of the shots he had fired had missed the target completely. In the brick-reinforced area where the spotters waited during the firing, Vasiliev switched off the lights that had lit the target. Obstinacy had brought him there, and was rewarded with the confirmation that his shooting had been pathetic, that of a recruit without talent. He slipped on the mud, regained his balance, then staggered towards the track and the start of the long walk back to where he had left the machine-gun . . . He hoped to get a ride back on a patrol vehicle to the ferry for the canal crossing.

They had closed up. Between them and the track was the last line of trees and then a few metres of waist-high scrub – where birches had been cut back and their roots had sprouted. Lofty had a good view of the track and could identify the stone, forty paces away, that was the kilometre marker.

Billy murmured, 'He's not here.'

Wickso whispered, 'It's early.'

Billy muttered, 'It's only two minutes early – and he's not here, shit . . .'

They had done the last fifty metres to the edge of the trees on their stomachs, going forward in the crawl. Lofty stood. He worked his body against a pine's trunk and made no outline. They'd rely on him, on the quality of his eyesight, he'd always been the best of them in darkness, and on the quality of his hearing. He was looking down the track, away towards the dull glow of distant lights that threw a faint orange sheen on the clouds where Ferret would come from. All the weapons were cocked, had been since they left the basher, and both Lofty's hands were on the grenade-launcher. He'd been tailed the last time, Ferret had. Billy had the job to watch right, Ham to the left, and Wickso took responsibility for behind them and the escape route. Lofty's firing finger lay on the trigger guard . . . He heard the movement, to the right. He felt Billy stiffen, muscles tightening. Lofty heard the slithering of feet in mud. He should have been coming quietly, but the feet weren't careful.

Lofty saw him.

Behind Lofty, Ham stifled a sneeze.

He was out to the right, moving at snail's pace towards the track. The shape was blurred, the arms and legs indistinct. Lofty strained to see him better. His heart pounded. Deep down in his guts, Lofty had not believed that Ferret would come . . . and he was there, and reached the track.

Again, behind Lofty, Ham gulped on his sneeze. Lofty slipped his hand from the launcher's trigger guard, reached back and found Ham's head, then his ear, then his cheek, and clamped the hand over Ham's mouth. Maybe the sound from Ham had not reached Ferret, maybe Ferret only sensed their presence. The shape, the figure – Ferret – paused in the centre of the track. He seemed to stand, irresolute, alone, and Lofty watched him, struggled to see him better. His hand slid from Ham's mouth and down to his tunic collar. Lofty held the collar tight in his fist and eased Ham up beside him. He could not see Ferret's face, only the black figure of the man in the middle of the track. The man seemed to turn, to study the trees ahead of him and the track behind him, the path along which he had come. Then he swung his whole body to face the sea and the beach . . . If he had thought he was followed Ferret would have crouched down or would have come into the trees, or would have found a ditch to lie in or an old trench, but he stood in the centre of the track.

Alongside Lofty, Billy's mouth was against Ham's ear. They passed Lofty. Neither was as skilled as Lofty at moving in forest or across scrubland. A branch snapped, a scrub sprig whipped back. They were bent low as they halved the distance to the track.

Frozen, unable to will himself to move, Vasiliev heard a deer, a fox or a badger coming close to him . . . not a patrol. When he was on patrol in the peninsula's forest they smoked and talked. The call came, and he sucked at air in astonishment.

In Russian, a strange distorted accent, 'Viktor, this way. Quickly, Viktor. Come to us.'

He should have run, did not. The fear, now, bled the strength from him. His legs were locked.

'Viktor, it's us, from Alice. Get to us. We cover your back. Come . . .'

Lofty heard the hissed whisper command Ham gave.

Ferret was beside the marker, on the track, on schedule. He did not move . . . Too frightened to run, poor bastard. Lofty had the weapon up to his shoulder and his finger was back on the trigger guard. Wickso panted beside him.

Billy moved. Ham followed him. Billy exploded in a sprint through the scrub and Ham followed him.

They reached Ferret. Lofty watched. They had him. The turn and the run back across the scrub and into the trees. No shouts, no instructions, no commands – only movement, speed. Disregard for noise, pace counted. When they came to him, Lofty peeled away from the tree-trunk that had sheltered him and led the charge. He sensed that Ferret had seized up, would have been the shock and the relief – and they dragged him like he was handicapped and useless. It was reckless chaos, and without Lofty leading them they would have charged into trees, fallen into the trenches, tripped on the old bunker roofs. It was the best moment in his life that Lofty could think of, the most fulfilment. Better than when he had been awarded the green beret at Lympstone and better than when he had passed the swimmer-canoeist course for entry into the Squadron, the best moment. They ran. Once Billy and Lofty, with Ferret between them, fell into a trench, but they were the living, not the dead who had gone to unknown graves there. They had the route out, the sunken dinghy. Lofty went past the basher, took the animal's path away from the fallen pine roots. Wickso would bring the kit from the basher – the inflatable bags, and the wetsuits.

The trees broke open in front of Lofty. The rain doused him and the wind carrying it caught at his tunic. He dropped down in the loose sand of the dunes. A way out, across the popple of the waves, were the red and green blinking lights of the *Princess Rose*. Lofty pulled from his pocket the beacon box that would guide the swimmer, Billy, to the dinghy, down on the seabed. He had the pencil torch in his hand.

A voice, shrill and terrified, babbled in Russian – it was a kid's voice.

'The bloody torch, Lofty, give it me,' Billy snapped.

It was ripped from his hand. The beam shone into the face, lit it. Ham swore.

The light pierced his eyes. Vasiliev wet himself. They were above him. The light bounced back from his face and he saw the black cream across their faces, on their hands, and the weapons.

The beam showed half of a kid's face, half of the terror in his staring eyes, the gape of his mouth, and they heard the stuttering breathing. Billy gazed up at the cloud ceiling and the rain racked down on him. Ham beat his fists in frustration into the sand. Noisily, Wickso lugged the gear after him, then dropped it, saw the face the torch half lit, and swore. 'Who the fuck is that?'

Lofty said quietly, 'Murphy's law – when something can cock up, it will . . .'

'Bloody helpful, Lofty. Stuff it, for fuck's sake,' Billy clattered.

'I was observing the obvious, I—'

Wickso said, 'What we going to do, Billy?'

Lofty said, 'Your job to think, Billy, always was.'

Billy said, 'I *am* fucking thinking, so quieten down.'

Lofty and Ham held the kid. Wickso crouched close to them and watched the trees with his back to the sea, the distant light of the *Princess Rose*, and they left Billy to his thinking as they always had. Lofty and Ham held him, but Lofty knew it was unnecessary. The kid was supine, terrified, and maybe he could see the bright lights of their eyes set in the black of the camouflage cream. The kid was going nowhere.

Billy said, breathing in fast bursts, 'He could be there, Viktor could be . . . Could have been five minutes late, or ten, but we'd bugged out . . . Have to go back, have to see if he's there. Got me?' The voice dropped. 'And there's the sunshine boy, wrong place at the wrong time. Witness. Eyewitness. Saw us, heard us, so we're not deniable. Can't leave him. Anyone got a better idea? Anyone else want to do some thinking? Yes, or no?'

Did he know? Lofty thought the kid knew. The eyes gazed up at them, popped and stared and pleaded. They were trained to kill, but the training was old. They had been taken back into civilian life of a sort, and the training had gone cold. Lofty thought it would be the same for all of them. His hands loosed the kid's battledress, and Ham's, and Wickso eased back in the darkness as if he wanted no part of it. But Billy wasn't challenged, never had been, not by any of them: his was the word of law. Billy had drowned the boy in the lough, and he had led them in the silence that confronted the Crime Squad detectives. Lofty knew there would be no volunteers, not for a killing in cold blood. Billy held out his hand for the torch and Lofty gave it to him. Billy took the torch and he shone it in turn – fast, raking movements – into each of their faces. Lofty twisted his head away from the beam, and Ham, and Wickso turned his back on it. When the beam moved away, they saw Billy's hand reach for four strands of dune grass and he snapped them off, broke one strand so it was half the length of the other three. He put the hand behind his back, where he couldn't see it himself, where he could shuffle the strands. His hand came back, hovered over his lap, and he shone the torch on the four strands of equal length.

'Short strand does it – you first, Wickso,' Billy said, and there was a tremor in his voice. Lofty hadn't heard it before.

Wickso's hand shook as he pulled the grass from Billy's fist, then Ham took his. Lofty's choice of two. Lofty, with Billy, had held the man down under the lough water and it had screwed his life. He walked and talked with ghosts as retribution. Lofty took a strand. The torch shone on to Billy's fist and he opened it: his strand was long. The torch wavered on and Wickso's hand opened: long. To Ham: short . . . Lofty let his strand drop.

'Just do it, Ham,' Billy said.

'No problem.'

Lofty knew he should have argued, should have kicked against it. He pushed himself up. Billy switched off the torch beam.

'Do it, Ham, so he doesn't get found.'

'No problem.'

'We'll give him an hour, an hour for Viktor, then it's abort. Be ready for us.'

'No problem.' The monotone answer.

Billy headed off the dunes, for the trees. Wickso was close to him, and Lofty had to scurry to catch them. At the trees, Lofty turned and looked back. He fancied, couldn't be certain, that there was a flash of a knife's blade and Ham stood high over where the kid lay. In the trees, Wickso stopped, threw up, then hurried on to catch Billy. They went faster than the first time, made more noise, didn't care. Lofty, clumsy, fell into a trench, a shallow zigzag in the forest floor. The ghosts closed around him, and the trees of the forest seemed to press against him and to crush him.

Locke was cruel and meant to be.

'They haven't called, and they should have. As soon as there's a hand on his collar, they'd have called. It's late . . . He's not bloody coming. I know it.'

He sat at the table, earphones on his head. She was by the kitchen's inner door. He was cruel because he wanted to wipe the composure off her.

'They wouldn't wait till they were on the beach, or till they were launched. They'll be hanging on and hoping. He's not coming. The whole bloody thing was a waste of time.'

She gazed back at him and gave him nothing. He wanted her to weep or turn away.

'Forget it, Alice. Forget him . . . He's not coming.'

He thought her steady gaze, unwavering, belittled him.

The second time . . . *Very good, Viktor, a session of outstanding value – and I want you to know that in London our experts are ready and waiting to receive this latest material, and they all have a huge admiration of what you do for us. Time you were gone, Viktor – and time, Alice, that you were in bed.* If Mowbray had smirked she hadn't seen it. And he'd yawned, like he had the first time, to signal their dismissal. They'd gone down the corridor running. Key into the door. No hesitations, no shyness. She'd said it out loud, told him that since the first time she'd gone on the pill, never before in her life been on the pill, and long enough since the last Gdansk trip to have given the pill's cycle time. Not a minute wasted. Clothes stripped off, his and hers, thrown down, shoes kicked away. The rooms either side would have heard their little cries. Each day, at her desk in the Service's section of the embassy in Warsaw, and each night at the little apartment the embassy rented for her, she'd pleaded for the day's and night's hours to hurry by. Him on her, then her on him, and fingers finding the secret places of each other. She thought then, and now, that the best thing she did was to make him lose the tension in his shoulders, arms and fingers, and in his mind, as if she lifted off him the burden of it. But hours went too quickly. Rolling away from her, coming out of her, slipping off the bed, dressing with fumbled hands because he gazed so wistfully at her as she lay on the bed, the door closing after him. Alice twisting on to her stomach and burying her face in the soft pillow and feeling the sweat of him on her and the wetness of him in her . . . and loving him.

They were on the beach, and the rain came off the sea and drenched them.

It was the turn of Jerry the Pole to fish. He thought it was with reluctance that the Russian, Chelbia, gave up the line. The fisherman, Roman, baited the hooks and cast the line out for him because he did not have that skill, then gave him the line to hold. The rain came from behind and soaked the shoulders of his coat and his trousers below its hem, and the sand caked his shoes. The bucket beside his feet was now half filled with fish caught and dragged in by the Russian, Chelbia . . . Roman had said that night, and driving rain, was always a good time to fish because the sand on the sea's floor was churned and food was thrown up for the cod, mackerel and plaice.

Jerry felt the sharp tug and whipped back his wrist. He chortled like a child at the weight on the line. 'I used to fish here when I was a small boy, but for fun . . . In the war I fished here for food, till we left. In my life this is the only beach I have fished from, but never at night.' He was pulling in the line and the slack tangled against his legs. 'Did you fish as a boy, Boris?'

The voice was quiet against the wind's song and the waves on the sand and the rain's beat. 'Only as a boy – I don't have the time to fish now. I used to fish with my uncle. He was a good fisherman. We went to the Kaliningrad canal, and what we caught was eaten – even the heads and bones went to make soup. I loved to fish.'

Jerry the Pole knew that the man, Boris Chelbia, was *mafiya*, and could not imagine why he was there on the Mierzeja Wislana – the body of him and the stature of him was *mafiya*. It reeked from his stance, his voice and his authority. The *mafiya* from Russia were not interested in properties in Wannsee, or the exclusive renovated villas across the Glienicker bridge that faced on to the Potsdam road. They bought the more expensive apartments, newly built, in the heart of the city. They had made their Berlin ghetto off Unter den Linden and in the new luxury towers sprouting across the old no man's land of the Wall – Mowbray's hunting-ground, where Jerry the Pole had been king, long ago. Not often, but sometimes, once a month and not more, Jerry the Pole made himself a plastic box full of sandwiches and, with a flask of coffee, took the S-bahn to the hunting-ground and his kingdom. He would sit on a bench in sunshine or in snow and the new apartments, new offices and new hotels would disappear from his eyes and be replaced by the grey concrete of the Wall, the guards in the watchtowers, the dogs and the guns; and he would feel the pride of involvement and achievement. When he was ready to leave the bench on Wilhelmstrasse or Leipzigerstrasse or

298

Friedrichstrasse, and the memories of the Wall had gone from his mind, he would see the new homes of the Russian *mafiya*, and he would watch them strut from their new Mercedes cars and he would envy their new clothes, their new confidence. The city was theirs: they knew it, and Jerry the Pole knew it. They did prostitution, and people trafficking, they smuggled cigarettes and cars, they were untouchable. When he took the S-bahn train home, and when he bought a newspaper, he could read of the murderous feuds for territory. They could be envied often but rarely crossed. The newspapers carried photographs of those who crossed them, and the blood in the gutters . . . And he had never seen one of them carrying a fishing-rod.

But he was not in Berlin. The fish was at his feet, and Roman knelt, ripped the hook from it and threw it casually into the darkness, into the bucket . . . He was on the Mierzeja Wislana, on a spit, two kilometres from the Russian border. Boris, the *mafiya* man, had been given ten successive casts by the fisherman. Jerry the Pole had had one cast. Roman took the line from Jerry's hand and gave it to the Russian, then skewered a shrimp on to the hook. The boldness came from his annoyance.

'So, Boris Chelbia, why do you wish to meet me?'

'I had a reason when I came – but I believe, at this moment, another reason makes it more valuable that we met. Do I talk in a riddle? Sufficient for you, I do import and export, into and out of Kaliningrad.' By now the Russian could throw his own cast. 'Now I am fishing . . . That is my business, my only business . . . I like fishing.'

The Russian turned and shouted into the wind and the rain. They were lit. A car's headlights blazed a cone down on to the beach and it caught them, threw their shadows across the sand and into the surf. Jerry the Pole thought it strange, amazing, incomprehensible, that he – the 'bottle-washer' of the Secret Intelligence Service of the United Kingdom, *no* pension – should be out and exposed on a foul night fishing by hand-line with a local and with a principal of the *mafiya* from Kaliningrad. He could see the lights of the buoys, tossing and winking, that marked the map line between Poland's and Russia's territorial waters. He did not know the plan that Mr Rupert

Mowbray had made, had not been trusted with it. He had no pension, no income, he survived on the frugal handouts of the German government. Soon, when the developers came with the architects, he would be turfed on to the street from his room across the Glienicker bridge. He sidled close to the Russian. Fuck the *Princess Rose*, whose lights rolled far out in the sea to the east, and fuck Mr Rupert Mowbray, who did not trust him, and double-fuck Mr Locke, who would not speak up for him in London about his pension.

'I am not, of course, a smuggler, but what an interesting place we are at . . . No fences and no Customs . . . To a smuggler it would be a place of great interest.'

The marker stone was a dull blur beside the track.

'Five minutes more,' Billy whispered.

Lofty heard Wickso's murmur: 'Five minutes only, then out.'

'You OK, Lofty?'

'Five minutes, then we quit . . . He's not coming. I'm OK.'

For near to an hour it had been unspoken. Nothing moved on the track. Lofty didn't need night-vision goggles to tell him that nothing, nobody, was coming. Four times Billy had called, used the owl's screech, and had won no response from the rain and the thickening mist. Billy's call had reverberated into the darkness and its shrill note had bounced back from the cloud ceiling, then dissipated into the mist – and nothing, nobody, came.

They sagged again into silence. Maybe they all thought – Billy, Wickso and Lofty – of the kid left behind with Ham. The short strand had gone to the right hand, Ham's, *no problem*. Ham would do it with a knife, or would throttle him, or would take him down into the water and drown him. Ham didn't do mercy.

Billy said he'd try one last time. The cry of the owl beat against the rain, the cloud and the mist, and was answered.

The cry came back, like a cock answered a hen. They were all taut, and Lofty stifled his breath. The answer came again, a low-pitched shriek – but behind them.

They were twisting in the scrub. The track in front of them was empty. They faced into the trees.

The shriek came again, and Billy called back.

Ham reached them. Crawling, free, behind Ham was the kid. Lofty gaped.

Ham said, 'Don't fucking interrupt me, guys, just listen. I was going to do him, slit his bloody throat. He couldn't scream, his voice was just a little whimper. He'd pissed himself and shit himself. I tell you, don't get up-wind of him, not if you haven't a peg on your nose. We'd used the name, hadn't we – Viktor? I had, Billy had. I'd got the knife out, and he found his voice – it was all about "Viktor". I start to listen. Then there's the full name. "Viktor Archenko". He's heard us use the name "Viktor", and he's blathering about the Viktor he knows. It's Viktor Archenko . . . You hearing me? It's only the same Captain, second rank, Viktor Archenko. I have a knife in my hand, two inches from his throat, and he's telling me about Captain, second rank, Viktor Archenko who is chief of staff to the fleet commander. I can't bloody believe what I'm hearing.

'I put the knife down. I put it in the sand where he can't see it. I tell him to cough it. He is a conscript, is Igor Vasiliev, and is doing his third year military service, and Viktor Archenko is his friend. It's what he called him, his *friend*. "How good a friend?" I ask. A good enough friend for Viktor to have gone into the water two or three days ago – I can't remember which, sorry – to fish him out when he'd been beaten and dumped in the docks for whistle-blowing on a weapons theft out of the armoury, and – detail doesn't matter – he drives him, and he talks to him . . . What do they talk about, a bloody conscript and the fleet commander's chief of staff? Archaeology. They talk about Malbork Castle . . . Alice and that dickhead Locke . . . the stop there, on the way to Braniewo. Doesn't take a rocket scientist to work out it's the dead-drop place. Easy enough to confirm. Call Locke up, ask him about Malbork Castle . . . I believed him. He was out shooting, it's been him on the range with that bloody machine-gun, but his shooting's been shit, and he came to the targets to see his spread.

'If he's conned me then he's done bloody well – God help me, I should know a lying shyster. He fired this morning and had a stack of bulls. He's the star, and he's going to shoot in a championship. Hear me, guys, be patient. His shooting was shit because of what he saw this afternoon, just after lunch. He was at the base, Baltiysk, and on his way to the headquarters block, in the hope of seeing his pal, the captain, wanting to tell him how well he'd shot in the morning session – it's where the encouragement comes from . . . He saw Viktor arrested.

'The way he tells it, Viktor came out of the building and was grabbed, handcuffs and a scuffle. Then he was thrown into a car, which went away fast. It was quick, quick enough for no one to see anything, 'cept the kid. That's professional. The base ticks over, unaware, but Viktor has been arrested. What's important, I think so, the car didn't shift towards the main gate and out, but away past the senior officers' mess, and that's the natural route – he's very exact – to the FSB's place . . . so, it's the heavy mob. The kid told me this and he was blubbering. He didn't act it. I'd put my life on it, I mean it. Viktor Archenko is banged up with the spooks. That's where we are, guys. He even drew me a map – I believe every word he told me.'

'Where does that leave us?' Wickso hissed.

'Up the creek, no pole,' Billy said.

'Time to get on the radio,' Ham murmured.

It hurt Lofty bad. Maybe of all of them redemption mattered most to Lofty. Billy would make the call on the radio, and would talk *failure*. The relay was Locke, and Alice. Alice would know that they had been too late, too slow – no one's fault – and that they had lost their man. The message would go to Mowbray on the ship. Mowbray would call London, and London would rubber-stamp the obvious. Abort, out, quit. Back at Tyne Cot by the end of the week. Sweeping leaves, tidying the beds, cutting grass, scrubbing the lichen off the stones, making the place fit for the families of the veterans on Remembrance Day, and the chance of exorcizing the guilt for ever gone.

Lofty heard Billy ask, 'And what do we do with him?'

Ham answered, 'Turn him loose – he won't cough on us.'

'No harm in it.'

Wickso chipped in, 'Why did he draw the map?'

Ham said, 'So we could go and get him.' Lofty had never heard, before, Ham speak like that, so serious, so lacking in cut and crap and sarcasm. 'So we could go and get Viktor out.'

'Tell him to fuck off,' Billy said.

Ham bent and whispered, Russian, in the kid's ear. He was gone. Another of Lofty's ghosts, the kid went up to the track, never looked back at them, never waved, and then the cloud caught him, and the rain and the mist. Twenty paces down the track and they'd lost sight of him. Billy was fiddling with the radio strapped to his chest, and Ham helped him. Wickso passed Lofty a stick of gum.

'Thanks – we were too late.'

Hope died.

Rupert Mowbray took the signal relayed to him by Locke. It was staccato, brief and without soul, and it wounded: 'Havoc 1 to Havoc 2. Ferret No Show. Delta 1 reports, confused, Ferret arrested and held by FSB on base. Confirm Delta team should Abort soonest. Out.' A prize had slipped from his fingers. He sat at the table in the master's cabin and the radio slid as the *Princess Rose* bucked.

He responded. His voice quavered as he spoke into the microphone. 'The boys on the ground, do they think there's anything they can do? Out?'

A brittle laugh answered him. 'Havoc 1 to Havoc 2. Are we ignoring standard radio procedures? I'll pass your query to Delta 1. Straw-clutching, aren't you? Nothing can be done. We should Abort soonest. Out.'

He slumped.

Lofty crouched to hear Billy, and felt a sense of joy.

'What you have to remember, guys, is that *Who Dares Wins*, the Hereford Gun Club, and *By Strength and by Guile*, the Poole regatta people, found all this was too dangerous. They copped out. Mowbray said, when we still had the chance to walk away, "He is one of the bravest men I have been privileged to know, and I – and you – are going to save that man's life." Is my life fucked up? Yes . . . I put paint on bits of paper, and I live where people can't find me. That's a life that's fucked. How's your life, Ham?'

'I've not a pressing appointment, not one that can't wait.'

'You fucked, Wickso, or are you in good shape?'

'Reckon that if I'm not back tomorrow they'll have to close A&E,

'cause they can't do without me. But they'll have to, till the weekend.'

'Lofty, we're all fucked up – you the same?'

'We have a hard time the week before the eleventh hour of the eleventh day of the eleventh month . . . As long as I'm back by then.'

All brittle answers, Lofty's and theirs. Bullshit answers.

A little quiet whisper from Billy, 'It's everyone or it's no one. It's the team or it doesn't happen. Has to be you, Ham, because you've the language and do communications. Lofty – because we'll need the bloody launcher and you're the best man on it. And you, Wickso – and I'm not dwelling on it – the medic. Me, I lead . . . if I could slim it down, can't, I would . . . We use the big three Ss – Speed, Surprise and a Shitload of luck. We have a wing, the map, a prayer, and not much else.'

Lofty reached out his hand in the darkness and caught Billy's fist, then Ham's gripped theirs, and Wickso's clamped them.

London's evening light threw smeared ripples on the river below them.

'You misunderstand me – what I have instructed is a reconnaissance, a probe. That's all.'

The voice boomed from twin speakers behind the wide desk, at each end of the window. The voice, scrambled and distorted, spoke to them with God's own tenor. It had a resonance of calm. Bertie Ponsford prowled between the speakers, his feet silent on the pile carpet, and Peter Giles was sprawled across the room's easy chair, picking at invisible dirt under his fingernails. The director general sat on his desk. His shoes dangled a little above the carpet and he whacked a rhythm, his heels against the desk's broad legs. Each in their own way, the DG, Giles and Ponsford, understood their affliction: they were second-guess men, and the action they could either sanction or countermand was far away. None of them could summon up a clear picture, only a vague image, of the coaster – the *Princess Rose* – heaving on her anchor chain out on the Baltic on a wild night. They depended on his counsel, and the beggar would know it.

'What I'm saying, the Delta team will push forward and examine the situation on the ground. They will move with great caution. I have been very specific about that. No risks are to be taken. Nothing will be done that compromises them. I am *almost* certain that there is nothing they can do for Ferret, but I would be ashamed if I was not *absolutely* certain that he is beyond our reach . . .'

The coffee was untouched, the biscuits uneaten. They listened, and the voice dominated them. To each of them, he seemed to stand with legs apart in the centre of the carpet, and the metallic tang of his tone carried an authority that was owned by none of them. In the old culture of the Service, men on the ground ruled and their initiative was backed by their seniors, but these were new times. They wriggled while he spoke through the speakers.

'I thank you for your anecdote from Grozny. An interrogator is called back to Moscow on a matter of urgency. It fits the mould. He will now be at the base at Baltiysk, a better bet than any you'll make on the Gold Cup. He will have had Ferret with him from early this afternoon, but I venture to suggest – from my considerable experience – that he will wish to keep Ferret with him, *in situ*, during his preliminary questioning. Myself, I'd not want to ship Ferret out until I had been through his quarters, his office, his telephone calls' list, his contacts, before he's off to the Lubyanka. We have a few more hours, probably until dawn, a little window is open. All that I suggest is a reconnaissance, an evaluation – then a speedy intervention or, more probably, an orderly withdrawal. I believe, I would emphasize it most strongly, that Ferret's loyalty to us demands we do what we can for him. We're up for it, but that's not what counts. It's in your hands, gentlemen.'

The DG held down the microphone's button beside his hip. 'Thank you, Rupert, and as eloquent as I would have expected. Can you wait a moment, please, while we discuss?' His finger came off the button. In the atmospheric crackle through the speakers were the merged rattle of a glass, the sharp yap of a small dog, an oath and a thud, then: 'Get out, you little bugger.' He threw another switch and the speakers died. The DG's feet beat harder on the desk's legs, the habit that had become addictive in the days after nine-eleven. It was a signal to Ponsford and Giles of the stress burdening him. 'I sense mission-creep here – but when did a mission of value not assume creep? When did a mission that was worthwhile not acquire a motion of its own? *Havoc*, Peter, the name given the mission, is that Rupert's or yours? Who called it "Havoc"?'

'Rupert did.'

'And, Bertie, you gave "Havoc" your blessing?'

Ponsford squirmed. He wanted out of the meeting, wanted responsibility off his back. 'Confusion and chaos, that's "Havoc". New names for operations are so difficult to find – I . . .'

The DG's heels made a drumbeat. 'In the ninth year of the reign of Richard the Second, fourteenth-century stuff, the military command of "Havock" was forbidden under pain of death. A tract entitled the Office of the Constable and Mareschall in Time of War, states "the peyne of him that crieth havock, and of them that followeth him" is a capital offence. You see, gentlemen, it was the medieval order to massacre without quarter. That's where we are – is it where we want to be?'

'I didn't see it that way . . .' Giles muttered.

Ponsford paced. 'It's only a name . . .'

'I believe you do Rupert a disservice – a very exact man. "Massacre without quarter." Very little that Rupert does has not been planned. All right . . . all right . . . May we go back to the beginning? Back to basics – why did we launch?'

'*Loyalty,*' Giles mouthed the word. 'And *duty* to a friend.'

Ponsford said, 'For the *reputation* of the Service.'

The shoes' heels pounded the desk's legs. 'Powerful ingredients – loyalty, duty and reputation – matters of pride and honour. Only reconnaissance, correct? I am trusting Rupert and that, I know, is unwise. It will have gone beyond his control and he will be a mere spectator. No massacre without quarter, understood? The young man there, Locke, he's sensible. By dawn they're off the ground, and out. Give Locke authority. First light, out. We should not forget that we revelled and oozed pleasure when we shared Ferret's material across the Atlantic, so we will at least try to fulfil our debt to the poor wretch. Out . . . by first light.'

'Mowbray's no longer running it,' Locke said. 'I've been given authority.'

She blanched. It was the first time he had seen Alice's shoulders droop. 'What will you do with it?'

'Let them amble about a bit.' A coolness in his voice. 'London won't bite on it, they're still digesting Rupert's nonsense about loyalty, duty, debts – the team can do reconnaissance, whatever that means, then they abort by dawn. I have control over them.'

'You'll enjoy that.'

'And what I also understand from London, they're now talking "damage limitation" . . . Your friend is being worked over by a senior interrogator. He'll crack. They all do. A bit of bravado, a little intellectual wrestling, then he'll break. Damage limitation and denial – the pity is they didn't think of it before they started this joke operation.'

In the kitchen's darkness he could not see her face. She said softly, without malice, 'As long as it's not you, Gabriel, who's damaged.'

While there had been no message from along the peninsula, beyond the fence and the watchtower, she had nurtured a hope. The message, when it had come, had slipped the last-chance faith in success from her fingers. It was smashed in shards on the floor at her feet.

'It won't be. They all bluster, then they crack.'

Bikov knelt in front of him. 'Viktor, stay awake.'

He forced his eyes back open.

'You have to listen to me, Viktor.'

He did not know if he had slept, or dozed, or whether his eyes had been closed only for a few seconds.

'We are going to go back, Viktor, over what you have told me.'

His eyes ached, his head throbbed, and the cold seemed deep in his body.

'And then, Viktor, you will sleep. Sleep a day and a night, and another day, if you want it.'

The candle's wick floated in the wax pool and the light from it puckered at his knees. It did not have the strength to reach to Bikov's face.

'Before you sleep, Viktor, I want to be very fair with you. I will repeat what you have said to me, and I will tell you the conclusion that I draw from it.'

He craved permission to sleep, to roll down on to the darkened concrete and curl up, knees against chest, but Bikov's hand reached past the candle and held his shoulder. He could not break the hold and lie on the floor.

'When I have told you what conclusion I draw, Viktor, you must think very carefully. You have the opportunity, then, to contradict what I suggest.'

His stomach hurt and pain nagged in the joints of his knees, hips and elbows, and the voice dripped into his ear.

'If my conclusion is wrong, Viktor, you should contradict it. If it is right, Viktor, you tell me.'

He struggled to concentrate, could not. He did not know what he had said.

'Can we start, Viktor, so that we can finish? And then you can sleep.'

He did not know that now a tape turned. Neither did he know that the lists of each logged telephone call he had made from his office and from his room lay in a file in a box, that more logs of each classified document initialled as having been read by him were also heaped in the box, photocopies of permission for him to go across the border, and records of every meeting attended . . . The box of evidence was filling. Nor did he know that a jet aircraft was fuelled and ready to taxi from a remote apron at Kaliningrad Military, that the cockpit crew were alerted to be ready for a dawn take-off, that a flight route to Moscow had been filed with Air Traffic.

'I am your friend, Viktor, and among friends only the truth is acceptable.'

Nor did he know that, far away in Chechnya, a gunship helicopter picked up a beacon's signal and located its origin as a shepherd's hut on a grassland plateau in the foothills below the Argun gorge, that the helicopter prepared to fire from its four underwing pods a total of thirty-two 57mm missiles, and would then rake the hut with its four-barrelled Gatling gun. Nor did he know who was responsible for the helicopter's flight.

'I am an honest man, Viktor, and you are. We are going to be honest with each other. Then you shall sleep.'

He tried so hard to remember the warnings Rupert Mowbray had given him. But he was across the candle from a friend, and the warnings had been about beatings, electric torture and drugs, not the dangers of a friend.

'We shall start, Viktor? Four years ago you learned from your mother, on her deathbed, that your father had been ordered to make an experimental test flight through the cloud of a nuclear explosion. It killed him. It had no scientific value. He was murdered and the killing weapon was wasting leukaemia – which you saw, but it was only four years ago that you learned the truth of the test flight. I suggest, Viktor, it was what made you turn to the opponents of Russia. You were a walk-in, you offered to spy.'

'No,' Viktor screamed. 'No – no—'

'A spy, Viktor, because of the murder of your father.'

'No.'

A silky soft voice massaged him. 'Viktor, I believe you. Of course I believe you. Your grandmother, gang-raped by troops from the Motherland, abandoned. Four years ago you learned of the rape and death of your grandmother . . .'

309

15

Q. Fifty-seven years after the German surrender, what Russian city is said never to have recovered from the Second World War?
A. Kaliningrad.

'If it had happened to my grandmother, Viktor, it would have been like a poison to me. To you, was it a poison?'

Better if he had not pared down his fingernails. He forced them into the palms of his hand, his fist clenched. He tried to make pain. Pain would hold his alertness. If he did not hurt himself he would slip back into exhaustion and betray himself. His fingernails were not long enough to make the pain bad ... He knew he hovered at the edge of collapse. The candle's last light played on his shoes and on Bikov's boots. The wick was too far burned for him to see Bikov's face. When he failed to make the pain, Viktor tilted his head up and looked for a focus point that would combat the drip of the voice, so near to him and so understanding.

'Viktor, I mean it with all sincerity. If it had been my grandmother I would have demanded vengeance.'

He could find nothing to lay his eyes on. The block, Piatkin's palace, was one of the old buildings of the base, German-built. Senior men would have used it when the base was in the hands of the German navy. Viktor had not been to this room before, but he had been in the outer office where Piatkin held court. The ceiling that he could not see now would be high. The room's walls, which were cloaked in darkness, beyond his reach, would be thick and the floor under him was solid concrete. To Viktor, the room was a tomb and the voice of a demon was in his ears.

'I don't hear your answer, Viktor. I was asking about vengeance, about poison . . . A young woman kills herself having left her baby boy on the steps of an orphanage. Do you not feel hatred?'

'I don't know . . .'

'Can you not trust me, Viktor? "I don't know . . ." If your grandmother had been mine, the hatred, the need for vengeance, would poison me.'

He blurted, 'No.'

'Vengeance . . .'

'No.'

'Together, they *poison* you.'

'No.'

He heard the sad sigh, then the syrup of the voice. 'I am disappointed in you, Viktor. I come to you as a friend. I admire you, and I respect you – but you give me no friendship and no respect. What do I have to do, Viktor, to be trusted by you? I have come to help you. You want to sleep, Viktor, and I want you to sleep. You have a burden on your back, Viktor, and I have come to share the weight of it, then to take it from you. When the burden is off, Viktor, you can sleep, and you will be at peace. Do you hear me, Viktor?'

'Yes.'

'First you learned of your father's death, then of your grandmother's death. The vengeance has to be vomited out of your mind. The hatred is there every minute of the day, and when you sleep there is no freedom from it. You will repay the killers of your father and your grandmother, repay them in kind. How? What is possible for you? There is only one way. You walk-in . . . Four years ago you were based with the Northern Fleet. I don't think there would have been Americans, but there would have been British ships and British businessmen, and you made your approach. Were you very frightened then, Viktor? What did you give them? A bundle of papers from a safe – plans and blueprints – as credentials? You were a spy . . . You want to sleep, Viktor, and it is very easy to sleep. You became a spy, yes or no? Answer the question and then you can sleep in peace. I am your friend. Yes or no?'

He gasped, 'No.'

Perhaps Viktor hoped to hear a little singing hiss of breath off the teeth of the man opposite him – frustration, irritation. He did not.

'Then, we shall move on . . .' Bikov said softly, calmly.

The searchlight's beam played on the *Princess Rose* and caught a porthole at the top of the ladder leading down to the engine room.

'I'm not going in there without this little piece of vermin,' Mowbray insisted.

He held the dog by the scruff of its neck as, once more, the mate unscrewed the steel plate that covered the hidden place between the hull and the engine-room's wall. The master was on the bridge, shouting into the radio link to the patrol-boat, and Tihomir had been given the job of hiding the old man. He didn't think they would be boarded. The light moved on and for a second time the patrol-boat circled them – but it was possible. He pushed the Englishman, who still clutched the dog, into the little black space, and heard a sigh of misery, and the dog's yelp, as he heaved the metal plate back into place. He worked frantically with his screwdriver to tighten the fastenings, then replaced the debris against the wall.

He stepped back.

'Why do we do this?' the engineer, Johannes, growled.

The grimace set at his mouth. 'Why do we do anything? Only for money.'

'She can blow us out of the water – it's an idiot's way to earn money.'

The mate asked if the engine was ready, and the engineer shrugged: the engine was ready.

'We were fools to take the money.'

The mate grinned. 'Big fools, but it was big money.'

Tihomir levered himself up the rungs. The searchlight beam fell on the little landing outside the accommodation cabins, below the bridge. The patrol-boat was a hundred metres off their starboard side and he could not look into the strength of the beam: it lit every paint scrape and every rust patch on the decks and the superstructure. He had brought the men their last meal before they had gone over the side and down into the launched dinghy. They had been very quiet, their voices had only murmured, and he'd thought that was the way of true fighting men – there had been nothing of the bravado and swagger of the mercenaries who had fought alongside him in the trenches by the river at Karlovac, his home. He had escaped his home: he wanted never again to see the trenches where the Serb advance had been stopped. It had been eleven years before but the sights, sounds, mutilation of the combat in front of his own city had been awful enough, too hideous, for him to stay. After they had scrambled over the side in their wetsuits with their weapons in the sealed bags, he had gone back down to the cabin. They had all eaten the food made for them by the Filipino cook-boy, as if a last meal was the most important; the plates had been clean. They should have been back five hours ago . . . It was all going to hell.

He climbed to the bridge. The master held the microphone against his lips but shouted as if it were necessary for his voice to carry across the hundred metres of water to the patrol-boat. Tihomir thought he shouted because he was afraid, and it was all crazy – crazy shit.

'I am doing no harm, I am an obstruction to no other vessel . . . No, I do not want a tug to tow us in . . . No, it is not necessary for us to be taken into Kaliningrad harbour . . . Yes, very soon the engine is repaired . . . Yes, I know that we are in prohibited sea space . . .'

But the money was big. A part of Tihomir's share would go towards paying for the course in advanced seamanship and navigation at the college in Genoa, and when he had that certificate he would gain a master's ticket. Another part would go to the restaurant bills in the next port he docked at. The ticket and the restaurants were all he looked for in life. The course would cost him 2000 euros, and the restaurants would cost him 100 euros a time; fine food and fine wine were the only luxuries he sought – if they came through this.

'I promise you that we will be gone by dawn. Look for us at first light and you will not find us, we will be gone . . . OK, OK, you send the tug at dawn if we are still here . . . The engine is very nearly ready for us to sail . . . I know you are doing your job, but I also am doing my job . . . By dawn we will be gone.'

'What was possible?' Tihomir thought it was crazy to imagine anything was possible. They must be back by dawn, the fighting men, or their retreat was cut off . . . In Karlovac, by the main square and close to the old barracks that had been built by the Bonapartists, was a church where the women, eleven years ago, had lit candles for the men in the trenches, and said quiet prayers. Each time he had come out of the trenches, before he washed the mud, blood and cordite stains off his body, he had gone to the church and added his prayer. The words came easily to him.

'You have my guarantee, the guarantee of a master mariner of twenty-four years, the guarantee of Andreas Yaxis, by dawn we will be gone.'

The searchlight beam was cut. A dull half-gloom settled on the bridge. The master sagged. Tihomir knew the subterfuge had almost failed, but had not. With the gratitude of a survivor, he said his prayer again, heard the rumbling thunder of the patrol-boat gathering speed as it turned away.

He went back below.

With his screwdriver he unfastened the sheet of metal plate.

The dog came out first. Hanging from its jaws was a writhing rat.

The old man blinked. 'Worth its weight in gold, the bloody little hero . . . Any fireworks over there?'

Tihomir shook his head. The dog pinioned the rat under its front paws then bit at the back of its neck and the squirming stopped.

'Ten minutes, ten minutes' recovery,' Billy whispered. He couldn't hide the panting in his voice.

Lofty was at his shoulder. The message was passed back. Less than a hundred metres in front of them was the canal, a black ribbon between the twin sets of shore lights on which the mist had settled like a greying pillow. Billy could smell the canal, salt water and engine oil. And the decay. They were hunched down beside a wooden building, their backsides resting on winter-flattened grass and weeds. On the open side there was cover from hazel and birch scrub. Above the far side of the building were dull overhead lights, but the building shielded them. Billy had a good clear view of the canal ribbon and the myriad maze of lights beyond it. He felt Lofty close up on him, and the others behind him. He knew that Wickso was the only one of them who looked after himself, kept himself fit, ran the pavements at night. Himself, he'd thought he was fit: he climbed Sgurr na Greine and Croit Bheinn for vantage-points where he could see eagles below him – he lugged his table-top and his paintbox up to summits. They had travelled a little more than eleven kilometres, and the load on Billy's back was like lead compared to that table-top and the box.

He tried to steady his voice. 'Guys, this is kind of a defining moment . . . We go on, or we go back. Nobody tells us what to do, not any more. Mowbray's on his fucking boat, out of it. Locke is the other side of the fence, out of it . . . We have a map which might be clear, might not, might be a genuine effort by that kid, might not . . . We all have to volunteer it, no one can stay back. Not enough of us for one to stay here, and three to go forward – I need all of you. So, what's it to be? Don't all speak at once. Guys, we have a few minutes. All lie up and get recovery time, then we talk. Then, it's go on or go back.'

The word in their dictionary was *yomp*. They had yomped a little more than eleven kilometres, but it wasn't the Brecon Beacons, it wasn't Dartmoor and it wasn't Woodbury Common – on the Beacons, the moor or the common they'd have done eleven klicks, seven miles, with the load on their backs in less than two hours. It had taken them three hours and thirty-four minutes, including the three five-minute recovery stops. It had taken time because there had been two sentries smoking and chattering near the firing-range munitions bunker, and they'd laid up to see the pattern the sentries walked. Then they'd skirted them, made a wide half-circle to get past and short, darting runs till they were clear. At the missile complex, they'd left the track and gone almost down to the beach because there was a watchtower and another bored sentry: they'd crawled to get round him and round the throw of the arc-lights above the fence. They'd had to duck off the track again when a lorry had lurched on it towards the missile cluster. At Rybacij, a dark mess of ruins from long ago, there had been a pair of stray dogs. At the old airstrip they'd covered four hundred metres on their stomachs. There was a gate a kilometre back from the canal, more sentries and a fence, and they'd waited by the fence a full ten minutes, the maximum Billy could spare, to check for patrols, before he'd brought Wickso forward with the wire-cutters . . . and he'd thought what they'd been through was a cup of piss compared with what was ahead.

The breathing behind him was softer and his own heartbeat was slower. He worked the calculations backwards from morning's first light at 06.15 hours. Billy's mind whirred with the figures, made the schedule they must keep to. The ten minutes was up, the minute hand had edged a faint luminous path, remorselessly, round his watch face. It was 00.48 hours . . . No time for debate now: go on or go back. If they succeeded, *if* they made the snatch, if they were on the beach at first light – 06.15 hours – they were meat, if they were on the beach at first light, without cover, they were carcasses. He cut ten minutes from each stage of what they had to achieve if they were to be on the beach and going for the sunken dinghy at 06.05 hours . . . By his watch, it was 00.50 hours. Twenty minutes to play with. There would be a hornets' nest behind them. There would be the four of them, and the passenger, and there was only twenty minutes spare in the schedule. There was always a fuck-up, guaranteed, but it could only delay them by twenty minutes.

'It's *now*, guys, or it's not at all – which?'

There had been no debate, and he hadn't expected one, or an argument. They nodded their assent grimly, like none of them had the stomach to make a laugh out of the moment. They ate into the twenty minutes he had set aside for guaranteed fuck-up as they wriggled into the wetsuits. In place of the suits and flippers the weapons that must be kept dry went into the bags. They would go bare-arsed into the water, without defence. When they left the protection of the hut they moved to the left and distanced themselves from the lights shining down on to the quay where a squat ferry-boat was moored. Twice they froze as they heard voices, casual conversations and music played from lit windows, and they saw men in uniform in the rooms with their tunics off. There was no alert, Billy knew it. The base rested for the night. They went catlike, hugging shadows, easing forward, stopping, waiting, listening, then scurried forward. In Billy's mind was a soundless curse: the men relied on him as their leader. They followed where he went, as they always had. In the cabin commandeered by Mr Mowbray there had been the admiralty chart, no. 2278, and he had glanced at it, but had not studied it. Chart no. 2369 was the one he had pored over because that had given them the route to the landfall on the beach. He had to lead towards the canal side, but also he scratched in his memory for a recall of the chart that covered the base, the naval harbour and the canal. They crept between shadows, always seeking darkness. For fear of them blinding him, he did not look across the canal at the lights. They reached the bank. Lit up, a patrol-boat powered down the centre of the channel, powerful, deadly. They were crouched beside a big drum of old wire cable, and between them and the start of the black ribbon was a high-stacked pile of pallets. A man pissed near to them, then lit a cigarette. It was thrown down and footsteps retreated. The final building they came to had no roof and its walls were pocked with bullet-holes, a relic of a long-ago war. Billy didn't care about others' wars, only his own. There was a drop of double his own height from the stone retaining wall down to the water. Oil gleamed back at him. He lay on his stomach, had left them behind by the wall with the bullet-holes. They had started late and it had taken two minutes longer than he'd allowed to reach the canal; the minute hand on his wrist told him more of the fall-back minutes were exhausted. He scrabbled, a heavy crab, to his right, and reached the worn stones where, in history, a ladder had been bolted to the canal side. Billy made the sign for them to close up on him, slipped on his flippers and went over the side. The third rung collapsed under his weight, and fell down into the water, splashing. He hung from the top rung – no shout came, no challenge. He went down. The water took him. He paddled, then reached up and took the weight of the first inflatable bag. It pulled him under and the cold, oily water was in his mouth and nose.

Billy and Lofty took the first bag, Ham and Wickso shepherded the second. They were blessed, he thought, by the blackness of the ribbon of the canal. He looked ahead now, had to, and land lights blazed in front of him. He struck out with his feet, kicked, and the bag supporting him and Lofty seemed to glide on the water. He only looked ahead.

'Christ—' Wickso's shout was strangled.

Billy looked his way and saw only the darkness, but Wickso's hand was off the bag and pointed up the canal, up-river. Billy's eyes darted that way.

He reckoned the ship was five thousand tonnes – give or take a tonne, as if that fucking mattered – and it ploughed up the canal towards the open sea. Where they were, treading water, it would pass within fifty metres of them. Now Billy heard the rumble of the big screw, and he saw the wave thrown out from the bow. They seemed, each of them, tiny and helpless.

Billy called, 'Ride it – all we can do is ride it.'

The ship towered over them, then the wave caught them and lifted them high and as they fell back a second wave thrust them back towards the canal's quay. Then they were sucked forward by the churn of the propellers. Billy clung to the bag with one hand and to Lofty with the other. The foam thrown by the screw dragged them down, he held on to the bag and to Lofty as if it were for life and for death . . . They bobbed. It was going away. In desperation, Billy kicked. He looked round. Ham and Wickso should have been close to them, but had been pushed back, and more time was lost before they had closed up. They crossed the centre of the canal channel, then the last of the ship's waves surged them towards the lights of the base. Close to the far quay they were confronted by a line of lights. They stayed in the dark water and he searched for a wandering sentry.

A half-sunken ship lay against the far quay. Its bow was under water, its deck awash up to the superstructure of the bridge. They paddled round it, then came to an abandoned landing-craft.

They used the ropes that tied it to the quay to drag themselves up. They were ashore . . . Quietly, each of them retched the canal water from their throats, then the bags were unzipped.

Ham sent the burst message: 'Delta 1 to Havoc 1. Arrived on location. Going forward. Out.' Billy took his weapon, the Vikhr SR-3 assault rifle. He armed the weapon and the noise seemed to deafen him, would have woken the dead. A road was in front of them, then darkened buildings, then the distant lights of the sleeping base that was home to the famed Baltic Fleet. They left the bags by the bollard to which the landing-craft was fastened. Four figures, black in the darkness, exploded across the open road towards the cover of the buildings.

*   *   *

In his cot, Igor Vasiliev tossed. Near to him a boy cried for his mother and far from him a boy writhed in a damp dream; others snored and coughed. A single dim lamp burned from the ceiling half-way down the dormitory block, and by the block's entrance a line of light spilt from under the door of the platoon sergeant's room.

He could not sleep, cuddled his pillow, and waking thoughts were nightmares. He had thought the man was going to kill him. The knife had been in the man's hand, and a fist had gripped his hair, forcing back his head to expose his throat. When he had gone to the targets, and the four ghost shapes had materialized from the forest, they had called for Viktor. He had babbled Viktor's name, Viktor Archenko's name, the name of the chief of staff to the fleet commander . . . *Viktor, Viktor* . . . his friend's name. The knife had been lowered. Stale water from a canteen had been given him, and he had talked – gradually calming – of Viktor, his friend. After the knife had been put back into its sheath, more water had been given him, and he had drawn the map. *Are you a friend, too, of Viktor, of Captain Archenko?* The man said he was. *You have come to save him?* No response. He had been led through the trees to the other men – and they had released him. He had gone back down the track to the firing position, had shouldered the weight of the machine-gun, tramped back and found a truck to give him a lift to the ferry. Back at the base, he had gone to the armoury and cleaned the weapon, without the usual care. He had been in the dormitory a few minutes before the lights were put out.

He could have told the truck driver that armed foreigners were ashore, could have told the NCO in charge of the ferry, could have told the lieutenant who had been at the armoury, could have gone and told the night duty officer in the headquarters building, could have gone to the senior officers' mess and waited respectfully at the outer door while Major Piatkin was called . . . could have knocked on the door of the sleeping room of his platoon sergeant and told him.

Could have . . . and had not. It would have been easiest to tell the driver of the truck, but with each opportunity passed up the next chance had become harder. It was stifled inside him. He did not know whether he had helped Captain Archenko, his friend, but he did know he was now a traitor to every conscript in every bed in the dormitory. He was washed with fear. He lay on his stomach, his side and his back. Sleep would not come.

'There has to be a dead drop, Viktor . . .' The purr was in his voice. It was imperative to Yuri Bikov that he showed no trace of annoyance. He did not think the prey could fight much longer. 'There is always a dead drop . . . I believe your dead drop was at Malbork Castle.'

It would be the tiredness that defeated his prey's resistance. The tape spool still turned in the outer office. He needed one grunted confirmation, only one. After the first acceptance of the questions he put, the first tremored, blurted or whispered, 'Yes,' the rest would come like a torrent. It was always that way. After the first acknowledgement of defeat, he would blow out the last gasp of the candle, slither across the concrete floor and his arm would be around his prey's shoulder. Then the confession would come. It would be coughed up, and spat out. It was the stalking of the prey that both intrigued and excited him, but in the moments after the start of the confessional he would feel, again, a sense of let-down. It was what the hunters told him when they went after deer or bear in the wilderness forests: the killing and gutting of an animal left nothing but a feeling of inadequate emptiness.

'Let us forget the walk-in, Viktor, at Murmansk or Severomorsk, and then the initial contact that followed it. You were transferred to Kaliningrad *oblast*. You were now within reach of your new friends. They would need a satisfactory dead drop. Not here . . . they would not want the dead drop near to Baltiysk. Inside the *oblast*, they would face the risk of identification and compromise – but you give what is, to them, a heaven-sent opportunity where all the risk is for you and none for them. You go to Malbork Castle. Every two months, because of your esteemed position, you are permitted to travel into Poland and visit the historic site of ancient history. Myself, Viktor, I have not been to Malbork Castle, I only have photographs to guide me. I imagine a great rambling place with dark corners and crannies on steep stairs and rubbish-bins. Ideal. You are in civilian clothes, you merge, you wander. You spend half a day in the castle, and in one corner, cranny or rubbish-bin there is a place where you leave documents, photographs or microfilm. They would not be there, your new friends, because to be there and to meet you face to face would put you in hazard, and them. They would come later. The pick-up from the dead drop would be a few hours after you had gone, or the next day. They are very satisfied with the arrangement – they are safe. The dead drop is at Malbork Castle, Viktor – yes or no?'

'No.'

'You see, Viktor, I don't criticize you. I understand you, I have sympathy for you . . . You would, of course, leave instructions as to the timing of the next dead drop, but you would not know how your package is received. Viktor, answer me a question.'

'What question?'

'I am inclined to believe you spied for the British, not the Americans – the Americans are more electronic, but the British go with old tradecraft, it is their style. How many packages from dead drops do you think the British receive each week? How many? That is my question.'

The trick was blocked by silence. The prey would see the man-trap laid for him. He would be aching now with tiredness, hunger, stress, but still had – just – the capability to recognize the trap. Bikov could not see his prey's face but he could hear the stifling of yawns, and there would be the pain of hunger, and the stress eating into him. The cold clung in the room.

'Not many, not many packages in a week. You might be the only provider of a package in a week. A man in London may have a diary in which he makes a red cross on the day you travel to Malbork Castle. You are the centrepiece of that man's life. Because of you, in London he has status – that is why he tells you he is your new friend. On your back, Viktor, that man's career prospers . . . One week there is a package from Viktor Archenko, the next week another man receives a package in Cairo, the week after a package comes from a ministry clerk in Beijing, and the last week in the month perhaps there are no packages. They have a big building, Viktor, by the Thames river in London. Two thousand people work there, but they have very few packages coming to it. In the crown of a man's career, Viktor, you are a jewel . . . But that man does not take a risk. No,

321

Viktor, the risk is left to you. That is the way they work. Your new friends have a toy and they play with it. I am your real friend, Viktor . . . so tell me that the dead drop was at Malbork Castle, yes or no?'

'No.'

The voice had a whistled thinness to it, and there had been a pause before the denial. Bikov sensed his prey's strength sank. It would not be long. The aircraft would be fuelled and ready. On the aircraft, the prisoner would be handcuffed, his eyes would be covered with adhesive tape and he would not be allowed to piss or shit, except in his trousers. He would be humiliated, and he would never again see his interrogator, but his ears would hear the playing of the tape from the first single word of confession through the torrent flow as it was transcribed by Yuri Bikov's sergeant. A car and a van would be at the military side of Sheremetevo, and Bikov would go home in the car to sleep. His prisoner would go on the floor of the van to the basement cells of military counter-intelligence. Bikov felt no sympathy, no remorse, no pity. He believed the collapse was close.

'I hear you, Viktor . . . Always remember I am your friend – not them. We shall move on.'

She did not reply.

Locke said, 'Didn't you hear me? They've called through. They're on the base . . . I don't know what the hell they think they can achieve.'

She sat on the bed. She could see him dully framed in the doorway, and she could hear the pent-up aggression in his voice.

'They've crossed the canal, they're inside the base. It's what you wanted, isn't it?'

Alice said, 'I suppose you hope they'll fail.'

'Don't pretend to yourself that you can read me.'

Alice murmured, 'Because if they fail then you were right from the start. Their failure will prove you right, and that'll be important to you.'

He turned from the door and moved away a pace, two paces, into the hall. He stopped. She thought he put up his hand and leaned against the wall, his arm taking the weight, but she could not be sure in the night darkness.

'I'm going out. I'll be gone some little time. I'd like you to listen out on the radio – you know the call-signs. Just listen out and relay anything relevant on to Mowbray. Do that, please.'

'Are you running away?'

He spun in the hall. The sudden movement of his body was clear to her, and he came back through the door and the bulk of him loomed closer to her. He strode towards the bed. She had been sitting. She slid down on to her side and curled her knees up; her arms were around her chest as if for protection. Alice thought he was going to punch her. She readied herself for the impact of his fist, ducked her head down. She could smell his body, unwashed since he had slept in the tunnel under the Gdansk railway tracks, and his breath. He bent over her. She stiffened. Alice felt his lips on her forehead, the damp touch of them. They lingered for a moment then moved an inch, and he kissed her a second time. The first two kisses were gentle; the third was pressed hard down on her forehead, catching strands of her hair. Then he was up and gone.

Back at the door, his voice was curt: 'Listen for the radio. I'll be some little time . . . Yes, running away. God watch you, Alice, God watch over the both of you.'

She lay on her side. The kitchen door was opened, then pulled shut, and she was alone with the silence.

Alice had known it was the last chance when the men had gone to the zoo park to lift Viktor out, and it had been another last chance when they had gone ashore and had been at the rendezvous point, but he had not shown. It was the third 'last chance' that had taken the men across the canal and into the base. She knew he was held, she knew the *Princess Rose* must sail by dawn: she understood that the third last chance was feeble. She could not believe she would see Viktor again. She felt a sense of personal shame because she had taunted Gabriel Locke, accused him of 'running away'.

The taunt at Locke had been her own act of self-defence. She would go back to Vauxhall Bridge Cross, where she would bury herself in her work and she would apply, after a fortnight's decent interval, for a posting away. She would be in Buenos Aires or Bogotá, or any bloody place, and one morning the Station chief would call her into his office, and she would be passed a sheet of paper with a brief, unemotional message for her to read: 'Inform Alice North that Moscow sources report execution of ferret last week following in camera trial.' She would read it, then feed it into the shredder, and she would be asked if she wanted to take the rest of the day off, and she would decline that offer. She would go back to her desk and busy herself with the low-level material from an Argentine police inform-ant or a Colombian interior-ministry official, or an agent from any bloody place . . . She touched her forehead and her fingers seemed to search for evidence that Gabriel Locke, who had said from the start that it would fail, had kissed her, but she found only her dry, furrowed skin . . . Wherever they posted her she would never forget Viktor. He was the only love of her life. Her fingers hovered on the amber stone at her neck.

Alice shook herself, pushed herself up, wiped her eyes, and rolled her legs off the bed. She smoothed her hair, then walked through the darkness and into the kitchen. A red light would flash on the commu-nications console when a signal came through from the team – no light flashed. She did not know why Locke had kissed her forehead, and she could not escape the shame of having taunted him. She sat down heavily at the kitchen table and began her vigil.

The third time . . . *I think that is everything, Viktor. You've done us proud, but then you always do. There's enormous admiration in London for what you achieve for us, and huge gratitude. In all honesty, Viktor, I can tell you that you are regarded as our supreme asset. I don't know when we'll meet again, Viktor, but it's been my privilege to work with you. Go carefully . . . Goodnight, both of you.* Mowbray had smiled at them and gone towards the bathroom as if to wash his hands of what they did in the rest of the night. They had known, she and Viktor, that it might be the last time. After the loving . . . walking on the frosted, crunching, crisp grass at the Westerplatte memorial, arms tight around each other. Him telling her to be brave, her telling him that they would be together, *one day*, for ever. The last kiss . . . The love had lasted.

The driver brought the final armful of branches. They were dry, had been sheltered from the rain by the canopy of the pines, and with the armful was a newspaper from the car. The headlights from the dunes splayed over the beach. Jerry the Pole watched as Chelbia knelt in his smart suit and packed the sheets of newspaper deep among the branches. There was a flash of gold. The flame gushed from Chelbia's lighter, the paper took and the branches caught. The fire crackled.

Jerry the Pole stood back. Roman, the fisherman, lifted fish from the bucket, some still quivering limply, and his knife ripped through the bases of their stomachs. His fingers casually flicked the guts on to the sand, and gulls screamed at the edge of the darkness. Jerry the Pole shivered but did not go near to the fire. Roman passed Chelbia a cod, still bleeding, then a mackerel and two plaice. Chelbia dropped the fish into the flames and chortled as they sizzled, spat. He looked up at Jerry the Pole.

'Do I do this at home? Do I hell! At home I eat at the Arlenkino or the restaurant in the Hotel Kaliningrad or at the Casino Universal, I pay through my nose. I pay for everybody. I go out to eat and it costs me five hundred American dollars. Here I eat for nothing, and what I eat I will enjoy . . . Fresh, grilled fish – the best. Come closer.'

A command. Jerry the Pole edged nearer to the fire.

'Closer.'

An order. Jerry the Pole would not disobey. At the café where his Mercedes was parked he had said that he would be on the beach. Neither the bastard Locke nor Miss North had gone to the café for him, or a message would have been sent. The café would now have been closed three, four hours. They would have had to come looking for him. He didn't care if they had to search for him. His *pension* was what mattered to him, and it was ignored. It was now past two o'clock, he should have been back at the car, curled up and asleep . . . Chelbia had asked him to stay, and he thought Chelbia was not a man whose request was wisely ignored.

He could feel the fire's warmth, and he stared down at the bubbling skins of the fish. Chelbia reached up and took his hand. Jerry the Pole felt himself pulled down and was too frightened to resist. Chelbia's face was close and smiling. He could not have broken the man's grip on his hand.

'I have enjoyed the fishing, and I will enjoy eating the fish. That was my good fortune when I came to find you, *you* . . . You work for the Secret Intelligence Service of Britain.'

'What is it you ask?' His hand was taken closer to the flames, the cooking fish, and the embers. 'I don't know why you say—'

'What are the names of the Secret Intelligence men you drive?'

'That's not true.' A flame played on the skin of his hand, scorched it, and the fish fat spattered on his skin.

'I want their names.'

'I can't—' The pain pierced the brain. The grip was now on his wrist and his hand was driven down into the flames and the reddened embers. 'Can't, can't—'

'Their names.'

'Rupert Mowbray – chief – and—' He saw his own skin curl, pop, and the agony rivered up his arm. He owed them nothing. The flames licked his hand, and there was acrid smoke seeping up from his shirt cuff and his coat. They had denied his pension. 'And Gabriel Locke is the junior, and there is Miss Alice North.'

'Why are they here?'

'To lift out, to take out—' His hand's skin had been white in the cold, then had pinked above the flames and the embers, now was blackening. 'Take out an officer from the base.'

'Which officer?'

'A captain, I think.' It was acute, stabs of pure needle-sharp pain. 'I think his name, I heard it, was – Archenko. Viktor Archenko. I think—'

'Archenko?'

He heard, through the pain and the scent of his own flesh burning, a sort of wonderment in Chelbia's voice, an astonishment. 'It is Archenko.'

His wrist was freed.

'A man I could do business with, mutually profitable business. Thank you, my friend, thank you.'

Chelbia dragged him up. Without his support Jerry the Pole would have collapsed. Chelbia manoeuvred him across the sand and into the spray of the surf. His hand was forced down into the water and the cold dulled the pain. Chelbia dried Jerry the Pole's hand with his own handkerchief, silk and monogrammed.

'What are you going to do?' he whimpered.

They came back over the sand. Chelbia said, 'I think the fish will soon be ready. I tell you, my friend, in five years only one man has confronted me, shown no fear of me – he is the best of men, a lion . . . I am going to eat the fish I have caught, and you will join me. I invite you to be my guest.'

Jerry the Pole clutched his hand and cringed. 'Thank you.'

'You have had, Viktor, three visits to Gdansk. Each was an overnight visit. On the three visits your delegation was supervised by a locally based political officer of the FSB, but a junior man. Inside the delegation you were the senior serving officer, and you would have behaved like a senior officer. You would not have stood at the bar half the night, you would have made excuses and said you were going to bed, perhaps to study papers for the next day's meetings. I have a plan, Viktor, of the Hotel Mercure. There is a fire staircase. I have a map also, Viktor, of Gdansk, and I estimate it would take an athletic man such as yourself about fifteen minutes of brisk walking to cross the inner city. Each night you were in Gdansk, Viktor, you left the hotel – yes or no?'

'No.'

'You went to the Excelsior Hotel and you were debriefed there by your handlers – yes or no?'

'No.'

If he looked into the small, wavering light of the flame he faced the voice and felt its persuasive softness. It lulled him. The voice merged with his hunger and his tiredness. He was slipping.

'They were magic hours for you with your handlers – yes or no?'

'No.'

'Each time you went and met your handlers it was like a liberation for you – yes or no?'

He clung to Alice. She was blurred. He reached for her.

'No.'

'I want to tell you, Viktor, why I think the night hours spent with your handlers would have been like a liberation to you, and were magic hours. You were flattered, you were made to believe you were a man of the highest importance, the centre of their world. It would have been a narcotic to you, because the spy is the man who is most alone in all the world. You soaked up the flattery. To them you were a hero, valued and trusted. Each wretched little piece of paper that you handed over they would have held in their hands as if it were priceless. They would have hung on your words, Viktor. You were the most important man in their lives, yes or no?'

Clarity came to her face, then slipped away. He held her against his shoulder, and the candle's warmth ebbed from her cheek through his shirt and reached his skin. He shivered hard, could not help himself. He knew he must hold on to her or he would sink.

'No.'

'And you told them of the deaths of your father and your grandmother – yes or no?'

'No.'

'Did they give you a woman, Viktor? They usually do. Dangerous to bring a whore into the hotel for one hour, a poor security procedure. Was there a secretary or a stenographer who was made available, Viktor? A woman – yes or no?'

He lay with Alice, their arms wrapped tightly around each other. If she left him he was gone, was alone in the darkness.

'No.'

'Viktor, do I seem stupid to you? Do I? We trust each other. We share our food, we share the cold, we share this room, we do not tell lies to each other. Am I stupid? A British woman stayed in the hotel where you were debriefed, the same woman each time on the matching dates that you were in Gdansk. A good fuck, Viktor – yes or no?'

He felt her arms loosening their hold on him. It was as if the skin of her hands, arms and body was greased, and she seemed to slip from the grip of his fingers.

'I don't think, Viktor, that they paid you. You are not a man interested in money. We are the same. What we own would go into a single suitcase. There is no sign in your room of luxury, of indulgence. I do not believe that money was involved . . . They would have liked that, Viktor. The Secret Intelligence Service of Britain is like the FSB – both loath to give out money. It has to go to committees, has to be authorized, then there is dispute over the scale and frequency of the payments. You were right not to demand money . . . You did not demand money because it would have demeaned your vengeance. You were pure, Viktor. It would have been important to you to be pure. And if you had demanded money you might have found that your cash value did not match the sweet flatteries they offered. A woman is cheap . . . Did she tell you that she loved you, Viktor – yes or no?'

He groped for Alice. She slipped from him. She was moving back and the candle's light made her a shadow . . . He reached for her but her arms were folded across her chest and she did not reach back for him. Without her he was lost. Every time, when he was in crisis, she was crystal-clear water in his mind and he could feel the touch of her, and her words soothed the fear. Now she drifted from him.

'But more important, Viktor, was your own safety. Spies do not retire, do not, one day, walk away and close down that segment of their lives. They are hooked, Viktor, they are as vulnerable as any addict with a syringe on the Moskovsky in Kaliningrad. The spy does not end up in a dacha with his secret secure . . . Hear me, Viktor. There are two options, only two – capture or flight. Now we are at the kernel of the matter, Viktor. Your handlers will have offered you the flattery and respect you craved, and the services of a woman, but they did not offer you flight – yes or no?'

He had lost Alice. She had slipped away and he could no longer see her face.

'I am honest with you, Viktor, I have never been anything else. First, they kept you in place too long. Last, they abandoned you. You are the innocent and they are the professionals. To them, in Britain, you are worthless. You should have gone, Viktor, a year ago, but I can hear their flattery, their sincerity, but it was all shit, Viktor – yes or no?'

The water seemed to close over him. She was not there to hold him. Viktor wept.

'A spy – yes or no?'

He thrashed, the drowning man's last throw for survival. 'No, no . . . no.'

Locke reached the fence. He stood beside the single bar set in it. It would not be a big step. He had already crossed a great divide, had killed a man. He did not know what he could do on the other side of the fence except purge himself. The instructors at Fort Monkton had taught covert movement in cities – how to move by foot on pavements, by taxi, by metro, by bus, by car – only one instructor had taught about movement cross-country. He remembered a sunny afternoon after a coach ride to the New Forest, near Brockenhurst, where a dozen of them, all novices, had sat in a semi-circle and listened to the one instructor, and titters had passed among them because it had all seemed irrelevant.

Locke ducked down and went under the bar. Behind him the fence was swallowed by the darkness.

16

Q. What part of Russia has been a 'historical military flashpoint'
since the thirteenth century?

A. Kaliningrad.

He had heard the two chimes of the clock set above the entrance to
the headquarters building. Bikov moved for the kill.

His voice was silky quiet. The last of the candle burned.

'I think, Viktor, in your place I would have done what you have.
You had motive from what was done to your father and your grandmother – I would have done it. You had the opportunity for the
necessary tradecraft, the castle at Malbork and the three visits to
Gdansk, and I cannot fault your procedures. Most important, Viktor,
you had access. That is where we are different.'

He studied each movement of his prey's body. He knew it was
close.

'Take me, Viktor, a humble half-colonel enduring the routine of
FSB life. I might have had the motive, but I have nothing to offer
that will wound. I am only a functionary, a bureaucrat and a pusher
of paper. I have no skills, no information that is wanted. Nothing
that is "secret" crosses my desk. My life is tedious . . . not yours.
Stamped on every sheet of paper in the fleet commander's safe is
"Secret" or "Classified" or "Most Confidential", and you, Viktor,
have the key to the safe. You have the vetting, you have security
clearance, everything in Admiral Falkovsky's safe is read by
you . . . Let me take you, Viktor, into the mind of a foreign intelligence handler . . .'

The head had gone down and the breathing had started to be
regular. He reached out, across the low flame, took his prey's

shoulder and shook it. Not a violent action, but merely enough to stall sleep. His prey's head wavered, then lifted.

'Thank you, Viktor. The mind of your handler. You want to sleep and you shall, soon . . . Because he owns you, your handler is a man of importance. He is one of very few, in an organization as gripped by inertia as mine, who has an agent in place. The papers come to him, from you, stamped "Secret" or "Classified" or "Most Confidential", and he passes them on to his customers – perhaps the Americans as well – and he has status, a foot on the pedestal of power. No matter that the documents, blueprints, plans you pass are of minimal value, Viktor – he has an agent in place and will keep him there as long as he can. Do you follow me, Viktor?'

His voice was a murmur. The wretch, addled with exhaustion, would be making stumbling attempts to watch for the man-traps, and would fail . . . Something nagged in Bikov's mind, was an irritant, but he could not place what he had missed. He pressed.

'I said "minimal value", Viktor . . . "Minimal value" because everything locked away in the fleet commander's safe is old. This crap state we live in, that you have cause to hate, has no secrets of importance . . . He, your handler, Viktor, is a man of great selfishness. I speak the truth. You are a plaything for his ego, he is a parasite on your back. When you last saw him, in Gdansk at the Excelsior Hotel, did he offer you a route out? Did he? There would have been, Viktor, fine words about admiration and obligation – but did he offer a route out? They always suggest a few more months, a few more weeks.'

He saw squirming movement: breakpoint was near . . . a few more minutes. It would be the hammer blow.

'You believe me, Viktor, don't you? I speak the truth . . . He is a selfish parasite – can you dispute that? Where is *he* now?'

Bikov was bent forward and the candle's flame played on his lowered chin. The puzzle was almost solved, but one piece did not fit. He could not identify what he had missed. It annoyed him. He slithered towards the kill.

'Where is he now? In his club? In a bar, or at home? Does he give a fuck about you, Viktor? Can you see him here now? Can you?'

The tears had returned, and the wretch's body shook. In the puzzle a round hole remained, but the last piece was square. He concentrated to drive the irritation, the annoyance, from his mind. He spoke across the candle's final flicker of light.

'You are lucky to have me as a friend, Viktor, because your handler has abandoned you. I am your true friend, your last one.'

He heard the choked weeping. It was the first time in an interrogation that he had missed a kernel point, and he did not know what it was, only that it eluded him.

Roman listened, and he thought of his daughter and his son and what this man could do for them.

'It's very simple,' Chelbia said. 'What I have learned, in import-export, always follow the simple way. What excites me – until I came to this beach I had no idea of what is now open to us. The unexpected is often the most exciting. Yes?'

Roman nodded. Chelbia ate fish with his fingers. Roman thought it incredible that a man who wore a suit that had cost as much as he earned in a year should sit on the rainsodden sand beside a fire and eat with his fingers. If either of his own children had eaten like that, or himself, stuffing food into their mouths, they would have felt his wife's slap on the back of the head. The Russian ate like a pig, and talked.

'So, simple . . . I bring the packages to the harbour in Kaliningrad. A fishing-boat from Kaliningrad takes the package out to sea, then has a problem and drifts into the restricted area. It is only a fishing-boat – who cares? Maybe I have to buy a man in the harbour office, but that is cheap. The fishing-boat goes close to the international boundary. He puts the package into the sea. It is weighted but it has a float . . . Everything is arranged. Roman puts to sea. Roman is separated from the other fishermen, but only by two hundred metres, and he finds the float. He picks up the package, and then he is back with the other fishermen. He lands with the package. Do you know, it costs me a thousand American dollars a week to put packages across the frontier on the Mamonovo to Braniewo road? And it will cost more because the Poles are, every day, more difficult. Later we shall talk, Roman, about what payment you will receive for lifting the package from the sea . . .'

Roman watched. The Pole, Jerzy Kwasniewski from Berlin but once from Krynica Morska, could not eat because of his burned

333

hand. When Chelbia had eaten all of the meat off a cod and a plaice, he lifted a mackerel from the glowing fire – and didn't flinch. He pulled off the head and threw it away to the gulls, then stripped the meat from the bones and fed Jerzy Kwasniewski as if he were a chick in a nest. He put little pieces into the man's mouth, and smiled at him. Many times Roman had burned his hands – from upset hurricane lights, from the oxyacetylene cutters – and he knew of the pain. He had winced as Chelbia had put the hand into the fire, but he had not intervened. Half of the mackerel went into Jerzy Kwasniewski's mouth, then Chelbia took the rest for himself, and spoke through mouthfuls of fish. He stopped only to spit out bones. He lifted up one of the shoes, drying by the fire, and examined it closely.

'When I want to know whether a man lives comfortably, or whether times are hard for him, I look at his shoes. Not his suit, not his coat. A man can get a new suit and a new coat off a dead man's back, from a charity shop. But it is rare to find shoes that fit comfortably when they have been worn by another man. I look at your shoes. They have been polished, but that tells me nothing. What is important, they are falling apart. An old man needs good shoes, and you do not have them. You have worked for the Secret Intelligence Service of Britain, now you drive for them, but they show little respect for you. If they gave you respect you would have the money to buy good shoes . . . Once a month you will drive from Berlin and you will meet with my good friend, Roman, and you will collect a package from him – four or five kilos in weight, the same size as a big bag of cooking flour – and you will deliver it to Berlin. You will be paid, and then you will buy new shoes.'

Roman remembered. Chelbia wiped his hand on his handkerchief, then smeared it across Jerzy Kwasniewski's mouth, then pocketed it. Chelbia reached out and took Jerzy Kwasniewski's scorched hand, then Roman's. All their hands were together. The deal was done. For money . . . Roman remembered the address given by the Father in the new church in Piaski in the last of the winter months. There had been hardship in the village, and for the first time that he could remember a holiday home owned by Swedes had been broken into and items of value stolen. There was no money in the village. The Father had told his congregation, the fishing families idle in the winter, of an old proverb: *The devil dances in an empty pocket*. The Father had said that poverty or an empty pocket leads to temptation or crime, and had told them that in history many coins were minted with a cross on the reverse so that the devil could not go down into the pocket if one of those coins was there. There were *zlotys*, a few coins, in his pocket, but none of them had a cross on the reverse. He held on to the two hands tightly.

Free at last from company, alone as he wanted to be, the engineer made good the engine. He crooned softly to himself and his thickened fingers moved with a lover's gentleness over the pistons, plugs and cables. He would not find another job at sea. None of the Lebanese-, Maltese- or Liberian-registered lines would want to employ a forty-seven-year-old engineer whose last ship, for more than ten years, had been a coastal freighter, a rust bucket. When the *Princess Rose* went to the breakers, so would Johannes Richter. The ship would be scrap, as would he. And there was no work in Rostock: Rostock was awash with unemployed engineers from the shipyards that had been, until 1990, the pride of the Baltic. He would go back to his apartment alongside the railway line that ran between Rostock and Warnemunde, and he would tend the balcony flowers. He would have money for his daughters, which was important to them but not to him. He had seen the determination on the team's faces as they ate their last meal . . . Win or lose, succeed or fail, they would be suffering hot pursuit when they came back. The patrol-boat had returned and had scoured them with its light – it would be out again when the pursuit started. The *Princess Rose* would sail towards the shore at speed, let them scramble on board, with or without their man, and then they would churn for the safety of the international sea boundary. Two extra sea knots might make the difference. In the engine room, he was below sea level. If she were holed by the patrol-boat . . . He had no fear.

The master's voice, from the bridge, boomed over his radio. 'Give it to me, Johannes. Give me the engine.'

The engineer threw the switches. He heard the rumble, the throb of the thing he loved. It was sweet. She rolled in a slackening swell, the engine idled . . . and he waited.

*   *   *

He had had only the one day in the forest near Brockenhurst to prepare himself.

It was almost a catalogue of disaster . . . If the radio in the watchtower had not been switched on, had not played dance music from a Polish station, he would have blundered against the legs of the tower. If the jeep on the track beyond the tower, by the inner fence, had not revved to full power to escape a pond of mud, he would have been on the track and caught in its lights. If a tree had not come down on the inner fence and collapsed it, he would not have known how to climb eight feet of mesh and two feet of barbed wire. He hurried, driven on, and his feet crackled over fallen branches.

The voice he heard was the instructor's, Walter's, when they had sat around him in the half-circle. Rumour had him as a one-time sniper, but now elderly and past a shelf-life; the gossip at Fort Monkton said he had killed men from the Derry walls over the Bogside and from the mountain overlooking the Crater District of Aden . . . Locke could hear his voice, but not distinguish what the damned man had said.

Birds, disturbed by him, screeched into the night off the pines' canopy, and once there was a bullocking charge away from him. Then he'd stopped, a statue, pounding heart, and thought it must have been a boar or a deer, until its stampede had died. He hurried until he could no longer force air into his lungs . . . and her face was always ahead of him, and her forehead, which he had kissed. Lower branches lashed his face, caught at his jacket, and twice he was in small bogs. Once his shoe was prised off his foot and he had to grope in slime to find it. There had been a boy, Garin, from the next farm to that of his parents. Garin went at night to a wood on the farms' boundary and could get close to a vixen's earth or a badger's sett, and not break a twig, not disturb them when he sat on the moss carpet. He had thought Garin Williams an ignorant little creep. Useless at language and literature, mediocre at maths and sciences, inept at history and geography – only able to walk in silence into an oak wood in the depth of night. He'd felt contempt for Garin . . . Now he would have cried out in relief if Garin Williams had been beside him, leading him.

They came back slowly to him, the words of the old sniper. The Book of Walter. About a stick, about being a blind man. About keeping off paths and looking for animal trails . . . and never putting down the weight of a foot before the ground was tested. About using the protection of trees, about never making a silhouette against a skyline, about never crossing the middle of a clearing.

Locke stood against a tree and took from his pocket the keys to his apartment in Warsaw, and some *zlotys*. He bent and laid them on the mould carpet at the base of the tree. Then, he moved forward, very carefully, testing with his shoe and with his hand held out until he came to a hazel bush. Breaking off a sprig seemed like a gunshot in the forest, and he waited until the sound had echoed away, then he stripped the side branches off it. It was his wand. The Book of Walter said that, cross-country, good boots should be worn and a camouflage tunic. Locke wore lightweight lace-up shoes, a grey suit, white shirt, and a red anorak with yellow piping.

He hoped Tasha, Justin, Charlie and Karen suffered, pleaded for them to be screwed, because they had talked and deflected when he should have listened to Walter and learned his Book. At the next big tree, brushed against by his wand, he knelt and scratched up a fistful of earth in his hand, spat on it to moisten it and wiped it over his forehead, cheeks and chin, on his wrists, the backs of his hands, and then put more on his anorak.

Locke moved forward. He found a trench system of zigzag pits and a bunker of concrete but didn't blunder into them because he had his wand, and had Walter – and Alice, not that she would ever know.

The base slept.

While it slept, a few radios played and a woman in married quarters screamed at her NCO husband. Close by, a baby cried, wind caught overhead wires, the sea was a distant murmur. A dog barked for attention, unheard. To save electricity in the base every second street-light was extinguished and those that were lit had been fitted with low-power bulbs. The base, sleeping, was a place of shadows. Brighter lights beamed from the windows of the senior officers' mess where Vladdy Piatkin and friends who massaged the conceit of the *zampolit* still drank. A lesser light shone down from the inner office of the fleet commander where he sat unmoving at his desk with a small key in front of him. A single dull strip light above the dormitory's doorway illuminated the young conscripts of the 'Ready' platoon. Arc-lights were above the guarded main gate, and a searchlight played over the base from a tower on the walls of the historic fortress. Cats, feral and-emaciated, moving on their stomachs, occupied the shadows between the lights. Only the cats knew that intruders stalked in their territory while the base slept.

They did not need to speak. On the paper map was the name of a street: Admiral Stefan Makarov. A low wooden hut on the street was marked: 'Shop'. Another square building was outlined: 'Gymnasium'. Ham peered down at the map he held. It was the map of a semi-literate kid, and they depended on it. Ham could see the street's name on the sign near the wooden hut where conscripts would have come to buy chocolate and soft drinks, and a solitary light was above the double doors of the gymnasium. Lofty opened the bag and his fingers groped inside it. They were at the end of a building, opposite the shop and short of the gymnasium. At the end of the street, Admiral Stefan Makarov, was an isolated three-storey building, a throwback to the days of a former regime. Ham thought that once a swastika would have flown from its roof. On the map it was double outlined and written beside it in a spider scrawl was the title: Federalnaya Sluzhba Bezopasnosi. It was hard for Ham to make out the scrawl of the map. They faced the side of the building. To reach it, they would have to cross open ground that was lit by every second light. An open jeep went past the side of the building, two men in it huddled against the cold, and the sound of it drifted away, as the lights caught the glare of a cat's eyes in a black corner.

'That's it,' Ham whispered. 'If the map's right, that's it.'

For stating the obvious Ham was rewarded with a sharp jolting elbow from Billy. It hurt him. Billy took Wickso's arm and pointed, a short-arm gesture, to the left side of the building, then reached for Ham and pointed to the right. Ham felt the fear. Back at Poole, long ago, the moment was called 'Fight or Flight' – go forward or go back. They listened to the night and the night's sounds, and the jeep had gone. Ham was shoved hard, like when he had done his first jump and the despatcher had heaved him out of the gate in the wicker basket of the balloon tethered eight hundred feet above a Dorset field. He crossed Admiral Stefan Makarov in a pounding charge and thought every man and woman, every officer, NCO and conscript in the base would have been woken. His harness, worn over the wetsuit, thudded against his chest and stomach. He held the Skorpion tight in his hands, as if it were salvation. He reached a door and shadow, and nestled into it. He listened, and heard only the radio's music, the woman and the baby, and the beat of his heart. He left the safe place, went past three more doors. The last doorway in the street was his goal. He looked across the open ground.

In front of the building was a saloon car. Between the car and the steps to a closed heavy door was a pacing sentry, his rifle over his shoulder. As he stamped backwards and forwards, the sentry raised his gloved hands to his mouth and breathed uselessly into them. Beside the door was a window, and Ham saw through it a second guard whose back was to him. The door opened, and a plastic cup was passed out. The man from the inside wore a pistol on his belt. The door was closed. Two drunks, in uniform, staggered along the far side of the lit area, one supporting the other.

He went back.

Ham told Billy what he had seen, then Wickso returned to them. Wickso said there was a fire escape at the back, unguarded, with a closed steel door on to each floor. Billy said they'd go through the back.

They were going into the building. None of the team disputed it. Lofty made spaghetti. He rolled it in his hands, about an ounce of it, and thinned the military explosive into a lengthening, narrowing strip. Wickso had the detonator and Billy had the firing box for the electric impulse. Lofty's hands moved fast. Ham thought himself a battleground survivor – had ever since he was a child in the playground – but his legs seemed fastened in clay. When Lofty had done the spaghetti he laid the strips carefully on Wickso's arms, like a woman's knitting-wool. Ham's grip on the Skorpion whitened his knuckles, and Billy had Lofty's grenade-launcher.

Ham thought of the police cell and, momentarily, wished he were there ... Billy had said they would need speed and surprise and a shit bucket full of luck. The bile choked in Ham's throat, and he hooked the mask on to his head.

339

In the quiet, with only the cats watching them, they headed to the back of the building.

He had been given friendship – had not been beaten, kicked, punched.

His body rolled in tiredness.

In the worst of his dreams over the long months before, Viktor had seen men in uniforms, men in heavy leather jackets and men stamping in and out of a cell with shit on the floor, and he had been scum to them – yet only friendship, sympathy, kindness had been handed him by the man in shabby clothes and mud-caked boots.

He hardly heard the words.

'I have it all, Viktor, I know everything . . . I know of your grandmother and your father, and the castle at Malbork and the visits of the delegation to Gdansk, and I know of the mistake you made. I shall tell you about your mistake, Viktor. A book of matches from the wrong hotel. Such a small mistake. You pocket a book of matches from a hotel that you did not visit, and a little sliver of suspicion is aroused – a worm turns. I don't expect, Viktor, you can even remember the moment you picked it up. A trifle, a small present for yourself, taking a book of matches and you don't smoke. You had no need for the matches, you gave them to another officer. They were used to light the cigarette of Major Piatkin, the *zampolit* . . .'

He rocked. He remembered . . . such a little moment, of such insignificance. And he remembered, too, the sharp, sneered anecdotes about Piatkin that so delighted the admiral when he told them, and his smiles and Falkovsky's bellied laughter. He remembered also the contempt that he, a senior serving naval officer, felt for the base's *zampolit*, who knew nothing of the science of naval warfare. The man was a clown, a fool. The man was mediocre. Piatkin was a grubby little shite on the take . . . and had brought him down. A rat gnawed at the base of a great house built of wood, and it crashed. Piatkin, whom he despised, had destroyed him. He did not see Rupert, or the men in the zoo park, or Alice. Above him, grinning and superior, was the face of Piatkin.

'How would you describe Major Piatkin, Viktor? A corrupted criminal? An imbecile? Or would you call him a counter-intelligence officer with a prying and suspicious mind? He undid you, Viktor. You are now alone. The words of your handlers were lies. You have only me.'

Captain, second rank, Viktor Archenko swayed and his voice was a hoarse whisper, 'What will they do to me?'

He saw a hand cup the tiny flame of the candle. A breath blew across it and into his face, and the flame died.

'Nothing, Viktor. You have been so helpful, and I am your friend and we are together.'

A hand was on his shoulder and a body slipped beside him, was warm. An arm held him close.

Bikov's major pushed the earphones off his scalp. He checked the spool still turned on the tape-recorder. He murmured to the sergeant that he should go down the stairs to the car and should start the engine. From his pocket, he took thongs for a prisoner's ankles, a hood and handcuffs. On tiptoe he followed the sergeant from the outer office and watched him go down the stairs. Bikov, he thought, was the finest interrogator he had known, the best. Without evidence, with no proof, the interrogator had bluffed his way to a confession. Incredible . . . On his mobile he called Kaliningrad Military and warned the pilot that they would be leaving Baltiysk within five minutes – with a prisoner. He cut the call and there was a mirthless quiet chuckle in his throat. *What will they do to me?* He had heard the whine on the earphones. *Nothing, Viktor* . . . Only a bullet in a prison yard. Or only a fall from the open hatch of a high-flying helicopter. It was hard for him not to laugh out loud.

They went up the rusted ladder. There was a light above it, they were exposed. They were on the steps below the little platform, the light shining on them. Lofty worked the explosive strip down over the hinges of the metal door and Wickso passed him up the small deto-nator, which Lofty sank into the putty. They were all breathing hard, and Lofty seemed to take an age. What he had told Ham, the kid on whom they depended had never been in the building and knew nothing of its interior layout, only that the office of the *zampolit* major was on the second floor. Each of them slipped the gas masks down. Billy gestured, like his nerve was going, that Lofty should go faster.

'A spy?'

The kill was made. He was on his haunches, he had pressed himself close to his prey and he held him tight in his arms. He was the mantis. The tape would be turning. That evening he would sleep in Moscow. The wretch would lie on a concrete bed in a cell, and in the rooms of the Lubyanka the lights would burn late and the bottles would be drained, and couriers would take the transcripts to the President in the Kremlin. A crisis would break and an ambassador would be summoned to receive an expulsion list – and it would be because of him, because of the skill of Yuri Bikov . . . He could not think of what he had missed, but he knew that one piece was outside the puzzle.

'Yes.'

'Can I hear it again, please? A spy?'

'Yes.'

He was not surprised that he felt no pleasure. The chase was done. He was drained, washed out. On the aircraft to Moscow, while the prisoner sat handcuffed, trussed, hooded, he would sleep.

'Each time you say it, Viktor, you will feel better, liberated. Again, a spy?'

'Yes.'

He saw a pit, a circle of discoloured concrete. The slot in the puzzle that troubled him was a circle. He bored on.

'Because of your grandmother and your father? Your dead drop was at Malbork Castle? You met your handlers three times in Gdansk? Everything that crossed the desk of Admiral Falkovsky you delivered at the dead drops or gave to your handlers?'

'Yes . . . yes.'

'They were British, the handlers who have abandoned you?'

He tried to read the sign above the pit, to complete the puzzle's picture. He was not listening for the answer. Bikov did not realize the stiffened tenseness that rippled in his prey's body. Without thinking, wearied, he repeated . . .

'Who have abandoned you.'

342

His prey twisted. Hands were at his throat. Nails gouged at his neck's flesh. He could not cry out. He was pushed down. His prey was above him, a knee in his stomach and little choking, crying sounds played in his ears. He could not breathe. *Who have abandoned you.* He tried to shout, could not . . . He saw the scraped picture above the animal pit, made out the faint outline of a hippopotamus . . . He heard a thud of noise beyond the closed door. The legs of his prey were above his and smothered his effort to kick, to beat his heels on the concrete, to alert his major and his sergeant.

For Bikov, the last piece of the puzzle was in place . . . a rescue from the zoo park, not *abandoned*. He should have . . .

The fingers tightened on his throat. He should have posted a guard . . . The second noise, from outside, was not the same dull thud, but a whipcrack of sound – the fall from a height of a metal dustbin on to concrete. His voice was a coughing gurgle. He should have posted a guard of naval infantry around the building . . . He felt himself failing.

The door opened and came across the room, flying free. Light blazed in his face. The fingers loosened. Grey gas smoke spread. Above him was the ceiling, around him were the bare walls and under him was the concrete floor. The fingers came off his throat and he gasped, drank in the smoke spreading from the ceiling, the walls and up from the floor. He should have . . . The figures were grotesque, huge, smoke swirling around them. The pain came to his eyes and his lungs burned and he rolled away, and a weapon barrel broke through his front teeth and bedded in his throat. He heard the command cry.

'Viktor, identify yourself – which is Viktor?'

The command was in his own language, but muffled. His eyes were open. He did not dare to wipe them, to cleanse them of the pain. There were three men in the room, black-suited with the water still on them, and the great masks guarding their faces. He saw the hand raised, then a torch shone sharply into his prey's face. The hands reached down. His lungs were filled and his eyes were coated in the smoke. Arms grabbed at his prey. He rolled to escape the smoke and the torchlight torturing his eyes. A shot exploded close to him, but he had rolled.

And then the room was empty.

He lay for a moment without moving. He heard the belt of feet going away. With his hand he groped to his side, where his prey had been, but his fingers caught at nothing. He started to crawl towards the open doorway, through the smoke gas, and twice he stopped because of the pain skewering him. Because he had rolled he had not been killed. On his hands and his knees, with his stomach scraping the concrete floor, he moved towards the open door. His eyes were closed as he went through it and hit the impediment, which was soft but not giving. He was coughing the smoke from his lungs and his throat, but if he opened his eyes the needles would make the pain come again. He would not have opened his eyes if his hands had not felt the wetness on the shape that blocked him. His hand was on the shirt of his major; it was blood-soaked. He felt for a pulse that wasn't there. His major's hand was resting lightly on the butt of the pistol in the shoulder holster. He heard the whine of the turning tape spools. His sergeant was beside the outer door and lay on his stomach, but his head was twisted to the side and he saw the twin bullet-holes in the forehead, within five centimetres of each other. Behind the sergeant was the close-barred door that hung, angled, from one hinge. He did not stop to feel his sergeant's pulse. There was a glass water flask on the table and Bikov snatched it, then doused his face to wash away the pain.

Out on the landing, the military policeman screamed in hysteria into his radio.

He had missed what should have been obvious to him, the zoo park . . . Across the landing, the steel fire-escape door gaped open, and the smoke was sucked into the night. He splashed the last of the water on to his eyes and coughed the gas out of his throat and chest. He used the table to push himself up.

He heard the foghorn blasts as the alarm sounded.

They ran. Loosely, the formation was a diamond. Billy in front, Wickso and Ham with the package, Lofty at the back with the launcher.

They ran because the darkened shadow corners of the base were gone. In response to the blast of the alarm and then the siren's call, lights snapped on in every window, and they heard those windows thrown open, and doors. Each time they passed a window or a doorway where a face peered at them, Ham shouted: '*Main gate – major incident – barricade yourself inside*.' Little went through Ham's mind as they ran, but paramount was the need to exploit the first minutes of chaos. He had shot both of them in the building and the blood had spurted up from the one who had groped for his shoulder holster and the droplets had bounced to the eyepiece of his mask and there were smears there from when he had wiped it. They were going towards the canal and Billy's back was only a blurry shape through the smears.

The package was a dead weight, and with each stride was heavier. He clung to the package, as Wickso did. Between him and Wickso there was a little gasp of pain. His mind focused. The package had no coat, no tunic, and the white shirt shone out each time lights trapped them. The package had no belt and clung to his trousers to stop them sliding down, impeding his stride. They ran past workshops, and the track Billy took was over gravel. He heard the whimper from the package's throat. He looked down.

The package wore no shoes, no boots. Its weight went down on the gravel and it shuddered. They were going under a high light. The face of the package winced. He saw the already shredded thin black socks. The package was a passenger. They carried him to the quay and, behind them, the shouting, the alarm blasts and the siren made a cacophony of sound.

Lofty covered them. Wickso hooked a little life-jacket over the package's shoulders and snapped the clasp.

Ham said, 'He can't run, he's no shoes.'

Billy threw the bags into the canal and the blackness of it seemed to call them.

They went down into the water.

The telephone rang, unanswered, on his desk, and the alarm pealed from the siren on the roof of the headquarters building. The fleet commander stared down at the key beside his hand. The curtains of the inner office were open and Admiral Alexei Falkovsky had expected to go to the window in time to see the tail-lights of the car driving towards the outer gate. Then he would use the key. Through the evening and the night he had thought only of the waters of the Tsushima Strait and the fate of a previous Baltic Fleet commander in chief, Admiral Rozhdestvensky, and the disaster visited on the navy's reputation then, which still lingered. A fist beat against his door, and a voice shouted his name with increasing impatience. It was eleven minutes past three o'clock in the morning. He had thought by now he would have seen the car drive his friend, his chief of staff, his *protégé*, away towards the main gate. His door was opened.

He yelled at the night duty officer, 'Fuck off, get out, fuck off away.'

He was told, 'The base has been attacked, a terrorist attack. Two of Colonel Bikov's colleagues have been murdered in the FSB building, but Colonel Bikov has survived. The terrorists are in flight and with them is Archenko. The base is now on black alert, the Ready platoon is about to move.'

He never looked up. His head sank, and his eyes rested on the key.

They spilled out of the senior officers' mess. The last of the drinkers lurched on to the step. Three had stayed with Piatkin, the *zampolit*, to gain a glimpse of the saloon car that would take Archenko away. As the *zampolit* on the base, he was always assured of having toady-ish men around him who would laugh with him and share his gossip. The three represented the network that augmented their service salaries with the sale of weapons, building materials, food from the kitchens to Chelbia, who paid well. At the moment the siren had started the telephone call had come and the steward had passed it to Piatkin. He, and the three others, shouted slurred orders into the night at any sailor or infantryman passing them, at any officer racing past in a jeep.

'Extra guard on the gate, seal the base.'

'Double the perimeter patrols – treble them.'

'Roadblocks on the Kaliningrad road, get them in place.'

'Reinforce the frontier, close the frontier – no traffic out, no trains – shut the airport. Mobilize the Ready platoon.'

Piatkin, swaying, started to run towards the armoury where the Ready platoon would be forming up, where he could take control.

The drink seemed to slosh in his body. Muddled, but already present, was a sense of impending disaster. He was responsible for base security. He would face an unmerciful inquiry. He ran towards the armoury, speeded on his way by the catastrophe that had enveloped him.

The queue snaked back out of the building.

One at a time, the conscripts were handed assault rifles off the racks, two empty magazines, and had to dig in a wide box for fistfuls of ammunition. Only one clerk served the queue. Half dressed, half asleep, the conscripts took what they were given and shuffled back outside.

Vasiliev was at the back. Maybe he had slept for two hours, restless and fitful, but no more. His head ached from the explosion of noise, the siren blasts and the screams of the sergeant. The sergeant, a demented ghost, had run down the length of the dormitory barracks stripping the blankets off them. Behind him the platoon formed up, and among the yawning, coughing and grunting was the scrape sound of ammunition being loaded into magazines, and the rattle on the paving of dropped bullets, and the yelling of the sergeant, and the shouting of the *zampolit*.

In front of him, an assault rifle was handed over and rounds were gathered up.

'Next.'

A rifle was thrust at him. 'No, I use the heavy machine-gun.'

'You use what you are given.'

'I should be given the NSV heavy machine-gun.'

The clerk threw up his hands in exaggerated complaint, then shuffled off to the back of the armoury. When he reached the far end he shouted for Vasiliev to come to help him. The sergeant called after him that the whole 'fucking platoon' was not waiting for him – he should catch them up at the headquarters building. Two heavy youngsters, the last in the dormitory to be half dressed, Mikhail and Dmitri, made the final length of the queue. Piatkin's voice rose above the sergeants; the platoon should go immediately to the headquarters building. He went past the desk and down past the rifle racks into the dim-lit recess of the building. Against the far wall was

Vasiliev's weapon resting on its tripod – as he had left it when he had come back from the range, and after he had cleaned it.

'Don't think I'm carrying it. You want it, you carry it. And how much ammunition?'

'Two hundred rounds, ball and tracer and—'

A voice, soft as zephyr wind, behind him said, 'He wants seven hundred and fifty rounds – ball and tracer and armour piercing – and he wants a second barrel.'

Vasiliev turned. The man close to him was slightly built and wore dirtied casual clothes. There was blood on his hands, caked dry, and his eyes were deep reddened as if from weeping.

The clerk snapped, 'And who are you to give orders in my—'

'I am Colonel Bikov, FSB military counter-intelligence. He wants seven hundred and fifty rounds and a second barrel, and he gets them whether I have to break your neck or not. And I want one 82mm mortar, and I want twenty-five para flares. How do you want your neck to be?'

He barely knew Mikhail and Dmitri. They were wide-shoul-dered, wide-gutted, and inseparable. He knew they came from the great wheat plains of central Russia, near to the Urals. He'd heard other conscripts say that Mikhail wet his bed at night and that Dmitri cried for his home and family. They had been one month in the platoon, and he had never seen evidence of that. Standing behind the shabby bloodstained man, the great swollen muscles of their shoulders burst inside the singlets and the open tunics, and their hands – big as hams from a smokehouse – reached for the 82mm mortar that the clerk pointed to, and the boxes for the mortar shells.

They had the machine-gun and its belts of ammunition, the mortar and the boxes. They struggled, the four of them, back down the length of the armoury shed to the door. The clerk shouted at them that he needed signatures.

A second platoon of naval infantry was reaching the armoury and had begun to form a queue.

Vasiliev struck out towards the headquarters building.

The command cut in the night air. 'You are with me. You take my orders.'

'Where do we go?'

'To the nearest point of water, where there are no fences and no regular patrols.'

He pointed towards the canal. Now Vasiliev led. His right hand on the barrel, and Bikov's on the shoulder rest, took the weight of the machine-gun; with their left hands they carried the ammunition box. Behind them, with the strength of farm-boys, Mikhail and Dmitri brought the 82mm mortar and the boxes of flares. They could not run, could barely trot. After a hundred metres, he thought the officer struggled, but he had seen his face and did not think this was a man likely to show his weakness.

Vasiliev said, 'May I ask, sir, did they take Captain Archenko?'

'They took Captain Archenko.'

'The sergeant said Captain Archenko was a traitor, and that terrorists had freed him and—'

'And murdered two good men – what is your name?'

'Vasiliev, sir.'

'Your given name?'

'Igor, sir.'

'Please, Igor, keep your strength and don't talk. Please, don't waste your strength.'

A searchlight played over the base, flitted between buildings and over roads, and as they struggled forward the light caught the glimmer of the canal.

The searchlight's beam tracked from the base to the beach below its mounting on the wall of the fortress. For a few moments its cone crossed the length of the sand and the sea wall then it raked on further and out on to the water. The beam had the power to penetrate the mist that had followed the rain. When it hooked on to a breakwater or a buoy marking a sunken wreck, it lingered, then moved on. It found a speck of white, traversed beyond it, and was jerked back. The cone of the searchlight's beam settled on five men, one in white and half out of the water clinging to something that the searchlight's crew could only identify as a floating black bag. One screamed into his radio what the searchlight showed them, and the other held the target. The target was close to the wall on the west side of the canal. The beam locked on to the swimmers.

Locke was away from the track and could move quicker on a cushion carpet of pine needles; the wand stick eased his path. There were no more brambles to catch at his clothes and tear his hands, and fewer of the hazels, which had whipped back on to his face when he'd blundered into them. He was beyond the line of trenches and bunkers, and he thought that this ground, now pine-planted, had been given up in that old battle . . . It was the first time in six years that he could remember being without the weight of the mobile telephone on his belt.

He felt a sense of peace . . . The phone was always on his belt in Warsaw and had been with him every working day, and every weekend day, and had been on charge at night, always within reach. The phone, its presence and its link to his work, had been confirmation of his status as an intelligence officer, a symbol of constant responsibility.

The mobile phone was in the pocket of Alice's coat, which hung on the back of a chair in the kitchen of the bungalow. Only when it was over, when she needed her coat, would she find his mobile phone. He wanted no contact with a world away from the sandspit and the forest.

Without the phone, he was free of them. He was liberated from Ponsford and Giles, and from Rupert bloody Mowbray. He was released from the spectral image of the dead man floating under the pontoon bridge.

He heard a whisper of sound that was alien to the motion of the high pine canopy and to the tread of his shoes over the carpet of needles.

Eight miles from his parents' farm, a direct line over fields and past rock outcrops and bracken slopes, was a quarry. Regular enough that a clock could be set to it, they had blasted a fresh fall of granite boulders each working morning at six a.m. As a child, in the school term, he had slept through the distant crack of the explosion, but in the holidays his father had pitched him out of bed and he had been frogmarched to the milking parlour to help. Every holiday morning, milking began at five forty-five a.m. Sourly, he had driven the cattle into the bays of the parlour, and every one of those mornings he had promised himself that as soon as he was able he would be gone from the cold, the cow shit and the smell of the farm. Ten minutes before the blasting, eight miles away, as the milk was sucked from the beasts' udders, a siren warned of the explosion. For ten minutes, if the wind was from the east, in the milking parlour he could hear it faintly.

It was the same sound. He knew they were running.

17

Q. Where is the longest sandspit in Europe?
A. Kaliningrad.

The third rung on the ladder had broken when they had gone down into the water, a second one fell away as they came back up out of the canal.

By Wickso's wristwatch, it had taken them seven minutes to swim the width of the canal, and for the last two they had been held in the pool of light. There had been no escape from it, nor was there now. Billy was up the ladder, lay on his stomach and reached back down for the first of the two inflated bags; Lofty was on a rung just below the waterline, and it gave. He fell back and the bag slipped down into the water and seemed, tantalizing, to float away from his arm's range. Lofty had to give up his hold on the ladder's stanchion to retrieve it. It was not difficult, because the searchlight was on them – but more time was lost . . . They no longer had *Surprise*. They had speed on their side and they still needed a shit bucket full of luck . . . *Speed*, but three of them, and the man they knew as Ferret, floundered in the water, with two inflatable bags.

Lofty grasped it and again launched himself at the ladder. He went up and heaved the bag past Billy's shoulder. Lofty was ripping the zipper on the bag, and then Ferret was up beside him and gasping. Lofty saw, in the searchlight's cone, the pallor of Ferret's face; the white shirt clung to him, his trousers were half down to his knees. One of his socks had come off in the swim and the sole of his foot was a lacerated skein of lines. Then Ham was up with the second bag, and Wickso. Lofty, on his knees, dragged the remaining

352

weapons out of the bags – what they hadn't needed for the snatch – felt that each of them had stayed dry, and threw at them all the reserve ammunition magazines.

He snatched up the grenade-launcher. They left the bags behind, and ran – each with their own scuttling stride – towards the shelter of the wooden hut. Finally, they had lost the searchlight.

The beam, almost angrily, seemed to Lofty as he looked back to thrash around for them, first it roved beyond them and it scuttered among the sheds and huts and buildings, then it swept back and lit the canal's quay. It retreated, searched the width of the waterway, and then it snapped up a rowing-boat. Lofty saw four men in the rowing-boat, and two bent their backs on oars. But finding the boat was an aberration for the searchlight and it swerved erratically back to the wooden hut.

None of them had spoken since the far side of the canal's quay, when they had been close to the half-sunken ship and the moored landing-craft. Then it had been Ham. Now it was Ham. 'He's got no shoes.'

'His problem,' Wickso grated. 'He'll have to manage.'

'We've got eleven klicks to do.'

'His feet are the last thing I'm worrying about,' Billy said.

A burst of shots hit the upper woodwork of the hut, and some might have sprayed into its roof of corrugated metal. They had escaped the searchlight's cone but not the ever-present and penetrating wail of the siren, and they could hear distant shouting and the roar of jeep engines. They ran.

There was glass and old iron scrap, sharp stone and rubble crunching under their four pairs of boots. Lofty was back marker, the last of the diamond's points. He heard each of Ferret's stifled cries, and he could see the man's weight flop on Wickso's shoulders and Ham's. Himself, he felt Ferret's pain. He remembered when he had turned in his seat behind the driving-wheel of the old Mercedes, and he had looked up past Ham and out through the opened door and he had seen the same face and the backs of the men who had blocked him. The man, Ferret, had protected them. And then he remembered Alice North beside the Braniewo road, in the farm gateway. It was owed to both of them.

Billy called back, 'Where we cut through, would a vehicle crash the fence?'

From Wickso, 'Probably would.'

Billy called again, 'How long does it take to hot-wire?'

From Ham, 'Less than a minute, but it's a diversion.'

They ran in the darkness. There were no more shots, but the shouting was louder, and headlights speared between buildings. They were among scrub bushes and nettle banks. They had to keep moving. Every dozen strides, Lofty would spin, face behind him and hold the launcher poised. If there was close pursuit, and if he fired, he confirmed their position – to shoot was the last resort.

The vehicle park was in front of them. It was wide and open, but there was a line of six lorries and a second line of three jeeps. Billy led them. None of them would contradict an order from Billy. He ran towards the furthest jeep, the one closest to the wire fence. He made the signs – Lofty would drive, Ham would hot-wire, Wickso would hold the torch. The noises behind them were louder, as if a wasps' nest were disturbed and the creatures with their stings ranged after them.

The package, Ferret, was dumped into the open back of the jeep and the breath subsided from him in a wheeze. Billy was beside him. Wickso held the torch close to Ham's frantic moving fingers, and a metal sheet clattered on to the jeep's floor. The wires jumped in Ham's hands. Lofty pumped the pedals. The engine shook, coughed, shuddered, and caught. They were aboard. He stamped on the accelerator. Bloody good thinking from Billy. No lights, but a cloud of fumes behind them, and he gunned the jeep into the mist curtain towards the fence.

Lofty clung to the wheel. Couldn't use the lights to guide him. Over potholes, bumps, heaps of stones, pitching and rising, crashing through the scrub. There had been a ditch, to take away rainwater, and he squirmed across it, lost traction before regaining it, and there, framed in the mist, was the fence. A light blazed, red, on the dash by his legs, but it was half hidden by the launcher across his lap . . . It would be Lofty's decision. He would go down on to the beach, and he could hear the sea, he would hit the beach and go along the tideline where the sand was hardest, no lights, and that would give them speed . . . The fence loomed in front of him. He took it head on, maximum power, and the jeep's bonnet bucked, and the tyres spun, then took again, and the fence's mesh screamed as it scraped over the engine covering. Its weight flattened the windshield, lashing into Lofty's face. He heard Billy's oath, and Ferret's howl, and the tearing of clothing – and they were through.

He spun the wheel towards the sounds of the sea.

The engine spluttered. The power died.

They skidded to a halt and the light, red, was bright against his legs. Lofty said, 'There's no fuel – the jeep's got no bloody fuel. We picked a jeep with an empty tank, we—'

Billy was already out, and Wickso, Ham and Ferret followed. He heard Ham's voice, sending the signal that would go as a burst transmission. Lofty slumped, then swung his legs out of the jeep and ran to catch them. Their first target was to reach Rybacij, then there was the open ground until the eight-kilometre marker from the ruined village.

They couldn't use the ferry because none of them knew how to start its engine.

'What will happen to him? What will happen to Captain Archenko?' he had asked, and in the confusion he had not been answered.

They had taken a rowing-boat from beside the entrance to the inner harbour, near to the north-west causeway, and the big boys from the farmlands had put their backs into the oars.

'Will Captain Archenko be killed?' he had asked, and was not answered.

They had landed. Soldiers, NCOs and officers, had milled around them, and then he had seen the way that the colonel took control. At first he had not spoken, had allowed the babble to float around him, but when the voices had died he had spoken with soft calmness, and he had given his instructions. He wanted a combat support vehicle. As soon as troops were armed and in formation, they were to be trucked up the far length of the peninsula, and should be deployed as a blocking force on the frontier. No other forces were to get ahead of him without his express permission. With a senior NCO, a full-ranking petty officer, to drive the vehicle – a UAZ-469 – they had gone north up the quay and there the colonel had inspected two abandoned black bags, sets of flippers and gas masks.

'He saved my life,' Vasiliev had said. 'He was the only friend I had.'

An arm had gone round his back, had squeezed him lightly, and they had again mounted up. They had driven to the vehicle park, and the colonel had been shown the single space where a jeep had been parked; he had seen the colonel's shoulders hunch as if tension caught them. They had followed the tyre-marks, their headlights showing the treads, and had gone through a broken hole in the fence, and then the headlights had spied out the jeep, and the shoulders had lifted as though a weight were shed. They went back towards the road up the peninsula and the first lorry of infantry thundered past them, towards the border.

They reached the destroyed skeleton buildings of Rybacij and drove to its far limit.

He persisted, 'I cannot kill my friend. I cannot . . .'

The colonel's hand motioned for the driver to stop on the track, and ahead of them was only the mist and the darkness. The colonel dropped from the vehicle, then his hand was out and it took Vasiliev's and helped him down. Then the colonel lifted, with Mikhail and Dmitri, the weapons and boxes from the vehicle. Behind them was a growing, widening line of infantry.

The colonel said, 'I don't ask you to kill your friend . . . I don't say that Captain Archenko, your friend, will be killed . . . He faces investigation that will be legal and fair, but rigorous. Igor, I want him captured, and I want the four terrorists killed who took him. Trust me, Igor. Will you trust me, do as I ask?'

He hung his head. He murmured that he would.

'Why do you have the machine-gun?'

'I train with it – Captain Archenko says I am the best.'

'For me, will you fire the machine-gun at the four terrorists? Will you, Igor?'

The eyes, lit by the vehicle's lights, were mesmeric to him and the gentleness of the voice soothed him. He was too young, too ignorant, to know how a cobra trapped a victim with its eyes before stabbing venom into it. It was as if they were alone and a gathering army was not behind them. He stammered, 'I will.'

'You are good with the machine-gun?'

'With that weapon I am the champion for the Naval Infantry of the Baltic Fleet.'

'You will show me a champion, the best – and you will trust me.'

Ahead of them was the airfield. Past the airfield was the missile site. Beyond the missile site was the shooting range. One of them had spared his life. He had seen the knife that the tall one had held and his throat had been bared, but his life had been spared.

'I will.'

'Site the weapon.'

Beside the track was a small promontory of sand and he heaved the machine-gun up it and began to prepare to shoot. He heard the colonel instruct Mikhail and Dmitri at what angle and at what range they should fire the first flares. He was a simple boy, and he felt a small spreading pride that he was *asked* and they were *told*. He thought the mist was lifting. He slapped the first belt, fifty rounds, into the breech and snapped the flap catch down. In the night was the clatter as he armed the machine-gun and he settled behind it. He trusted the colonel, as if the colonel were his newest friend. The colonel crouched close to him.

'I'll feed for you.'

'It's not necessary, sir, but . . .'

'You are Igor, and I am Yuri. We are together. It is better if I feed for you, Igor, and spot for you.'

He was a conscript, a creature of no importance. The colonel of counter-intelligence was a man of stature. Vasiliev did not know why so important a man lay beside him and held the belt of tracer and ball and armour-piercing ammunition. To the side of them, down on the track, was the crack as the first flare was fired from the mortar.

He had not seen it climb, but he saw it break out. The flare, to Locke, seemed suspended in the skies, merged in the thinning mist, until it began to fall slowly and he lost it.

*　　*　　*

Alice heard the burst message come in as the console bleeped and the light blinked at her. She played it back. Ham's voice was detached, curious and metallic, distant.

'Ferret picked up. Reached west side of Morskoy canal. Moving out. All hell broken behind. Out.'

She sat on the chair with her coat hooked behind her, and shared the kitchen with the darkness. Her mouth gaped. She could make out the walls and the units, the pictures and the line of hanging saucepans. Her mother would have liked the steel saucepans, the wood units and the pictures on the walls . . . She tried not to think of him. She should not have had to receive the message, or to pass it on: Locke should have done it. But, Locke – the coward – had run away, would be sitting against a tree or on the beach or . . . She cursed him. Turning to the radio, she hit the code buttons that would scramble the relayed message.

Her voice was clear, sharp. 'This is what I've just received. Stand by for verbatim. "Ferret picked up. Reached west side of Morskoy canal. Moving out. All hell broken behind."That's all I've got . . . God, I feel so useless.'

She cut the transmission.

On the bridge, the master could feel the motion of the engine as it turned over. He heard the muted cry of the siren carried over the water, then there was the laboured noise of feet on the inner ladder and the bridge door burst open.

He stared ahead, out through the window, but the mist masked the few scattered lights of the shore where it was closest to them. Where the wind lifted up the siren call, at the base, he saw nothing. He thought Mowbray had run from the cabin, then thrown himself at the ladder.

The voice bellowed behind him, 'They've lifted him. They're on their way.'

'But they've raised the dead,' he said grimly. 'How far have they come?'

'This side of the canal, they're legging it. I always said it could be done. Damn the doubters – make ready.'

'They raised the dead, and they have too far to come.'

'The doubters – fuck them – said it was not possible. It will be a triumph for—'

'Is it close pursuit?'

The master turned. He saw Mowbray blink, then bluster, 'Nothing that they can't handle. They're trained men.'

'Don't listen to me, listen to the night. What do you hear? You hear nothing? I hear the sirens. I hear the alarm. Can I tell you what is at Kaliningrad?'

'I know what is at Kaliningrad.'

Mowbray's bark betrayed his fear, the master thought. What he knew from his life at sea – the barking men, the men with certainty, were always those who harboured fear. 'At Kaliningrad naval base is a brigade of Naval Infantry, and in coastal defence are two artillery regiments and a missile regiment. Behind them are interceptor aircraft, bombers and attack helicopters, and in the base are frigates, destroyers, patrol-boats and . . . Do you want more?'

Mowbray snarled, 'When did you enlist with the doubters?'

'A few minutes ago, Mr Mowbray, when I heard the sirens.'

'They're incompetent, they're Russians – they'll be chasing their own backsides, won't know where to look, where to run. I know Russians – fools.'

'It will only take one good man,' the master said. He saw the anger in Mowbray and thought, from his experience of men, that anger ran with fear.

'And we have the night, and we have the fog.'

'We have the night for two more hours, and fog is not a friend to be trusted – it lifts.'

'You took the money.'

The master swivelled away. The door slammed shut behind him. He had taken the money and looked for more. He wanted a grove of olive trees and an orchard of lemons and a little villa with a view from the patio on the hillside above Korinthos . . . and he was a man of his word. He would do what he could. It was many years since he had accompanied his wife to church, but he prayed then, on his bridge, that the mist on the water would stay down. For the first time he saw flares in the sky, one high and one in dying descent over the land.

He checked the dial to confirm the power was there, then wrenched back the lever and heard the first grating roll of the anchor chain as it lifted.

The sheet of paper trembled in Ponsford's hand. 'I don't quite believe it to be possible. My God . . .'

He passed the paper to Giles, who held it in front of his spectacles. It was only a line and a half of text . . . How many times did the damn man need to read it? Five times, six? The paper was returned, and Giles's head shook as though he could not credit what he saw.

He reached for the telephone. Giles frowned. They were in the annexe off the central communications unit – in vernacular, the 'War House' – on the floor below the basement library. In the annexe were two canvas camp beds, a table with a plate of sandwiches under clingfilm, a hot-drinks vending-machine, and a wall screen on which a large scale map of the Kaliningrad *oblast* and Polish territory east of the Vistula river was displayed. The message had come through a glass door at the annexe's far end, where technicians worked at a bank of machines. It was years since Ponsford had been in the room but Giles – Special Operations – would have been there more often, when the map showed Kabul or bloody Herat or fucking Kandahar. He lifted the telephone and his hand still trembled.

'Who are you ringing?'

'The DG – who else?' He dialled.

'I doubt you'll find him.' Giles pursed his mouth.

He listened and the phone rang out. 'Ridiculous – course I will. On a night like tonight, course he'll be in place. A damn great bed he has up there, wardrobe, fresh clothes, shower. He'll be there. Why shouldn't he?'

'Please yourself, Bertie.' Giles shrugged.

A voice answered. Messages for the director general were being diverted to the night duty executive. Would the caller please wait for the connection. Ponsford dropped the phone.

'I'd never have thought it.'

Giles grimaced. 'You're good on a cliché or two, Bertie. A hot summer, a tinder-dry forest and the potential for disaster, what do they do, Bertie?'

He said savagely, 'They cut a bloody fire-break.'

'Bullseye, Bertie. "They cut a bloody fire-break" between themselves and the action. All of them up on the fifth floor achieved their eminence by cutting bloody fire-breaks.'

'Bastards,' Ponsford murmured.

'Look at it from their view, Bertie. They've sanctioned, on the record and minuted, a reconnaissance – nothing more. A fire can't jump a good wide break. The team went over the canal, and lifted Ferret, and now: "All hell broken behind." ' His finger stabbed up at the map on the screen. 'Twelve kilometres from the canal to the embarkation point, quite a stride – a fair stride – you'd agree on that. What I'm saying, Bertie, dammit, the team have it all to do.'

'Don't ever accuse me of liking the man, but you sell Rupert Mowbray short . . .'

'Mowbray? Rupert bloody Mowbray?' Giles snorted in theatrical derision. 'For Christ's sake, Bertie, don't tell me you think Mowbray's in charge. He's on a bloody ship miles from the action – and it is action. It is at a level of all-hell-broken-behind arse-puckering action. Locke, the pompous little prat, and the only sane one out there, is the wrong side of the frontier, and can in no way influence events. You know what I've learned about covert special operations? You set up a system of command and control, best bloody men given the job, and they're always too far back. Every time you believe there'll be a steady hand on the tiller, there never is . . . We never learn. Yes, nothing personal, not you but *we* . . . We don't learn as we chase the goddamn glory.'

'Without offering offence, I think your attitude is negative,' Ponsford said sombrely.

Giles laughed, not with him but at him. The laugh split his sallow face. 'Bertie, it'll be in the hands of men we don't know. On their side and on our side. Believe me, or not believe me? We can pump up a picture on that imbecile damn kids' screen of the fleet commander of Baltiysk – Admiral Alexei fucking Falkovsky – and we can play war games with his potential reactions . . . waste of time. On their side it will depend on the qualities of some bloody platoon commander, or an NCO, or even a wretched little conscript with a hole in the seat of his bloody camouflage pants. On our side, it's a hermit, a con-artist, a drop-out and a bloody hospital porter. It's the little people's turn to take charge.'

Giles went shambling towards the door. Ponsford stared at the screen.

'Sorry, Bertie, a bit over the top . . . Just going for a breath of air.'

Locke was the modern man.

The modern man looked after himself, because no one else would. He ate the food that would not destroy his body with cholesterol, he drank sparingly and never to excess, he kept his muscles fit, he pursued the advancement of his career by saying the correct things to principal people, he let the newest technological electronic innovations take the strain of his life, and he was *sensible*. He stood out in a crowd as the one marked for advancement, he would prosper and progress . . . After Fort Monkton and after the days in the probationer classes in the lecture rooms at Vauxhall Bridge Cross, after being made up to a fledgling officer in the Service, Locke had been told that if he kept himself clean he had a fine future beckoning, might get to assistant deputy director general or even to the loftiness of deputy director general. Because the latest human-resources regulations demanded it, he had seen his assessments from his last year on home posting, and from his first year on overseas posting in Zagreb – before his transfer to Warsaw. They glowed: he was 'nobody's fool', he was an officer 'not afraid of work', he was a man 'with an aptitude for decision making/taking', he was 'an independent thinker'. It had all collapsed. His career, his future, had crashed with the same finality as an outdated computer system.

He ran in a madman's delirium. He felt no tiredness in his lungs and no pain in his legs. As his career disappeared over a faraway horizon, he ran towards the distant daylight.

Three times lorries had gone past him up the track towards the fence. There was no going back. Locke, alone among all of them, knew how it would end.

Ahead of him, far away, the flares burst and dangled, then slid lower on their parachutes, until they were lost among the dense set of the trees. He understood the pattern in which they were fired. They reached up into the mist and burned through it; they would throw the clearest light on the beach, and would cover the dunes and the sea, to push the team and Ferret away from the beach, and keep them moving. Soon, Locke thought, amid the beat of his heart and the crackle of his feet on dried brushwood, he would hear gunfire.

The team struggled to keep the pace. To their left was the airfield and the track. Between the dunes, on their right side, and the track, the ground was caked sand and grit stone with clusters of knee-high scrub that had been stripped of foliage by the autumn's gales. They would have gone faster on the beach, and Ferret would not have had to be half carried, half dragged, but the flares that tracked them were brightest over the beach.

Each time a flare was fired, streaming up into the night mist like a celebration firework, Lofty turned and crouched and held the rifle butt against his shoulder. His finger lay on the trigger guard of the grenade barrel clipped to the underside of the rifle's stock. He could fire a grenade to a maximum of four hundred metres, but the flares were launched at what he estimated to be a thousand metres or more, and the mortar that spewed them was always beyond range. The lorries had taken a blocking force ahead. Behind the mortar was a line of lights, guns' beaters, always and inexorably driving them towards that block. It was as though, uncannily, the mortar's crew knew the team's pace and matched it.

The flares would kill them, but they could not stop and wait for the mortar's crew to be within range of the grenades. They pressed on and stayed a few metres outside the slow drop of the flares' light. Billy suffered.

Lofty was the oldest of them, then Billy, then Wickso, and Ham, but Billy was suffering the worst. When they moved in the diamond, their speed was set by Billy, and Lofty knew it had slackened. It was 05.05 hours. They were late on the schedule, ten minutes minimum already, and Billy was going slower. They were near to the end of the airfield, and after the airfield was the missile site, then the start of the firing range, then two thousand metres to the targets, then five hundred to the point on the beach level with the sunken dinghy . . . At least ten minutes late, but could have been more. They had to up the pace.

Lofty hissed, 'Keep it going, Billy. We're all with you. Has to be faster, Billy.'

In the Squadron, they would have cracked the pace, but that time had gone, had run as sand through their fingers. He could hear the pants of Billy's breathing and the stumbling steps of Ham and Wickso with Ferret. They must go faster. He thought of the stones in their geometric lines, and the ghosts in the darkness. He heard the rustling of leaves he should have cleared . . . Another flare went up to the right of them and he could see the emptiness of the beach and the ripple of white waves breaking. He knew the mist cleared hesitantly, and he knew that the flare tracked them.

'Go faster. You can do it, Billy. You have to.'

They spilled from the vehicle.

Vasiliev, the conscript, sagged under the weight of the machine-gun, then dropped it down on to the centre of the track, between the ruts. For a moment he was alone, and the colonel was beside the farm-boys, whispering to them as they set the mortar and adjusted the base plate. Then he crawled across the ruts, lifted the loaded belt and held it ready in his hands.

'This time you shoot, Igor.'

'Yes, sir.'

'I am not "sir". I am your friend. I am Yuri. This time you shoot, Igor.'

'Yes . . . This time I shoot, Yuri.'

'Because you are the best – and I know nothing – tell me how you shoot.'

The voice soothed in his ear. He lay behind the machine-gun, and the butt was tight against his shoulder and his left fist clamped on the grip of the butt; his right hand's trigger finger rested against the guard. The voice massaged in his ear.

He recited: 'The rounds are 12.7mm calibre. There are fifty rounds in the belt, and each ten are made up of one that is armour-piercing, seven that are ball and two that are tracer. I have to shoot, for accuracy, in short bursts, a double tap on the trigger, because this is a suppression weapon, and after the first aimed round then it is impossible to hold the sights on the target. The muzzle velocity of the round is eight hundred and forty-five metres per second and—'

'How do you feel, Igor, when you shoot?' The voice was soft silk.

'I feel like I dream,' he said quietly. 'A dream of happiness.'

The colonel whistled sharply. He heard the crack of the mortar firing.

At full elevation, the 82mm mortar threw the shell a distance of 1100 metres. It exploded, the flare burst, the parachute opened, at an altitude of 400 metres. With the parachute restraining its fall, the flare would be in the air for a minimum of four minutes. When it lit the skies, the mist under it seemed to shrivel and it bathed the ground in increasing white light.

This time Lofty hadn't bothered to turn. At last they were going well ... It was the eighth flare that had been fired, and for the first two the team had thrown themselves on to their stomachs – Ham and Wickso had lain over Ferret's body – and they'd watched the speck of light climb, had seen it burst, realized its light would fall wide of them, and hurried on. When the third flare had been fired they had settled to a crouch, then Billy had cursed at the wasted time, and they'd started out again on their shambling run. For the fourth, fifth, sixth and seventh flares, they had kept going, and Billy's judgement was vindicated because the flares lit the beach and the sea.

Lofty looked up, shouldn't have done – the light blinded him. The flare had burst directly above him, and hung over him. He blinked, ducked his head, rooted. When he looked around, they – like him – were stock still, as if caught in a photograph: he could see the wrinkles in their wetsuits, Ferret's clinging shirt, the stitching of the webbing, and the blood over Ferret's feet. Then Billy hit Wickso, a downward chop, Ham threw Ferret to the ground, then Ham and Wickso had hold of the knees of Lofty's suit and dragged him down. After the report of the burst a great silence lay over them, and the light squeezed away the mist that each of them had thought was their protector. It mocked them, seemed not to move away from them. It hovered, an eye, over them.

They were on sand, stone and grass tufts, among the low scrub bushes, and Lofty knew that the schedule ticked.

He was on his stomach and lay half across Ferret. He could feel the man's shivering. 'What we going to do, Billy?' he pleaded.

'What's its range – how far's it back?'

'A thousand at least – I can't touch it.'

Billy murmured, 'And maybe they can't touch us.'

'We got to run, Billy, we can't stay down. We—'

Billy snarled, 'Don't tell me what we can't fucking do. Right, we run – Jesus—'

They pushed back up on to their feet, and the poor bastard – Ferret – had his feet straight into stone shards. One foot was bloodily ripped and on the other the sock was shredded. Ham and Wickso had him up like he was a casualty. The three stumbled into Billy, who hadn't moved, and Lofty saw how Ham elbowed Billy aside and he half fell. Lofty caught him. He could see, from the light above them, the froth in Billy's mouth and the spittle on his lips. 'You good, Billy?'

'Course, I'm good. Don't I look it? I'm doing back marker. *Move.*'

Lofty had always done what Billy told him. He moved. Billy had been the sergeant, Billy was the leader. It was his role. Billy had told him to hold the man's head under the water and Billy had told him what to say to the Crime Squad detectives. He moved because Billy told him to.

'You're good, Billy.'

'Just doing back marker, be right behind you.'

Lofty went past Billy. Ahead of them was a shadowy line, like the mark of the tide. The edge of the flare's pool was their goal. They were running. Ferret's stride matched Ham's and Wickso's, and Lofty was close behind them. He fancied the flare was dying, that the pool of light shrank and the shadow seemed to come to meet them. The darkness beyond the shadow was the target. In the light, the mist was reduced to small summer's-day clouds. He was close up to Ham and Wickso, and he caught Ferret's trouser waist. They pulled Ferret and he pushed him. The shadow and the darkness past it were almost within their reach. The light had gone to dusk. They were past the end of the runway, and . . . Dusk to daylight, the moment after another flare climbed, spilt its light, hung. The little knot of them around Ferret ran, and Lofty – in that sunlight – realized he no longer heard Billy's wheeze, his boots, the cursing.

Then, far behind him, 'Get on, you bastards. Run. Go, keep going.'

'In your own time, Igor, shoot in your own time.'

'But not Viktor, not Captain Archenko?'

He could see the white light on the white shirt, and the shirt bobbed between three men. His vision was good, above average, but the magnification of the sight ensured that he saw also the back of Viktor's head. Twice it was thrown back as if in a spasm of pain. He thought Viktor would have been unable to run, but the men around him pressured him on, and held him up. Behind them, a fourth man dropped steadily back . . . Igor Vasiliev, in his twenty-second year, the son of a taxi-driver from Volgograd, had never experienced combat. His father had urged him to volunteer for his conscription into the units of Naval Infantry. Naval Infantry were not sent to Chechnya. Anything was better than being posted to Chechnya. Igor Vasiliev had never fired his chosen weapon at a human target. He steadied himself. The target in the cross-hairs of the sight was dropped now from the group that supported his friend. His voice, soundlessly, recited the detail of the firing mechanism of the gun, as if that process would further calm him. 'Gas-operated, belt-fed and air-cooled, with horizontal sliding wedge breech-block . . . unfinned barrel with conical flash suppressor . . . ammunition fed into the breech in non-disintegrating belts . . . capable of penetrating 16mm of armour at five hundred metres . . .' His target was at 1150 metres, without protection, and was now twenty paces adrift of the group. He had only ever fired on the range, at stationary raised targets. The back of the man, broadened by the wetsuit, filled the crossing point of the hairs. The target fell, then picked itself up, tried to run again. His finger rested on the trigger . . . He hesitated.

'So that I can know you are the best, Igor, and I can be proud of you – shoot.'

To kill a man, he squeezed the trigger gently.

* * *

The tracer went past them, bright flying light at waist height, with a whip's crack. Another round was at knee level and spattered on a stone. The third seemed deadened, lifeless. They ran on . . . Then Billy screamed.

One cry, short, cut . . . Billy's scream stifled. One more double tap, then only the sound of their running and the battering of their magazine pouches on the webbing . . . He knew what he would see. As he ran, Lofty twisted his head and looked back into the flare's pool of light. He howled into the sunshine of the flare's daylight, 'Billy's down – hit – fucked.'

He turned. More shots hissed past him. A weight collided with Lofty, smacked him down. Wickso, bent low, cleared him and scurried towards where Billy had fallen. Lofty lifted the launcher towards the light that dropped on them and fired, reloaded and fired again. Away beyond the pool of light were explosions, twenty seconds apart, and way short of a target.

He crawled to them.

Wickso was crouched over Billy. Lofty saw the raised hand and in the fingers was a syringe. Lofty heard Billy's moan. Then he saw Billy's right leg. It was off above the knee. He knew that what had come past them were the bullets from a heavy machine-gun, but he hadn't before seen the damage they made – a raw, amputated leg, and the black of the wetsuit was hacked to shreds. He could see the blood and the flesh and splintered bone. The amber stone, wrapped in adhesive tape, heaved on Billy's chest. Two more bursts came over them, but they were high and he thought they were aimed at Ham and Ferret who would be running for the new shadow line as the flare fell lower.

'Get them off him,' Wickso shouted.

Lofty's hands were in the webbing pouches of Billy's harness. He saw Billy's eyes, open but gone someplace else. He groped for the grenades in the pouches.

'Is he all right?'

'Don't be daft, Lofty.' Wickso was savagely quiet, like he was the professional. ' "Is he all right?" It's taken his fucking leg off. No, he's not "all right", and not likely to be.'

He had four more grenades, and Wickso plunged the syringe of morphine into Billy's stomach through the gap he had made by wrenching apart the flaps of the wetsuit.

'Don't you do a tourniquet?'

'Not bloody grenades – get the bloody boots. What for, a tourniquet? They'll shoot him anyway . . . The boots are for Ferret.'

Wickso held Billy's hand. Billy couldn't speak. The lustre had gone from his eyes. Lofty heard the revving of a distant engine and, far away, there were headlights that fell well short of them. He pulled the boot off Billy's right foot, wanted to apologize but couldn't find the words, jerked at it till it came away. The second boot was off to the side. He reached for it, gripped the wetsuit leg, and blood dribbled on him. He closed his eyes, did it by touch, took the second boot.

On its parachute the flare sank to the ground and guttered.

He saw Wickso, with the indelible pen, write the single letter on Billy's forehead, M – morphine . . . Lofty fired one more grenade towards the advancing vehicle, and knew it was wasted. The vehicle tracked them and would always be beyond the range of the launcher.

Wickso ran well, and Lofty could match him, but the ground was open and the vehicle pursued them. They caught Ham and Ferret.

Ham had Ferret's weight and was going slowly. Fingers fumbled with the laces of the boots. The boots went on to Ferret's feet, over the wounds and the blood. Ham asked for Billy as the laces were dragged tight. Wickso said that Billy was dead. Lofty knew time had gone – time they could not spare – and that the schedule was wrecked. Lofty reckoned it a good lie – it was against the ethic of the Squadron to leave a man, wounded, in the field . . . It was right to lie – and Ham seemed satisfied. As they ran, faster than before, Ferret striding with them, Ham sent the signal. As he sent it, Wickso tripped on a jutting root and pitched forward, swore and nearly brought Ferret down with him. Lofty realized it, then: Ferret had not spoken a single word since they had lifted him out of the bare room – not a syllable, a word, a phrase, a sentence – but he would have known they were being hunted to their deaths. Behind them, the vehicle's engine was clear in the night. Would there be a stone for Billy, or for any of them? If there were one for Billy, Portland stone, a mason might carve on it: 'He was deniable.' Like the rest of them.

To stretch his stride, Lofty punched Ferret's back.

Alice relayed the signal. She recognized Ham's voice, and the gasp for air. Then there was a curse, and she thought that was Wickso's – because there was the West London whine in the oath – and she strained for Viktor's voice, but it was not there. She sent the signal, brutal and short, to Mowbray on the *Princess Rose*. Stripped of the call sign and the signature – 'delta 1 down. proceeding to rv. eta one hour' – the signal was a pickaxe blow into her stomach. It would be dawn in an hour.

18

Q. Where did a spy report, in the summer of 2000, the redeployment of Tochka missiles, nuclear warheads fitted, with the capability of targeting NATO bases in Europe?

A. Kaliningrad.

The beach was lit to an ochre glow. The daylight fell on it beyond the point where the fence came from the trees. The colour softened on the dunes. Roman stared through the gap between Chelbia's turned shoulders and the hunched silhouette of the Pole who had come home, and he thought the beach up the peninsula was tarnished gold. With his good eyes and his good hearing, Roman watched the gradual descent of the flares and the firefly-red specks of the tracer and listened to the faint clatter of the machine-gun.

Out of the side of his mouth, Chelbia asked, without turning, 'Is it normal for them to exercise at night?'

'No, it is not normal.'

Chelbia persisted, 'On occasions, do they exercise at night?'

'A few times – what is normal is that they do not have the ammunition or the fuel to exercise either at day or night. What is more normal is that the soldiers go to pick potatoes or turnips from the fields.'

Chelbia shrugged. 'Then I do not understand what is happening.'

'Look, look – there you have your answer.'

Roman pointed, not to the distant daylight that made a bogus dawn but at the yellowed sand where the fence came down to the sea. He saw the ant-sized soldiers and the tiny shapes of lorries whose headlights shone on to the dunes. Then more light came because the searchlight from the tower roved over the beach. Only once, fourteen years before, had Roman seen soldiers on the beach, lorries' lights, the searchlight shining down from the tower, and flares fired beyond the fence, and had heard the rippling crack of gunfire. A week later he had been in Krynica Morska to ask the garage there for help in the repair of the engine for his boat. A police sergeant had been at the garage because the tyres of his car needed replacing. While the plugs and washers on the engine had been changed and the tyres fitted, the police sergeant had told Roman of an emergency in the closed military area across the border. A sailor had bludgeoned his officer, then fled towards the fence. He had been captured – and the police sergeant had not known his fate, but had smirked at the thought of it. From the north and the south there had been a closing cordon, and to the west there had been the sea and to the east there had been the lagoon. Roman had often thought, in fourteen years, of the blundering flight of the sailor, and of the dragnet that had scooped him up.

Chelbia gazed into the night, at the dropping flares that made dusk come over the beach. 'What are you telling me, Roman?'

Living in Piaski village, fishing and minding his own business, never concerned with the riots of Gdansk down the coastline, never offering an opinion on politics, never drawing attention to himself or being in trouble, Roman had found it impossible to place himself in the mind of that fleeing sailor. But in his jeans hip pocket there was now a roll of American dollars, given to him by Chelbia who was a criminal.

His voice was hoarse. 'A man runs, is hunted – that is what I am telling you.'

Chelbia nodded, as if the answer satisfied him. Roman saw him take Jerzy Kwasniewski's hand, the burned one, and heard him say quietly, 'A man runs, is hunted – would that be Archenko?'

Roman felt the pain, himself, as the fist took the burned hand.

The Pole squealed, then said falteringly, 'Archenko was to be brought out in the evening, eight or nine hours ago.'

Chelbia let the hand drop away, mused, 'When I met him I thought he was a lion. He came to me with a hand grenade. He said he would kill me if I did not obey him. How many people make a threat on my life? Very few, I tell you. And I believed him. I believed he would kill me. Did he want money, as you do? I had brought a lorry full of weapons from the base, for export . . . He came to me and threatened to kill me, and would have. What he wanted was the return of *one* weapon from the hundreds that had been loaded on to the lorry. One. Why did he want one machine-gun from so many? He had the determination of a lion, and its arrogance. I gave him the one weapon, and I offered him an arrangement that would have made him a wealthy man. He refused me. I offer you an arrangement, and you gobble it, because you are greedy. He runs, and is hunted. Let us stay to watch his fate.'

In the last light of the distant flares, before they died, Roman saw the smile on Chelbia's face.

The Pole blurted, ingratiating, 'You can see the lights of the ship. The ship waits for Archenko. It is *hoped* to bring him off the beach to the ship.'

'I tell you something, Kwasniewski . . .' Again, Chelbia took the burned hand, but his fist must have been tighter on it because the scream was shrill in the night air. '. . . should you betray me as you betray Archenko and the people who help him, if I ever thought you betrayed me, having taken my money, I would break your spine with a sledge-hammer – and, believe me, I would enjoy doing it.'

Around the car on the dunes a crowd was gathering, faint shapes against the trees. Roman heard his wife call his name. He answered her. She stumbled down from the dunes and strode at him across the beach. Gulls scattered. He saw her in the light of the fire. She scolded him. She had been to sleep, she had woken, her bed had been empty, she had thought him dead, hurt, washed out to sea. She had come with an escort of neighbours and fishermen, dragged from their homes in the emergency . . . Her voice pealing and warming to the attack, she shouted at him. She wore her heavy boots and her wool robe, and the hem of her nightdress peeped below it. Her words cudgelled him, and he heard the titter of his neighbours and his fishing friends. He reeled from her assault.

'My fault,' Chelbia said softly. 'Boris Chelbia, madam, apologizes. I detained your husband . . . Sincere apologies.'

She buckled. A flask of fresh coffee was opened, and it was passed first to Chelbia. He held them in his hand, all of them. Roman watched for the next flare to be fired, and he listened for the next burst of the machine-gun. A man ran and was hunted, a ship out at sea waited, and the cold bit into Roman's body.

They were between the dunes and the fence of close mesh, topped with razor-wire.

The fence ran parallel to the beach and behind it were the bunkers and silos of the missile batteries. Above it were three watchtowers and arc-lights. The ground they crossed was bare dirt with no scrub bushes. It was serrated with gullies and short, slight ravines where years of rainfall had fashioned shallow drains. More flares were fired, but not the machine-gun, and for close to a kilometre it was possible for them to scurry forward, using the gullies for cover. Twice they had been fired at from the missile batteries' watchtowers, but the weapons used had been short-range assault rifles. Bent double, hustling, they hugged the ground. When a gully petered out they would go in a crabbed crawl out of it, then scramble, then drop down into the next. Wickso was in front. Ham could hear the blistered breathing of Lofty close behind him. The ground, carved with the natural trench lines, gave them a chance – a small chance.

One of Ham's hands clung to the Skorpion machine pistol, the other was buried in the sodden material of Ferret's shirt. He had as little feeling for the weapon as for the package. Emotion had always come hard to Ham Protheroe . . . No feelings of affection for the men he had trekked and trained with in the Squadron. No feelings of love for his parents, who had now shut him out of their lives. No feelings of sympathy for the widows and divorcees who had bought him dinners and fine wines, who had 'lost' their credit cards, and who had welcomed him into their beds. The emotions of affection, love, sympathy were all alien to him. His mind was a vacuum, emptied and cleansed.

In front of them was more scrub. With the scrub they would lose the hiding-places and sunken gullies. The clouds of mist had now shrunk to isolated pockets. They would be exposed. When they broke into the scrub and no longer had the gullies for cover, they must dance from cloud to cloud or they would be exposed.

It was best for Ham that he had no emotion, and a short horizon, as he propelled Ferret forward.

The flares came faster and the cover was more difficult to find. For the first time, Ham loosed his hold on Ferret's shirt and let him run alone.

'Tell me – because I am ignorant – how you fire.'

He lay behind the machine-gun. The voice was a whisper. The words were sweet honey and lulled the conscript. He did not realize it, but loyalty was passed. Only Captain, second rank, Viktor Archenko had ever spoken to him with the same respect. His father, when Igor had lived at home, had not shown him respect, and did not now when he returned home for annual leave; his father still talked to him as if he were a child and not a champion shot with the NSV heavy machine-gun. His platoon sergeant and the instructors on the range had shown him neither respect nor friendship, and others had tried to drown him when he had protested at the theft of the weapon that was his. The officer who supervised the range, and the men in the armoury, had not shown him respect, even when they had known that he was chosen to represent the Baltic Fleet in championships, nor had the conscripts with whom he lived in the barracks dormitory. He did not think of Viktor Archenko, who had followed his triumphs, who had talked to him of the castle at Malbork, who had requested he drive the car on occasion into Kaliningrad. He was captivated by the new friendship offered him, and by the respect. In those night hours, loyalty was transferred.

A simple boy, Igor Vasiliev would not have understood that he was a marionette in the subtle, sensitive fingers of a master puppeteer.

'I shoot well because I am fit, strong.'

'Most men would have their shoulder broken by the recoil?'

'It comes back not as a blow to the shoulder but with the impact of a heavy push, but you must have the strength to hold it so that your aim is not lost.'

There were four flares in the air, coming down like steps on a

375

ladder. When he had last seen them, four men and not five, they had moved like fleeing rabbits, darting and weaving over a short space of ground, then going down. The last time he had had them and the sight's cross-hairs had wavered over them, he had thought he had the opportunity to shoot, but then had lost it. Each time he went to the firing range he saw that ground over which they ran. He knew the ground close to the firing range as well as he knew the end of the street in Volgograd, Ulitsa Lenina, where his parents lived. So many journeys to the range, bumping in the back of lorry transport, had meant he knew the ground in front of the missile batteries. He knew the sunken rain gullies, and as loyalty had passed he had told the man, who now lay beside him and held the ammunition belt, where the scrub began again and at what range the flares should be fired. He concentrated.

The voice, a murmur with the wind, did not disturb him. He knew they must break cover and waited for them.

'I could not do it. I would panic when I saw the target – how do you control the breathing?'

In his own words he could not have explained it. It was natural to him, his given gift. He used the language of the instructors: 'You must always stay calm. The breathing must be controlled. When you shoot you have an exhilaration, an excitement, and that can destroy your aim. You must not gulp your breath, then try to hold it in full lungs, or the exhilaration will make your head pound, your brain split. You exhale, and you pause to shoot – not hold the breath, but pause. It is a difference. You must always keep your mouth open when you shoot because if your mouth is closed the noise of the discharge will destroy your hearing.'

'I understand, Igor. There.'

The men broke cover.

The flares were above them. The diamond shape was smaller. One was ahead. In the width of the diamond was his friend, the white shirt clear to see, and another black-suited figure was running close to him but not near to him. The fourth man at the back was behind his friend. The loyalty ebbed but had not died. The cross-hairs wavered off the man behind, and his friend, and he eased the butt's grip fractionally, and they snatched at the target running alongside his friend . . . Caught it, lost it when it ducked, then wove, found it again.

He held the target. It was his skill that the cross-hairs were locked on the magnified spine of his target. His finger slid from the guard to the trigger bar.

Ham ran.

A flare came down in front of him, the parachute sagged and the charge burned its last light. He skipped to avoid it. The parachute's cords were clear in the daylight from the three flares still floating above him.

The moment he cleared the cords that hung – a frosted spider's web – from a scrub bush, Ham was at his full height. Instinct then, in his next stride, made him duck.

Some men, under fire, wove. Some ran tall and believed in immunity. Some ducked as if to make a smaller target. Ham ducked, and did not know that the cross-hairs leaped from the width of his body by the lower spine to the back of his head.

Ham heard nothing, knew nothing of the shot that killed him.

Ham did not hear its report travelling far behind the bullet. He saw nothing of the ground and the scrub that rushed to break his fall. Ham knew nothing of the blood, tissue, brain parts, bone fragments that spattered in an arc.

Lofty fired twice back behind him. Wickso unhooked the radio from Ham's body. They sprinted towards where Ferret crouched, and they wove, ducked, went doubled, and when they reached Ferret they snatched him up. They cleared the line of the missile batteries' fence. The formation of the diamond was broken.

She sent the signal on.

She knew the tang of Wickso's voice. Different from Ham's. Ham's was quieter, less snapped, the vowels better formed. There was something bored in Ham's voice.

The signal – 'DELTA 2 DOWN. PROCEEDING TO RV. ETA 25 MINUTES' – was transmitted to the *Princess Rose*.

As if she drowned, her life seemed to slide before her.

She was Albert and Ros North's 'little angel'. She was the spoiled girl-child and the apple of their eye. She was the kid who expressed no gratitude, the kid whose ambition was to break from them and make her own way. She was the girl who slipped from them, but never so far as to be without the safety-net of a trust fund. She was creeping towards middle age and, after Rupert Mowbray's retirement, her career had plateaued.

Other single women of her age, at Vauxhall Bridge Cross, schemed their way into the lives, and the hotel bedrooms, of senior executive-grade officers and were available when the divorces came through. The senior men searched for women who understood the constraints of security. She'd heard it said often enough that the requirements of secrecy destroyed every marriage fashioned in heaven, but outside the confines of Vauxhall Bridge Cross . . . She had kept away from all invitations to a quick restaurant meal and a hotel fling. She had the memory of Viktor, and an amber stone at her neck . . . She had nothing. She felt the love drain away from her, lost on a sandspit in Eastern Europe.

She thought them – Wickso and Lofty, who ran with Viktor, Ham and Billy – the best men she had known. She sat at the table in the holiday-house kitchen, the console in front of her, and dreaded hearing the bleeping that would alert her to the next transmission and the red winking light. The worst man she thought she had known was Gabriel Locke. Her fist clenched, she hit the table.

Far behind Locke, starting out from the border fence, was the cordon that had spilled off the lorries. He thought of home, his childhood. His mother, the women from the neighbouring farms and their children used to make a line high up on the bracken slopes above the grazing fields. They would beat through the bracken and over rock outcrops to drive the foxes down towards the hedgerows where the men made a second cordon, where his father was. The child, Locke, had hated it. The foxes were flushed out and driven down to the guns. The vixens, it was said, were worse than the dog foxes because they would take the lambs born in spring to feed their cubs. If it had been merely the culling of vermin Locke might have accepted it, might have acknowledged the necessity of it. It was the screaming of pleasure, the shouting of enjoyment, as the guns thundered, as the foxes keeled over that he had loathed. He had refused to be a part of it and on those Saturday mornings when the beaters and the guns had formed up, he had gone into the outbuildings or the barns and hidden. Their excitement at the chase and the thrill of it was something he despised in his parents and the kids off the neighbouring farms. He had seen, of course, what the foxes did to lambs and he had known that the alternative was the laying down of poison, but deep in him, carried into his manhood, was an elemental fear of a cordon driving a prey towards the guns. The line was behind him and ahead were the flares, which he saw through the pines, and the occasional cracked rumble of a heavy weapon.

The forest was deep, close-set, around him. He blundered on towards the flares' light and the machine-gun.

Now he was among the old trenches and the bunkers. He had no care for the old craters he stumbled into, or for the rough concrete angles of the sunken bunkers that scraped the skin off his shins. Low branches whipped his face and where there were thickets of thorn they tore at his jacket and ripped at his trousers. He thought of the men who had been here, down in their holes, in their trenches, in the bunkers, and two lines pressing them into an ever-diminishing sector. No escape. Had the men who had been there wanted to escape? Had they believed what they did, fighting from trench to trench, bunker to bunker, was worthwhile? Had they dreamed, in their last hours, that in half a century their names would still be spoken? When the flares ahead were highest, as they reached their zenith, slivers of light rained down between the pines. He had seen an anti-tank weapon half buried in the needles, and rifles, and a little pile of mortar shells still identifiable but richly coated in the forest lichen. He found two skeletons, entwined as if they copulated in death, arms hugging each other's white ribcages, and he thought of the comradeship of death. Gabriel Locke believed he walked, ran, stumbled in a Valhalla of heroes.

His shoe kicked the skull. It rolled away from him. Still strapped into its helmet, it bounced against a tree-trunk and he felt the shock from his toes to his ankle and his knee. Was the name of the man who had lived in the skull still spoken by an old, infirm woman? He fell.

He gasped for breath and steadied himself against a mess of tangled roots. The roots of the gale-destroyed pine towered over him, and the last flare fired threw a trellis of fine shadows on to his face. To gain better support he moved closer to the wall of roots and earth at the base of the toppled tree – and he fell. Branches collapsed under him. His arms thrashed . . . He had closed his eyes, in reflex, to protect them as he had gone down into the hole. Blinking, he groped his hands out so that he could push himself up. Softness under his fingers. The light showed him the bergen pack and the four envelopes laid on it. He picked them up, and slipped them into the inside pocket of his jacket.

He crawled out of the hole. He knew he was close to them. The trees now thinned and the light was brighter. He stretched his stride and ran faster towards the bursting flares.

Igor Vasiliev had seen one body, but only a snatched glimpse of it in the vehicle's headlights. They had pitched and lurched past it as the petty officer steered between the thickest of the scrub and the highest of the dunes.

The petty officer braked the vehicle two metres short of the second body.

The ground beside the body was a small knoll. It was the natural place for him to settle the tripod. He was out of the vehicle and Mikhail and Dmitri heaved the weight of the heavy machine-gun over the side of the open back of the vehicle and he caught it, dropped it down and pressed hard on the tripod legs to settle them. The colonel was beside him with the belts, and then the farm-boys were lifting out the mortar, and . . . Vasiliev looked at the body. Because he had never before fired in combat, he had never seen the crippling damage caused by a 12.7mm calibre bullet. He saw the throat and the chin and the lower jaw . . . nothing more. He dropped down behind the machine-gun. The upper jaw, the nose, cheeks, eyes and upper skull were gone.

He stared, saucer eyes, at what was not there. As the vomit rose in his throat, he heard the snap of the colonel's order.

The vehicle's headlights were killed, the body became another shape in the darkness.

The arm was around his shoulder. The voice soothed, 'You are the best, Igor . . .'

The vomit, foul-tasting, slid at his teeth and dribbled at his lips. He coughed it on to the ground. With his sleeve, he smeared it from his mouth.

'There are admirals and generals, commanders and brigadiers, captains and colonels. They are the great men, and they are helpless now. Because you are the best, and have the skill, you alone are important. You . . .'

Vasiliev said, 'The barrel is warm now. I did well to get the first hit when it was cold. With a cold barrel, the bullet can fall short. The barrel shoots better when it is warm.'

Locke saw them. He was in the last line of the trees. In front of him were a carnival's lights. It was like when the fair came at the Whit holiday to Haverfordwest where he had been taken as a child; like the fireworks over the Thames on Millennium Night when he had been alone on the Embankment with the crowds because everyone else he knew had already sealed their arrangements. The flares burned above them and the tracer rounds came past them and captivated him, as had the lasers over the river. The flares lit the ground and the tracers showered red sparks on impact.

They were, he estimated, a little more than a half-mile from him, perhaps a thousand yards. Three flares were up and they were Locke's markers. The flares tagged them. To find them he had only to look where the light fell brightest.

Darting figures, tiny at that distance, they came towards him. When they crossed the fiercest of the light's pools, he could see the white shirt – see it well. Harder to make out were the black-draped figures. Because he was exhausted, and getting breath into his lungs was an increasing struggle, it was difficult for Locke to count and to concentrate on what he saw. He had a long view of the white shirt and the spurts of progress it made, but he could never be certain of more than two of the dark shapes that scurried close to it. The tracer came in flat lines beside them or over them. Only two . . . He stood against the cover of the trees . . . They seemed to him to run twenty or thirty paces, then he would lose them, then they came on again: the white shirt and the two, where there should have been four.

He had no sense of danger, no feeling of threat. It was where he had wanted to be, had chosen to be. He had heard the crack of the last flare's detonation and the rumbled thud of the weapon firing . . . Far behind were the sounds of the cordon's beaters. But fear was gone from him. He pushed away from the last line of the trees. There was no going back, never had been that chance.

Locke ran.

Another cascade of flares was fired and more tracer came in scarlet lines. Together they guided him.

He no longer stumbled, was light-footed, didn't fall. He was a free spirit. The trenches were behind him, and the bunkers, and the old, abandoned weapons, and the skeletons and the skull. Beyond the point he aimed for he saw the pinpricks of headlights, and they wove a meandering way towards him. He did not feel the scrub tearing at his legs, cutting into his trousers, nor the grit stones wedged between his socks and the inner soles of his shoes. The darkness clawed at him.

He heard them.

Not voices, but the wheezing gasps of breath. For a moment they were outlined against the skies, then had gone, then were back. The gasps were closer.

Locke called out, his voice thin in the night's air, 'This way, I'm here, it's Locke.'

An answering coughing grunt from the darkness. 'Locke? Fucking hell—'

'It's me, Locke.'

'You got back-up?'

'Just me.'

They were on him, came from among the scrub bushes and a black shape bounced into him, flattened him. A hand caught him and dragged him up. The white shirt veered past him. The hand freed him and the breath had been knocked from him. They'd gone on. For the first few of his strides after them, Locke thought he would not catch them. What had he expected? A bouquet of roses, a cup of tea from a Thermos, his hand shaken, his back slapped and thanks spoken? He tried to stretch his stride, legs heavy now, lungs emptied, pain in each muscle. The white shirt was a dozen paces ahead of him and the black shapes were alongside it, only two.

He called again, after them: 'Where are the others?'

From the panting to the right, 'Having a crap . . . Where the fuck do you think they are?'

'Where are they?'

From the left, 'Down . . . they're down.'

For a moment, Locke did not understand. 'Dead? Is "down" dead?'

Through the whistle of the breath, 'Ham dead, no fucking head. Billy down, hit . . . Maybe dead, may not be.'

'You left him?'

'Prat – this isn't the fucking Queensberry stuff. Why are you here?'

The line of trees was set against the sky. The wall of darkness the trees made beckoned them, seemed to scream for them. He had closed the gap. If he had reached out, thrown himself forward, his fist might have caught a grip of a wetsuit or the white shirt's collar. As they went past the high earth mound where the furthest of the targets were displayed, a flare burst over them. The trees reached for them. He saw Lofty and Wickso grab the shoulders of the white shirt and thrust it down. Then they were crawling on their stomachs. Because he ran and they crawled, he beat them to the trees, then dived and the wet of the ground was in his nose and the needles were in his mouth. He looked behind him. He could see each piece of the pines' bark, each cone on the lower branches, each needle on the fronds. For a moment, at half his height, Wickso knelt and raised his right arm as far as he could. The light cascaded on him and he gave them the finger. The tracer round speared at them, the bullets hammered into the trunks, and needles, branches and cones scattered over them.

'I came to help.'

'Lofty, I ask myself why would anyone come here to help?'

'Wickso, he's either got God, bad – or too much sun, worse. Give him Ham's—'

The weapon was forced into his hand. They were gone on their stomachs. More bullets hit the trees above them, or whined away off stones, and the tracers showered sparks. As he slithered after them on his knees and elbows, Locke held tight to the weapon's stock. At Fort Monkton, on the indoor range there, he had fired a Walther P5 on the indoor range, fired it for half an hour at a time on two afternoons. The instructor had said he was 'bloody useless' the first time. He had treated it as a laugh, a side-show, two afternoons off from the real business of electronics available to new officers. Shooting had seemed an unimportant distraction, as useful as instruction in covert movement through woodland as taught in the New Forest . . . As a child he had never fired his father's over-and-under shotgun . . . All his marks on electronic communications, theatre analysis, report-writing had been marked with the red stars of distinction. They were all up now and charging.

'What is it, the weapon?'

Lofty's grunt: 'Skorpion, Czech – 7.65 calibre, blow-back, selective fire . . .'

'I don't know how to use it.'

Wickso's hiss. 'Then fucking well learn.'

He winced. The difference now: he could see the trees. He could hear the sea on the beach, and he could see the tree-trunks without the aid of the flares' light.

'Take it down.' Having given the order, Piatkin stepped aside.

The pain throbbed in his head, but he was sober at least. The Military Police corporal, a huge bull of a man on whose bared right arm a tattooed girl danced, readied himself in front of the door, sucked in a gulp of breath, then swung back the sledge-hammer.

The door panel disintegrated at the third blow.

The corporal reached through the splintered panel and turned the key. He threw open what remained of the door, then moved away. Piatkin, alone, would enter. Behind him, and behind the corporal, were the men who staffed the fleet commander's outer office – all except the chief of staff, Captain, second rank, Archenko.

The bastard. Piatkin swore.

The desk was sideways on to the door. The top drawer of the near desk leg was open, pulled back, and the key was still in it. The pistol was on the floor. The chest and arms and what remained of the head

384

were on the desk. The head's fall had toppled the inkwell: part of the blood flow, merged with ink, was a delicate purple rivulet that was staunched against an opened carton of Camel cigarettes. The top of the head and much of the blood was on the ceiling, around the lamp fitting.

The deputy fleet commander was in Moscow. The head of operations was in Severomorsk.

Piatkin felt hatred for this man who had been Archenko's protector. He saw again the cold faces of the men who would sit in judgement on him. He ordered that the room be sealed, that the body of Admiral Alexei Falkovsky be left. If *he* failed they would flay the skin off his back.

He stamped towards the operations room in the bombproof bunker under the headquarters building.

Vladdy Piatkin, the *zampolit*, did not know how he could distance himself from the catastrophe engulfing him.

'Tell me, Mr Mowbray, because I think it is fair now to ask, why exactly did you bring us here?'

Mowbray bit at his lip. 'How far are we off the shore?'

The mate said that they were five nautical miles from the beach. For an hour, in almost total taut silence, from the bridge, they had watched the flares and the racing lines of tracer in front of them. The master had now called for full power. The *Princess Rose* surged towards land, not high and proud but low with the weight of her cargo. Dawn dribbled above the tree line, which he watched.

'Why, Mr Mowbray?'

He stood at his full height. 'I had a vision of what was necessary. A secure floating platform for a fall-back plan . . . We could launch from it, slip ashore, pick up our man, return under cover of darkness to the platform, then move beyond their territorial waters.' His voice tailed off. 'That was my vision of a fall-back plan.'

'We are late, too late.'

Grandly, as if he addressed his students, Mowbray retorted, 'I never acknowledge failure. It is unacceptable, failure is.'

The mate, behind him, spoke with a gentle sadness. 'If we like it or do not, failure is with us, Mr Mowbray. It has happened.'

He turned, spat, '*Unacceptable*. Failure never has, never will be, acceptable.'

The mate's binoculars were handed to him. The mate pointed towards the dim, distant lights of the naval base. His sight was not as clean as the mate's, and with the binoculars at his eyes, he fiddled with the focus. Then . . . First he saw the moving lights, then the spreading bow wave. Then he made out the dark gun-metal shape of the patrol-boat, the arrow of its bow wave aimed straight at the *Princess Rose*.

'Please. I beg of you, what is possible.'

The conscript, Igor Vasiliev, clung to the vehicle's open side as Bikov directed the petty officer away from the track. It pitched, rolled through the scrub and he held the machine-gun locked between his knees. He felt pride. His skill was recognized. They crossed the scrub and rolled up on to the summit of the dunes, and the beach, open, rolled out in front of them.

His name was called quietly. Ponsford had been dozing. He jerked up from his chair, and went to the glass door. The signal was printed out on flimsy, low-quality paper. He reflected – and it was a near-treasonable offence to speak it – that bloody accountants now ran the building. His mind roved: another victory for the paper-clip counters, cheap paper for signals into the annexe off the central communications unit. He glanced at his watch. Twenty-five minutes since the last signal had been given him, and two hours since . . . Where the hell was Giles? He scraped his memory: *Just going for a breath of air.* The technician passed him the second signal.

Nothing could be read from the faces. The technicians who serviced the War Room in the lower basement could mask their feelings whether the message they passed on was of triumph or disaster. For the second time, no frown or glint of concern marked the young man's face. And they never commented on the signals. Ponsford took it.

He shook.

The second signal – 'DELTA 2 DOWN' – seemed to kick him harder than the first had, wounded him more sharply. He had never seen the men, never met them, knew them only from the old service photographs on their files, and it had been Peter Giles's responsibility to check them out, and Mowbray's. He realized how long it was since Giles had gone for his 'breath of air'. The technician was back through the glass door and had sat again and swivelled his chair to face the equipment that brought in the signals. The technicians were all younger men and women, in love with their gear, and he wondered if they had hearts, read the signals they deciphered and cared. His mind was fogged. On the screen where before had been the blown-up map of the Mierzeja Wislana sandspit, which became the Baltijskaja Kosa on Russian territory, there was now a cartoon head and shoulders, crudely drawn as if at the kitchen table by Giles's grandson, then left unfinished as if the child had lost interest. The cartoon's head was an empty circle. No eyes, no ears, no mouth, no features. Why had Peter Giles drawn it while he'd slept? So long ago, a lifetime, Rupert bloody Mowbray's voice had boomed: *I thank you for your anecdote from Grozny. An interrogator is called back to Moscow . . . will now be at the base at Baltiysk . . .* A man of importance, of authority. An unknown face filled the screen. Giles had said: *It's the little people's turn to take charge.* Bertie Ponsford needed to share his burden.

Through the intercom link he told the technician that he was off to find Mr Giles. 'Won't be long.'

Ponsford took the lift up to the atrium floor. Some of the smokers used the terraces above the Thames at the back of the building for a 'breath of air', others preferred the fire escapes; a few went out through the electronic gates at the front, swiped their cards and huddled in the driveway. The atrium, silent except for a single polishing machine, was to Ponsford like any American chain hotel before it woke – a Holiday Inn or a Marriott – empty of soul, devoid of heart. They stayed in such hotels when they went 'across the pond' to make a pretence that a Special Relationship existed. Did it, hell. He gazed around among the tall pot plants. It was a barren place, and it was his life . . . Soulless, heartless, barren – the working home of Bertie Ponsford.

He went on to the terraces. Christ, were they actually screwing? In the shadows a couple crouched, then parted, and eyed him with hostility. He looked at all the rails, at the benches, and into other shadows. He wondered if he knew them, then wished them *bon voyage*. They'd have been from the recently expanded Afghan Desk, the cocky crowd, newly important, and the time difference for their theatre meant there was always a night shift fully rostered. Bloody hell, having a ride on the terraces . . . Methodically, he checked the fire escapes. He came back into the atrium and walked to the main entrance. He knew all the names of the older night staff who manned the principal doors of the building. If he spoke to them, used their given names, they beamed proudly – and Ponsford felt popular. He had almost forgotten why he had started out on this night mission through the dull-lit, hushed building. On the Service's business, two men were down.

'Morning, Mr Ponsford.'

They were all either from a Guards regiment or were paratroop veterans or had served with the Marines. They wore crisp uniforms with pride, with medal ribbons, and he could have shaved off the reflection from their shoes. He knew that one and all of them had hated the move from the shabbiness of Century House to the Yankee cleanliness of Vauxhall Bridge Cross.

'Hello, Clarence – you can help me. Have you seen Mr Giles?'

'Not since he left, sir.'

'No, no . . . he was just going for a breath of air.'

'I don't think so, sir. Had his coat on, and his hat, and had his briefcase. Said he was going home, sir.'

Ponsford held the wall for support. He seemed to hear a rasping, angry whine. He refused to – damn well would not – accept that the whine was from the polishing machine's motor. A chain-saw's engine pierced his mind, and the fog cleared. A chain-saw, with a big bloody blade, would cut a fire-break.

'You staying on, sir?'

'Yes, I am, Clarence,' he said, sucking the breath through his teeth.

'Big show, sir, is it? Don't see many of them, these days.' The old soldier laughed. 'But you're not going to tell me, sir, are you?'

'No, no, I'm not.'

He turned away from the main entrance, through which his long-standing friend, Peter Giles, had gone. They'd been on the same induction course and had gone up the ladder together. And now the beggar had run for safety – each man for himself – had scuttled behind the fire-break. He went back to the lift that would take him down, again, to the War Room. If those who had survived, and Ferret, were going to make it out they would be close to the beach by now. The ratchet of the chain-saw's teeth clamoured in his head.

19

Q. Where do the tourist agencies claim Russia's most breathtaking and unspoiled beaches are?

A. Kaliningrad.

She heard the message.

Alice listened.

Wickso's voice, laconic, and the brevity of old messages was gone, was clear in her headset.

'Delta 3 calling in to Havoc, whatever number Havoc has. We are on the treeline. Dunes, beach and sea are in front of us. It's lit by flares, all of it, it's bloody midday here. I am with Lofty and Ferret. We have to cross the dunes and the beach, get into the sea, raise the dinghy, then . . . They've got a heavy machine-gun on us.'

She thought Wickso teased her. He seemed so close, with the sharp edge in his voice, as if he were beside her. He was close, as a crow flew: she remembered the quiet courtesy with which Wickso had passed coffee from his flask, in the farm gateway near Braniewo, when Ham had told her of the failed pick-up in the zoo park – Lofty had had his arm round her for comfort. She heard him, crisp in her headset.

'Have to use the dinghy. Have to get over the dunes and the beach . . . They've a blocking force between us and the frontier – to be expected, actually. We're being squeezed. Well, that's the way it goes . . . oh, and Locke showed up.'

Her mouth gaped, and then her teeth seemed to chatter. He had said: 'I'm going out. I'll be gone some little time.' The voice droned on, as if careless to interception. She sat very still, her hands pressed the headphones tight against her ears.

'He sort of pitched up, like it was just before closing time, like this is Last Chance Saloon. Why? Said he'd come to help . . . We're about to go for the beach. If we get out of the saloon – no, no, when we get out of the saloon, you owe me a drink, ma'am . . . Going now. Out.'

She clicked to 'Transmit'. She couldn't match the laconic mood in his words. She quavered, 'Received for onward transmission. Anything further, send direct to Havoc 2. Not to me. Change to necessary frequency. Communicate direct with Havoc 2. Out.' She was too shaken, too beaten, to offer her personal encouragement. It would have insulted them, she'd thought fast, to have wished them luck – and luck was already beyond the reach of Billy and Ham. She should not clutter their minds with emotion . . . Viktor would have been beside Wickso. It would have been unprofessional to ask for the microphone and the headset to be passed by Wickso to Viktor. What to say? 'How's the weather where you are? . . . I love you . . .' Nothing to say, and if she had heard his voice sharp in the earphones, she would probably have cried – and that would have been unprofessional.

She tipped the earphones off her head and snatched her coat off the chair.

She left the door to the kitchen open behind her and as she ran for the back fence she heard its hinges sing in the wind.

She caught her coat on the wire as she scrambled over it. She ran between the trees. When they were on the beach, when they had gone into the water, when the flares lit them and the machine-gun fired on them, there would be no more transmissions. She wanted to see it, the last-chance drink in the saloon. She must be there, must be a witness. It was owed them . . . The binoculars rattled in the pocket of her coat, bounced on something. She could not identify what they hit against, and did not care. She reached the path between the trees.

A car came behind her and its lights blazed on her. It swerved to pass her, and a man waved cheerfully at her, as if it were not exceptional for a young woman to be stampeding through a dump village, out beyond nowhere, at dawn. She passed the church. The car had stopped there. She saw that the man who had waved to her wore a priest's habit. Should she follow him inside, beg a candle and light a flame for them? She did not break her stride.

She ran towards the dunes and the beach, and in front of her a scrum of cars, casually abandoned, threw down guiding lights.

Alice North ran as if the devils chased her. She was responsible. She had gone to Rupert Mowbray with the transcribed minutes of the meeting. She had worked his vanity, she felt the guilt. She had to be there on the beach to see it finish.

The cool of the wind blustered on her as she came to the dunes' summit.

It was where she had shown Gabriel Locke a grave. At the front of the parked cars, where the dunes fell away to the beach and the shore, the engine of a saloon ran, the driver revved it and its lights speared down. She saw the crowd of men and women standing around a low fire. She stumbled in the loose sand of the dunes. The crowd stood in silence. She slowed and walked the last steps to join it, and she saw from the flames the sombre stare in their faces.

Near the fire, beyond the crowd's backs, the gulls pranced and scrapped for fish heads. She wondered if Gabriel Locke would soon be carrion. She didn't know why he had gone out into the night for 'some little time' and what he could do 'to help'. She saw Jerry the Pole, and the blackened mess of his hand, clenched like a claw, and she followed his eyes down the beach.

Where she looked, the beach had an eerie brightness.

The flares dispersed the dawn's first shadows and the night's rain mist melted under them. The dunes, the beach and the sea close to the sands were exposed and the light, garish in its intensity, left no cover and no hiding-place. From the edge of the tree line to the last fall of the dunes was, Wickso estimated, seventy-five metres. The width of the beach from the dunes to the shore where the sea rolled in little ripples then fell back was a further 150 metres. From the surf to the sunken dinghy was an additional 100 metres. Running or swimming, there was no protection. Far out to sea, far beyond the light pools, was the hulk of the ship, and he saw from its bow wave that it came towards them, grey and remote.

'Who goes first, Wickso, you or me?'

'Not him,' Wickso grinned and looked down at Ferret. 'And can't be Locke . . .'

Locke murmured something that Wickso barely heard, about 'watching the backs'. He held the Skorpion away from him, as if it might bite.

'. . . between you and me, Lofty.'

'I'd like to.'

'You go first, then, Lofty.' He unfastened the bleeper from his webbing. It made a shrill repetitive howl, but long blasts. He hooked it on to Lofty's webbing, where it could be seen and heard easily. When Lofty was closer to the dinghy the bleeps would come shorter; when he was over it they would be shortest. 'We'll follow when you get into the water. Two targets. No call to make life easy for them. When we get to you, you'll be under and breaking the bottles. If there was a second way, I'd take it. It's what we've got.'

He heard Locke mutter again about 'covering fire'. 'Look, I didn't ask you to trip along, don't know why you did – just fucking shut up.'

Lofty heaved the launcher into Wickso's lap, then took all the grenades he had from his pouches – there were six left, not that it mattered, and a seventh up the tube. All that had been fired had been wasted. Lofty was off his stomach and seemed to crouch, like a sprinter in the blocks.

'If I don't—'

'Don't even go there, Lofty. That's crap.'

'Yes, yes.'

'You can do it, Lofty, and we're right behind you.'

He saw the tremble of Ferret's body, and his arms seemed to be in spasm; his hands were clasped together as if to break the shaking. It was a quick gesture, meant as kindness: Wickso took Ferret's neck in his hand and squeezed hard. Ferret choked . . . Give him something else to think about, Wickso reckoned. And he needed it, they all did . . . It would take Lofty, in the wetsuit, a clear fifteen seconds to reach the beach, then twenty-five to reach the water-line, then . . . He was left with the waifs and strays. He squeezed Ferret's neck again, hurt him some more. Not kindness now, but to ready him.

He barked at Locke, 'You just follow me, stay on my shoulder. I don't hang about for you.'

He felt the fear squeeze his guts worse than he had squeezed Ferret's neck. He had seen Billy and Ham. He knew the hitting power of the machine-gun, and he knew the skill of the man who fired it. The fear cramped his stomach.

Lofty was rocking – waiting for the gun. There was a dullness, a darkening. Two flares down, and another drifting lower to the beach. A gloom spread across the dunes, the sands and the sea.

Wickso snarled, 'For fuck's sake, Lofty, get on with it – or do you want a bloody cup of tea first?'

Lofty was up and the shadows spread on him. He took a first hesitant step away from the trees. He would have heard the whip in Wickso's voice, and perhaps the fear was infectious. The darkness seemed to creep over the open dunes and down on to the beach. He was clear of the trees. To Wickso it was like the crack of the pistol . . . the flare burst above him, hung, and the light blistered away the shadows. Lofty shambled away from them.

Wickso understood the trick played on them. The flares had been allowed to die. The marksman or the man who directed the marksman wanted them flushed from the trees. The bait was to let the flares fall, to re-create the natural murk, to get them out and unprotected. The brightness, the return of daylight, fell on Lofty. Wickso watched, willed him on. Maybe Lofty had covered a quarter of the ground, gone a quarter of the way across the dunes. Trying to sprint, but not able to because the sand under his feet was soft, giving. He had asked too much of Lofty but, then, too much had been asked of all of them. Lofty was the simple one, the one who was led, the one who raked leaves from graves, Lofty . . .

He said, emptiness in his voice, 'When we start there is no stopping. You don't stop for me, I don't stop for you. We follow Lofty.'

Lofty had crossed half of the dunes, then there was the open beach where kids in that sunshine might have played. The big man ran and his boots slithered, slid in the giving sand. Wickso pulled Ferret up, and kept a tight hold on his collar. He tensed. Wickso stabbed a backward glance at Locke. He saw a vacant stare. He cleared spit from his dried-out mouth, coughed it. Lofty was going over the edge of the dunes.

*   *   *

394

'Take him.'

He heard Bikov's voice.

The sight was set for 1200 metres. He had tracked the target for ten seconds, from the moment the target had emerged from the tree-line. He had held the target, running but not well, from the flare's burst. The fitness instructors made the conscripts sprint on the loose sand of the dunes by the ruined village of Rybacij. He knew how hard it was to go fast on the dunes. Magnified for him, the target's knees pumped but could not gain good grip.

His finger was on the trigger's bar. He paused his breath, squeezed the bar, and the thudding weight pressed into his shoulder. The noise exploded around him.

As he watched the tracer round go, the target went down. The target, in the scope sight, broke its stride, stopped, stood upright, then fell. The target was not pitched sideways, or backwards or forwards; it subsided. The target collapsed.

His finger eased from the trigger bar.

Vasiliev said, 'I tell you, Colonel Bikov, there is not another man, not a conscript or an instructor NCO or an officer, who could have hit a moving target at 1200 metres – only me. You have seen me shoot . . . what am I, Colonel Bikov?'

'You are the best, Igor.'

'The barrel was warm. I did not need the help of the tracer because my first shot was perfect. You will not see better shooting, Colonel.'

'When the last of them makes the run, and Archenko – and they must – I will see better shooting. You are supreme.'

'Did you see, Colonel, that I made what we call a "beaten zone"? It has the shape of a cigar, one that an officer would smoke. Inside the beaten zone of a heavy machine-gun, no target can survive. The "beaten zone" is the margin of error, caused by the shift of the tripod's feet, thirty metres long, two metres wide. When I shoot, anything in the "beaten zone" is dead.'

'I salute you, Igor.'

He heard only the praise heaped on him. He did not take his eye from the sight as he nudged the cross-hairs away from the body, black under the bright light, and traversed them back towards the trees, where the target had come from. Had he taken his eye from the sight, twisted his head, let his gaze wander down the line of bullets waiting for feeding into the breech, then he would have seen the eyes of the colonel, and he would have known that they did not match the honey of the words . . . and had he looked beyond the eyes, where the mortar was set up, he would have seen the anger that misted the faces of the farm-boys and the contempt of the petty officer. He did not. Vasiliev – proud, the exhilaration pounding, the best – did not know he was despised, detested.

As the flare fell, two more were fired. He was his own man. He had no more need of the friendship of Captain, second rank, Viktor Archenko. His excellence was proven. He watched the trees and waited for the last of them to break, and for the glimpse of the white shirt in the cross-hairs.

The arm came up.

They saw the black sleeve and the hand that was stained with dirt and blood, and it was clenched as if to withstand pain. It was rigid. Wickso couldn't help himself . . . The arm was raised above a gently rippling lake of grass stems, as if it had been thrust up from deep water and now broke the surface. Wickso wanted to weep.

The arm fell back, as if the water closed over it.

'Give it a minute,' Wickso said.

The treeline was a refuge. While they stayed there, harboured by the pines, they were safe. His mind rambled . . . He kept his hand on Ferret's shoulder and felt the pounding of the blood in the veins that wound around the upper spine. Locke was behind him, and ignored. He could see all of the dunes and most of the beach and he could see, clear, the water, could make out each small, surging wave. Out beyond the waves and the white caps was the ship. She seemed to come so slowly, and far to the east of her, but coming faster, was a bow wave – bright white in the gloom. If he could see the bow wave, Wickso knew it, they were late, the schedule was gone. The dawn came. He sent a signal.

No frills, no favours – no call-signs, no sign-offs, no chatter. Delta 3 was down, they were going for the dinghy.

The minute was exhausted, and another.

Wickso said, 'Just one more minute, get our breath back, then we'll hack it.'

He was thankful he couldn't see Lofty. The waving grass stems, thin and green-yellow, hid Lofty. And more thankful that he couldn't hear Lofty . . . Wickso knew about death in the field. Lofty, he hoped, was unconscious. If he was still alive, but critically wounded, his pulse rate would be slipping to twenty or thirty, down from sixty to eighty, slipping towards the coma, on the route between life and death, and the coma would stifle what was left of the heartbeat. Lofty, Wickso hoped, was now clinically dead and within twenty minutes – after the creeping brain damage – would be biologically dead. Another minute had gone. He loved Lofty, could have wept for the big, quiet man who was now down on the dunes, hidden by the grass stems.

'We give it one more . . .'

Ferret turned his head, looked up at him.

'We give it one more minute, do you understand me?' Wickso spoke more slowly, to a child, and held up a single finger. 'One more minute.'

'I understand English. You do not have to speak carefully. I understand everything you say.'

'Sorry. I didn't know. Sorry, sir.'

'I am Viktor – do we have one more minute?'

Behind him, from the side of his vision, Wickso saw that Locke had discarded the Skorpion and his hand now lay on the grenade-launcher; he could make out the deep-ploughed shadow lines in Locke's forehead as if he studied it to find a truth.

Locke said, 'You have to go, you don't have one more minute.'

Wickso flared, '*We* go when I say we go. We go when *I* am ready to go. I run this bloody show. We go when I decide it is the right time.'

Locke said, 'You don't have another minute.'

Viktor said softly to Wickso, 'I understand that you are frightened. I am frightened. For three weeks I have been frightened, sometimes beyond control, sometimes within control, but frightened. It does not make you a lesser man . . . Too much is asked of you. You are the bravest of men . . . It is better that you acknowledge the fear.'

Locke said, 'Fuck the fear – just get moving.'

Wickso twisted his body. He hit Locke, caught him with a clenched-fist punch to the side of the chin and saw the head jerk back. When the head was back, he hit it again. His third punch split Locke's lip. He was over him and the blows came in a frenzy. Wickso had seen Billy without his leg and Ham without the upper part of his head, and he had seen Lofty's arm raised in the pain spasm. Locke did not fight him and did not cover his face, just stared back, and with his fingers Wickso would have gouged the eyes, but he was pulled off. Viktor held him, smothered him, held his arms tight so that he could not reach Locke's eyes. In front of him was the stretch of the open dunes and the beach that had no cover and the sea where the mist had lifted, and he saw himself magnified in the cross-hairs of a gun sight.

Wickso panted, 'We go when I say we go.'

'Victory has many fathers, but defeat is a lonely child.'

Maybe he had read it but he did not know in what volume. Perhaps he had been told it but Bertie Ponsford could not recall when or by whom.

The technician had brought the signal through the glass door dividing the annexe from the Central Communications Unit. Four, five times he read it, willing the words to disappear, change, be erased. 'DELTA 3 DOWN.' He could not alter it.

Bertie Ponsford felt the loneliness.

He turned and faced the screen. The outline of a head with no features stared down at him. He was not the best with matters technical. He had been on the courses where senior officers were drilled by hard-faced, patronizing young women, in the arts of electronics. He could manage the Chinagraph pencil that linked to the screen's image – pathetic, really, that he could only *manage*. He put crude hairs on the head's scalp, and ears. He did not attempt the eyes, because he did not know whether they were tight set or wide, or a mouth. He brought slight life to the opponent, the enemy, but he did not know the man – all he could be certain of was that one of Giles's *little people* had bested him.

He cleared his table.

Bertie Ponsford thought they played a game, an old man's game. But others had intruded, younger men, who did not know the rules.

Younger men had spoiled the pleasure of the game by barging into it. He gathered his papers and files together and placed them in his briefcase.

The technician had his back to him and was deep in a magazine. His going was not noticed.

He followed in the footsteps where the director general had led, where Giles had gone. He justified himself. To cut a fire-break was sensible.

The lift surged him up to the Russia Desk floor. If he hurried he would be clear of the building before the first of the day shift came on.

His hurried, heavy footfall clattered down the corridor past the numbered doors, past the notice-boards where holiday lettings were advertised and invitations were posted for players for Sunday-morning sports teams and where the in-house orchestra and Light Opera and Dramatic Society advertised, and the newest amendments to health and safety 'in the workplace' regulations were posted, and he swiped his card for entry to his office.

It was all so damnably normal.

To keep it *normal*, Bertie Ponsford would need a fire-break – a bloody wide one. From the start of the adventure his name had been loud in the minutes. He checked that all of his papers were off his desk and in the safe. Without a fire-break, he would be destroyed. He took down his coat from the stand. It had been a dream. He looked out of the window and saw the early commuters on the Embankment across the river, and the first speeding buses. Whether he survived or whether he was swept away he would never again speak with Rupert Mowbray . . . He remembered Mowbray's leaving party. All the older men drunk, and all the younger officers eyeing them with embarrassment, or amusement, and the talk had been of the glory days when the writ of the Service ran wide. The decanter and the crystal glasses had been presented, and then – in his cups – Mowbray, moist-eyed, had told them of the worst morning he had experienced in forty years with the Service: the shocked, hushed gloom in the little corner of the Broadway building, when the news had come through of the execution of Colonel Oleg Penkovsky. 'Handkerchiefs out, and bottles from cupboards, not a single silly little frightened giggle – like the mourning wake for an esteemed friend. A man of infinite courage lost because we didn't get off our bloody arses or lift a finger for him.' Nobody, then, had told Mowbray he was talking second-class rubbish. Then the talk had gone back to the glory days . . . Old men jerking off – and he, Bertie Ponsford, was one of them.

He closed the door after him.

Down the length of the corridor he scraped the head of his battery razor across his cheeks, chin and upper lip. By the time the lift dropped him in the atrium, he thought he had made himself passably decent. His last gesture, before the doors opened and exposed him, was to straighten his tie. Crisis? What crisis? Already the first of the day shift were busy swiping for admission. He slipped towards the main entrance.

The cool morning air caught him. The street-lights still burned but the dawn negated their power. The first cars were arriving, being flagged through the outer gates. The early cyclists in their gaudy Lycra kit were dismounting. The stream on foot pressured round him. He stood on the pavement, looked for a taxi.

'Morning, Mr Ponsford,' the voice trilled behind him. 'Off home, then?'

He turned. Clarence beamed at him.

'Yes, off home.'

Clarence winked. 'All done and dusted, is it, Mr Ponsford?'

'Where's my best bet for a taxi?'

'Taxis are always best across the bridge. Been a good night, has it? If it's not impertinent, Mr Ponsford, well done.'

'What do you mean?'

The second wink was heavier, and a grin. 'Just my little joke, Mr Ponsford. The likes of a gentleman such as yourself don't stay overnight unless it's for something worth the sweat – a big, *big* show, what the Service is about – like old times . . . No offence.'

He went on his way, far from a spit of sand in the eastern Baltic. He cleared his mind. He would be behind his fire-break when the final message came in, with the phone at home off the hook. He would be in bed, and secure. He would be safe from the fate of Ferret, and from Mowbray's team, and from young Locke, whom madness had caught – not his worry.

He walked briskly up the pavement and began to wave for a taxi. Others could take the strain, were welcome to it.

The problem lay at Piatkin's table.

Military and air-force officers now hustled for space in the operations room, and generals were reported on the road from Kaliningrad. The problem was his – the ship out in territorial waters. He was watched. By default, he had assumed responsibility, but now the weight of it hung on him. Ringing through his mind was the accusation: the failure of security could only have been caused by his incompetence or by his intention. He would rot in premature retirement, or in gaol. In the crowded operations room, the only free space was close to him ... the ship. He was told the ship's history, its engine failure in Gdansk and the repairs, its loading, then the repeat failure. He was told it had been boarded, checked, and found to be above suspicion. The ship, named to him as the *Princess Rose*, was now under power, moving towards the beach, and a patrol-boat closed on it. The commander of the patrol-boat *demanded* instructions. Many times Vladdy Piatkin checked the chart map. As a *zampolit* attached to the Baltic Fleet he had a rudimentary knowledge of naval affairs, but it was slight ... The ship flew the flag of convenience of Malta. Alarm bells, as shrill as the sirens that had tipped him out of the senior officers' mess, pealed in his head. If he panicked, ordered the patrol-boat to fire on the ship prematurely, he would be gutted by the inquiry board that would follow. Nobody, none of the uniformed, medal-ribboned officers, stepped forward to help him. He broadcast his order.

'Intercept, then escort away from the coastline. Do not open fire unless you face resistance and can confirm the ship is engaged actively in the land action. Get the fucking thing out of the area.'

The master said, 'I am now three nautical miles off shore ... They are too late ... We did what we could. It is not our fault, Mr Mowbray. We are a coastal cargo ship, not a boat for war. In four minutes, a maximum of five, we must turn. In four minutes, or five, the Nanuchka is with us. We have to turn and plead our ignorance, our stupidity, a further problem with the propeller drive, and we have to hope we are believed – or we will be boarded. We will stay as long as we can, Mr Mowbray, but I do not see them on the beach. What can I do?'

He felt aged, wearied . . . There wouldn't be a car at the airport. No bands, no alarms, no welcoming line of greeters. Felicity would meet him. He would go home and empty the dirty clothes out of his bag, and while the washing-machine thundered in the kitchen he would pour himself Scotch, and tell her if 'they' phoned she should tell 'them' that he had gone to the common to walk . . . not that they would phone. Without fuss, the process barely visible, he would be airbrushed from the memory of the Service. He would never again be called upon to lecture at the Fort; he would never receive the invitation to an old farts' reunion, he would be removed from the mailing list of the former officers' news sheet, his lifetime's work would be undone. A letter would come from the vice chancellor, signed by a secretary, three lines at most, relegating his chair in strategic studies to the bin. So unfair . . .

The dawn was settling on the tarpaulin covers of the holds filled with fertilizer sacks. The flares were still pitched high over the beach, but the clarity of their light was lessened by the slow sunrise behind the forests' trees. He could see the detail now of the approaching patrol-boat's bow wave . . . Maybe five minutes were left, perhaps six, and then it was doomed. Who could he blame? 'They' would blame him – who would *he* blame? Locke, of course. Locke would be the scapegoat of his personal bitterness.

'You should do what you can,' Mowbray said brusquely. 'Do what is honourable.'

He was relaxed. The colonel's hand soothed his shoulder. He had shown he was the best and he would show it again. Vasiliev lay behind the heavy machine-gun and waited for the last of them to break cover. In his mind, across the dunes and the sand and the sea, he created beaten zones within which the bullets would have killing accuracy.

Viktor said, 'It is too many minutes.'

Locke heard Wickso say, 'Nearly there, nearly.'

He asked, 'How do you use the launcher?'

He thought Viktor was now at the edge of control, as if he stood on a pit's edge and looked down and saw only the darkness of the abyss. Locke watched Viktor reach out to take both of Wickso's hands and pressure them together, to give the man strength. He thought Viktor had good hands, powerful, and they enveloped Wickso's and killed the trembling. To Locke, it was as though Viktor had woken from a sleep, and the morning light showed him reality.

Viktor said, 'We have two choices – we run and take the chance, or we surrender and take that chance. I cannot surrender.'

Scorn in Wickso's response. 'You can't do it, you wouldn't know how. Have to dive, have to break the compressed air bottles, have to get the engine going. You couldn't—'

Locke asked, 'What's the firing procedure for the launcher?' Quite a handsome man, he thought, and not flattered by the photograph in the file or by the picture that Alice had shown the team. Locke never, in the normal times of his life, looked at another man and was taken by his appearance: it would have denigrated him. Viktor was, to him, fine-looking. The jaw, mud-spattered, jutted at an angle of defiance. Alice loved the man . . . He had kissed Alice. Alice and Viktor would remember him.

'How do you fire the grenades from the launcher?'

Viktor said, 'I am going for the water. You stay if you want to, take the chance with them. For me, fast death or slow – I choose fast. We have no more time.'

'I hear you,' Wickso said.

'How many grenades do we have, and what is their range?'

In his inside pocket were the four letters. He should have given them up, he had not. The envelopes were nestled against his chest. Wickso gave no answer to Viktor. The light broadened in front of them and the flares had less power and Locke could see the silhouette of the *Princess Rose* and the white V-wave coming closer to it. He knew what he would do. He heard the murmur from Wickso about retrieving the bleeper from Lofty – God, had they only one of them? Pathetic . . . He saw Wickso lift himself up from his stomach, then the fist tightened on the snub machine pistol Wickso held, then the discarded Skorpion was given to Viktor. Wickso was on his feet, and

Viktor was beside him. The dunes stretched away from them, and the beach and the sea . . . He had been to Hereford, had been given the demonstration of close-quarters fire-power in the 'killing house': trussed up, gagged, blindfolded, they had played at hostages, as the stun grenades and gas and the live rounds had blasted, wafted and cracked around them – his memory was of the silence in the room, then the shattering noise and speed of the assault. In the afternoon they had been shown the use of explosive charges, then had been sent on their way. What he could recall was the strutted contempt of the Special Forces officers for them, because they were mere civilians. Words were few, the language of their bodies was explicit . . . He remembered the liaison man, at the meeting at Vauxhall Bridge Cross: *I don't think my people would be that keen on a trip in there, not to Kaliningrad*. He was there, the men who had stormed the 'killing house' were not. He felt no arrogance because conceit was long ago purged from him. He was there, had chosen to be, as they had chosen not to be.

'I lead,' Wickso said. 'Run zigzag, head down, run like the goddamn wind. In the water you dive, keep down, the dinghy's a hundred metres . . .'

He felt calm. 'How do you fire the bloody thing?'

Locke groped at the pouches on Wickso's webbing and snatched out the grenades. He filled his pockets with them. He stood. In the far distance he could hear the cordon moving forward from the frontier fence. They had used up too much time. The flares hung in a lighter sky. Too much time.

'Count to fifty, then go. Give me fifty.'

He started to run.

Locke heard Wickso's hiss, 'You get left, you know you get left behind.'

He didn't turn, didn't wave a last time.

Locke heard Wickso's shout, 'It's loaded. Just use the under-trigger. Fires a blank bullet into the grenade. Reload it down the barrel, tilt the barrel and let it slide in. Maximum range is four hundred metres, that's top. Burst radius is five metres, fuse delay is four seconds or contact. The ones marked phosphorus are best, better than explosive. The bolt action on the launcher puts the next blank in the breech. Go close, go in on top of them. Phosphorus will burn them.'

The shout faded.

He ran the zigzag, as they would, and he felt the cold of the morning on his face.

She saw them, two not three.

A chattering excitement broke around Alice. The crowd edged away from the fire: it gazed up the beach and over the fence that ran down to the waterline, over the military vehicles and the soldiers on the sand, past the more distant line of troops.

Two men ran on the dunes. Alice held the small binoculars hard against her eyes. She could see them clearly because the flares, in descending height, were over them, and because the low pulse of the sunlight caught the ground on which they ran. They were good binoculars – not Service issue, but a present from her father. Everything from her father was the best. With ten times magnification, and sunshine daylight to look into, it was easy for her to see them both. A few minutes earlier, a lifetime gone by since, she had seen – as had the crowd – a single figure, black-suited, break from the trees. In the circle of the lenses, the angry red tracer had surged to meet him. She had seen him go down. No movement for a moment, then a hand raised . . . and dropped. After that there had been no more tracer dots, but she fancied she heard, on the wind, muffled cheers from the cordon that merged with the sea's beat.

They were so small, so far from her, but she could make out through the lenses the leading man, black, and the figure a pace, or three, behind. She saw the white shirt and the pinhead of blond hair . . . She could not see Locke. The lenses held the two of them: around them was the expanse of the dunes and ahead the open beach and the sea. There was no cover. She had thought it was the big boy, Lofty, who had gone down . . . She thought it was Wickso and Viktor who came in haphazard angled lines across the dunes, towards where he'd fallen.

It seemed to Alice as if the crowd watched it like it was vaudeville, a show. She had been to Rome, last year at the convent school, with her parents. The second day they had 'done' the Colosseum. Her father had been interested in the logistics of building the place, her mother had seen only the multitude of stray cats living there, and the teenage Alice had been quietened by the thought of a great multitude revelling in the excitement of watching death. When the one she thought was Lofty had gone down, the crowd had indulged itself with a noisy sigh – it was only a show, an acrobat's fall from a high wire. If she continued to watch with her binoculars she would see the tracer come, and the white shirt might drop and the pinhead of fair hair might fall . . . Where was Locke?

She took the binoculars from her eyes. She compressed them, dropped them into her pocket.

She heard the rattle as she loosed them . . . She could not watch . . . Her hand, in her pocket, felt the shape the binoculars had fallen against . . . She could not watch it. She took the mobile phone from her pocket. Not hers.

The excitement grew around her. She turned away. Whose phone? Where had the phone come from? She had her back to the flares, but the machine-gun had not fired – the fucking machine-gun would wait till they were on the beach. She switched it on. It warbled, vibrated, and the screen lit. A text envelope was displayed. She clicked . . . The text would show her whose phone had been placed in her pocket. She knew . . . She had heard the message on the radio: *Oh, and Locke showed up*. She read the text.

GABRIEL, PROBLEM OUR END. POLISH POLICE ANXIOUS U HELP THEIR ENQUIRIES INTO DEATH OF RUSSIAN CONSUL GUY IN GDANSK. CAN U HELP QUERY. LIBBY.

She understood. She was only a General Service officer, not the full shilling, but she knew why he had slept in the railway station at Gdansk, why he had kissed her, why he had walked out into the night, why he had *showed up*, why he did not run on the dunes.

Alice saw the crowd's faces. Titillated enjoyment, macabre pleasure, gallows-watching, the mob in the Colosseum. She took Jerry the Pole as her focal point. He was her target, and he alone would understand her language.

'You bastards. You poor, pathetic bastards. Get your kicks cheap, don't you? It's not fucking Saturday-night television – it's men's lives. Decent of them – right? – to make some bloody entertainment for you. You are sad. In the whole damn lot of you, there's not as much guts as in their little fingers. You are cowards ... cowards ... c owards. Enjoy the bloody show while it lasts – pity you won't ever see a show like this again. Bad bloody luck. Do something—'

The voice was accented English, soft-spoken. 'But what, my child? What is *something*? What do you want them to do?'

She turned. He had driven the car that had passed her, and he had waved to her. The wind pressed the priest's habit against his legs and tugged at the white of his hair.

'Something.'

'If there is something that can be done, it will be. Enough of profanity, my child – we are all in God's hand. They are simple people, but they are not cowards.'

'Just do something,' Alice said.

20

Q. Where do the lost graves lie?
A. Kaliningrad.

'When they are half-way, the middle of the beach,' Bikov murmured.

'I can't see the middle, I only have the sight—'

'The middle of the beach.'

'I only have the vision from the sight 'scope – where is the middle?' Vasiliev snapped. 'You tell me, you have to call it.'

'I'll call it.'

'It's all you fucking have to do, call it. Spot. Is that too much? Just tell me when to shoot . . . Which target?'

'Not yet, a moment.'

Now Vasiliev – the conscript from Volgograd – thought the colonel was shit. He, Vasiliev, had the machine-gun. He had the target in the cross-hairs. He had the power. All that was asked of the colonel of Counter-Intelligence (Military) was to call the shot and spot, and he hesitated. Did he not understand the breathing pattern that was necessary? The caller, the spotter, the feeder of ammunition was a servant. He could have taken them on the dunes, two scrambling figures with the sand slipping loosely away under their feet. He could have fired when they slithered down the last slope from the dunes to the beach, each breaking their fall with their hands. But each time he could have taken them, fired, the murmur in his ear had been that he should wait.

They ran. For moments he had the two of them in the 'scope. Then it was none of them, then one. He thought they went slower, as if the impetus of the charge from the trees was slackened. He thought it was more from the sun than from the flares but pricks of light bounced from the beach and played in his eyes. He blinked. By closing, opening, squeezing shut, opening his eyes he lost the focus of the aim and the cross-hairs showed him only the beach. He swore, edged the 'scope sight the fraction required. A cormorant fluttered in it. There was a colony of cormorants . . . Distraction, and he swore again. He had them. The black figure had stumbled, had slid to its knee, the white shirt checked, reached down and dragged the figure up. The moment was perfect.

'Do I fucking shoot?'

'A moment.'

'What do you wait for?'

'The middle.'

He should have been allowed to shoot in his own time. The machine-gunner was the principal. In infantry tactics, as taught him, the machine-gunner was free to fire as the best moment was presented. He knew his breathing was bad. He gulped air. His right hand clamped down on the guard above the iron frame of the butt, it was tight against his shoulder, but his left hand reached forward. He did not have to look to click the sight a notch further, to take in another hundred metres. They were no longer together in the sight. He wavered between them. Either the black figure or the white shirt. They were both targets, no more and no less. He had no emotion for the figure he did not know, or for the man who had been his friend. He made the click and his finger drifted back to the trigger guard.

'Which? Fuck you, which one?'

The petty officer's voice rang in his ear. 'Don't speak like that to a senior.'

'Fucking make your mind up.'

The petty officer's voice dropped. 'He's a good man, Colonel. Archenko is popular, well liked. I don't mean . . .'

The same murmur from Bikov. 'I respected him.'

'I don't mean to diminish his guilt. He has the best reputation of any officer – efficient, fair, we trusted him.'

'And strong, the best of officers.'

Vasiliev screamed, 'Which?'

The murmur had gone cold, like ice crusted it. 'In your own time. One or both.'

409

Vasiliev snatched his eye up from the 'scope sight. He gazed out, over the barrel. He saw the dunes and the width of the beach, and the two tiny figures of men, black and white, in the middle of the gilded beach. Without the magnification they seemed to move at snail's pace. His eye darted back to the sight. He saw empty sand. He twisted the sight to the right – saw only the beach space. To the left – a blur, then sand and gulls. He made the adjustment. Vasiliev snatched in the air, filled his lungs. He held them. Beyond them, soft focus, was the shimmer of the sea. His finger went from the guard to the trigger bar. Mouth open, he allowed the breath to seep from his lips. He had them, he began to squeeze. He paused on his breath, gentle.

He heard the whistle of its approach.

The grenade exploded.

Vasiliev flinched.

The shrapnel sang.

By flinching, turning away his head, twisting his exposed shoulders, he jarred his aim. He saw sand, dirt, debris, hanging in a little cloud. It was not near him. His eye was back to the sight. He heard the petty officer spit, contempt. Where he looked for them there was only the cloud's mist. He fired. He could not see the beaten zone. The tracers beaded from the barrel, then were lost in the cloud. The colonel fed the belt. The butt pressured his shoulder and the thunder of the weapon was buried in his ears. He kept his finger on the trigger – not double tap, not releasing. The cloud cleared. He still had his finger on the trigger bar, depressing it, all his strength on it, when the belt was exhausted, when the brass cases no longer flew to the side.

'Arsehole,' the petty officer snarled. 'So far away it would not even have cut your pretty-boy face. You missed.'

'A belt. Give me a belt.'

The petty officer grabbed the ammunition belt that hung from Bikov's neck. Vasiliev had the breech plate up. He snapped the first round of the belt into the breech, rearmed the machine-gun. They were near to the water's edge. His breathing was fast, uncontrolled. He raked the sight on to them. He saw his friend's head, and the white shirt. They were running, each holding the other's hand, the

410

black arm and the white arm, each pulling the other along. He gasped to fill his lungs.

The petty officer scorned him: 'You said you were the best, and you fucking missed.'

Not a squeeze, a jerk. He had them both. His finger wrenched on the trigger bar. Both were in the cross-hairs, would be in the beaten zone . . . Silence. Not the hammer blow but only the metal scrape of the working mechanism going forward. A jam. The breath sighed out of him. For a moment his mind blanked. It was empty. He heard the petty officer's shout, and the murmur of Bikov, but not their words. He scraped his mind for the answer. There was no instructor to help him. Not the calm of the firing range. He recocked. He squeezed the trigger . . . Silence. He lifted the breech plate and pulled the belt clear, but the first round was still wedged in the chamber. Fingers in. No feeling in them and clumsy movements as he prised the round out – an armour-piercing round with the black-painted tip and the red ring on the cartridge rim, and if it had detonated as he'd reached his fingers into the breech it would have taken off his face. He freed it from the belt, dropped it. He laid the second round of the belt in the breech, whipped the plate down, and armed the weapon again.

'You arrogant shite, you're fucking useless!' The petty officer crouched close to him.

They were going down to the water. He had to wait. 'Regain control of breathing,' the instructors said. His heart pounded. He made another click on the 'scope sight. He breathed hard, twice.

'Where did it come from?'

'Just shoot – pretty boy.'

'I don't know,' the murmur answered him. The hand gently moved on his shoulder. 'In your own time . . . I don't know.'

He stared into the sight. He had the breathing. Finger to the trigger bar. They were at the water. He thought it was the sun, not the flares. Where the sea came to the shore, where the waves ran to their limit, the light was silver and reflected back. The brilliance burned his eye. The light danced on the crests and he saw the splash as they hit the waterline. He could not look into the sight, but he fired.

*   *   *

He thought they were in the water.

Locke had blasted off the grenade, but it had fallen far short of the source of the tracer.

He did not understand why the firing that had brought Lofty down had been short bursts, but the firing aimed at them on the beach had been a never-ending cacophony of rounds . . . and he had not understood why there had then been the delay. They had reached the water. He crawled forward. The scrub tore at his coat and his trousers, and scarred the hands that held the launcher. The blast of the machine-gun had started again . . . He must get forward.

They still held each other's hands.

The spray leaped around them. Wickso held his hand until the shelving of the beach had the water at their knees, and they could no longer run. Out beyond them, the sun playing on the hull's rust, was the *Princess Rose*, and closing with it was the bow wave. The bursts were wild – once they had been so accurate. Wickso did not know why they now spattered the sea in a great arc around them.

Wickso shouted, 'There's no other way.'

'Never was.'

'We go for it.'

'We are brothers.'

'Stay with me.'

The bleep rang in Wickso's ear. He loosed Viktor's hand. Together they dived at the wave breaking ahead of them. The tracers seemed to ignite the water. It was twelve years since he had swum hard . . . with Billy, Ham and Lofty, in rough winter seas, off a beach of grey pebble, into Murlough Bay off the Antrim coast on an away-day from the Ballykinler camp. Flippers, then. The flippers were discarded, were back in the tree line. He could not have run in them across the dunes, could not have stopped at the shore to ease them over his boots. He swam crawl and only his arms and the tip of his head made a target. He did not look back.

There was more firing, but with the sea-water in his ears he no longer heard the impact of rounds into the water or the shockwave as they went overhead. But the bleeper, prised off Lofty's webbing, was close and the ringing tone was ever shorter. He was far away from the beach, he glided away from Billy and Ham, and the memory of Lofty's eyes staring up at him, mute and pleading, on the dunes. They had gone past Lofty, almost tripped on him, and Lofty's hands had been on his stomach and the hole was big enough for an orange to have settled in, and he hadn't stopped to feed him morphine, only to snatch the bleeper. A burst hit the water ahead of him. He didn't know whether Viktor was labouring behind him, or was a carcass on the tide. The bleeps came together, and he sucked the air into his lungs.

He dived.

Something worked . . . The bleeper was good. His hands groped into sand, then a rock, then he saw the shape of the deflated dinghy. His first touch was against the engine, and he clung to it, then began to feel along the side of the sunken shape. The breath bubbles careered past his eyes. He found the bottles, broke them. The dinghy corkscrewed as it inflated. The engine's propellers smacked his knees and the side came up hard under his chin. He was dazed, hurt, and he kicked out and up.

Wickso broke the surface. The salt of the water was in his mouth, and he spat. The dinghy floated away from him. He flailed with his arms, lashed with his feet. A dozen years ago, as a member of a Squadron, he would have been rolling over the dinghy's smooth side with an otter's agility. He struggled for a grip on the rounded side, clawed it, then slowly heaved himself up, over, and into it. He felt the strength ebb from his body. He floundered, gasping.

He threw the switch. The cough of the engine was reluctant, then it caught.

He saw the bobbing fair hair and the white shirt. The head and the body had drifted a full forty metres past where the dinghy had surfaced. The head and the shirt floated and there was no beat in the arms.

Wickso gunned the engine.

He was too far back, but the desperation trapped him.

He lay on his stomach and laid out in front of him were all the grenades he had.

Locke had not come close enough, and knew it, but he tilted the barrel up.

★　★　★

413

'The dinghy. Take the dinghy, Igor.'

The gases burst into Bikov's face, and the cartridge cases spilled out in front of him. The noise reverberated in his ears. He fed the belt and followed the line of the tracers.

He saw the small black figure in the dinghy lifted up, as though on an elasticated rope, then keel over. Perhaps the man had fallen on the rudder arm, because the dinghy now careered in pointless tight turns, and each turn took it further from the scrap of white that stood out on the sea's growing colour. Grenades exploded near them. Bikov ignored them.

'Well done, Igor. It is proven. You are the best.'

'I knew it. It was not my fault that the round was damaged, that the weapon jammed.'

The grenades sighed as they flew, like stones thrown by kids. They cracked, like little fireworks that carried no danger. He thought they were fired at full elevation and some were beside them and some cleared them. He wondered why one man had stayed behind, and made a futile sacrifice by firing without skill, with no purpose . . . He loathed the boy.

'Igor, did Captain, second rank, Archenko tell you about Malbork Castle?'

'He did.'

'Igor, did Captain Archenko encourage your skill with the machine-gun?'

'Yes.'

'Igor, it is what I heard – did Captain Archenko go into the water of the docks to save your life, and did you thank him?'

'But I did not know the truth of him.'

He hated the boy. It was rare for Yuri Bikov to hate. Too many, in his opinion, interrogators hated – despised – the men they were tasked to question. Hate seldom came to him. He did not *hate* his wife who bled money from him and who denied him access to his daughter. He had not *hated* Ibn ul Attab whom he had tricked and deceived in a Chechen cave. He did not *hate* Archenko with whom he had shared a plate of food, by candlelight. Hatred, he would have said, demeaned him . . . but he hated the boy.

No more grenades were fired. For a moment he imagined one

man bunkered like a rat in a hole with the launcher useless in his hand, and a pouch or a pocket empty. In a moment, a minute – a few minutes – he would order the infantry line behind him to move forward to flush out the man. It puzzled him, briefly, that the gesture of sacrifice had been so futile, not pressed home. He pondered it . . . Looking up he saw the speck that was Viktor Archenko's head, rising and falling in the water, and he thought that, very slowly, the man edged towards the dinghy as it surged on its futile course.

'Igor, what should happen to Captain Archenko?'

'For his treachery, Colonel, he should die.'

'Igor, at your hand?'

'I have his head in my sights. It would be a difficult shot, across water and with so small a target, at that range. I could do it . . . but I think it better not to.'

'Igor, why is that?'

'To drown is slower.'

'Igor, shoot the dinghy.'

He held the belt and was ready to feed. He heard the sucking-in of breath. Speeded thoughts. The conscript would be a celebrity, and famous for an hour, given a medal, and when his service had expired and he went back to a shit-hole existence in fucking Volgograd he would boast of his skill, boast till he bored everyone around him. Traitors became heroes. *Rehabilitation* was the Russian way . . . What then the future of the celebrity executioner? Seen from a grimy window in the Lubyanka, an old man shuffled in the square in carpet slippers, grey-haired and needing a stick to support him – the execution retired from claiming victims. *He worked with two buckets beside him. One had eau-de-Cologne to hide the smell and the other was filled with vodka. All he stopped for on a busy day was to reload his pistol and to drink the vodka.* He would have been a celebrity, then a bore, then forgotten.

Two bursts, double tap and short.

'Is it sunk?'

'He is alone in the water, Colonel. When he tires he will drown. I correct myself – he is already tired, he will drown soon.'

Bikov looked up. He gazed out on to the sea. The sunlight had replaced the flares. The ship, even at that distance filthy and humble,

415

had slowed and the patrol-boat circled it. He thought it had been a plan of daring, or of desperation. A boat off-shore, a team landed in darkness for a snatch, a race back to an embarkation point, a sunken dinghy, departure from territorial waters before dawn. Time had beaten them. Why would they have done it? He shook his head, almost with a sense of sadness. Yuri Bikov, colonel in military counter-intelligence, had no friends that he would have risked his life for. It had been *idiocy* . . . What confused him most: Archenko was nothing, was of minimal importance, Archenko was not worth the price of it. He went to the petty officer and ordered that the extended line of infantry should come forward, should be alert, should look for a single man – probably without ammunition – and they should rout him out. The petty officer slouched away . . . He remembered the Argun gorge, where he had been to save the life of a man he had not met. He felt humility, and understood.

Then Bikov sat on the dunes sand beside the tripod legs and felt the sun's early warmth on his face, and sometimes he watched the lines of ants that moved past his boots, and sometimes he watched the faraway fair pinhead of an exhausted man who would drown. He smiled at the conscript. 'Igor, would you like to drink vodka?'

In his deadened ears he heard the surprise from the boy he hated. 'No, Colonel. Why do you ask? Thank you, no.'

He loaded the last grenade. It had the markings of phosphorus. Locke felt a sense of shame.

He had not sufficiently pushed home his attack.

The grenades had been launched from too far back. They had fallen randomly, had failed to break the aim of the machine-gunner. He had not gone close. In a frenzy, he had reloaded. He had spilled the grenades from his pockets, had laid them out in front of him and, hands trembling, had forced them down the barrel and fired, and fired again.

His name would not be spoken. He thought himself too late, but he crawled forward. Flies buzzed him, the sun snatched on his skin. The dinghy was sunk, Wickso was lost. He had looked back once, had seen the fair hair and the white shirt in the water. Viktor lived, but it was too late . . . His father would have known about revenge, would have put down poison for the rats if they came into the chicken coop behind the kitchen and ate eggs, would have thought nothing of the rats' death agonies.

He had hoped to save Viktor, but he had not pushed forward far enough. It was about revenge. A set book at school, text to be learned for examinations, the same sunlight in the classroom, the words of Shakespeare's merchant Jew: '. . . revenge. The villainy you teach me I will execute, and it shall go hard but I will better the instruction.' But he had only one grenade, phosphorus, left. As he slithered forward, the snake, Locke could see the light glint on the barrel of the machine-gun and the two men close to it.

It had sunk from his sight.

With the dinghy was Wickso.

He was alone. He felt the burn of the sun on his face. He could manage only little movements of his hands and stunted kicks with his feet, but that was sufficient to keep him afloat. The waves lifted and dropped him, but the ebb tide's current carried him further from the shore. From his eyeline, with the spray breaking in his eyes, he could see the ship and he thought it had stopped, or if it had not stopped it had slowed.

Alone, as his grandmother had been when his father was born. Alone, as his father had been when he had obeyed his orders and had flown into the spread of the mushroom cloud. Alone, as he had been at the dead-drop site at Malbork Castle, and alone as when he had turned away from the fence in the zoo park . . . He would float out to sea, until he could fight no longer, then he would drown.

He tried to cry out, and had no voice, and Billy, Ham, Lofty and Wickso could not hear him. He gave them his silent thanks . . . And he tried to shout to the shore that they should finish him, show him mercy, but the words lay in his throat with the salt taste.

Viktor drifted.

The patrol-boat came round them again, and the voice distorted by the loudspeaker instructed that they turn or they would be rammed . . . Then it turned towards them and foam blossomed from the Nanuchka's propeller screws. Its sharp bow lined up on them.

The master shouted from the bridge, 'If I could do anything I would. I cannot.'

Rupert Mowbray stood at that point on the deck, against the rail, where the impact would come, and he held out his arms wide and challenged them, made a target for them.

The mate was at the base of the accommodation block, below the bridge, and he had brought up an armful of the white china plates from their mess room and he threw them in futile anger, one at a time, into the path of the patrol-boat.

The engineer, framed in his hatch and above his ladder into the depths of the ship, bit on his lip and clutched an ugly spanner.

A madness caught them all. From each of them was an inane gesture of defiance.

But the master swung the wheel and the *Princess Rose* turned. The patrol-boat came past them. Its fenders scraped the hull of the condemned cargo tramper. They lurched from the scraping blow. The master wept. Mowbray spat. The last of the mate's plates shattered beside the forward gun crew. The engineer dropped the spanner and it clattered to the deck by his feet. They looked far back. They could see, all of them, the little bobbing head in the water.

Mowbray intoned, 'Dammit, gentlemen, the end of an old man's dream and the end of a young man's life do not make for a pretty sight.'

The patrol-boat was alongside them. Ahead of them was the open horizon of the Baltic Sea.

Her binoculars dropped from her face.

She turned on the crowd. 'He's in the water. What are you going to do?'

Alice saw the uncomprehending faces. She went to Jerry the Pole, who looked away. She kicked his shin. 'Tell them – he's in the water. What are they going to do for him?'

Jerry the Pole limped away from her, then shrugged. 'They know he is in the water. What do you expect them to do?'

She rasped, 'Tell them, and ask them.'

They were told, they were asked . . . The fisherman grimaced and shrugged, nothing could be done. The Russian waved his hands, and the light caught the jewel on his finger ring: nothing was possible. Of the villagers, men and women, some laughed and some were sombre and some turned from her gaze. She had the burned hand of Jerry the Pole in her fist and she led him from the fisherman and the Russian, made him stand in front of each man and each woman and repeat her demand: *What are you going to do?* A woman, big-bellied and big-bosomed, who would have recognized emotion, romance, love, helplessness, tried to comfort her and hold Alice close, but she was pushed away.

She rounded on them, 'If he were one of yours, what would you do? Leave him, turn your backs on him?'

Alice was beside a boat. It was sturdy, pulled up high on the sand, one among many. She put her weight against it and heaved. Her feet slipped away in the soft sand, and she could not move it. No one helped her. She looked up. The crowd had made a half-circle around her but were too far back for her to reach them and pull them forward to help. They watched. She strained and the boat did not move, was bedded in the sand. She heard the scream of gulls. She dropped her shoulder against the boat's planks. She panted, gasped . . . She heard the voice, and a murmur of response, then the sharper reply.

Alice did not have the language and did not understand.

The priest was beside her, his shoulder against hers, his weight with hers. Then the fisherman's shoulder, then the Russian's weight.

Jerry the Pole told her, 'The Father says we should launch. They say there is a machine-gun. The Father is a man of great learning. He spoke words of Latin to them, as on a Sunday's mass. They will launch.'

The boat moved. All the men's shoulders, and the women's, were against it. It scraped the sand, gathered momentum.

'Ask him,' Alice demanded of Jerry the Pole, 'ask him what he said.'

It was relayed. The Father grunted beside her, '*Quem Dei diligunt, adolescens moritur.*'

Jerry the Pole said, 'It is what he told the village last year when a fisherman was lost at sea. It is from the words of Plautus . . .'

She was a convent girl. Alice said softly, 'I understand what he says. "Whom the gods love die young." He speaks a truth.'

'They will face the machine-gun.'

The boat skidded down into the water and the crowd pushed it until they were waist deep. The fisherman was in it first, then the Russian, then Jerry the Pole. Then Alice scrambled up and over the side. The engine rattled, dark smoke coughed, it surged.

The crowd was on the beach. The priest stood in front of them, stern, his hands tight across his chest, but she saw him break the hold and he made the sign of the cross.

The boat, on full power, crashed the waves' crests.

Locke heard the popping of gunfire.

He was the snake in the grass. He had left the scrub and was now on the dunes, and he slithered a path on the sand between the grass tufts. The sand was in his mouth and nose and he blinked to keep it from his eyes. It was in his shirt, his trousers and shoes, but he kept the launcher's barrel clear of it. He wriggled forward on his stomach. There must be no sand in the barrel for the last grenade – white phosphorus. Each little contorted movement took him further from the gunfire, and nearer to them. With the gunfire, merged with it, were their voices.

The young man knelt, the older man stood. Their shadows fell across the machine-gun. Though the sun was behind him, the older man had his hand over his eyes, and the younger man pointed over the dunes and the beach towards the sea.

The younger man laughed. 'What do they think they are doing?'

The older man said, 'They are too far out for the cordon to hit them. The shots fall short.'

'Don't they know about me – about the quality of my shooting? When they are close I can sink them.'

'Yes, because you are the best . . .'

A line of troops idled behind them. Locke, squashed down in the sand, watched. He had sufficient Russian to understand the words, but the older man's insult confused him. The gaze of all the troops in the line had followed the young man's pointing gesture. He thought he was a little more than a hundred metres from them, from the machine-gun. He would go closer . . . The flies were around his face, crawled on his skin . . . The young man laughed louder, and pointed again, but the older man looked away.

He squirmed deeper into the sand. Very deliberately, Locke turned his head. The grass tufts were in his face. He laid the launcher down, careful that the barrel was clear, then used both his freed hands to part the grass. He looked where the younger man had pointed. He saw the boat, out past the point where the fence ran down into the sea. It threw a crisp spray from its bow, coming along the coastline but keeping its distance from the beach. He freed the grass strands, slid his hands over the sand and moved more grass. Locke saw the fair-capped head and a hint of the white shirt . . . He had the chance.

It would be better than revenge, it would be fulfilment.

He thought he was blessed.

He heard the young man ask, 'What will be my reward?'

'A parade, a band, a medal, and fame – if that is what you want.'

'I will wait until they stop to lift him out, then I will shoot.'

He turned his head. The place he lay in had become a nest. He would wait there. He would only move when there was no chance of failure. The troops lounged behind the two men, and held their rifles casually, but he thought their attention would quicken when the machine-gun was readied to shoot.

Chelbia said, 'I identify you, Miss North, as an intelligence officer, a lady of importance. Myself, I am only an insignificant businessman, and I make a small living from the trade of import and export. Now I and my friends do something that is a madness, the play of lunatics. I do not look, Miss North, for financial reward, but for *co-operation*. I look for doors to be opened and for eyes to look away . . . My colleague, Jerzy Kwasniewski, he is an old man, in the twilight of his years. He has no pension after a life-time of service. He should have a pension . . . We are all in the hands of God, also in the hands of Roman, who is an excellent and honest man, and he has the need of a faster boat. Miss North, do we get a fast boat, a pension and co-operation? They are trifling requests. I think it is important, Miss North, as we go to save your agent, that we have your word they will be given us. Your word would be a satisfactory guarantee . . . Do we have your word?'

'Whatever you want, Mr Chelbia, you shall have.'

* * *

421

The young man flexed his hands, wiped his eyes, then arched his back. He dropped down, took the machine-gun's butt and worked it against his shoulder for the final time. He was grinning. The older man, as if his knees had stiffened, came down heavily beside him and lifted up the belt in his hands, his elbows taking his weight. The troops were alert now and little nervous whispers passed among them.

'You are ready?'

'When they slow to pick him up . . . then I am ready. Do I have your friendship, Colonel?'

'You have my friendship, as Captain Archenko had yours . . . To betray your friend, Igor, is worse than betraying your country. Shoot and enjoy it.'

He saw the mouth of the young man pucker, and the hand that meandered close to the trigger guard came up and wiped fast at an eye. The face of the older man was impassive.

'What should I do?'

'You must do what you believe is your duty.'

The hand cocked the weapon, the finger was back on the trigger guard. The breath was drawn in . . . The eye that had been wiped was now at the sight.

Locke clutched the launcher and drew up his knees.

He launched himself, and life passed before him – not the past, but the future.

Locke saw . . . Hands reached down to catch the collar of the white shirt and the body was lifted up and fell hard into the boat's bottom.

He ran. The head tilted away from the sight, but the finger stayed on the trigger, and the tracer round streamed out, but high. First, confusion on the face, then irritation, and anger. The older man gaped.

Locke saw . . . The elation creased Rupert Mowbray's face, and he punched the air, then snapped down the radio's switch for transmission.

He charged. He felt a great calm. Tiredness had gone from his legs. Behind them, behind the tripod and the machine-gun, the troops were rooted, and two big lads by a mortar were statue still.

Locke saw . . . Careering from the bottle's neck, the cork thwacked into the ceiling of an office, and the champagne spilled into the glasses held high by Bertie and Peter.

He rushed them. The sand no longer skidded from under his shoes. He was at peace. The older man turned away and his hands were lifted and covered his face, and the belt was dropped. Officers shouted, troops lifted their rifles.

Locke saw ... The palms of the hands beat on the conference-room table as Americans, Canadians, Israelis, French and Germans of the intelligence community applauded the conclusion of the director general's briefing on Operation Havoc.

The barrel of the machine-gun waved towards him. It was as he wanted, and all fear was gone. He barely heard the first rifle shots fired at him, and the tracer of the machine-gun spitting wild and wide of him.

Locke saw ... They walked hand in hand, among trees, where spring flowers bloomed.

The barrel of the launcher was aimed at the young man and the tripod and the machine-gun. The first blow, a hammer's, was against his arm. The second, a pickaxe's, was at his hip. He staggered twice, but held the aim. He was a dozen paces from them. He was falling. He looked into the little pit hole of the machine-gun's flash suppressor. He pulled the trigger. The grenade squirmed out, hit the right tripod leg, ricocheted to the side, rolled, and lay. Another blow battered him. He went down. He was on his knees. He stared at the barrel. There was the burst of the cloud of phosphorus, and the blast of the firing of tracer and ball and armour-piercing bullets.

Locke saw ...

The technician's magazine was on the floor beside his chair, discarded. The signal was decoded. He pulled the paper from the printer and went to the glass door.

The annexe off the central communications unit was empty. Two beds not slept in, two chairs not used, a table cleared and the screen empty.

In the unit, without natural light and with recycled air, the technicians were permitted to dress down. His trainer shoes flopped quietly over the annexe carpet as he circled the table. Where were they? He called back to colleagues that he intended to deliver the signal personally, by hand. He wanted to be the messenger who lightened tired faces, made the smiles crack exhausted mouths. He padded out, and took the lift up.

He knocked on the director general's outer door respectfully. A sharp voice called for him to enter. A young man was hitching his coat on the stand, and an older woman was switching on the computer console. A younger woman was busy at the coffee-machine. Was the director general in? He was not, he would not be in the building till the afternoon. He walked away.

Back down the corridor, back down two floors in the lift. Another door.

Had Peter Giles arrived yet? Another languid and disinterested answer. No, had had a late night, but would be back in tomorrow. He was asked, as an afterthought: Something urgent or can it wait? He clung to the single sheet of paper, as though it were his personal property and he alone was charged to deliver it, and closed the door after him.

The technician descended another floor, traversed another corridor, rapped another door.

Had they seen Mr Ponsford? No, he'd left a voice-mail, had stayed late and had now gone home, was not to be disturbed – could someone else help? They could not. He left them, at Russia Desk, to their coffee and their computers, and to the gutting of yesterday's Moscow newspapers, to the transcripts of yesterday's radio news broadcasts. Irritation itched at the technician.

He had been on duty through the night. Through the signals, he had lived *their* night. He knew them as the Delta team, with their call-sign numbers, and they were all *Down*, bloody down, gone, history – and the high and the mighty who knew them and who had sent them had left and not yet returned. He was only a lowly technician, and he lived in a Hackney bedsit. He would try to sleep away the day behind thin curtains that could not suppress the daylight. 'Try' to sleep, but it would come difficult because he had read each of the signals. He had been with them.

He did not know of a hut above the beach of a Scottish loch, where a man had painted in the shadow of Beinn Odhar Mhor, but he knew Delta 1 was *down*. Nor did he know of a file marked 'Not To Be Continued With' in a locked cabinet in a south-coast police station, but he knew Delta 2 was *down*. He did not know that early-morning winds blew leaves against lines of gravestones at a Passchendaele cemetery, but he knew Delta 3 was *down*. Nor did he know that trolleys were hurried down the corridors of a West Midlands hospital, carrying the victims of the morning's first traffic accident and of the first coronary attack, but he knew Delta 4 was *down*. He had been with them through their last hours.

The technician came into the atrium. He stood among the storming flow of the Service's staff coming to work. He had thought he was proud to work there. The technician could not believe he would not see one of them – the director general with his bodyguard, Peter Giles who had the limp from his hip problem, Bertie Ponsford with the pinched face of a hunter – but the sea of movement swam round him and he did not see them. He had read the first line of the signal, and could have punched the air.

He did not know who Ferret was, what was Ferret's importance, why men's lives had been lost that Ferret should be brought out, or what were the prospects of an alien, in exile. He had been with Ferret during the long dark hours, had run with him, gone into the water with him, and could have cheered out loud at his rescue. Nor did he know that Alice North would leave the Service, would live with Ferret and help him earn a meagre living as a translator of Russian documents after his brief usefulness had been leached from him.

He saw Clarence. Clarence had his raincoat over his uniform tunic, would be going home after his night shift – Clarence was the eyes and ears of the great and monstrous building. Had Clarence seen the director general? Had not set eyes on him. Had Clarence seen Mr Giles? Gone home, definitely not come back. Had Clarence seen Mr Ponsford? Not since he left, looking for a taxi.

The technician did not know about fire-breaks. Nor did he know that within two years awards for Other Buggers' Efforts would be discreetly listed in a New Year Honours List, and that Giles and Ponsford would go in the company of their wives to the Palace.

Clarence winked, then whispered, 'Was it a big show? You know what I mean – an "old times" show. Did it work out?'

'At a cost.'

'Well, it's the show that matters, isn't it? I'm glad to hear it worked out.'

He saw Clarence strut away, like a goal had been scored, like his team had won something, as though *at a cost* did not matter. The technician took the lift back to the lower basement. He knew who was Havoc 1. He could put a name – *Oh, and Locke has shown up* – to the call-sign, but not a face.

He did not know of a farm in west Wales where the morning's milking was finishing, or of a body that had floated under a marina's pontoon, or of a dead drop that had failed at a castle in eastern Poland, or of a kiss, or of the moment when a machine-gun had fired and a grenade of white phosphorus had exploded.

The technician settled at his desk and punched through the numbers for internal mail.

He did not know of a colonel in casualty with severe arm burns who, on discharge from a military hospital, would resign his commission and go far to the east for a job in a lumber factory, never talking of the cause of his scars – or of a conscript in intensive care because the phosphorus had spattered his face and hands and had fire-licked through his uniform, who would go home and would drive his father's taxi in the night on the streets of Volgograd when his disfigurement could not be seen – or of the funeral with full military honours of the admiral who had commanded the Baltic Fleet, at which successive senior officers queued to praise his memory.

He sent the signal away.

He did not know of letters, bloodstained, that would be retrieved from a scorched body, holed by a hundred rifle shots, which would be returned after an interval that was decent, along with the bodies. Or know that Rupert Mowbray, under the arc-lights at the border crossing at Braniewo, would say, side of mouth, 'Just like the Glienicker bridge. It's comforting to know that little changes,' and Libby Weedon would nod agreement as Russian soldiers used the dark small hours of the morning to carry forward the five unmarked coffins to the waiting hearses, then hurry away because Mowbray had a plane to catch and a lecture to give in Bologna to the Italian Service that afternoon.

426

The technician cleared his desk, briefed his replacement, put on his coat.

He did not know that after that decent interval the intelligence men of old enemies, new friends, would drink together, chuckle, and forget together.

The technician left the building for his bus, and his home with the thin curtains and his bed.

What he did know – he no longer heard the machine-gun, as he had through the night, but he saw a beach where the sea had not yet wiped away the footprints of men who had run for the water, and the sun caught the bloodstains and nestled on discarded cartridge cases, and the gulls wheeled, and the silence had fallen.

The technician felt the anger hurt him.

It had been a big show – but at a cost.

'The best practitioner currently working in the UK . . . quite simply
the most intelligent and accomplished'
Independent

'In a class of his own'
The Times

'One of the modern masters of the craft'
Daily Mail

'A master of the thriller set on the murky edges of modern war'
i

'A stylish writer'
Observer

'One of the most venerable names of the thriller genre'
Independent

'Richly imagined novels that bristle with authenticity'
Washington Post

'The dabbest hand in the industry . . . a master'
City AM

'The pace leaves you breathless . . . he is the master of the thriller
genre'
Edinburgh Evening News

Continue reading to find out more about the thrillers that have
earned Gerald Seymour the title of 'best thriller writer in the
world today' (*Telegraph*) . . .

THE CORPORAL'S WIFE

'Seymour is, quite simply, one of the finest thriller writers in England,
every bit the equal of Frederick Forsyth and Robert Harris.'
Daily Mail

A young woman determined to live her own life in an
oppressive society.

A rag-tag team of men sent to bring her out of it against all the odds.

THE CORPORAL'S WIFE is a hugely suspenseful thriller
about escaping one of the world's most explosive hostpots – Iran.
It is an epic, nail-biting story of courage and betrayal, a brilliant
glimpse into a closed society and the way the secret services
operate on both sides of the line between politics and morality.

'This is another masterly performance from an author whose
recent work turns individual spying missions into ambitious ensemble
dramas mixing action scenes and love stories with espionage.'
The Sunday Times

HODDER

THE OUTSIDERS

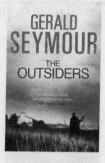

'Once again demonstrating his ability to probe the moral murkiness of the spy trade and create an absorbingly diverse ensemble, Seymour crafts a sophisticated, reader-teasing tale.'
The Sunday Times

MI5 officer Winnie Monks has never forgotten the death of a young agent on her team at the hands of a former Russian Army Major-turned-gangster. Ten years later, she hears the Major is travelling to a Spanish villa and she asks permission to send in a surveillance unit.

There is an empty property next door, perfect to spy from – and as a base for Winnie's darker, less official plans.

But this villa isn't deserted: the owners have invited a young British couple to 'house sit' while they are away.

Jonno and Posie think they are embarking on a carefree holiday in the sun. But, when the Secret Service arrives in paradise, everything changes.

'Those [Seymour] sends off into dangerous territory are, in fact, his readers. With each book, we enter a dangerous universe, and are totally involved with utterly plausible characters, faced with moral choices that are rarely straightforward.'
Independent

HODDER

A DENIABLE DEATH

AN EPIC NOVEL OF HIGH COURAGE AND LOW CUNNING, OF LIFE
AND DEATH IN THE MORAL MAZE OF THE POST-9/11 WORLD.

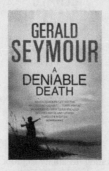

'Gerald Seymour is the grand-master of the contemporary thriller and
A DENIABLE DEATH is his greatest work yet. Gripping, revealing
and meticulously researched, this is a page-turning masterpiece that
will literally leave you breathless.'
Major Chris Hunter, bestselling author of *Extreme Risk*

YOU WATCH. YOU WAIT. THE HOURS SLIDE SLOWLY PAST.

A WHOLE DAY. THEN TWO.

YOU LIE UNDER A MERCILESS SUN IN A
MOSQUITO-INFESTED MARSH.

YOU CAN'T MOVE, LEAVE, OR RELAX.

YOUR MUSCLES ACHE FROM CLENCHING TIGHT FOR SO LONG.

IF YOU ARE DISCOVERED, YOU WILL BE TORTURED THEN KILLED.

AND HER MAJESTY'S GOVERNMENT WILL DENY ALL
KNOWLEDGE OF YOU.

'Great storytelling . . . you just have to read this novel . . . absolutely gripping.'
Eurocrime

HODDER

THE DEALER AND THE DEAD

THE ARMS DEALER BETRAYED THEM.
THE SURVIVORS WANT REVENGE.

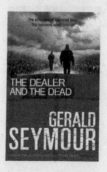

'*The Dealer and the Dead* is Seymour firing on all cylinders
and his rivals need, once again, to look to their laurels.'
Independent

In a moonlit field near the Serbian border, Croatian villagers waited for
an arms shipment that would never come. They will never forget that night,
or the slaughter that followed.

Eighteen years later, a body is discovered in a field, and with it the identity
of the arms dealer who betrayed them. Now the villagers can plot their revenge.

For Harvey Gillott, it was all a long time ago. But now the hand of the past
is reaching out across Europe, to Harvey's house in leafy England. And
it's holding a gun . . .

'The final scenes are brilliantly orchestrated . . . Without doubt, *The Dealer
and the Dead* is one of the finest thrillers to be published so far this year.'
Yorkshire Evening Post

HODDER

THE COLLABORATOR

CORRUPTION. BETRAYAL. REVENGE.

'A dense, intensely satisfying thriller from one of the modern masters
of the craft, Seymour's latest novel will remind the world just how
phenomenally accomplished a thriller writer he is.'
Daily Mail

Eddie Deacon has a new girlfriend. She's beautiful, clever and Italian.

And then she disappears.

What Eddie doesn't know is that Immacolata Borelli is the daughter of
a merciless Naples gangster. She can no longer live with her conscience and
has decided to collaborate with the police to bring down her own family.

But the Borellis will not lose their empire without a fight. They will use
or destroy anything and anyone to prevent her from talking.

Including Eddie.

'Tight writing and meticulous research . . . Seymour paints the streets
of Naples and their dark denizens with an artist's brush that lingers equally
on the grime, the glitter and the blood.'
The Times

HODDER

HARRY'S GAME

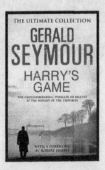

THE ICONIC THRILLER BY THE GRAND-MASTER OF THE CRAFT

THE MASTERPIECE THAT MADE HIS NAME
IN A NEW EDITION WITH FOREWORD BY ROBERT HARRIS

'Absorbing from beginning to end . . . the sort of book
that makes you lose track of time.'
New York Times

A British cabinet minister is gunned down on a London street by an IRA assassin.
In the wake of national outcry, the authorities must find the hitman. But the trail is
long cold, the killer gone to ground in Belfast, and they must resort to more unor-
thodox methods to unearth him. Ill-prepared and poorly briefed, undercover agent
Harry Brown is sent into the heart of enemy territory to infiltrate the terrorists.

But when it is a race against the clock, mistakes are made and corners cut. For
Harry Brown, alone in a city of strangers, where an intruder is the subject of immediate gossip and rumour, one false move is enough to leave him fatally isolated.

'Evokes the atmosphere and smell of the back streets of Belfast
as nothing else I have ever read.'
Frederick Forsyth

'A tough thriller, vibrant with suspense.'
Evening Standard

'Devastatingly good . . . you can smell the mean streets where the terrorists hide.'
Spectator

'First rate . . . Edge-of-the-seat reading.'
Washington Post

HODDER

CRIME
LINES

Your direct line to the finest crime and thriller writing.

For content exclusives, author interviews, top writing tips, competitions and articles visit Crime Lines, the new crime and thriller community from Hodder & Stoughton.

 /Crime Lines www.crime-lines.co.uk @CrimeLines